Look for these exciting Western series from bestselling authors
WILLIAM W. JOHNSTONE
and **J. A. JOHNSTONE**

The Mountain Man

Preacher: The First Mountain Man

Luke Jensen, Bounty Hunter

Those Jensen Boys!

The Jensen Brand

Matt Jensen

MacCallister

The Red Ryan Westerns

Perley Gates

Have Brides, Will Travel

The Hank Fallon Westerns

Will Tanner, Deputy U.S. Marshal

Shotgun Johnny

The Chuckwagon Trail

The Jackals

The Slash and Pecos Westerns

The Texas Moonshiners

AVAILABLE FROM PINNACLE BOOKS

WHITE LIGHTNING

A TEXAS MOONSHINERS NOVEL

WILLLIAM W. JOHNSTONE

and J. A. Johnstone

PINNACLE BOOKS
Kensington Publishing Corp.
www.kensingtonbooks.com

PINNACLE BOOKS are published by

Kensington Publishing Corp.
119 West 40th Street
New York, NY 10018

Copyright © 2020 J. A. Johnstone

All rights reserved. No part of this book may be reproduced in any form or by any means without the prior written consent of the publisher, excepting brief quotes used in reviews.

This book is a work of fiction. Names, characters, businesses, organizations, places, events, and incidents either are the product of the author's imagination or are used fictitiously. Any resemblance to actual persons, living or dead, events, or locales is entirely coincidental. To the extent that the image or images on the cover of this book depict a person or persons, such person or persons are merely models, and are not intended to portray any character or characters featured in the book.

PUBLISHER'S NOTE

Following the death of William W. Johnstone, the Johnstone family is working with a carefully selected writer to organize and complete Mr. Johnstone's outlines and many unfinished manuscripts to create additional novels in all of his series like The Last Gunfighter, Mountain Man, and Eagles, among others. This novel was inspired by Mr. Johnstone's superb storytelling.

If you purchased this book without a cover, you should be aware that this book is stolen property. It was reported as "unsold and destroyed" to the publisher, and neither the author nor the publisher has received any payment for this "stripped book."

All Kensington titles, imprints, and distributed lines are available at special quantity discounts for bulk purchases for sales promotions, premiums, fund-raising, educational, or institutional use. Special book excerpts or customized printings can also be created to fit specific needs. For details, write or phone the office of the Kensington sales manager: Kensington Publishing Corp., 119 West 40th Street, New York, NY 10018, attn: Sales Department; phone 1-800-221-2647.

PINNACLE BOOKS, the Pinnacle logo, and the WWJ steer head logo are Reg. U.S. Pat. & TM Off.

ISBN-13: 978-0-7860-4416-0
ISBN-10: 0-7860-4416-0

First printing: October 2020

10 9 8 7 6 5 4 3 2 1

Printed in the United States of America

CHAPTER 1

Loud, angry voices sounded up ahead and caught Pike Shannon's interest. He didn't recognize any of them, but the men were upset about something.

Then he heard a voice he *did* recognize. It belonged to his old friend Andy Burnett.

"I reckon I'd better go see about that," Pike said to the young woman who had been strolling along the main street of Warbonnet, Texas, with him on this pleasant evening.

"Blast it, Pike, don't go looking for trouble," she told him. "You're a peaceable man now, remember?"

"That's a fine thing, a Ramsey telling somebody not to go looking for trouble."

Belle Ramsey punched Pike on the arm with a hard little fist and said, "Don't you go making sport of my family, Mr. Pike Shannon."

"Sorry," Pike said, and meant it—mostly. "I reckon it's just a matter of habit."

True enough. The Shannons and the Ramseys had been enemies since the old days in the hills of Arkansas. It had been a blood feud then, and the violence was one reason Pike's great-grandpappy, old Garvan Shannon, had moved the family to Texas. Such generations-long clashes tended to wipe out entire families, and Garvan wasn't going to stand by and let that happen to his, no matter how many grudges he and the other Shannons might hold against the no-good, dad-blasted Ramseys.

Garvan had had no way of knowing that eventually the Ramseys would wind up in Texas, too, also in Warbonnet County, and the current generation would cause all kinds of trouble for Pike and his family. Only a few months earlier, the Shannons and the Ramseys had gone to war over their moonshining operations—which had also come with them from Arkansas—and the ruckus had cost too many lives.

One of the men who'd died, Doak Ramsey, had been Pike's archenemy, a kill-crazy lobo who eventually had turned against his own cousin, beautiful, red-headed Belle, and slashed her face with a knife. The injury had healed, but she would always carry the scar.

As far as Pike was concerned, it didn't make her any less pretty—although it still went against the grain, sometimes, for him to say or even think anything good about a Ramsey.

None of that kept him from walking with her of an evening, now and then, like tonight. He'd been enjoying himself, and he thought Belle was having a fine time, too. He hated to interrupt that companionship.

But Andy Burnett was an old friend, and it

sounded like he might be in some sort of trouble. Pike couldn't ignore that.

"I'll be right back," he told Belle.

"Not hardly," she shot back. "You're not leaving me here while you go charging off to get in a fight. I'm coming, too."

Pike knew from experience what a waste of time it was to argue with her, so he didn't even try. He just headed on down the street with long strides.

Pike was a tall, broad-shouldered, dark-haired man who moved with an easy grace. His face, revealed by light spilling through some of the windows he passed, was rawboned and weathered enough that it was just shy of handsome. He carried a Colt .45 on his right hip. He had made his living with that gun during the long years when he'd been away from his family and his home in Warbonnet County.

Now he was back, and since the trouble with the Ramseys was finished, he hadn't had any need of the revolver during the past few months. That didn't mean he was going to stop carrying it. He had packed iron on his hip for so long that he wasn't sure if he could keep his balance and walk without it.

He spotted a group of men in the street ahead of him and could tell that was where the angry voices came from. They were standing in front of the hardware store, which hadn't closed down for the night yet.

Enough light came through the store's open door for Pike to see tall, lanky, fair-haired Andy Burnett standing in the center of the group. Andy nearly always had a grin on his pleasantly homely face, but not tonight, surrounded like this.

"What makes you think a no-good moonshiner like you has any right to put up election fliers, Burnett?" one of the men crowding around Andy demanded.

"I got the same right as any other man in War-bonnet County," Andy replied hotly. "And I haven't brewed any 'shine in months. I even dismantled my still."

"You're still a criminal," another man said. "You can't run for sheriff!"

Pike stopped short. This was the first he'd heard about Andy running for sheriff. He knew that a special election had been called to replace the murderous Doak Ramsey, who had finagled his way into the job before justice caught up to him, but the idea of Andy Burnett pinning on a lawman's badge took Pike totally by surprise.

Because, as a matter of fact, Andy *was* a moonshiner, or at least he had been until recently, just like Pike and his family and several other people in the county who had had stills set up. *Somebody* had to cook white lightnin' if folks around here were going to have anything decent to drink, since there had been one of those so-called local option elections a while back that made liquor illegal and turned this whole part of Texas dry.

It was a loco idea, but people had voted for it. And the sheriff had to enforce the law, unless he was actually an owlhoot like Belle's cousin Doak had been.

Pike spotted a piece of paper tacked to the wall of the hardware store next to the door. He stepped closer and saw that, sure enough, written on it in big letters was ANDY BURNETT FOR SHERIFF— AN HONEST MAN FOR AN HONEST JOB.

Andy was an honest man, Pike couldn't argue with that. And being sheriff was an honest job, if your name wasn't Ramsey. If that was what Andy wanted to do, Pike supposed it was all right with him.

Not with these obnoxious townsmen, though. Half a dozen of them clustered around Andy. One of them suddenly reached for the sheaf of papers Andy held in his left hand. More fliers he'd intended to tack up around town, Pike thought.

Andy jerked the papers back, out of the man's reach, but when he did, another of the men grabbed him from behind, pinning his arms to his sides.

"Now you can get 'em, Fritz!"

The man called Fritz snatched the fliers from Andy's hand. Another member of the fledgling mob said excitedly, "Let's make him eat 'em!"

"That's a good idea," Fritz said. He crumpled one of the papers into a ball as he stepped closer to Andy. "Open up, Burnett. We'll see how you like the taste of your own lyin' words."

As Pike stepped forward from the shadows, he said, "That's enough."

He didn't raise his voice, but it was deep and powerful enough that even at a normal level it seemed loud in the quiet street. Fritz jerked around in surprise, and a couple of the other men turned toward Pike as well.

"Shannon!" one of them exclaimed. "Watch it, Fritz. He's a gunslinger!"

"We're not packing iron, Shannon," Fritz said, "and this is none of your business."

"You're ganging up on a friend of mine, and that makes it my business." Pike hooked his thumbs in the gunbelt supporting the holstered Colt. He wasn't going to accept at face value Fritz's claim of them being unarmed. Anybody who looked like he was trying to haul out a smokewagon was liable to regret it.

Fritz sneered and said, "We're just lettin' Burnett know that respectable folks won't stand for the likes of him running for sheriff. That's a job for an honest man . . . the one thing this blasted handbill of his gets right."

"Is that so? Who'd you vote for last election? Doak Ramsey?"

Pike's acerbic words made the men frown. One of them muttered, "We didn't have any way of knowin' that Doak was a crook."

"Other than the fact that all the other Ramseys and their kin are crooked as a dog's hind leg," Pike snapped.

Too late, he remembered that Belle was standing right behind him. He wanted to turn to her and emphasize that he didn't include *her* in that statement, of course, but he didn't figure it would be a good idea to take his eyes off this bunch. Individually, they might not have much sand, but even coyotes grew backbones when they were in a pack.

Fritz said, "Who we did or didn't vote for then don't have a thing to do with *this* election. We've already had one dirty moonshiner worm his way into the sheriff's job. We don't need another."

"Then campaign against him and beat him at the ballot box, the way things are supposed to work. Threatening him like this is just pure cowardice."

"Pike, I was handling this," Andy spoke up in a surprisingly cool voice. Pike understood that his friend's pride was probably hurt right now. Andy didn't like it that Pike had had to step in to help him.

But Andy had helped out during the war with Doak and the other Ramseys, so as far as Pike was concerned, there was a debt owed to him, to say nothing of their friendship.

"Give him his papers back, and then you boys scatter," Pike ordered in a hard voice. "Go home. It's getting late, and your families probably expect you."

"You go home, Shannon," Fritz said. "You don't even live in town. Go on back to that so-called horse ranch your family runs. Probably a bunch of horse thieves, if you ask me. Probably not a horse on the place that wasn't stole!"

That was going too far. Pike clenched his hands into fists and stepped toward the loudmouth.

Before he could throw a punch, Fritz suddenly flung the sheaf of papers into Pike's face and yelled, "Get 'em!"

CHAPTER 2

Fritz must have thought that with Pike and Andy outnumbered three-to-one, the outcome of a fight was a foregone conclusion.

It was, but not in the way that Fritz believed.

Pike didn't flinch as the papers flew around his face. He had had bullets singing past his ears on many occasions, so a stack of electioneering hand-bills wasn't going to bother him.

He set his feet and met Fritz's charge with a straight, hard right that slammed into the man's jaw. The force of the blow shivered up Pike's arm to his shoulder.

Fritz went backward as if he'd been swatted across the face with a two-by-four or kicked by a mule.

At the same time, Andy leaned back against the man who was still holding him, jerked both his legs up, and straightened them in a double-barreled kick that caught one of the other men in the chest. That hombre flew backward, too.

The force of the kick made the man holding Andy stagger and loosen his grip. Andy twisted free and whirled around, bringing up his left elbow as he did so. Andy was a mite on the scrawny side, but he packed a lot of power in his ropy muscles. The elbow cracked against the man's nose and blood spurted as he howled in pain.

Two more of Fritz's cronies charged at Pike from different directions. He ducked the roundhouse punch that one of them swung at him, grabbed the man around the middle, and heaved him up and around into the other attacker. They crashed together, their heads smacking into each other with a dull thud. Both of them collapsed like rag dolls.

That left just one troublemaker out of the original half-dozen still on his feet. He stood there for a second, looked back and forth between Pike and Andy, and then turned and ran for dear life. He never looked back as he disappeared into the gathering shadows.

Pike looked around at the men lying on the ground and moaning. He said, "I'm glad I didn't have to shoot any of you idiots. Next time think twice before you gang up on somebody."

Belle stepped forward and extended the sheaf of papers.

"Here you go, Andy," she said. "I picked them up."

"Thanks, Belle," he said as he took them from her. "I'm much obliged." He looked at Pike. "To both of you. Although I could have handled that bunch."

Pike doubted that, but he just nodded and said, "Yeah, but I needed the exercise. Been getting a little rusty from just sitting around most of the time. I appreciate you letting me pitch in like that."

Andy lifted the stack of handbills.

"I was about to tack the rest of these up around town," he said. "You two want to come with me?"

"I wouldn't mind," Pike said. "I want to ask you about this sheriff business."

"What is there to ask?" Andy said as the three of them started along the street with Belle walking between him and Pike. They left the troublemakers groaning behind them. "I'm running for sheriff, just like it says here."

"I just never figured you for the peace officer type."

"Well, I got to thinking that I'd like to raise my kids in a county where all hell wasn't bustin' loose all the time, like it was when, uh, when Doak was the sheriff . . . No offense, Belle, him being your cousin and all."

Belle snorted and said, "I've got just as much reason to hate what Doak did as anybody. More reason than most." She didn't have to mention the scar on her face for Pike and Andy to know what she meant. "So if you believe that you can keep things pacified around here, Andy, then more power to you, as far as I'm concerned."

She paused, then added, "Not that I've forgotten how you said that all the Ramseys are crooked, Mr. Shannon."

"Aw, shoot," Pike muttered. "I would've said present company excepted, but I didn't get a chance to."

"That's all right," Belle said magnanimously. "Just don't forget that when it comes to the Ramseys, I *am* the exception."

"Not likely to," Pike said.

He was grateful that she didn't press him for an explanation of that comment. To tell the truth, he wasn't sure *what* he felt about Belle Ramsey. She was exceptional, though, no doubt about that.

To change the subject, he jerked a thumb over his shoulder at the men they had left behind them. "Why'd those fellas try to gang up on you like that?"

"Oh, that was Fritz Durham's doing," Andy said. "He kept egging those other boys on. Fritz has never liked me since he decided that I'd gotten the better of him on a horse trade. It figures he'd look for any excuse to give me some trouble. Some fellas just can't let go of any old grudge."

Pike grunted. He'd never had any run-ins with Durham himself, but he'd never heard much good about the man, either.

For the next half-hour, they walked around War-bonnet as Andy used a hammer tucked behind his belt and a pocketful of tacks to put up the handbills.

"Is anybody running against you?" Pike asked.

"Lester Scroggins," Andy replied. "He worked as a jailer for a while under the previous sheriff, before Doak was elected, so he's got some experience in the law business. I probably won't beat him"—Andy shrugged—"but I didn't figure it would hurt anything to give it a try. And Scroggins isn't a bad sort. If he *does* win, I don't reckon it'll be the end of the world."

Belle said, "That's a good attitude to take. If I could vote, I'd vote for you, Andy."

"I'll vote for you," Pike said. "And I'll tell Dougal and Torrance and Fiddler they ought to vote for you, too. That's four, right there. Or at least three. Torrance is contrary enough that he might not, just because I said he should."

Andy chuckled and said, "It'll probably take more than that to get me elected, but I appreciate it, Pike."

When he had tacked up all the fliers, he got his horse from one of the hitch rails, said good night, and headed home, leaving Pike and Belle to finish their walk. Belle lived in a boardinghouse here in town these days. She said, "Since we've already been all over town with Andy, I reckon I'd better call it a night and head on home, too."

"The café's still open," Pike said. "We could stop and have a piece of pie."

"It's a little late to be eating. Almost time to turn in, in fact."

"My grandpappy Dougal says it's always a good time for pie."

"Well, I wouldn't want to dispute the word of a man as wise as Dougal Shannon," Belle said with a laugh. "All right. Pie it is."

But as they strolled down the street, Belle added, "This idea of going to the café wouldn't have anything to do with you wanting to see Sophie Truesdale, would it?"

"Sophie's never there in the evening like this," Pike said. "Johnny Quinlan closes up the place for her at night."

"You know Miss Truesdale's schedule, do you?"

"Well, not necessarily." Pike didn't like the way Belle's sharp tongue made him feel defensive. "I've just been in there in the evening a few times and talked to Johnny. That's how come I know."

"I see." Belle paused, then added coolly, "I noticed that you call her Sophie, instead of Miss Truesdale."

"That's her name," Pike said.

"They ought to call her Miss Tight-laced, Stick Up Her—"

"Hold on there," Pike said quickly. "The two of you aren't still feuding, are you?"

Belle didn't answer the question directly. Instead she said, "I don't see why you'd be defending her, Pike. After all, she's a Dry. If it wasn't for her and that blasted Women's Christian Temperance Union, a person would be able to get a drink around here." She waved a hand to indicate the buildings up and down the street. "Doesn't it still strike you as wrong that there's not a saloon as far as the eye can see?"

"Well . . . it's odd, I'll grant you that."

Pike had been in scores of frontier towns, from the Rio Grande to the Canadian border and all the way out to the Pacific Ocean, and as far as he could recall, Warbonnet was the only one without any-place to buy a drink. He assumed that Clarkston, the county seat of Chaparral County, just north of Warbonnet County, and Bolivar, the other town up yonder, were the same way since that county was dry, too, but he hadn't been there yet since returning to these parts.

Warbonnet hadn't been like that, either, when he left home years earlier. It had been a wide-open, even wild, cowtown.

But no more. Things had changed. The frontier was getting civilized, the way frontiers always did, sooner or later, and he supposed that getting rid of all the saloons was just part of the process.

"But that's the way things are now," he continued. "We just have to get used to 'em."

Belle looked over at him and shook her head.

"Never thought I'd see the day when Pike Shannon got all tamed down like a fat old housecat," she said. "All my life I heard about what a hell-roarer you were. After you left these parts and we started hearing stories about all the trouble you were getting into in those other places, some of the boys worried that you'd come back one of these days and start in to wipe out the Ramseys." She shrugged. "Which is sort of what happened. But now . . . What do you do all day, Pike? You're bound to have a still out the woods somewhere. Don't you?"

Pike shook his head and said, "Hand on the Bible, I don't, Belle. I'm just a horse rancher now. Torrance and I work with the stock. It keeps me busy."

That was true. He'd heard rumors that a few moonshine stills continued in operation in the county, but the Shannon family didn't have anything to do with them. Pike and his brother Torrance and their grandfather Dougal were all law-abiding men now. That made the boys' mother, Mary, and their sister, Vanessa, happy. And leading a peaceful, lawful life, although quite a change for Pike, had its advantages, and he was learning to appreciate them.

"All right, I suppose I believe you," Belle said. Pike thought she sounded a mite disappointed. "If we're going to get that pie, we ought to go ahead and do it. It *is* getting a little late."

They walked on toward the café. As they approached the neatly painted building, Pike saw yellow lamplight spilling warmly through the curtained windows. The place always had a homey feel to it, the food was good, and the pie was always excellent. That was Sophie's specialty.

That . . . and getting under Belle Ramsey's skin. Although, after the dustup a few months earlier, Sophie had helped the doctor care for Belle's injuries while she was recuperating.

Pike opened the door and stepped back so Belle could walk into the café first. He started to follow her, then had to stop short as she came to an abrupt halt. He looked past her to see what had caused her to throw on the brakes.

A young woman with thick blond curls pulled back and tied at the back of her head stood behind the counter. She wore a blue-flowered dress, a white apron, and a surprised expression that hardened into a frown as she saw Pike there behind Belle.

"Well, don't just stand there letting flies in," Sophie Truesdale said.

CHAPTER 3

"Where's Johnny?" Pike asked. It was probably a dumb thing to say, he thought, but it was the first thing that came to mind.

"Mrs. Quinlan was taken ill," Sophie replied. "Nothing serious, I don't think, but Mr. Quinlan thought he should stay with her this evening. So I told him I'd deal with the café, of course."

"Of course," Belle said. "You're nothing if not helpful and considerate of others, Miss Truesdale."

"Thank you, Miss Ramsey," Sophie responded. Her voice, as well as Belle's, sounded about as cold as an icicle hanging from a porch roof after a blue norther came through. She went on, "What can I do for the two of you?"

Pike glanced around. There weren't any other customers in the café. He said, "We thought we might get a piece of pie, but it looks like you're fixing to close up for the night—"

"Nonsense," Sophie interrupted. "There's still pie. Would you prefer apple or peach?"

"Peach," Belle said.

"Yeah, that'll be fine," Pike said. "Thanks."

"Sit down at one of the tables," Sophie said, "and I'll bring it to you. Do you want coffee, too?"

"Might as well, if it's not any trouble."

"No trouble at all," Sophie said sweetly. "It's my pleasure."

The way her eyes were glittering, though, Pike didn't believe it really was a pleasure.

He and Belle sat down at one of the tables, which like all the others was covered with a blue-checked cloth. He couldn't help but glance back and forth between Belle and Sophie. They were quite different, Sophie with her fair complexion and blond hair, Belle with her rich golden tan and thick auburn hair, but alike in that each girl was pretty enough to plumb take a man's breath away.

Sophie came out from behind the counter and brought over two saucers, each with a slice of pie on it, then followed that with cups of coffee.

"Thanks," Pike said. He had taken off his hat and set it on the floor beside his chair. To make conversation, he added, "Have you heard that Andy Burnett's running for sheriff?"

Judging by her expression, Sophie hadn't. She said, "Really? I wouldn't have expected that."

"I was mighty surprised," Pike said.

"Well . . ." Sophie said as she lingered beside the table, "I don't have anything against Mr. Burnett, but I'm not sure I'd be able to support him in the election."

"Why not?" Belle asked. "Because he used to cook moonshine?"

"It *is* illegal to brew, consume, or possess alcohol in this county."

"Yeah, thanks to you and your friends."

Sophie smiled and said, "I'll accept that as a compliment. All too often, the battle against immorality is a thankless mission."

"I didn't mean—"

"I assure you, Miss Ramsey, I know exactly what you meant."

Faced with the imminent prospect of a catfight breaking out right in front of him—and unsure of what he'd do about it if it did—Pike quickly picked up his fork and took a bite of the peach pie.

"That's mighty good, Sophie," he said. "Don't tell my ma, but I don't know anybody who makes better pie than you do."

"Thank you, Mr. Shannon. That's good to hear as well." Sophie nodded to both of them. "Enjoy. I'm going to clean up a bit in the kitchen. If you wouldn't mind, turn the Closed sign around on the door when you leave."

"Sure." Pike reached for his pocket. "I can go ahead and pay you."

"There's no charge. What is it they say in saloons? 'It's on the house.'"

"Oh, now, you don't have to do that—"

"I insist. Good evening."

With her back stiff, Sophie went behind the counter and then disappeared through the swinging door into the kitchen.

"That's just like her, the stuck-up little busybody," Belle said. "Makes her snide little comments and then runs away."

"After everything that happened a while back, I

thought the two of you were almost getting to be friends," Pike commented.

"You did, did you?" Belle snorted. "Sometimes, Pike Shannon, I don't think you know a thing in the world about women."

As he swallowed another bite of pie, Pike figured he couldn't argue with what Belle had just said. He knew guns and horses and fighting . . . and making moonshine.

In a perfect world, that ought to be enough.

Pike smelled pipe smoke before he reached the ranch house and knew Dougal and Fiddler were sitting out on the porch, puffing away on their corn-cob pipes. He made a face in the darkness as he rode toward the house. He knew those two old codgers would question him about how his evening had gone.

To tell the truth, Pike wasn't sure *how* it had gone. Parts of it had been all right. He had enjoyed the walk with Belle, at least starting out. Even the ruckus with Fritz Durham and his cronies had held a certain appeal. It was good to move around and get in on a little action again. Got the blood pumping, something that Pike had missed.

But then there'd been the tense confrontation between Belle and Sophie, which was both awkward and confusing. Despite what Sophie had said about the pie and coffee being on the house, he had left a silver dollar on the table when they finished, trying to be discreet about it so Belle wouldn't notice.

Maybe she had, maybe she hadn't, but she didn't say anything about it.

She had even kissed him on the cheek when he took her back to her rooming house. Pike would have liked to get a better kiss. He and Belle had sparked a few times, and her kisses had a way of shaking him right down to his toes. But tonight he was glad for that quick brush of her lips when she could have turned away without anything and he wouldn't have been surprised.

He sure as blazes didn't want to have to explain all that to Dougal and Fiddler.

Luckily, he had something else to distract them with, he thought as he walked to the house after putting his horse up in the barn.

"How's Warbonnet tonight, boy?" Dougal asked from one of the rocking chairs lined up on the porch. A little orange glow came from the bowl of his pipe as he sucked in on the stem.

"Mighty quiet," Pike replied. "How else would you expect it to be?"

From one of the other rockers, Fiddler said, "It does seem that the town is a much sleepier place than it once was."

Pike could see the two of them in the light from inside the house. Dougal Shannon, his grandfather, was a big, barrel-chested man with a long white beard and a thick thatch of white hair. Fiddler was about half Dougal's size and mostly bald except for a fringe of graying hair around his ears and the back of his head. He had weak eyes and wore thick spectacles.

To this day, Pike didn't know Fiddler's real name.

That was what everybody called him because he was so good at playing the fiddle, drunk or sober.

He had been drunk when Pike first met him, in the Warbonnet County jail. Fiddler had his own grudges against Doak Ramsey and his deputies. He had become a staunch friend of the Shannon family and had moved in here at the ranch. He was especially friendly with Pike's widowed mother, Mary, something that Pike didn't allow himself to ponder too much. As long as Fiddler made his ma happy, Pike wasn't going to interfere.

Pike leaned against the railing that ran along the edge of the porch and thumbed his hat back. He said, "I ran into Andy Burnett in town."

"What's Andy up to these days?" Dougal asked.

"He'd picked up some handbills he had printed at the newspaper office."

"What sort of handbills? He tryin' to sell something?"

"Yeah, himself," Pike said. "He's running for sheriff in that special election."

The rocking chair creaked as Dougal sat forward sharply.

"Runnin' for sheriff?" he repeated. "Andy? Andy Burnett?"

"That's right."

"What in blazes *for?* Andy's never been a lawman. He's a farmer and a rancher and a . . . a . . ."

"Moonshiner?" Fiddler suggested. "I was under the impression that he'd given up that enterprise, just as you folks have."

"As far as I know, he has," Pike said. "He claims he wants to make the county a better place."

Dougal puffed hard on his pipe for a moment and made clouds of smoke swirl around his head. He took the pipe out of his mouth and jabbed the stem at Pike.

"Make the county a better place? I'll tell you what'd make the county a better place—"

From the open doorway, Pike's brother Torrance said, "Yes, we know, Grandpappy. You want them to repeal the results of that local option election and make Warbonnet County wet again. Maybe that will happen one of these days, but for now, you know what the law says."

Dougal snorted.

"I know what the law says. I also know right from wrong. And it just ain't natural for a man not to be able to take a drink now and then!"

"Theoretically, I agree with you," Fiddler said. "However, having suffered the torments of Hades in freeing myself from the grip of demon rum, I can't say that I'm displeased with the current state of affairs." He sighed. "If liquor were to become freely available again, I'm not sure that I'd be able to withstand its sweet temptation."

"Oh, sure you would," Dougal said. "Mary would keep you on the straight and narrow."

Pike refrained from pointing out that Mary Shannon had never been able to keep her husband Elijah from making moonshine, or her son Tyree, either. And her youngest son, Pike himself, had gone off and become a hired gun, riding dark, lonesome trails all over the West. Even her middle son, the bookish Torrance, had a hot temper and had gotten in trouble now and then. So maybe Fiddler was right and it was better that he wasn't tempted.

Torrance came on out onto the porch and asked, "Did I just hear you say that Andy Burnett's running for sheriff?"

"That's right."

Torrance thought about that, nodded, and said, "I'd vote for him. Andy is a good man, and once he sets his mind to something, he sticks with it until he gets it done."

"That's what I think," Pike agreed.

Dougal scratched at his beard and said, "What do you reckon he'd do, though, if he had to arrest some, uh, friends of his for cookin' 'shine?"

"I hope we never have to find out," Pike said and meant it.

CHAPTER 4

Over the next three weeks, life continued as normal on the Shannon ranch. Pike actually enjoyed helping Torrance and Dougal care for and train the horses they raised. After years spent on lonely trails, never knowing when somebody was going to try to kill him, with little human contact other than his fellow hired guns and whatever soiled dove whose company he'd paid for, being around family and genuine friends was a welcome change for Pike.

True, sometimes he got to feeling fiddlefooted and wanted to be out on those trails again. Now and then he missed the tang of powder-smoke, and figured it was time to go see the elephant. But mostly he was content.

Feelings over the election were starting to heat up in Warbonnet. The day before the election, Andy Burnett rode over to the Shannon ranch and found Pike and Torrance out on the range, checking one of the pastures where they kept their horses.

"Howdy, Andy," Pike greeted him. "What brings you out here?"

Andy thumbed his hat back and said, "I came to ask you a favor, Pike. There's going to be some speechifying in town tonight. Folks have asked both me and Lester Scroggins to talk. They've even built a platform in front of the courthouse for us to stand on while we're giving our speeches." He shook his head. "Man alive, I sure do hate the thought of having to get up in front of a bunch of people like that and talk."

"I would, too," Pike said. "I'm afraid I can't help you with that. If you want somebody to give you a hand figuring out what you ought to say, you need Torrance. He's a lot better with words than I am."

Andy looked over at Pike's older brother and said, "No offense, Torrance, but I sorta know what I want to say already."

"That's fine, Andy," Torrance assured him. "It's always best for a politician to speak from his heart, anyway."

"What I need, Pike," Andy went on, "is for somebody to watch my back. Several people have warned me that Fritz Durham is still going around town trying to stir up trouble against me." He paused, then burst out exasperatedly, "Dang it, I'd give him the blasted horse back if I thought that'd satisfy him. I reckon he's got such a burr under his saddle by now, though, that it wouldn't do any good."

"So you want me there in case a fight breaks out?" Pike said.

"That's sort of been your line of work for the past

decade, hasn't it?" Torrance asked dryly. "Didn't anyone ever hire your gun to help out with an election campaign?"

Pike glared at his brother, his annoyance compounded by the fact that Torrance was right. Pike *had* been involved in an election up in Montana that had turned into a pretty bad shooting scrape. But that wasn't going to happen here in Warbonnet County. Fritz Durham was an obnoxious son of a gun but not a killer. His specialty was bluster, not bullets.

"I don't think you're going to need my help," he told Andy, "but I'd like to hear what you have to say, anyway. So sure, I'll be there."

"So will I," Torrance said. "There's nothing I like better than a good, spirited debate between candidates. In fact, maybe we'll bring the whole family. It would make a good outing. I'm sure there'll be a big crowd, and Ma and Nessa can visit with their friends in town."

That actually sounded like a good idea, Pike thought—as long as there was no trouble.

"Thanks, fellas," Andy said. "You're right about there being a crowd, Torrance, and kind of a fandango at the same time. Not anything as big as Fourth of July, mind you, but the town's got a brass band together to play some songs, and there are supposed to be tables of food set up at the Baptist church. I think you and the folks will enjoy it. Everything should be gettin' underway around sundown."

"We'll be there," Pike promised.

Andy nodded, waved, and rode away. As they watched him go, Torrance said, "You should have asked him how much he's going to pay for your services."

Pike narrowed his eyes.

"I'm just gonna be there as Andy's friend, and you know it. Sometimes you're just a blasted pain in the rump, Torrance."

Torrance shrugged and said, "I'm going to check on those horses on the other side of the creek."

He nudged his mount into motion and headed for the line of trees that marked the course of Coyote Creek. Pike watched him go and sighed. He loved his brother, but he didn't believe that he and Torrance would ever get along as well as they should. The past, and the differences in them, would always be too much between them.

The idea of going to Warbonnet for the campaign speeches was welcomed by the other members of the family, just as Torrance had predicted.

"I've been needing to get into town to pick up a few things at the mercantile," Mary Shannon said when Pike and Torrance told her about Andy Burnett's visit. "I'm sure a canny businessman like John Strickland will stay open since there'll be a crowd in town." She swatted Pike lightly on the arm. "And you should have told Andy to come on to the house and say hello. I'd have been happy to give him a cup of coffee or some cider."

"I reckon he had other things on his mind, Ma, like that speech he's got to give tonight. And I just never thought of it."

"You were raised to be more hospitable than that. Next time think of it."

"I need a few things from Mr. Strickland's general store, too," Pike's sister Vanessa said. "And Julie Bassett said she wanted to introduce me to her cousin who's visiting from Dallas the next time I came into town."

"This cousin of Julie's is a fella, I suppose?" Torrance said.

"Heavens no! I don't have time for any fellas, especially ones from *Dallas*."

Nessa was the youngest of Elijah and Mary Shannon's children and the only one who had inherited their father's bright red hair. It was long and straight, at the moment tied into a ponytail that hung far down her back. She was a slim, athletic girl, as much at home on the back of a horse as she was in a kitchen or parlor. She could handle a rope, too, and was a good shot with a rifle.

When Doak Ramsey had been elected sheriff and started his iron-fisted and ultimately violent rule of Warbonnet County, he had hired several deputies. Some of them had been relatives, some not, and among those who weren't related was a young man named Joe Eagleton. He had gotten to know Nessa, and what might have turned into an actual romance had begun to develop between them—if all hell hadn't broken loose, claiming Joe as one of its victims.

Nessa had moped around some after his death, but they hadn't been close enough for her to be absolutely brokenhearted. So Torrance's thought that

Julie Bassett's city-bred cousin might be a young man wasn't unreasonable.

Nessa's vehement reaction told Pike that maybe she had been a little more upset about Joe than she had let on, though. Maybe she was still getting over losing him.

Belle had told him that he didn't know anything about women, and that included his own sister, he figured. He had been around plenty of ladies—but most of them were ladies of the evening, and he hadn't been interested in learning how their minds worked.

Mary and Nessa fussed around getting ready to go into town. Torrance and Fiddler even shaved and put on clean clothes. Pike and Dougal didn't see any point in going to that much trouble. All they were going to do was listen to politicians speechify, even though one of those fellas was a friend.

When everybody was ready, Fiddler helped Mary up into one of the rear seats of the wagon while Nessa climbed in without any help. Then Fiddler and Dougal settled onto the driver's seat, with Dougal taking up the reins, while Pike and Torrance swung up onto their saddle mounts. The Shannon family headed for Warbonnet.

This part of north central Texas was pretty country with the late afternoon sunshine splashing all over rolling, thickly wooded hills, broad grassy valleys, and the occasional rocky upthrust like the flat-topped hulk of Warbonnet Peak, which was visible in the distance on the far side of the town named for it.

The trail from the ranch merged with the road that ran alongside the Brazos River, which was a deep, greenish-blue right now because it hadn't flooded in a while. Pike had seen the river turn into a brown, roaring monster when too much rain fell upstream. At the moment it was peaceful, with a steady flow that rippled here and there where the water passed over limestone ledges in the broad bed.

The sun was still just above the western horizon when they reached Warbonnet. The raucous strains of a patriotic song being played by the brass band were audible as they neared the settlement. Other people were on the road, on horseback and in buggies and wagons. Looked like the campaign event was going to draw a good crowd as Andy had predicted, Pike thought. Of course, country folks would seize just about any excuse to go to town, even listening to politicians talk.

The road turned into Main Street, and up ahead it was crowded with people. Mary leaned forward and said to Dougal, "Get as close to the store as you can before you park, but I think we'll have to walk a ways."

"Sure," Dougal replied. He guided the wagon team expertly and a few moments later maneuvered the vehicle next to a hitch rail in front of the blacksmith shop. "I reckon this is the best we can do."

"That's fine, Dougal," Mary said, patting her father-in-law on the shoulder. "Strickland's is right there in the next block. You did a good job."

Fiddler hopped down to help her from the wagon. Nessa, wearing a split riding skirt, just threw her leg over the tailgate, balanced there for a second, and

jumped easily to the ground. Pike and Torrance
swung down from their saddles and looped their
reins around the hitch rail while Dougal tied the
team next to their horses.

The six of them joined the crowd streaming
toward the courthouse, where the stand for the
candidates to speak had been built. Kids ran around
playing and yelling. Dogs chased them, barking ex-
uberantly. The brass band, which had assembled
next to the wooden platform, made up for any lack
of talent with the enthusiasm they put into their playing, or at least they tried to. The whole scene was
rather chaotic, but it was chaos of a pleasant sort.

As dusk began to gather, men went around light-
ing the coal oil lamps set on poles that served as
streetlights. Around the speaking stand itself, torches
had been placed to light it up brightly. Once they
were lit, as well, people assembled in the large open
area in front of the courthouse, and on the broad
lawn behind the stand, to listen to the speakers.

Pike and his family were close enough to the
platform that they had a good view of it as the two
candidates for sheriff climbed the steps. The doleful
expression on Andy Burnett's face made it seem
more like he was climbing the steps to the gallows,
rather than a speaker's stand.

Lester Scroggins, on the other hand, had a big,
cheerful smile on his lips under curling handlebar
mustaches. Wearing a rather garish checked suit,
he waved at the crowd and grinned even bigger as
people responded with cheers and applause. One
man cupped his hands around his mouth and yelled
over the din, "Attaboy, Lester!"

The previous mayor, G. Ellsworth Heath, a distant relative by marriage to Doak Ramsey, had ske-daddled from Warbonnet after Doak's death. The manager of the local stage line office, Abe Mill-worth, had been appointed as acting mayor by the remaining members of the town council who hadn't also taken off for the tall and uncut in the wake of the moonshine war between the Ramseys and the Shannons.

At some point, there would have to be a special election to select a regular mayor, but for now, every-one seemed to be satisfied with the job Millworth was doing. He mounted the platform following Andy and Scroggins and waved his arms to get the crowd's attention.

"Folks, settle down, settle down, please!" Mill-worth called in a rather reedy voice. He was a short, scrawny hombre with a ragged brown mustache. "Quiet, please!"

When that didn't get any response, Millworth put two fingers in his mouth and let out a loud, piercing whistle that cut right through the hubbub. The crowd fell silent, and even the kids and dogs hushed.

"That's better," Millworth said. "Now, settle down, folks, because we're gathered here this evenin' on serious business. Tomorrow, as you all know, we're fixin' to have an election to determine who's gonna be the new sheriff of Warbonnet County. The town council and I have prevailed on the two candy-dates for the job to come here and say a few words to us about how they intend to uphold law and order in the county. I reckon most of y'all know who they are . . . Lester Scroggins!"

He flung out his left hand toward Scroggins, who stepped forward, clasped his hands together, and pumped them over his head in the manner of a victorious prizefighter.

"And Andy Burnett!"

Millworth waved his right hand toward Andy, who shuffled ahead a couple of paces and waved shyly at the crowd, still looking like he'd rather be almost anywhere else.

In the crowd, Pike leaned over to Dougal and said quietly, "Andy looks like he's afraid they're going to tar and feather him."

"With some o' this bunch, I wouldn't put it past 'em," Dougal said with a snort.

"You two hush," Mary said. "I want to hear what they're going to say."

Up on the platform, Millworth went on, "Lester and Andy flipped a coin a few minutes ago to see who was gonna get to go first, and Lester won. So, without any more beatin' around the bush, here's Lester Scroggins!"

The band started playing again. The loudmouth from earlier once again bellowed, "Attaboy, Lester!" More applause followed.

Scroggins let it go on for a minute or so, then waved his hands for quiet.

"It's a tree-mendous honor for me to be here this evenin', folks!" he began. "Just like it's an honor to be runnin' for the position of sheriff of Warbonnet County! As many of you are aware, I have extensive experience when it comes to law enforcement—"

"You locked me up plenty o' times when I was

snockered, Lester!" a man called, causing a wave of laughter.

"And that never kept us from bein' friends, because you knew I was just doin' my job, Curley!" Scroggins responded with a grin as he pointed a finger at the man who had spoken. "I give all of you my word that if I'm elected sheriff, I'll do that job, too, without favor or prejudice and with fairness for ever'body! I'll enforce the laws rigorously and even-handedly! Warbonnet County will be a bastion of law and order!"

"I don't know what a bastey yon is, but I like the sound of that," a man in the front row of the crowd said. He whistled and started to clap.

Torrance said to Pike, "It sounds like Lester's got the crowd won over before Andy even says anything."

"Give Andy a chance," Pike replied.

"Oh, I will, I will. I'm not sure everybody else will, though."

"Lester Scroggins is a pompous windbag," Pike muttered.

Fiddler said, "He was a decent jailer. Never treated me bad when I was behind bars, unlike some of the others."

Up on the platform, Lester Scroggins continued to talk, pacing back and forth now and waving his arms around like a hellfire-and-brimstone preacher as he exhorted the crowd about the honor and privilege of serving the law and the community. Pike had to admit that it was a good speech. Andy appeared to think so, too. He even applauded when Scroggins finally finished and stepped back. Scroggins magnanimously gestured for Andy to proceed with his own speech.

Andy swallowed so hard Pike could practically hear the gulp from where he was. He walked up to the front of the platform, cleared his throat, and began, "Friends, neighbors, citizens of Warbonnet County, I'm grateful to you for giving me the opportunity to—"

"Can't hear you!" somebody shouted from the back.

That was probably true, Pike thought. Compared to Scroggins's booming tones, Andy was about as quiet as a church mouse. Pike remembered times in the past when Andy had lifted his voice loud and clear in raucous song as people stomped and danced and men played guitars and fiddles. Unfortunately, moonshine had been involved in all those instances, and Andy was stone-cold sober tonight.

Andy cleared his throat again and made another try, saying, "Thank you for having me here tonight. My name's Andy Burnett—"

Again he was interrupted, but not with a request to speak up this time. Instead, a loud, harsh voice yelled, "Why do we even let this no-account trash up there? Andy Burnett's got no business runnin' for sheriff! He's nothing but a lowdown moonshiner!"

CHAPTER 5

Several men bulled their way to the front of the crowd, ignoring the indignant comments from the people they shoved past. The would-be trouble-makers carried ax handles and held them in such a way it was obvious they were prepared to use them as clubs.

Pike recognized the burly shape and jowly face of the man in the lead, Fritz Durham. He had thought the voice was familiar when Durham yelled and interrupted Andy's speech.

Abe Millworth stepped up to the edge of the platform and said, "Hold on there, Fritz. You can't go bustin' in like this. Lester got to talk, and now Andy gets his chance."

"But he doesn't deserve a chance, that's what I'm saying," Durham replied. "A lawbreaker shouldn't even be allowed to run for sheriff. That's just common sense, blast it!"

"Now wait just a minute," Andy said. Anger made his voice stronger than it had been. "I've never been convicted of any crime or been put in jail. And no matter what you think, Fritz, it's not against the law to make a good deal in a horse trade!"

Durham's jaw tightened in anger as he glared up at the platform.

"Are you denying that you used to make moonshine?" he demanded. "It'll be a waste of breath if you do, because dang near everybody here knows better." Durham cast a disdainful glance at the crowd. "Shoot, probably half of these folks *bought* white lightning from you at one time or another!" He shook the ax handle in his hand at Andy. "And as for horse tradin', the way you associate with horse thieves like the Shannons makes it clear you approve of breaking the law that way, too."

"Now wait just a goldang minute!" Dougal bellowed as he elbowed his way forward, shaking off Mary's hand as she tried to catch hold of the sleeve of the work shirt he wore under his overalls. "You can't talk that way about me and my family, mister! I never stole a horse in all my borned days, and neither did any o' my kin!"

Durham sneered at him.

"You expect me to believe that, old man? Everybody knows the Shannons have been criminals from 'way back. You're just a bunch of white trash hillbillies from Arkansas—"

Torrance lunged to try to grab Dougal's arm as the old-timer took a swing at Durham, but Dougal was too fast for him.

Durham ducked under the wild punch, though, and jabbed his ax handle into Dougal's stomach. It was a vicious blow that made Dougal double over in pain.

As for Pike, he hadn't tried to stop his grandfather from walloping Durham. He figured that whatever happened, Durham had it coming. And Pike was ready and willing to take part in dishing that out, so he was moving in quickly as Durham rammed the ax handle into Dougal's midsection. Durham didn't have time to get himself braced before Pike's right fist crashed into his jaw and drove him back into his companions.

"Stop it, you men!" Abe Millworth yelled from the platform. "Stop that dadgummed fightin'!"

No one paid any attention to him. Durham's friends had caught him and kept him from falling, although his hat had flown off when Pike punched him. He straightened up, shouted a curse, and charged at Pike as he swung the ax handle back and forth.

The men with him, who were similarly armed, were right behind him. As the crowd scattered to let them through, it looked like Durham and the others might overrun Pike and hammer him to the ground with the wooden bludgeons.

Once they had him down, they could kick and stomp him, maybe even fatally.

But before that could happen, Andy Burnett sailed off the platform and landed right in the middle of them, flailing around him with hard, mallet-like fists. His punches sent men reeling every time one landed.

Andy wasn't the only one to come to Pike's aid. From the side, a compact but powerful dark-featured man tore into the bunch of troublemakers, sending blows into the ribs and faces of men with devastating effect, even though the punches didn't travel very far. From the corner of his eye, Pike recognized Sam

Crow, a good friend and another former fellow moonshiner.

Dougal had recovered from being jabbed in the belly and was getting in on the fight, too. So was Torrance, who was a mild sort nearly all the time despite his impressive size. But he wasn't going to stand by and watch any of his family being attacked without striking back.

Pike was only vaguely aware of all that since most of his attention was centered on Fritz Durham. He bobbed and weaved and ducked as he avoided the wild, lashing swings of the length of hardwood wielded by Durham. Durham grunted like an animal as he flailed at Pike.

Any man with a club like that in his hands could be dangerous, but Durham was clumsy and slow and far from an expert fighter, relying on his strength to make up for any shortcomings. Pike got the opening he'd been waiting for as Durham left himself wide open after one particularly erratic swing.

Stepping in swifly, Pike hooked a left into Durham's ribs. Durham grimaced and let his arms sag. Pike whipped a right to the man's jaw again, and this time it landed cleanly enough, and with enough force, to make Durham's eyes glaze over. He let go of the ax handle, and it clattered to the street.

Durham was still on his feet, though, so Pike hit him again, this time with a left. Durham went over backward, and there was no one to catch him this time. His friends were busy brawling themselves. Durham crashed down on his back and made dust fly up from the ground.

Even armed with the hardwood cudgels, the other

troublemakers were proving no match for Torrance, Dougal, Andy Burnett, and Sam Crow. Torrance was big enough that he'd been able to spread his arms wide and plow down two of them. Dougal snatched up a fallen ax handle and walloped one man across the back with it, making him pitch forward on his face. Andy and Sam had knocked another two men off their feet. The two who were left threw down their clubs as one of them yelled, "That's enough! We don't want no more trouble!"

"You're gonna get it anyway," Dougal said as he shifted his grip on the ax handle he held and got ready to wade in on them.

"Hold it!" Andy said before the burly old-timer could start swinging. "They said they'd had enough, and the rest of the bunch look like they have, too. Fight's over."

Pike heard the stern, powerful tone in his friend's voice, and inspiration struck him. He pointed a finger at Andy and raised his own voice to say to the crowd, "You hear that? That's what an honest sheriff sounds like! I don't need to hear any speeches from Andy Burnett. I saw with my own eyes how he dealt with this mob and put a stop to the trouble! You saw it, too, folks!"

For a couple of seconds following Pike's words, silence hung over Warbonnet's main street. Then a man in the crowd called, "Good job, Andy!"

"Yes, sir, mighty fine!" another man added. Several people began to applaud, and that clapping welled up and filled the street.

Andy looked surprised. Up on the platform,

Lester Scroggins appeared nonplussed and not very happy. He hadn't budged to help break up the trouble.

Abe Millworth waved his arms for quiet and said, "Andy, you still got a right to finish your speech if you want to."

Andy shook his head.

"No, that's all right, Mr. Millworth," he said. "I guess I'm not much of a talker."

Torrance slapped him on the back and said, "Actions speak louder than words, anyway."

Millworth shrugged and said, "All right, I reckon if that's the way you want it . . ."

He motioned for the brass band to start playing again. The musicians launched into another patriotic tune.

Andy turned to the Shannons and Sam Crow and said, "I sure do appreciate you fellas pitching in like that."

"Somebody needed to stop Durham from bellering like an old bull," Pike said. He watched as a couple of Durham's friends helped him to his feet. The man still looked pretty glassy-eyed. He didn't even glare at Pike or Andy as he and the others shuffled off into the crowd.

Torrance said, "Durham's liable to try getting even with you, Pike."

"I don't think so," Pike said with a shake of his head. "He's full of hot air, but not much else. I reckon he's had enough."

"I hope so."

While they were talking, men started coming up

to shake Andy's hand and slap him on the back. Andy looked a little uncomfortable at all the attention, but he managed to smile and return the handshakes.

Andy would never be a natural politician, Pike thought, but he was an honest, forthright man, and sometimes that might be enough.

The crowd began to thin out as folks spread along Main Street to shop, visit with friends, or listen to the music from the band. Mary said, "Nessa and I are going down to the store now."

Fiddler said, "I'll go with the ladies and make sure they're all right." The little man hadn't gotten mixed up in the brawl, but that was probably for the best. He had stood between Mary and Nessa and the combatants, ready to protect them to the best of his ability in case the fight had started to spill in their direction.

"We'll be around," Pike said to his mother with a nod. "See you later at the wagon."

He and Torrance and Dougal left Andy surrounded by well-wishers and strolled along the street. Dougal sighed and said, "At a time like this, a fella ought to be able to go into a saloon and get a drink."

"How about a piece of pie instead?" Pike suggested.

"At Miss Truesdale's café?" Torrance said. "I can understand why you'd want to do that, Pike."

Pike frowned.

"You don't understand anything," he said in a surly voice.

Torrance just laughed and clapped a hand on his grandfather's shoulder.

"Come on, Grandpappy," he said. "We'll be Pike's chaperones."

Pike clenched his jaw and kept a tight rein on his temper. He didn't want to start another brawl so soon after the first one was over, especially not with his own brother!

CHAPTER 6

The café was doing good business when the three Shannon men got there, which was no surprise considering how many people were in Warbonnet this evening. People were sitting at all the tables, but a few stools at the counter were open. Dougal asked one of the customers to move over so he and Pike and Torrance could sit together.

Sophie, looking pretty but a little harried in a green dress with the usual apron over it, came along the counter to stand across from them and ask, "What can I do for you?"

"Apple pie and coffee for all three of us," Dougal said. "I'm buyin'."

"Of course, Mr. Shannon."

Sophie's face was a little flushed, and a couple of curling strands of her blond hair had come loose and hung on the sides of her face, framing the attractive features.

"You look like you could use some help," Pike commented.

"I've got Mr. and Mrs. Quinlan both working in

the kitchen this evening while I handle things out here," she said as she reached for cups and saucers for the coffee. "I can't complain. It's times like this that allow the place to actually turn a profit."

"You know what'd make it even more profitable?" Dougal asked. He leaned forward and went on in a confidential tone, "If you were sellin' a few shots of white lightnin' under the counter!"

Sophie stopped in the middle of pouring the coffee and looked up with a horrified expression.

"Why, I could never—" She stopped when she saw the grin on Dougal's whiskery face. "You're just having some sport with me, aren't you, Mr. Shannon?"

"Maybe," Dougal allowed.

"Well, I don't think I'll be selling any illegal liquor in here anytime soon."

"That's probably a good thing," Pike told her. "If you got caught at it, Andy Burnett might have to arrest you if he's elected sheriff."

Sophie put the saucers and coffee cups in front of them and asked, "Do you think he'd really do that? Arrest someone for making or selling moonshine, I mean? Given his history . . ."

"If Andy gets the job and swears to uphold the law, he'll uphold the law," Pike said. "He might not like it all the time, but he wouldn't go back on his word."

"Well, then, perhaps I'll hope that he wins the election tomorrow. Now, that was apple pie you wanted . . .?"

She got three enthusiastic nods in response.

The pie was delicious, as always, and even better

washed down with cups of Sophie's excellent coffee. When they were done, Dougal slid two silver dollars across the counter to Sophie.

"That's too much," she told him. "One will cover it, and you'll have change coming back—"

"No, ma'am, you just keep the extra," Dougal told her.

"That's very generous of you."

"Be a good thing for this café to stay in business. Warbonnet needs folks like you, Miss Truesdale."

She frowned a little and said, "I'm surprised to hear you say that, Mr. Shannon, considering my beliefs when it comes to consuming alcohol."

"Not at all, ma'am. Y'see, without folks like you tellin' other folks they shouldn't be drinkin' 'shine, they might not be so likely to do it. I reckon you know what the Good Book says about forbidden fruit and all."

Sophie's lips thinned in disapproval for a second, but then she took Pike by surprise when she laughed.

"I suppose you're right about that, Mr. Shannon," she said. "So you and I, even though we're on opposite sides, we fulfill a function for each other, symbolically speaking, that is."

"Yeah. I think. I get a mite confused when you start addin' in them fancy words."

Torrance chuckled and said, "Take my word for it, Grandpappy, she's right."

Sophie looked at Pike and asked, "Do *you* have any thoughts on the matter?"

Pike held up his hands defensively.

"Only that the pie and coffee were mighty good,"

he said. "That's about as deep as I want to do any thinking this evening."

"Just remember that the three of you are welcome anytime, despite our philosophical differences."

"You keep makin' pie that good," Dougal said, "and we ain't likely to forget."

They left the café, ready to walk back down the street and rendezvous with Mary, Nessa, and Fiddler at the wagon. Mary and Nessa should have had time to finish their shopping by now.

The three men had hardly started on their way, though, when Pike spotted Belle Ramsey making her way through the happy crowd as she came toward them.

Torrance noticed her, too, and said to Pike, "Good thing Miss Ramsey didn't come along and happen to look through the café's front window while you were gobbling down Sophie Truesdale's pie."

Pike drew in a deep breath.

"I swear, Torrance," he said, "it's like you're trying to goad me into taking a swing at you this evening."

Dougal said, "You two boys stop pokin' at each other. I know, it's natural for brothers to get in scrapes, but we're tryin' to be peaceful and law-abidin' these days, remember?"

"How long do you think *that's* going to last?" Torrance asked with a snort. "Pike must be champing at the bit to start some trouble by now. It's all he knows how to do."

"Keep it up and you'll find out whether or not you're right," Pike snapped.

He turned his back on his brother and grandfather and stepped forward to intercept Belle. As he nodded and pinched the brim of his dark brown hat, he said, "Evening, Belle. Were you around for the, uh, speeches earlier?"

"Speech, you mean," Belle said. "I heard Lester Scroggins get up there on the platform and run his mouth for a while, but Andy didn't get to say much before all Hades broke loose, did he?"

"He said enough . . . and he showed why he ought to be the one who's elected sheriff tomorrow."

"Well, I hope you're right. I've known Andy for quite a while. He's a very decent man."

Pike nodded and said, "Nobody who knows him could ever disagree with that."

"Where are you headed now?"

Pike nodded in the direction of Strickland's Mercantile and said, "Back to the store to meet up with my ma and Nessa. They had some shopping to do after the ruckus was over, so Torrance and Grandpappy and I . . ."

"Did what?" Belle asked as his voice trailed off.

"We've just been, uh, walking around some," Pike replied. He cast a warning glance at Torrance and Dougal, not that he believed it would do much good. Torrance was liable to spout off anyway.

Instead, Torrance didn't say anything, but Pike saw the way his mouth tightened. He was trying to keep from laughing out loud. Dougal looked pretty amused at his discomfiture, too.

"I'm surprised you didn't go down to the café," Belle said with a sweet, innocent smile that Pike didn't believe for a second was genuine. "That seems to be one of your favorite places in Warbonnet."

Torrance couldn't hold it in anymore. He burst out laughing.

Pike jerked his head around and snapped, "Blast it, Torrance—"

"Oh, leave him alone," Belle said. "I know that's where you were. I saw you coming out of there a few minutes ago and thought I'd have a little fun."

"Fun, eh?" Pike repeated.

"It was pretty amusing watching Pike Shannon, the notorious gunslinger, squirm like that. And just for your information, Pike, I don't care what you do. You can go in there and moon over Sophie Truesdale as much as you like."

"I wasn't mooning over anybody. We just had pie and coffee. All three of us. And now we're walking down to the store, if you'd like to come along with us."

"I wouldn't mind saying hello to Mary and Nessa," Belle replied with a shrug. "I'm not walking with you, though. We just happen to be going in the same direction."

"However you want to think of it," Pike said. He started toward Strickland's again.

Belle fell in beside him. Torrance and Dougal came along behind. Pike could hear them talking, but the street was noisy enough that he couldn't make out what they were saying.

He had a hunch that was probably a good thing.

Mary and Fiddler were sitting in the wagon, talking and laughing, when the others got there. Pike thought again that he wasn't sure how he felt about his mother having a gentleman friend, even though he liked Fiddler. He was glad she seemed to be happy, though.

Several crates and canvas bags were in the back of the wagon already. Nessa emerged from the store carrying another bag and placed it in back with the others. Then she said, "Belle, it's good to see you again," and the two girls hugged. They had gone through quite an ordeal together during the final showdown with Doak Ramsey and his men, and that had created a bond of friendship between them.

They chatted for a while about mutual friends and goings-on in the county, and then Nessa said, "You need to ride out to the ranch sometime soon for a visit."

"I'd like that," Belle said. "You think I'd be welcome?"

Eyebrows arching, Nessa looked at her in surprise and asked, "Why in the world wouldn't you be?"

"Well, my last name *is* still Ramsey, and the Ramseys and the Shannons have a history of not getting along."

"History is right. Ancient history. None of that matters anymore." Nessa looked at Pike, who was leaning against the hitch rail waiting for everyone to get ready to go. "Isn't that right, Pike?"

"Belle's just about the last of the Ramseys in these parts," he said. "Seems like it'd be a mite foolish to hold that against her now."

"So you wouldn't mind me riding out to the ranch sometime, Pike?" Belle asked.

"I reckon you know I wouldn't."

"Well, then, I'll keep it in mind." Belle cocked her head to the side. "Here's an idea . . . If Andy wins that election tomorrow and becomes the sheriff, he could hire you as one of his deputies, Pike."

"A Shannon?" Pike exclaimed as he straightened from his casual pose against the hitch rail. "Wearing a lawdog's badge? That's never gonna happen!"

Torrance said, "You know, that's actually not a bad idea. It would give you an excuse to stay on the straight and narrow, Pike. If you're still determined to do that, that is."

"Just forget it," Pike said, shaking his head. "I'm not a star packer, never have been, never will be."

With that, he jerked his reins loose from the hitch rail and swung up onto his horse. As he turned the animal, he looked down at the auburn-haired girl and said, "You're welcome at the ranch anytime, Belle."

Then he heeled his mount into motion, weaving skillfully around the people, horses, wagons, and buggies in the street and heading out of Warbonnet without looking back, unsure why he was so annoyed—

And wishing he had a nice healthy slug of white lightning right about now, to smooth the sharp edges off of whatever burr it was that had gotten under his saddle!

CHAPTER 7

It looked to Pike as if the turnout for the election was actually smaller than the crowd that had gathered in Warbonnet the previous evening for the campaigning. But he supposed that probably wasn't unusual. People had come to hear the speeches to be entertained. Making a mark on a piece of paper and dropping it in a box wasn't nearly as much fun. And of course, the women and children who had been on hand for the festivities weren't voting today.

The voting was done in a meeting room on the first floor of the courthouse. After casting his own ballot, Andy Burnett waited under a shade tree on the lawn for the results. Pike, Dougal, and Sam Crow, all of whom had also voted earlier, kept him company.

"I've been with you when you were waiting for your kids to be born, Andy," Sam said. "I don't think you were this nervous for any of those."

"Well, havin' kids don't put you in a position where you might get shot at," Andy replied.

Dougal grunted and said, "Sometimes it does. It

all depends on what sort o' deviltry those kids . . . and grandkids . . . get up to."

He looked meaningfully at Pike, who heard the comment but chose to ignore it.

"Seems like a pretty good mix of fellas who are voting," he said to Andy. "Quite a few from here in town, but I've seen plenty from out in the country, too."

"And you think the country folks are more likely to vote for me, while the hombres from town pick Lester?"

Pike shrugged and said, "They've probably had a chance to get to know Lester better. But they saw the way you waded in and handled that trouble last night, and that's got to count for something."

"It ought to count for a lot," Sam Crow said. "Lester never budged when the ruckus started. Just stood there watching it with his mouth hanging open."

Andy nodded and said, "I never even thought at the time that it might help my chances of winnin'. I just couldn't stand by while my friends were in trouble."

"And people understand that," Pike said.

"I hope you're right." Andy looked at the courthouse and mused, "You know, when I first got into this, I never figured I had any chance of being elected, and I told myself right from the start that I didn't really care whether I was or not. But now that the day's here . . . I reckon I do care. I'd like to win. I think I'd do a good job."

"So do we," Pike said as he clapped a hand on his friend's shoulder. "And in a few more hours, we'll find out if you're going to get the chance."

The voting ended at six o'clock. It would take a while to count the ballots, but the expectation was that the result would be known by sundown, which occurred around seven o'clock at this time of year.

Lester Scroggins showed up at six-thirty, an impressive figure in a checked suit, embroidered vest, string tie with a silver clasp, and a big, cream-colored hat. Quite a few of his friends and supporters were with him as he came up to Andy, took the big cigar out of his mouth, and extended his other hand.

"Just wanted to wish you luck, Burnett," he said, "and may the best man win."

Scroggins's attitude made it abundantly clear who he believed that to be.

Andy shook hands with him anyway and said, "Thanks, Lester. You ran a clean campaign, and I appreciate that."

The editor of the local newspaper stood nearby scribbling notes for his story about the election in the next edition of the paper, Pike noted. He didn't trust journalists, himself. He had seen too many stories about things he had witnessed and even taken part in, where most if not all of the details were wrong or out of context. As far as he was concerned, journalists were just as fanciful and even more dishonest than the fellas who wrote dime novels, because those drunken hacks weren't pretending to be writing anything other than fiction.

Someone in the crowd called, "Hey, here comes Abe Millworth and Oscar Calhoun!"

Calhoun was the Warbonnet County clerk, a balding, medium-sized man with a round, genial face.

He had a piece of paper in his hand while Acting Mayor Millworth carried the box in which the ballots had been placed. As the two men came along the walk from the courthouse entrance to the street, the crowd surrounded them and the noise level went up considerably.

People stepped aside to let the two candidates move forward to meet the officials. Calhoun and Millworth came to a stop. Calhoun waved for quiet. It was slow in coming until Dougal and several other men added their voices to the request, calling, "Settle down! Settle down, blast it!"

When everyone had quieted down enough for him to be heard, Calhoun cleared his throat and said, "We have the results of the special election for sheriff of Warbonnet County. But before announcing those results, I want to thank Mayor Millworth, Mr. John Strickland, one of our respected businessmen and citizens, and Mr. Hiram Bosworth, pastor of the First Baptist Church, for helping to count the ballots and making sure everything was done correctly and accurately."

Calhoun cleared his throat again, prompting a man in the crowd to call, "Just tell us who won, Oscar!"

"All right, all right," Calhoun said. "Lester Scroggins received 754 votes—"

Whoops and cheers and applause came from Scroggins's supporters. Lester himself waved both hands to the crowd and grinned hugely.

"And Andy Burnett received 789 votes," Calhoun went on when the racket died down.

This time, a surprised silence hung over the crowd

gathered in front of the courthouse. Oscar Calhoun continued, "That means Andy Burnett is the new sheriff of Warbonnet County!"

Pike let out a rebel yell, took his hat off, and waved it in circles over his head. That prompted an upswell of shouting and clapping and whistling as those who had voted for Andy celebrated his victory.

Andy himself just stood there looking stunned.

Dougal slapped him on the back and said, "Good job, boy! You won!"

"Yeah, I . . . I reckon I did," Andy said. A smile spread slowly across his face as well-wishers gathered around to slap him on the back, grab his hand, and pump it enthusiastically.

Lester Scroggins still looked as stunned as Andy had a moment earlier. Clearly, in his mind he had been pinning on the sheriff's badge already. But, as realization soaked in on him, he swallowed hard and pushed his way through the crowd to confront Andy.

The tumult stilled abruptly again as the two men stood there in front of each other. Pike wasn't sure how Scroggins was going to react to losing, and from the tense expressions on the faces of the onlookers, neither was anybody else.

But after a couple of seconds that seemed longer, Scroggins stuck his hand out and said, "Congratulations, Andy. I know you'll make a fine sheriff."

"Why, thank you, Lester," Andy said as he clasped his erstwhile opponent's hand.

Lester grinned.

"I hope if you find yourself in need of a jailer, you'll keep me in mind," he said. "I *do* have considerable experience."

"I'll sure keep that in mind," Andy promised. "As law-abidin' as Warbonnet County has been lately, though, I'm not sure I'll have to lock up all that many folks."

"Let's hope it stays that way."

It was an admirable thought, Pike mused, but he wasn't sure how practical it was. There might be a lull in lawbreaking at the moment, but chances were, it wouldn't last.

He had offered his congratulations to Andy already, so he drifted back to the edge of the crowd on the courthouse lawn. As he did, he noticed Sophie Truesdale standing there, looking nice in a brown dress, with her hair loose around her shoulders and down her back.

"Hello, Pike," she said.

"Evening, Sophie. I, uh, almost didn't recognize you outside the café, without your apron on."

"Oh, really?" she replied, and the hint of coolness in her voice told him that his feeble attempt at humor had been misguided. "Maybe you should make an attempt to see me outside the café more often. You could join me for church services Sunday morning. I believe Pastor Bosworth's sermon is going to be about the virtues of self-control."

"I, uh, I've never been much of one for going to church . . ."

"There's a meeting of the Women's Christian Temperance Union next week, too. I'll be there. You don't have to be a woman to attend."

Her attitude was starting to get under his skin. He said, "Why is your bunch even meeting anymore? You won, didn't you? Warbonnet County is dry."

"Right now it is, but who knows how long that will last?" Her smile was almost a smirk. "There's no telling when someone might decide to take up moonshining again, especially now that Andy Burnett has been elected sheriff."

"Making liquor's against the law. Andy will uphold that law."

"You sound awfully certain about that, Pike. But it's been my experience that people never really change."

"Is that right? Well, that's good to know, I reckon." With stiff, exaggerated politeness, he tugged on the brim of his hat and said, "Reckon I'll bid you a good evening, Miss Truesdale."

As he started to turn away, she said, "Pike, wait. I didn't mean . . . Well, what I said doesn't necessarily apply to everyone. Some people *can* change. It's just . . . very difficult."

"That's true. I reckon somebody's got to have a good enough reason to want to."

Pike looked across the lawn, through gaps in the crowd, to where Andy had been joined by his wife and three young'uns. The kids looked excited, but Deborah Burnett, although she was smiling, seemed a mite worried, too. Pike could understand that. When Andy pinned on the sheriff's badge, he would be taking on a lot of responsibility—and possibly danger, as well.

"Andy's got a good reason . . . four of 'em, in fact," Pike went on to Sophie.

"I hope you're right, Pike," she said.

He nodded to her, a little more friendly-like now, and left her standing there at the edge of the crowd.

He believed her when she said the gibe about people not being able to change hadn't been directed at him.

But even so, she was right. Deep down, he wasn't sure that he *had* changed since returning to Warbonnet County. For a while he had found himself up to his neck in lawbreaking and gun smoke, and even though the past few months had been peaceful enough, he sensed that old restlessness inside him. The need to raise hell, shove a chunk under the corner, and spend some time on the knife edge of excitement and trouble.

Maybe Andy Burnett would be able to keep Warbonnet County a peaceful, law-abiding place. In a way, Pike hoped that would be the case.

Because he knew, no matter how reluctant he was to admit it, that he was eager for any excuse to cut loose his wolf again.

CHAPTER 8

Andy Burnett reined his horse to a stop, thumbed his hat back, frowned up at the top of the wooded hill in front of him, and sniffed the air.

The sharp tang he detected was unmistakable to him. He had cooked enough 'shine that he had smelled it many times. That was sour mash.

Somebody had a still nearby, and they had been operating it for a while, otherwise they wouldn't have had the sour mash starter to use for the next batch.

The Brazos River was behind him. He hipped around in the saddle and looked along the stream. He had sent his deputies, Lem Cranepool and Jack Humphries, to search farther along the river. They were still in sight but facing the other way, about a hundred yards apart. Andy didn't want to yell or fire a shot to get their attention, because doing that would alert the moonshiners that somebody was around.

Of course, they probably knew that already. With a vantage point like that hilltop, they'd be fools if they hadn't posted a lookout to keep an eye on the surrounding countryside.

Even knowing that he might have been spotted, Andy had a job to do. He pulled his hat back down tighter on his head and kneed his horse into motion. He spied a faint trail weaving its way up the slope and started toward it.

He had to watch where he was going, but he also kept lifting his eyes to the slope above him, watching closely for any sign of an ambush.

Twenty years earlier, there might have been Comanches lurking among the post oaks and live oaks. The Indians might be gone, pushed 'way out into West Texas and then onto reservations, but that didn't mean trouble wasn't waiting for him.

He had received several reports that people had smelled something suspicious out here in this area five miles southeast of town. Not only that, in the past month since taking office he'd had to make half a dozen arrests for drunk and disorderly conduct in Warbonnet.

None of the men he had put behind bars would admit where they had gotten the liquor, and since they had all paid their fines, he'd had no choice but to let them go. The amount of trouble a fella could get into for taking on a snootful of booze wasn't bad enough to scare any of them into talking.

Over and above the evidence of those fellas he had locked up, Andy had heard numerous rumors about moonshine being available in the county again. A few men had sidled up to him and suggested— unwisely—that he must be the one who'd gone back into the 'shine business. Being sheriff was a perfect cover for an operation like that, as Doak Ramsey had proven . . . for a while, before his crimes had all caught up with him.

Andy had kept his temper and advised those hombres that as sheriff, it was his job to arrest anybody making, transporting, selling, possessing, or consuming liquor. Some folks might not believe that, even yet, but it was exactly what he intended to do.

As he followed the trail higher, his nerves felt like they had ants crawling along them. Not for the first time since being sworn in as sheriff, he thought that he had made a huge mistake by going after the job. He wasn't afraid for himself, not really, but Deborah and the three little ones were depending on him. If anything happened to him, what would they do? How would they get along?

And yet, if every man felt that way and nobody was willing to tackle the jobs that might prove to be dangerous, the world would descend into chaos, and pretty darned quick-like, too. Somebody had to step up and defend law and order—

The swift rataplan of hoofbeats interrupted his brooding thoughts and made him haul back on the reins. As his horse came to a stop, he turned to look back down the slope.

Jack Humphries was riding fast toward the foot of the trail. He must have spotted Andy about halfway up the hill, because he grabbed his hat off his head, waved it in the air, and yelled, "Sheriff! Hey, Sheriff!"

Andy grimaced. Jack had served as a city marshal's deputy up in Fort Worth, so he should have known better than to start hollering like that while they were hunting lawbreakers.

From the crest somewhere off to Andy's right, in the direction the trail had been meandering, a rifle suddenly cracked. Andy's head jerked toward the sound, then back to Jack Humphries. He watched in horror as Jack toppled backward out of the saddle with his arms flung out to the sides.

The deputy's right foot caught in the stirrup. The horse, spooked by the shot and Jack's sudden tumble from his back, whirled around and bolted, running at crazy angles because of the weight dragging from the stirrup. Andy saw the way Jack bounced loosely on the uneven ground and knew that the man was dead, probably drilled cleanly by whoever had fired from the hilltop.

The guard might have been dozing and hadn't known anyone was around until Jack started shouting. He had reacted quickly, gunning down the man who was approaching the still, but once he had time to think about it, likely he would realize that Jack had been yelling at *somebody*.

He might have even heard the word *Sheriff.*

That meant the moonshiners would not only be ready for him, Andy realized, but also that they might come looking for him in order to keep him from getting away.

He wheeled his horse around and started back down the trail as fast as he could go. Unfortunately, the way the narrow path twisted among the trees and brush, he couldn't build up much speed.

More hoofbeats sounded, this time from above him. They were after him, all right.

"There he goes! Get him!"

Andy bit back a curse as he heard the shout from his pursuers. The next second, guns began to blast. The dull flatness of the reports told him they were handguns, and he was still within range. The crackle of branches as slugs whistled through the brush not far from him was proof of that.

He thought about pulling his iron and firing up the slope at them, but he discarded the idea. He wasn't a gunhand like Pike Shannon, and shooting uphill was tricky even for a skilled marksman. Being on horseback made it even more difficult.

No, even though running away grated on him, especially when he had seen Jack Humphries killed right in front of him, he knew that he was outnumbered and outgunned, and if he tried to shoot it out with the moonshiners, he'd just wind up dead.

That wouldn't do Jack or anybody else any good.

Andy bent low in the saddle to make himself a smaller target as another bullet whined past him, uncomfortably close to his head. He yanked his horse around a bend in the trail and saw the end of it, where it opened out onto the fairly level ground between here and the river, half a mile away.

As he looked in that direction, he saw another rider galloping toward him and recognized Lem Cranepool, his other deputy. Cranepool was a leathery, middle-aged man with a drooping gray mustache. He had been a cowboy and a freighter and had also worked as a lawman in various places. Andy considered himself lucky to have been able to hire him. As Cranepool had put it, he was "gettin' a mite too long in the tooth to keep workin' for forty a month and found."

Now Cranepool was riding fast enough that the wind pushed the brim of his hat up against the crown. He must have spotted Andy as he rode out into the open and realized the sheriff was under attack, because he pulled his Winchester rifle from a saddle boot, guided his horse with his knees, and started cranking off shots at the men chasing Andy down the hill.

Andy waved Cranepool off, figuring they would both head for the river, get back to Warbonnet and gather a posse, then return to this hill and raid the still—assuming it was still there. Knowing that they had been discovered, the moonshiners might have broken down the apparatus and fled by then.

Andy heard the ugly thud of a bullet striking flesh, and at the same instant, his horse leaped under him, almost unseating him. When it started running again, its gait was unsteady. Andy knew the horse had been hit, and from the way the animal slowed and began to flounder, the wound was a bad one. Andy yanked his rifle from its scabbard and kicked his feet out of the stirrups.

It was a good thing he did, or else he might have been pinned when the horse went down less than ten strides later.

Andy landed running, but he threw on the brakes quickly as several slugs kicked up dust not far from his feet. He turned and dived back behind the horse, which was lying on its side, wheezing and breathing its last breath. Andy shoved away the rage he felt at the poor animal being shot down like that. He couldn't afford it right now. He had to stay cool-headed and keep his wits about him if he hoped to survive.

The horse wasn't very good cover, but it was better than nothing. Andy tried to shrink himself as small as he could as he heard a couple of shots smack into what was now a carcass. He didn't lift his head until he heard hoofbeats from the direction of the wooded hill. He risked a glance and saw two men on horseback emerging from the trees. They blazed away with handguns as they charged toward him.

He shoved the Winchester's barrel over the horse's body and fired. One of the attackers jerked in the saddle but didn't appear to be hit. Andy figured he had come close enough to spook the fella, but that was all.

With dust and powder smoke in the air and sweat in his eyes, he couldn't see well enough to make out any details about the men trying to kill him. He worked the rifle's lever and was about to take another shot when hoofbeats drummed up behind him and a second rifle cracked swiftly. Lem Cranepool had disregarded the order to veer off and had come to his rescue instead, Andy saw when he glanced back over his shoulder.

And the bushwhackers didn't care for the fact that the odds had evened up. As Cranepool and Andy threw lead at them, they whirled their mounts abruptly and charged back into the trees.

Caught up in the heat of battle and furious that they had killed his horse, Andy leaped to his feet and said, "Haul me up there behind you, Lem, and let's go after them!"

"Wouldn't be a good idea, boss," Cranepool drawled. He held the rifle in his right hand and extended the left to Andy. "Come on up, but we'd best light a shuck outta here. No tellin' how many more of the varmints are up there. They could be drawin' a bead on us right now."

Andy realized the deputy was right. He clasped Cranepool's wrist, put his foot in the stirrup, and swung up behind the man with Cranepool's help. Cranepool heeled the animal into a run, although it couldn't muster up as much speed now, carrying double like this.

Andy looked at Jack Humphries's body when they passed it. Normally he was a mildspoken man, but a curse ripped out of him at the sight.

"I know what you mean," Cranepool said. "Hate to leave him, but we can't carry him back in. We'll send the undertaker with a wagon."

"And I'm going to find the men who did this," Andy vowed. "They may have taken off for the tall and uncut by the time we get back out here, but that doesn't matter. I'll track them down and bring them to justice, no matter what it takes."

"And I'll help you," Cranepool said as they reached the river and turned to ride northwest along it toward Warbonnet. "But it might be a good idea to see if you could recruit some more help, too."

"What are you talking about, Lem?"

"If you're huntin' men, sometimes the best one to do it is a fella who's been hunted his own self. He knows how they think."

Andy nodded slowly, even though he was behind Cranepool, and the deputy couldn't see him. He had a hunch he knew what Cranepool meant, and it wasn't a bad idea.

Of course, Pike Shannon probably wouldn't see it that way.

CHAPTER 9

Stripped to the waist on this hot day, Pike hammered on a horseshoe he held on the anvil with a pair of tongs. The rhythmic blows rang loudly here in the small blacksmith shop on the Shannon ranch.

Pike wasn't much of a smith, or a farrier, either. Torrance was considerably better at both jobs. But Torrance wasn't here, and Pike's horse had thrown a shoe somewhere. He hadn't been able to find it, so he was trying to come up with a replacement.

When he paused in banging the hammer against the shoe, he heard a horse approaching. Leaving the horseshoe and the tongs on the anvil, he switched the hammer to his left hand and stepped into the shop's doorway to see who was coming.

Even though he didn't have a shirt on, his gun-belt was strapped around his hips, and the Colt .45 rode easily in its holster. A man might not expect trouble, but he was wise to be prepared for it.

Pike relaxed as he recognized the man riding toward the ranch headquarters. Andy Burnett had come for a visit.

Or maybe it was official business, Pike thought, although he wasn't sure what the sheriff of War-bonnet County might want with him. He was just a peaceable, law-abiding rancher these days—like it or not.

Andy saw Pike standing in the door of the black-smith shop and turned his horse in that direction. He reined in, nodded, and said, "Howdy, Pike. Good to see you."

"Likewise, Andy. Or should I call you Sheriff Burnett?"

A solemn look came over Andy's face as he said, "I'll always be Andy to you, Pike, but as a matter of fact, I *am* here in my capacity as sheriff."

Pike tried not to grimace. He hadn't actually expected this visit to turn out to be an official one, but it seemed he was wrong about that. He said, "Hold on. I want to put this hammer up and get my shirt on. Wouldn't want to be arrested in the half-dressed state I'm in now."

Andy frowned and asked, "Who said anything about arresting you?"

"Why else would the sheriff ride all the way out here?"

"To ask for your help," Andy said.

Pike could tell from his friend's expression that something serious had happened. He said, "Ride on over to the house. I'll be there in a minute."

Andy nodded and turned his horse. Pike went back into the shop, set the hammer on the anvil, and shrugged into his shirt. He buttoned it and tucked it in while he walked to the house.

By the time he got there, Andy had dismounted

and was standing on the porch, talking to Pike's mother and Fiddler. The two of them must have heard Andy's horse and come out to greet him. Mary and Fiddler were smiling, so Pike figured Andy hadn't told them the real reason he was here.

"You just sit down there in one of the rockers," Mary told Andy as Pike climbed the steps. "I'll get some glasses of nice cool lemonade and be right back."

Andy smiled and said, "I'm much obliged to you, Miz Shannon. It was a pretty warm ride out here from town."

"I imagine it was." Mary fanned her face with her hand. "It's turning out to be a scorcher today."

She disappeared into the house. Fiddler gestured toward the four rockers lined up on the porch and said, "Let's sit down, gentlemen. Unless you'd rather talk to Pike alone, Sheriff Burnett . . . ?"

"No, that's all right, Fiddler. I expect the news will be all over the county by nightfall."

"What news is that?" Pike asked as the three of them sat down. Andy had taken off his hat while he was talking to Mary. Instead of replacing it on his head, he rested it on his knee.

"One of my deputies was killed earlier today," he said.

"Good Lord!" Fiddler said. "What happened? Was it an accident?"

"No accident. A no-good, bushwhacking moon-shiner shot him."

"You're gonna have to explain that," Pike said grimly.

Quickly, Andy sketched in the details of the brief

fight at the hill southeast of town. He concluded, "My other deputy, Lem Cranepool, thinks that Jack must have spotted something up on the hill, maybe some smoke, and was riding to warn me when they gunned him." He shook his head. "I reckon we'll never know for sure. But Jack's dead, no matter what. And I'm gonna get the men responsible for it."

"You said you wanted my help," Pike reminded him.

Andy nodded and was about to respond when the door opened and Mary came out onto the porch carrying a tray with four glasses of lemonade on it. The drink was cool enough, and the day hot enough, that beads of sweat formed on the glasses almost instantly.

She stopped short and said, "My, you men look serious. Did I interrupt something important?"

"Andy was just telling us about something bad that happened today," Pike said. "One of his deputies was shot and killed by some varmints operating a moonshine still southeast of town."

"Oh, no." Mary's eyes widened, and she suddenly looked unsteady on her feet.

Fiddler was the closest to her. He sprang up and took the tray from her hands before she dropped it. He turned and handed it to Pike, then took hold of Mary's arm and said, "Here, let me help you sit down."

When she was in one of the rockers, she patted his hand and said, "Thank you, Fiddler. That shouldn't have thrown me for such a loop. It's just . . . I hoped Warbonnet County was going to be a nice, peaceful place to live now."

"Yes, ma'am, I reckon we all did," Andy told her. "But I've been hearing a lot of rumors that moonshining has started up again in these parts. And now that I have proof of it, I'm gonna have to try to put a stop to it."

"I understand, I just—" Mary looked up suddenly, and anger glittered in her eyes as she went on, "Andy Burnett, you don't believe that the Shannon family had anything to do with this, do you?"

"No, ma'am, of course not," Andy replied hastily. "I mean, after all the trouble with Doak Ramsey and his bunch, Pike and Dougal didn't exactly give that Texas Ranger their word that they'd never cook up any more 'shine, but—"

"We haven't," Pike said, his voice flat and hard. "Especially not now. We wouldn't put you in that position, Andy."

The sheriff nodded and said, "I appreciate that more'n you know, Pike. I swear, the possibility that you folks might be involved in what happened to my deputy, or any of the other lawbreaking going on around here, never even entered my mind. Just the opposite, in fact. Lem Cranepool came up with a good idea, and I agree with him. The best man to help me track down those varmints is sitting right here."

He looked directly at Pike.

"Who, me?" Pike burst out.

"You've hunted men, and you've been hunted," Andy said bluntly. "And you know moonshiners, too. Tell me anybody else in Warbonnet County better suited to finding the men who murdered Jack Humphries."

Fiddler said, "He has a point, Pike."

Pike glared at the little man for a second, then turned his attention back to Andy.

"I'm sorry about what happened, but I've said all along that I won't wear a badge. I don't have any interest in being a deputy." Pike snorted. "That fella Scott tried to tell me I ought to be a Ranger, and you saw how far he got with that idea."

"I know the way you feel, Pike. That's why I'm not asking you to be my deputy. I'm asking you as a friend. Nothing official about it."

Pike's frown deepened. Andy was a pretty smart hombre. He had known that Pike would turn him down flat if he'd asked him to pin on a badge.

But he had always had trouble saying no to a friend. That had gotten him in trouble more than once in his life.

And now it looked like it might do that again.

Pike leaned forward in the rocker and clasped his hands together between his knees. He said, "If I try to find the fellas, I'll do it my own way. I've never been very good about following any sort of rules."

"That's another good reason not to ask you to let me swear you in as a deputy."

Fiddler chuckled and said, "I believe you've thought this through, Andy."

"I've tried, believe me. Well, Pike, what do you say?"

Pike glanced over at his mother, who said, "It sounds pretty dangerous to me. But then, you've never really listened to me about taking the safe way, have you, Pike?"

"I reckon not."

Andy said, "If you want to talk about this with Torrance and Dougal before you give me your answer—"

"That's not necessary. I'll make up my own mind, you know that. And I don't reckon it'd hurt anything for me to look into it."

"I'm mighty happy to hear you say that."

"I reckon you've already taken a good look around, out where it happened?"

Andy nodded and said, "Yeah, Lem and I gathered up some men and rode back out there when the undertaker went to get Jack's body and bring it in. The still was already gone."

"No surprise there."

"Looked like they were in the middle of a run but just put out the fire, dumped everything, loaded up the still, and left. We found wagon tracks and what looked like two or three riders with it."

"Anything that might tell you who they were?" Pike asked.

Andy shook his head.

"They cleaned up after themselves pretty good. The only thing they left behind was this."

He reached into his shirt and pulled out what appeared to be a folded piece of cloth. He handed it to Pike, who unfolded it and said, "What is this?"

"I think it's a piece of a sack that had sugar in it. They'd have needed sugar for the mash."

Pike rubbed his finger over the coarse fabric. A few tiny white grains clung to the tip. He licked them off, then nodded and said, "That's sugar, all right." He held the cloth up and studied it more closely. "There's something printed on here. N . . . E . . . T. Net. Looks like it's just part of a word, with the first and last parts torn off."

"I saw that," Andy said. "All I could think of was a fishing net." He shook his head. "It didn't make any sense to me."

"Me, either, but it's something to keep in mind, I suppose. You want this back?"

Andy waved a hand and said, "No, you keep it, just in case you find something it ties in with."

Pike folded the scrap of cloth and put it in his pocket, then said, "What do you intend to be doing while I'm trying to find those bushwhackers?"

Andy sighed.

"You know, at first I was so mad, I was bound and determined I was gonna track them down myself. But I was elected sheriff of the whole county, to enforce all the laws, and I can't ignore my other duties to go after this bunch. I'll still investigate any other moonshining I hear about, because that's my job, but as for tracking down those killers . . . I'm going to be relying on you, Pike."

Pike nodded slowly.

"I'm sorry if I'm putting too much of a burden on you—"

Pike lifted a hand to forestall Andy's apology. He said, "It's not too much of a burden, don't worry about that. I didn't know that fella Humphries who was shot, but I don't like the idea of anybody gunning down a deputy just to protect a still."

Mary seemed to have gotten over her shock at hearing the news. Her voice was firm as she said, "That's right. Your father, God rest his soul, and your grandfather and your brothers may have cooked plenty of 'shine in their time, but they never hurt a lawman or anybody else. They were moonshiners, not outlaws. Pike, whether you need it or not, you have my blessing to help Andy put a stop to this."

"Thanks, Ma," Pike said as he reached over and clasped her hand for a moment. Mary Shannon was a pioneer woman, and as such, she had a fierce streak in her that came out now and then. "I'd appreciate it if you wouldn't say anything about this to Torrance or Nessa or Dougal. I don't want Torrance griping at me about it, and Nessa and Dougal might worry."

"Well, I suppose I can do that. You boys didn't drink your lemonade," she went on. "It's a hot day, and there's no need for you to go thirsty, especially you, Andy, since you have to ride all the way back to Warbonnet."

"Thank you, Miz Shannon." Andy lifted his glass and drank deeply of the cool, tart liquid. "That's mighty good."

Mary smiled and said, "If Dougal was here, he'd tell you it'd be better with a splash of 'shine in it."

"It's fine the way it is," Fiddler assured her. "Very tasty."

Andy finished his lemonade and stood up, saying, "Reckon I'd best get back to town. Pike, thank you again. If there's anything I can do to help you—"

"I'll let you know," Pike promised. He stood up and followed Andy out to the hitching post where the sheriff had tied his horse.

Away from Mary and Fiddler, Andy lowered his

voice and asked, "Are you sure about this, Pike? I don't want to take advantage of our friendship."

"You're not," Pike assured him. "I'm glad to give you a hand, Andy."

In truth, he was more than glad to break up the monotony that life here on the ranch had become. He loved his family and enjoyed being around them, but he had spent too many years on lonely trails, never knowing when or where danger might strike. Finding the men who had killed Jack Humphries and helping Andy deal with the moonshining moving back into Warbonnet County was just what he needed.

He could almost smell the powder smoke already.

CHAPTER 10

The terrain in the far northwestern corner of Warbonnet County was the most rugged in the county, with numerous hills dotted by rock out-croppings and separated by brush-choked gullies. The twisting course of the Brazos River became even more serpentine as it wound through those hills, often running between high, thickly wooded bluffs.

The landscape became less rough and sloped gradually downward to the southeast, so that by the time a rider reached the opposite corner of the county, he was traveling through flat fields planted with sorghum and cotton.

There were no farms up here. The soil was too poor for that. It was decent country for grazing cattle, though, because thickly grassed meadows were tucked away between some of the spiny hills. There was also a road that meandered down toward Warbonnet from the settlements farther west and north.

Pike had followed that road up here today. He reined in as he came in sight of a building beside the trail a couple of hundred yards ahead of him. It was a fairly large structure but had a squatty look about it. Roughly built of thick wooden beams on the upper half, above big chunks of red and tan sandstone, it had a sagging wooden porch on the front and a rickety-looking barn off to one side.

Somebody had painted BENNETT'S TRADING POST in ragged red letters on a wide board and nailed it to the front of the awning over the porch. A wagon was parked in front of the building and three horses were tied up at a hitch rail, so it appeared the place was doing a little business. The horses had a dusty, weary look, as if they had been ridden hard.

Pike had been here before. In fact, he had run into trouble at the trading post when he first rode back into Warbonnet County.

However, that was months in the past, and he hoped to pick up the trail he was looking for here. Something had stirred around in the back of his mind when he studied that scrap of cloth from a sugar bag Andy Burnett had given him, and later that evening, it had come to him what it was.

He heeled his horse into motion again and rode slowly toward the trading post. He was still about fifty yards away when a shotgun boomed inside the building. A couple of seconds later, the front door slammed open and two men charged out, twisting around as they did so to fire revolvers back into the building. Smoke and flame spouted from the gun muzzles.

Pike reined in again, uncertain what was going

on. The two men leaped from the porch to the ground, ignoring the steps, and lunged for the horses. They wore long dusters that flapped around them as they practically leaped into the saddles on two of the mounts.

Another man appeared in the doorway, spewing curses and shouting, "Come back here, you no-good thieves!" He waved a shotgun—surely the one Pike had heard go off a moment earlier—and then tried to draw a bead on the two men as they jerked their horses around.

One of the fleeing men fired again. The man with the shotgun screamed as he fell back in the doorway and dropped the double-barreled weapon.

The two outlaws hauled their mounts the rest of the way around and kicked them into a gallop that sent them pounding along the trail straight at Pike.

The brief glimpse he'd had of the man with the shotgun had been enough for him to recognize Edgar Bennett, the owner of the trading post. Pike didn't like Bennett, but he hoped the man wasn't hurt too badly. Right now, Pike had a use for him.

And that meant he also had a good reason to stop the two men who, evidently, had just robbed the place.

They probably expected him to get out of their way. To ensure that, they threw several wild shots in his general direction. Pike reined his horse around so the animal was crossways in the trail and drew his Colt. The gun came up fast and smooth, without hurrying, and he squeezed the trigger as the barrel leveled on the chest of the rider who was closest to him.

The Colt roared and bucked. The outlaw rocked back as the slug hit him, then flopped forward. He stayed mounted, but he wasn't guiding his mount anymore. The horse shied toward the edge of the trail and started trying to buck the deadweight that smelled of blood off its back.

The man went flying, hit the ground hard, and didn't move. The way he landed like a sack of grain told Pike he was either dead or close to it.

Seeing that, the other man realized that he needed to regard Pike as a serious threat. Instead of continuing to fire wildly, he took aim and triggered a shot that whipped past Pike's ear, much too close for comfort.

As Pike returned fire, he noticed that this man clutched a canvas bag in the same hand that held the reins. That bag probably contained the loot from the trading post, Pike thought.

No matter how good a marksman a man was, shooting from horseback was always tricky business. Pike's bullet was well-aimed, but the outlaw's horse jumped to the side just at the wrong instant, and the slug that should have hit the outlaw in the chest drilled him through the right arm instead.

The impact slewed the man halfway around. He had to drop the bag and grab the saddle horn to keep from falling off the horse. He yelled a curse and tried to raise his gun again, but his wounded arm refused to work. He even fumbled his grip on the revolver, and it dropped to the ground.

Without the rider banging his heels against the horse's flanks, the animal slowed. The man was able to get hold of the reins again and bring the horse to a stop. He sat there glaring at Pike, who rode up carefully with his gun held ready.

The man cussed him out, up one way and down the other, then said, "This was none of your business, mister. Why'd you have to horn in?"

"I've got my reasons," Pike answered. He wanted to see how badly Edgar Bennett was hurt. He gestured slightly with the Colt's barrel and went on, "Turn that horse around and ride on back to the trading post."

Cursing bitterly, the man started to turn his horse. As his left side swung around toward Pike, he let go of the reins, slid that hand underneath the duster he wore, and plucked a Smith & Wesson pocket pistol from behind his belt.

Pike hadn't spotted the hideout gun, but he had been halfway expecting a sneaky move like that, so he was ready. The outlaw simply wasn't fast enough to raise the gun and fire before Pike's Colt roared again.

The bullet punched into the robber's chest and drove him off his horse. He landed on his back in the road and spasmed a couple of times before his final breath rattled grotesquely out of his throat.

Pike took a glance at the first man he'd shot to make sure that hombre hadn't budged. Satisfied that both of the outlaws were dead, he rode on quickly to the trading post.

As he came up to the building, Edgar Bennett

stumbled out onto the porch again. Pike was glad to see that the man was alive and on his feet. In fact, he didn't even see any blood on the dirty apron Bennett wore, or anywhere else on the man's disheveled clothes.

To steady himself, Bennett clung to one of the posts that held up the awning over to the porch. He was a short, fat man with a little mustache, double chins, and a few strands of greasy black hair combed over the top of a mostly bald head.

Pike brought his horse to a stop again and said, "I thought you were shot, Bennett."

The trading post owner cursed and said, "Not through any fault of that blasted owlhoot I ain't ventilated. He did his best to kill me. But his bullet hit my shotgun and knocked it clean out of my hands. Hurt like blazes. I couldn't even feel my fingers for a couple of minutes. Plumb ruined a good gun, too, blast his ornery hide!" Bennett squinted bleary eyes past Pike at the bodies in the trail. "They're both dead, ain't they?"

"They are." Pike nodded toward the third horse, which was still tied up at the hitch rail. "Was there another man with them?"

"Yeah, but I done for him with my shotgun. The three of them came in and wanted whiskey. I didn't trust 'em, right from the start, so I sort of moseyed along behind the counter until I could reach that scattergun of mine on the shelf underneath it. I hadn't had a chance to grab it when they pulled their irons and told me to clean out the till."

Bennett leaned over and spat into the dirt before continuing his story.

"They had the drop on me, so I didn't have any choice but to do what they said. I filled the bag one of 'em tossed on the counter, and I don't know what would've happened after that. I got a hunch they would've gunned me down like a dog. They had that sorry look about them."

He shrugged and went on, "But right then, Jasper Cole drove up in his wagon and stopped, and they told me to keep my mouth shut and waited for him to come in. When he did, one of the varmints walloped ol' Jasper with his gun butt and knocked him out. But that distracted 'em enough for me to get my hands on my Greener, and I blowed one of 'em down. The other two lit out with my money. You know what happened after that, Shannon." Bennett's eyes narrowed. "By the way, what happened to that poke full o' money?"

Pike turned in the saddle and pointed along the trail.

"Fella dropped it when I shot him," he said.

Bennett seemed steadier on his feet now as he started down the porch steps, saying, "I better go get it."

"What about that hombre you mentioned? Jasper?" Pike said sharply. "Hadn't you better check on him?"

"Oh, he's all right," Bennett replied with a negligent wave toward the trading post, not looking back. "He's got a hard head."

He started trudging toward the dropped money bag. Pike shook his head in disgust and got ready to dismount. If Bennett wasn't going to make sure Jasper Cole was all right, he supposed it was up to him to do so.

He hadn't swung down from the saddle yet when a man suddenly reeled into the open doorway from inside the trading post. He wore a duster like the other two owlhoots, and his face was covered with blood, as was his left arm and side.

Pike realized instantly that this was the third robber, the one Bennett had blasted with a load of buckshot. Most of the charge must have missed him, because he definitely wasn't dead, no matter what Bennett had believed. As curses spilled from the man's mouth, he thrust the gun in his right hand toward Bennett's back.

Pike had holstered his Colt, but he drew and fired before the outlaw could pull the trigger. His slug hit the man in the head and dropped him like a rock.

At the sound of Pike's shot, Bennett yelled incoherently, jumped about a foot in the air, and then made a stumbling turn to see what had happened.

He saw Pike sitting there on his horse with a wisp of smoke curling from the muzzle of his Colt. The third bandit was a bloody heap on the porch.

Pike started to reload and drawled, "That's another one you owe me, Bennett." He fixed the trading post owner with a hard gaze, adding, "And I aim to collect."

CHAPTER 11

Using a rope, Pike dragged the other corpses back to the trading post. The outlaws' horses were grazing nearby, calm now that the shooting was over. He led them back and tied them to the hitch rail with the other one. When he was ready to leave the trading post, he would tie the dead men over their saddles and take them back to Warbonnet.

Judging by the gaunt, beard-stubbled looks of the three hombres, they had been riding the owlhoot trail for a while without being very successful at it. The fact that they would stoop to robbing an isolated trading post like this was another indication that they weren't exactly notorious desperadoes.

But Andy Burnett might have wanted posters on them. Pike wasn't interested in claiming any bounty, although he supposed if he had any money coming to him for killing the three of them, he would take it.

It was more a matter of identifying them. They might have kinfolks somewhere who would like to know what had happened to them, no matter how grim their end had been.

There had been a time, Pike reflected, when after trading bullets with scum like this, he would have dug a shallow hole and piled them all in it, at best. At worst, he would have left them where they fell for the buzzards and coyotes.

He supposed that returning home and spending time with his family had softened him somewhat. He figured that if he had wound up dead during his long self-exile from Warbonnet County, he would have appreciated it if someone had let his folks know.

With that chore done, he went into the trading post and found Edgar Bennett knotting a crude bandage around the head of a grizzled old-timer sitting at one of the tables. The man had some dried blood on the side of his face from the cut that Bennett was bandaging, a result of being pistol-whipped.

"How are you feeling, sir?" Pike asked.

"I reckon I ain't ready to be planted yet," the man said, "and considerin' the way things could'a gone, I'm mighty thankful for that." He stuck out a gnarled paw. "I'm Jasper Cole, cook over to the Diamond C."

Pike shook hands with him.

"Pleased to meet you, Mr. Cole. I'm Pike Shannon."

"Oh, I know who you are," Cole said. "I reckon most folks in Warbonnet County do. You're the fella who got rid of Doak Ramsey and his sorry bunch."

"Well, I had a lot of help," Pike said with a shrug.

"And you cleaned up them three owlhooters who was tryin' to rob Edgar here, he tells me. That's a good day's work."

"It's a start, anyway."

Neither of the other men asked him what he

meant by that. Bennett stepped back and said, "There you go, Jasper. That'll do you until you get back to the ranch. Now, what can I do you for?"

"Just come to pick up a few supplies. Didn't know I was gonna walk into somethin' right out of a dime novel!"

Pike sat down at one of the tables and waited while Bennett gathered the supplies Cole wanted and loaded them in the old ranch cook's wagon. As Cole drove away, Bennett came back into the trading post and eyed Pike warily.

"You said you aimed to collect on what I owe you. How much do you want, Shannon?"

"If you're talking about money . . . not a blasted cent," Pike said. "What I want from you, Edgar, is information."

Bennett's forehead went back a long way, and most of it creased as he frowned.

"I don't know what kind of information I'd have that you would want," he said. "I just run this little trading post, never do much business—"

"That's bull," Pike said. He stood up. "You said those owlhoots came in and wanted whiskey. They knew you sell moonshine here, didn't they?"

Bennett said, "Selling moonshine's against the law. So's drinkin' it."

"That never stopped you from doing a good trade in it, back in the days when Doak Ramsey was supplying you."

This was the first place Pike had stopped after entering Warbonnet County, months earlier. It was obvious the place was a saloon as well as a trading post. Bennett wasn't making any secret of that in those days, even though according to the law, he wasn't supposed to be selling liquor.

But since the county sheriff was the one *selling* him the 'shine, Bennett hadn't bothered hiding it. Pike had sampled the stuff, and it wasn't bad. Not as good as the old Shannon family recipe, of course, but perfectly drinkable.

Then he'd had a run-in with some fellas who'd been on the prod and picked a fight with him, having no idea that they were some of Doak Ramsey's deputies. That ruckus had started the whole war with the Ramseys . . .

Those memories flashed through Pike's mind, but he put them aside as Bennett said nervously, "All that's in the past, Pike. I'm a law-abidin' man—"

"Stop it," Pike interrupted him. "You wouldn't know law-abiding if it came up and slapped you across the mush."

"Hey, now, you got no cause to talk like that! I appreciate your help, but that don't mean you can come into my own place and insult me."

"Take it easy, Edgar," Pike said coldly. "I'm not looking to cause trouble for you. I just want to know who you're buying 'shine from these days."

"I never said I was buying 'shine . . ."

Bennett's voice trailed off as Pike's cold eyes seemed to bore into him. Quietly, Pike asked, "So, if I go behind the counter over there and have a look around, I won't find any jugs of white lightning?"

"All right, all right, blast it! A fella named Norvell Grant brings me a load every couple of weeks."

"Norvell Grant," Pike repeated. "Can't say as I recognize the name."

"I didn't know him, either, until he showed up one day a while back with a jug and let me sample it. Said if I liked it, he could get me as many of them as I wanted."

"Was it good?"

Bennett's head bobbed enthusiastically as he said, "Mighty good. As good as anything Doak Ramsey ever sold me." He started to look worried again. "Listen, Pike, after you busted up Ramsey's operation and you and your friends stopped cookin' 'shine, I tried to go straight and stop selling the stuff. I really did. Getting out of that business cut deep into the money I was making. Mighty deep. But I figured it was the right thing to do."

Pike didn't believe that for a second. Edgar Bennett had never been concerned about doing the right thing, only about making money. If he had stopped selling moonshine, it was only because his supply had dried up and he had no choice.

"I understand why you'd be upset," Bennett went on. "I didn't know you and your family were gettin' back into the business. I thought that you'd quit, and with Andy Burnett being sheriff now, it just never occurred to me that you'd want to start cooking 'shine again. But I'd be happy to buy from you, Pike, and tell Grant to take a flying leap. From what I've heard, Shannon whiskey was always the best—"

"Hold it right there." Pike stopped him. "I never said we were making moonshine again."

"But . . . if you don't want to sell to me . . . what's this all about?" Bennett asked with what looked like a frown of genuine confusion.

Pike reached in his pocket, took out the folded

piece of cloth Andy had given him, and tossed it to Bennett.

"Take a look at that. That's a piece torn off one of the bags you use to put sugar and flour and coffee in, isn't it?"

It would have been no use for Bennett to deny it. All Pike had to do was look around on the shelves to see several bags with BENNETT'S TRADING POST stenciled on them in the same script used on the scrap of cloth.

"Yeah, that's what it looks like," Bennett admitted. "Some slicker from a company in Dallas came in here one day and convinced me that putting the name of my place on the bags I use was a good idea. Said it'd make my business a lot better. So I bought a few hundred of the blasted things from him. It's gonna take me years to use them up!" He shook his head. "You just can't trust folks from Dallas."

Pike thought he was probably right, but that was neither here nor there. He said, "You've been doing more than buying 'shine from Grant, haven't you, Edgar? You've been selling him corn and sugar to make it with, haven't you?"

"No, sir," Bennett replied, shaking his head. "I don't recall ever selling anything to Grant except some chewin' tobacco."

"Then who *have* you been selling sugar to?"

"Anybody who comes in and asks for it." Bennett was starting to sound exasperated now. "I don't know. I can't remember everything I sell to everybody who comes in here. Shoot, I sold some just a little while ago to Jasper Cole, didn't I? You were sitting right there and watched me do it!"

As much as it galled him to agree with anything Edgar Bennett said, Pike had to admit that he was right. Sugar was a common commodity. Since Andy had found that scrap of cloth at the location of the still on the other side of the county, it was clear that the moonshiners had bought some sugar here. Pike had hoped that Bennett was doing a major business supplying them. If Bennett was to be believed—and what he said had the ring of truth to Pike's ears— then that wasn't the case after all.

However, Pike's ride out here had brought him something even better: the name of one of the men now peddling white lightning in Warbonnet County. He didn't know Norvell Grant, but he figured it was time he made the man's acquaintance.

"You said Grant makes his deliveries every couple of weeks?"

"That's right," Bennett said.

"When will he be coming by here next?"

"He's due three days from now, as a matter of fact."

"What's he look like?"

"He's a good-sized fella. Has dark hair and a mustache and sort of a lumpy face, if you know what I mean. Nobody would ever call him handsome."

"Does he deliver the moonshine by himself?"

Bennett shook his head and said, "No, he's always got a man with him. Not always the same fella, though. I guess he doesn't want to take a chance on somebody holding him up. That 'shine's valuable, not to mention the money he collects from the places that are buying it."

"And what places are those?"

Bennett shook his head again, more emphatically this time.

"I don't know, and I'll be honest with you, Pike, I wouldn't tell you if I did. I'm not gonna get somebody else in trouble with the law. I just know I've heard talk that there are several places in the county now where a man can get a drink if he wants one."

"All right," Pike said. He didn't press the trading post owner. He supposed even a rat like Edgar Bennett could have a few shreds of honor left. "What time does Grant usually show up?"

"Along around the middle of the day, I'd say."

Pike nodded and said, "Here's what we're going to do . . ."

CHAPTER 12

Pike and Andy Burnett went through the wanted posters in the drawer of his desk in the sheriff's office but didn't find any that matched the three men Pike brought into Warbonnet late that afternoon.

Afterward, they went down to Cyrus Malone's undertaking parlor, where Andy studied the faces of the men laid out in the back room. He commented to Pike, "I reckon they never did anything big enough to get themselves on reward dodgers."

"That was my thinking," Pike agreed. "But I still didn't care for hearing bullets so close to my head. A small-time desperado can kill you just as dead as Jesse James could."

"Oh, sure, ventilating them was self-defense on your part, no doubt about that," Andy said, nodding. "There'll have to be an inquest, but I've got your statement, and I'll talk to Edgar Bennett and Jasper Cole, too. That'll be enough for the coroner's jury, I expect. You won't have to be there."

"The old-timer didn't see anything," Pike pointed out. "He was out cold the whole time."

"Yeah, but he can testify to what happened to him, and that'll back up Bennett's story." As they left the undertaker's place, Andy went on, "What were you doing out there, anyway, Pike?"

"Just decided to take a ride in that direction and say hello to Edgar."

"I didn't know you fellas were friends," Andy said shrewdly. "In fact, considering what happened the last time you were there and the fact that he testified against you at your trial, I wouldn't figure you'd have much use for the fella."

"All that's water under the bridge, as they say. I'm not the sort to hold grudges."

"Uh-huh," Andy said, clearly not convinced.

Pike didn't want to tell him that the visit to Bennett's Trading Post had produced a lead to whoever was bringing moonshining back to Warbonnet County. Pike had always been one to play his cards close to his vest. He would continue to do so until he had something definite to tell Andy.

He rode home but didn't say anything to his family about what had happened earlier in the day. No doubt they would hear gossip about the three dead men Pike had brought in, the next time they went to town, but for now he didn't see any reason to bring it up.

Instead he spent the next two days working around the ranch with Torrance and Dougal, moving horses around from pasture to pasture and training some of them to work on cutting out cattle from a group.

They kept a small herd of cows on the ranch for just that purpose.

A good saddle mount that also had good cow sense was worth a considerable amount of money. Pike had already seen plenty of evidence that the ranch was successful and would just continue to be more so as their reputation as a source of fine horse-flesh grew and spread.

Somehow, though, the thought of doing honest work for the rest of his life, no matter how lucrative it might be, just rubbed him the wrong way. At least to a certain extent, Shannons had always been rene-gades and scoundrels, going all the way back to their origins in Ireland, and maybe he had too much of that outlaw blood flowing in his veins to ever be completely comfortable with a normal existence.

And yet what was he doing? Working for the law! Even though it was unofficial and he wasn't wearing a badge, right now he was on the side of respectabil-ity, whether he liked it or not.

On the morning of the third day after the battle with the robbers at the trading post, Pike saddled up to ride northwest again.

"Where are you going?" Torrance asked when he met Pike leading his horse out of the barn.

"Feel like taking a ride," Pike replied.

"I thought we were going to work on gentling some more of that proddy stock today."

"Some of us don't believe in working every single day of our lives," Pike said. "A fella's got to stop and take a deep breath every now and then. Clear his mind."

"You rode off just a few days ago and were gone

all day." Torrance didn't bother trying to keep an accusatory tone out of his voice.

"And I might just ride off for longer than that, one of these days," Pike snapped, quickly running out of patience with his brother as he usually did.

"Yeah, I wouldn't be a bit surprised if you did."

Pike had been about to swing up into the saddle, but he stopped short and turned to glare at Torrance instead.

"What in blazes do you mean by that?"

"Well, it's not like that would be the first time you ran off and abandoned your family," Torrance shot back.

"I didn't abandon anybody. Pa was here, and so were Tyree and Dougal, and you were even mostly grown by then. The four of you were perfectly capable of handling things around here."

"That doesn't change the fact that you turned your back on all of us, just so you could ride off and become a gunman and hired killer."

It was all Pike could do at that moment not to hammer his fist into Torrance's smug face. The only thing that held him back was knowing that if he did, his mother and sister would find out and be upset by it.

That . . . and the bothersome thought that to a certain extent, Torrance was right. Boil things down to their essence, and that was what Pike had done. He'd had his reasons for doing it, and he wasn't a man given to brooding and regrets, but still . . . Torrance had a point.

That didn't change things now. He put his foot in the stirrup and stepped up into the saddle.

"I don't know when I'll be back," he said. "You and Dougal just carry on without me."

"Sure," Torrance said coldly. "What else would we do?" He shrugged. "Anyway, we're used to it."

Pike's jaw tightened as he held back an angry retort. He lifted the reins and heeled his horse into motion. He rode away from the ranch, knowing that Torrance would tell the others he was gone—and make him look as bad as possible in the process.

Maybe they would feel differently about things once they found out he was trying to help Andy quash the moonshining operation moving into the county and deliver justice for the slain deputy.

First, though, he had to find out who was actually behind it.

And that meant finding and following Norvell Grant.

"Grant hasn't been here yet, has he?" Pike asked Edgar Bennett.

The trading post owner swallowed hard and shook his head.

"No, he hasn't. He should be showing up pretty soon, though, if the past is anything to judge by." Bennett lifted the bottom of the grimy apron he wore and used it to wipe nervous sweat from his face. "You'd best get your horse out of sight in the barn if you don't want Grant to see it."

Pike nodded. He was the only one in the trading post other than Bennett, and he hoped it would stay that way until Norvell Grant showed up.

"You know I'm takin' a big chance here," Bennett

went on. "Grant strikes me as the sort of hombre who wouldn't take it kindly if he knew I put you on his trail."

"There's no reason for him to know," Pike said. "I don't intend to jump him or anything like that. I just want to find out where he goes after he leaves here."

"You want to follow him back to whoever's cooking that 'shine. I know good and well what you're up to, Shannon."

Pike started to turn away from the counter, then stopped and pointed a finger across it at Bennett.

"Just remember, Edgar, if I suspect you tipped off Grant about me, even if you didn't, I'll be back to settle up with you. So be mighty careful . . . and stop sweating like that! You look like a man who's about to climb the gallows."

"That's how I feel," Bennett muttered.

Pike left him there behind the counter, got his horse from the hitch rack, and led the animal into the barn. He left the saddle on the horse but put him in a stall where he could get some grain and water. He closed the barn door to make it look unused.

Then Pike climbed the ladder to the hayloft, which was empty now because not many men stabled their horses here while visiting the trading post, and Bennett kept sacks of oats on hand to feed those few animals.

A small door was cut into the wall above the loft floor where bales had been unloaded in the past. Pike opened it and looked along the trail. From here, he had a good view of anyone who approached the trading post.

He waited there only twenty minutes or so before

he heard hoofbeats and the creak of approaching wagon wheels. Staying back in the shadows where he wouldn't be seen, Pike watched as a good-sized, sturdy-looking wagon pulled by a team of four mules rolled along the trail and came to a stop in front of the trading post.

The man handling the reins matched the description of Norvell Grant that Bennett had given him. If anything, he was even uglier than Bennett had made him out to be. Beside him on the seat rode a rail-thin man with a jutting, rust-colored beard on his angular jaw. He had a shotgun resting across his knees. A Winchester was lying on the floorboards behind their feet, too.

Both men wore holstered handguns. They looked like they were ready for trouble, all right.

The wagon bed was filled with crates. While the bearded man tied the mules to the hitch rail, Grant went around to the back and lifted the lid off one of the crates. It wasn't nailed down. He reached in, brought out a couple of one-gallon glass jugs full of clear liquid, and turned to carry them into the trading post.

Edgar Bennett had come out onto the porch to greet the men. He said, "Howdy, Norvell." Pike was glad to see that he looked and sounded less apprehensive now.

Grant said something in response to Bennett, but Pike couldn't make out the words, just the rumble of his voice. Grant carried the jugs on inside, followed by the bearded man who brought in two more.

For the next few minutes, Pike watched as the two

men unloaded jugs of moonshine and took them into the trading post. He kept count. Bennett was taking delivery of twenty jugs.

The last time Norvell Grant came out of the building, he was bouncing a small canvas pouch on the palm of his hand. That pouch was filled with gold coins, Pike guessed, the payment Bennett had made for the 'shine. Pike continued watching as Grant pulled a metal strongbox from under the wagon seat, unlocked it with a key he took from his shirt pocket, and placed the pouch inside.

A moment later, he and the bearded man were ready to go. The bearded man untied the mule team and Grant took up the reins. They left the same way they had come, following the road northwest.

Pike waited until they were out of sight before he got his horse and led it out of the barn. Bennett was standing on the trading post's porch.

"I guess you saw what you wanted to see," Bennett said with a bitter edge in his voice. "Are you gonna turn me in to the sheriff now?"

"I told you all along, I'm not interested in you, Edgar," Pike said. "Did you know the man who was with Grant today?"

"Yeah, he's come along to help with the delivery before. His name's Ruel Blake. Never says anything, but you can tell he's a mean one by the look in his eyes. I'd hate to have to cross those two . . . even if I was a gunhand like you, Shannon."

"I'm not planning on crossing them. All I want them to do is lead me to their boss."

With that, Pike mounted up and rode away from the trading post. Turning his back on Bennett like that made the hairs stand up a little on the back of his neck. He figured Bennett would like to put a bullet right between his shoulder blades. The thing was, Bennett didn't have the guts to do that.

He might have tipped off Grant and Blake, though, despite the warning not to do so, in which case the two moonshiners might have an ambush waiting for Pike somewhere up ahead. He needed to keep his eyes and ears open, so that he wouldn't ride right into trouble.

And if Edgar Bennett *had* betrayed him, Pike would see to it that the trading post owner regretted that decision—sooner rather than later.

CHAPTER 13

Pike had tracked many men in his life. He knew how to do it without being seen, and even though he had been away for a long time, he still knew War- bonnet County. Being careful not to let himself be skylighted, he chose a course that took him parallel to the road, with enough high ground and gaps be- tween the hills that he could see the wagon from time to time.

Even with his skills, he almost lost his quarry for a while. He had to cut over to the trail and backtrack along it until he came to another, even smaller road leading east. Recent wagon tracks turning onto it told him that Grant and Blake had gone that way.

Half an hour later, he watched from a thick stand of trees atop a hill as the wagon stopped at a log cabin and Blake unloaded half a dozen jugs of moonshine while Grant collected some coins from a gangling, overall-clad settler who had to be run- ning a tavern in the cabin to supplement his income from the hardscrabble farm.

As the afternoon went on, Pike saw the pair in the

wagon wander across the northern half of the
county and make five more deliveries, none of them
as large as the one to Bennett's Trading Post. But
assuming they had dropped off jugs of moonshine
in other places before reaching Bennett's, it was still
a good day's work and must have brought in a considerable amount of money for whoever was behind
the liquor trade.

For some reason, Pike didn't believe that was
Norvell Grant. He knew he was judging on appear-
ances, but Grant just didn't strike him as the sort to
mastermind a big moonshining operation. Grant
was nothing more than a competent delivery man.

Late in the afternoon, Grant turned the wagon
northward. Pike continued following, hanging back
as much as he dared so that Grant and Blake wouldn't
spot him.

After a while, he realized that they must have
crossed the county line into Chaparral County by
now. He was sure of it a short time later when the
smaller road the wagon was following intercepted
the main road between Warbonnet and Clarkston,
the county seat up here. Pike saw a sign that read
BOLIVAR – 5 MILES. Bolivar was the only other town of
any size in Chaparral County, the terminus of the
railroad spur line that ran down from Fort Worth.

This was enemy territory, Pike mused. Chaparral
County, like Warbonnet County, was dry, its citizens
having voted in the local option election to make
liquor illegal. And like Warbonnet County during
Doak Ramsey's time as sheriff, Chaparral County
had a thriving moonshine business. The man in
charge of it was Solomon Henshaw, who, rumor had

it, also had his greedy fingers in just about every other criminal activity in these parts.

During the Shannon-Ramsey war, Pike had cleverly ruined a budding alliance between Doak Ramsey and Solomon Henshaw. Now, with Doak dead and gone, Henshaw might well believe that the door was open for him to expand his criminal empire into Warbonnet County. Setting up a new moonshine trade in the county would be the first step in that plan.

All that was certainly plausible, Pike decided, but he had no proof of it. That was why he continued following the wagon, now close to half a mile ahead of him.

As they came closer to Bolivar, more riders appeared on the road, along with several buggies and wagons. Pike closed up the distance between him and his quarry, not wanting to lose them after following them for half a day. With other folks on the road now, coming and going, it wasn't likely Grant and Blake would notice one more rider behind them.

Dusk was settling over the landscape, and lights began to appear up ahead. That would be Bolivar, Pike thought. He moved up even closer and saw the wagon with its load of now-empty crates rattle along the main street for a couple of blocks before turning down an alley between a hardware store and a café.

Pike nudged his horse over to the side of the street and quickly dismounted. He looped the reins around a hitch rail and stepped up onto the boardwalk in front of the buildings. Without wasting any time, but also without hurrying so much as to draw attention to himself, he moved along the planks to the alley mouth and glanced around the corner of the hardware store.

The wagon was just pulling into an open area behind the café. Pike stepped into the alley and edged along the wall. He wished the shadows had been a little thicker. If Grant or Blake happened to look in here, there was a good chance they would spot him.

Ever since he had started trailing them, though, he had gotten the impression that they weren't worried about being followed. Maybe they were just confident, even more so now that they were back in their home county.

At any rate, Pike heard them talking, and then a door opened and closed. They had gone into the café through the back door.

Satisfied that they had no idea they'd been followed here, Pike moved faster now, stepping into the open area next to the wagon. He saw a lighted window on the other side of the building and slipped over to it, stopping with his back against the wall next to the uncurtained window. He took off his hat and leaned in to have a look.

The window didn't open into the café's main room but rather into a private chamber with a rectangular table where a man sat with a plate of food and a mug of what looked like beer in front of him. Clearly the café didn't abide by the no-liquor law, if that actually was beer in the mug.

The plate was piled high with steak, potatoes, gravy, and a couple of biscuits. The man had taken off his black hat and placed it on the table, revealing a thick shock of white hair over a weathered face. Despite his white hair and craggy appearance, the man didn't seem old. He had the vitality about him of a man in the prime of life.

Pike recognized the man as soon as he laid eyes on him. That was Carl McConnell, Solomon Henshaw's chief lieutenant, having dinner here in the back room of this café.

If Pike had had any doubt that Henshaw was responsible for the moonshining in Warbonnet County, it was dispelled in the next minute as Norvell Grant and Ruel Blake entered the room, each man also carrying a plate of food and mug of beer. They joined McConnell at the table.

Grant set his food and drink down and pulled out the key to the strongbox from his pocket. As he slid it across the table to McConnell, he said, "There you go, Carl. Everybody paid up, just like they were supposed to."

The window was open because of the warm evening. Pike heard every word. In his gravelly voice, McConnell asked, "Where's the box?"

"Why, I left it on the wagon," Grant replied. "It's sort of heavy, and I figured since you'd be drivin' back up to Clarkston with it anyway—"

McConnell put his knife and fork down, glared at the two men, and said, "You idiots. You left that much money just sitting there where anybody could come along and walk off with it?"

"Nobody's gonna see it, stuck up under the seat the way it is, and anyway, nobody around here would dare lay a finger on the boss's money. They know they'd wind up buzzard bait in a mighty big hurry if they did anything that foolish."

"Not everybody around here knows who that wagon belongs to," McConnell grated. "Now go out there and get that strongbox and bring it in. And it blasted well better still be there!"

"It will be, it will be," Grant mumbled. He sighed and jerked his head at Blake. "Come on, Ruel, gimme a hand with it. Sooner we get it done, the sooner we can have our supper."

Blake didn't say anything, and his sour look didn't change.

In the gathering darkness outside the window, though, a grin had spread suddenly over Pike Shannon's face.

He turned quickly away from the building and moved alongside the parked wagon. The stolid mules hitched to the vehicle ignored him. He groped in the darkness under the seat, found the handle on one end of the strongbox, and pulled it out. Taking hold of the handle on the other end, as well, he lifted the box.

It was heavy, all right—heavy with the loot Grant and Blake had collected for the moonshine deliveries. Pike was strong enough that he didn't have any trouble handling it by himself. He hurried into the alley and back to the street where he had left his horse.

The hardware store was still open, but no customers were going in or out of the place at the moment. Pike put the box under his left arm and untied his horse's reins, then balanced the strongbox on his saddle horn and swung up. He put the

box under his arm again and reined the horse away
from the hitch rail.

Behind the café, somebody yelled in surprise and
alarm. Pike smiled as he heeled his mount into a de-
liberate walk that wouldn't attract any attention.
More shouts sounded in the night.

He shifted the strongbox so it was more in front
of him, knowing that his broad back would conceal
it. Behind him, Norvell Grant and Ruel Blake would
be running around frantically, like chickens with
their heads cut off, looking for whoever had taken
the money.

Right now, they were on foot, but within minutes,
more than likely, they would grab horses and expand
their search. Pike wanted to take advantage of the
time he had. As he reached the southern edge of
town, he nudged his horse into a little faster pace.
He had to be careful about asking too much of the
animal, since it was carrying more weight than usual
with the extra burden of the strongbox.

The money itself meant almost nothing to Pike.
If somebody back in Bolivar had noticed him carrying the strongbox and put Grant and Blake on his
trail, he was prepared to toss the strongbox into a
gully and take off for the tall and uncut if he had to,
rather than shooting it out with them.

All he really wanted to do was serve notice on Carl
McConnell, and by extension Solomon Henshaw,
that their dominance over Chaparral County wasn't
complete. Somebody had dared to defy them. And
if that could happen once, it could happen again.

Pike estimated that he was a mile or more out of

Bolivar when he heard rapid hoofbeats drumming far behind him. He reined in and tossed the strong-box down in the road. He knew he had a little time before the pursuit could catch up, so he dismounted and drew his gun.

A well-placed shot knocked the lock and hasp loose. Pike opened the box, took out several pouches of coins, and stuffed them inside his shirt. There were a few greenbacks, too, and he took those as well. The loose coins he slung into the weeds beside the trail and threw the strongbox after them. Some lucky pilgrim might come across the coins.

Then he mounted up again and put his horse into a ground-eating lope. As the swift rataplan of hoofbeats grew louder behind him, he moved even faster, then turned off the road into a thick stand of trees.

Full night had fallen by now, and a three-quarter moon hung in the eastern sky, casting silvery light over the landscape. Pike worked his way to the top of a hill where he stopped, turned, and looked back down at the road.

After a few minutes, he saw two riders gallop past and knew they had to be Norvell Grant and Ruel Blake. Unless they found where he had thrown those coins and the strongbox, they would have to return to Bolivar empty-handed.

Carl McConnell wouldn't be happy about that, and neither would Solomon Henshaw.

Giving in to the impulse might have been a mis-take, Pike reflected. Now Henshaw would at least suspect that he had an active enemy in the area, and he might be more careful in the future.

But that didn't matter. Now Pike knew who *his* enemy was, and he was dangerous, too. As Henshaw and McConnell would find out.

With a grim smile still tugging at the corners of his mouth, he turned and rode cross-country through the night toward home.

CHAPTER 14

"There you go," Pike said as he set the greenbacks and the pouches full of coins on Andy Burnett's desk. "Use it to do some good for the county, and if you want to thank anybody, you can say much obliged to Solomon Henshaw."

Andy looked up from staring at the loot and exclaimed, "Henshaw!"

Like everybody else who had been involved in the moonshine business in this part of the state, he knew the name of the man who ruled the criminal roost in Chaparral County.

"That's right," Pike said. "He's got men delivering 'shine to at least half a dozen places in the northern half of the county."

"How do you know that?"

"Because I followed them."

Pike picked up one of the chairs in Andy's office, turned it around, and straddled it as he told his friend about everything that had happened the day before, including his daring foray into Bolivar and his theft of the strongbox from the wagon. The only details he left out were the locations of the places where Grant and Blake had delivered the jugs of white lightning.

Andy noticed that and said dryly, "I don't reckon you want to tell me exactly who's dealing 'shine in Warbonnet County these days."

"I don't know the name of everybody who lives in the county, Andy, and I sort of disremember all the places I followed those hombres to yesterday."

"I figured as much," Andy said, nodding slowly, "and I'm not surprised. If things were turned around, my memory might not be very good, either." He paused, then added, "You know, you just confessed to committing a serious crime in a neighboring county. I could arrest you for robbery and hold you for the sheriff of Chaparral County."

"You mean it's against the law to recover ill-gotten gains from a criminal?" Pike nodded toward the money still lying on the desk. "Anyway, I turned it in to the law, didn't I?"

Andy leaned back in his chair and chuckled.

"Never mind. I'm more interested in stopping Solomon Henshaw from moving into the county." The sheriff's face grew more serious. "You said his men were delivering 'shine. I reckon it's likely they cooked it up in Chaparral County. You think the still that was set up southeast of town belonged to Henshaw, too? The one where Jack Humphries was killed?"

"That makes sense," Pike said. "If Henshaw's trying to support a booming trade in two counties, he can't count on his stills up there in Chaparral to produce enough for the demand. He'd have to have some operating down here, too. He's probably supplying the buyers in the northern half of the county from his existing stills—that's what I saw yesterday—while taking care of the southern half with 'shine cooked down there. But all the profit, no matter where it's from, goes back in Henshaw's pocket."

"So it's Henshaw we have to put out of business." Andy opened a drawer in the desk, reached inside, and took out something that he slapped down in front of him. "I know you don't want to wear this—"

"I sure as blazes don't," Pike said as he abandoned his casual seat on the chair and came to his feet. He looked at the deputy sheriff's badge on the desk as if it were a diamondback rattlesnake.

"If you're going to take on this job, it'll be better if you're an official representative of Warbonnet County," Andy argued. "That's what you want, isn't it, to put Henshaw out of business?"

"I've never met the man," Pike said, "but I've heard plenty about him, none of it good. I've never agreed with this whole idea of making liquor illegal, Andy, you know that. But Henshaw's mixed up in other things that are a lot worse, in my opinion. Hitting him through his moonshining operation is as good a way as any of making sure he doesn't hurt folks."

"I can't argue with that. We sure as shootin' don't need anybody from Chaparral County coming down here and causing trouble."

Pike smiled. County rivalry was a powerful thing in Texas. He had heard more than one tale of counties practically going to war against each other over some slight, real or imagined.

"So why don't you take the badge?" Andy went on. "That way you'll have some legal standing."

Pike shook his head.

"If I pin on a badge, that means I'll be working for you. I'll have to tell you everything I'm doing and get you to agree with it. I can't work that way, Andy. I'll let you know what I've done—maybe—but only after I've done it."

Andy put his hands on the desk and pushed himself to his feet.

"I can cut you a lot of slack, Pike," he said, "but that only goes so far. You bend the law too far and I won't have any choice but to regard *you* as . . . as . . . ."

"An outlaw?" Pike grinned. "You can say it. And if you think I'm going to lose any sleep over some star-packer thinking I'm an outlaw, well, you're quite a few years too late for that."

"I didn't know you thought of me as just some star-packer," Andy said stiffly.

"Blast it, that's not what I meant—"

Andy stopped him with a gesture.

"No, it's all right, Pike. I understand. I really do. And right now I'm more interested in results—which means Jack Humphries' killers being brought to justice—than I am in anything else. So I suppose we've got a deal. You do what you can, and I'll stay off your back as much as possible."

Pike nodded curtly and said, "Sounds good. And if I wind up needing some help . . ."

"You know where to find me," Andy said.

* * *

Pike had gotten home pretty late the night before, after everyone was asleep—or so he had thought. No one had said anything unusual to him or questioned him that morning when he got up, ate breakfast, and said that he had to ride into Warbonnet for a while.

But when he got back to the ranch and went into the barn to put his horse up, he found Nessa there mending some of her tack. She set it aside, stood up from the stool where she'd been sitting, and said, "Just what is it you're up to these days, Pike?"

"What are you talking about?" he asked. "What makes you think I'm up to anything?"

She gave him a pitying look.

"You might be able to put things over on Torrance and Grandpappy, maybe even Ma, but not me. I can see right through you, Pike Shannon." A worried expression came over her face. "You must be getting ready to leave home again. Maybe for good this time."

"What?" Pike shook his head and stepped forward to put his hands on her shoulders. "Nessa, I'm not going *anywhere*. Not for good. Sometimes I might not be around for a little while, but I'm coming back."

"Unless you can't, because . . . because . . ."

"Well," he said, "I reckon that's a risk we always run. Some folks say that getting out of bed is the most dangerous thing any of us do day after day."

"Whoever said that never knew you!"

Pike had to laugh at the intensity with which she said that. He drew her into his arms for a hug and patted her on the back as she rested her head against his chest.

He realized that what he had just told her was true: he didn't want to leave his family again, not for good. Despite the restless feelings that welled up inside him from time to time, despite the occasional urge to follow those dark, lonely trails, now that he had spent time at home and gotten to know his family again, he didn't believe he would ever be complete without them. Even Torrance, as annoying as he could be.

Pike regretted that he hadn't gotten to say goodbye to his father and his oldest brother Tyree, both of whom had died while he was gone. But his father's death was what had brought him back here, so that was *something* good that had come from it.

"Do you feel better now?" he asked Nessa.

She straightened and nodded as she looked up at him. She was a tough girl. Emotion might have threatened to overwhelm her for a moment, but her eyes were dry.

"I'm fine," she said. "But I'm going to hold you to that promise about coming back. And if one of these days you don't . . ." She gave a defiant toss of her head that made her long red hair swirl. "I'll come and find you, and you'd better have a darned good explanation."

Pike laughed and slipped his arm around her shoulders.

"And I'll hold you to *that*," he said.

It would be a while before Norvell Grant and another of Henshaw's men made any more deliveries in the northern part of the county, if what Edgar Bennett had told Pike was right, so for now Pike turned his attention to the other prong of Solomon Henshaw's two-pronged attempt to move his criminal activities into Warbonnet County.

Andy Burnett had told him about some of the reports he'd received of suspicious activities in the southern half of the county that might be connected to moonshining. Pike intended to check them out and see if he could locate more stills. If he could, he intended to wreak havoc with their production.

Later that day, he rode up to the edge of a cultivated field in the river bottoms, five miles from where Jack Humphries had been killed. Out in the middle of the field, an overall-clad man was trudging along behind a plow being pulled by a swaybacked mule.

Pike reined in and thumbed back his hat as he sat his saddle, not wanting to ride across the rows the farmer had already plowed. He knew the man's curiosity would get the better of him, and sure enough, after a couple of glances over at him, the farmer pulled back on the mule's reins. He left the plow and walked toward Pike, pulling a bandanna from the pocket of his overalls to wipe sweat off his face as he did so.

"Something I can do for you, mister?" the rawboned homesteader asked.

"Looking for Nelson's Ford," Pike replied.

The farmer scowled but pointed south.

"That way another half-mile," he said. "Be obliged to you if you'd ride around this field and not cut across it."

"Sure," Pike said. "I'm told the ford is a good place for a man to water his horse . . . and quench his own thirst, too."

The scowl deepened on the farmer's lantern-jawed face. He snapped, "So you're another one come to partake o' that devil's brew."

Pike put a puzzled look on his face and shook his head.

"I'm afraid I don't know what you're talking about, amigo."

"Sure, you don't," the man scoffed. "Folks in this county voted to do away with that sort of thing, but that don't stop you fellas who got to have your white lightnin', does it?"

"Somebody's making white lightning down at the ford?" Pike asked in mock innocence. He knew good and well that this farmer, whose name was Abner Richardson, had complained to Andy about all the comings and goings around his farm, lots of strangers riding by and wagons rolling past in the dead of night.

Richardson turned his head and spat.

"I don't know a thing about it," he declared. "Just be on your way, mister. The Good Book says we're supposed to hate the sin but love the sinner, but right now I'm havin' a hard time doin' that."

"Sure, whatever you say," Pike responded with a shrug of his shoulders. He turned his horse to ride around the field, as the farmer had requested.

"And stay off my property," the man called after him. "I don't want the likes o' you around my family."

Pike just lifted a hand and waved without turning around. The farmer's outrage put a smile on his face. Richardson had confirmed that something was going on at Nelson's Ford, a low-water crossing of the Brazos. Pike had heard of it but had never been there.

He entered an area of thick woods that grew on both sides of the river as it twisted its way through this part of the county on its way to the Gulf of Mexico. The heavy growth reminded him of the forests in East Texas and was indicative of the way Warbonnet County served as a borderland of sorts between eastern and western Texas.

He came to the Brazos, which was fairly deep at this point, and turned to follow a narrow trail along its bank. The trail was wide enough for a single rider, and the trees crowded close on Pike's left. The banks were steep and dropped off seven or eight feet to the water.

However, the river widened as he continued following it in a generally southeast direction. He could tell the water wasn't as deep because he could see riffles where it flowed over the rocky bed. The banks dropped lower until their edges were only a foot or so above the river's surface. Heavy rains upstream usually led to flooding in this part of the county.

Pike rode around a bend and saw a limestone shelf that extended all the way across the river. The rock jutted up high enough that the water was only a few inches deep where it flowed across the shelf, which was wide enough for a wagon to cross it. The river dropped off the other side, falling a foot in a miniature waterfall. This was Nelson's Ford, where riders had been crossing the Brazos for a long time, going back to the days when only the Comanche had roamed this part of the world.

An area on the opposite bank had been cleared off.

A building made of unpainted, rough-hewn planks sat in the open space. A sign attached to a post stuck in the ground read NELLSON'S FORD STOAR.

Pike rode across the ford, letting his horse pick its way at its own speed. As he did, he studied the building. No horses were tied in front of it, but he did see some wagon tracks to the right of the store, leading to a rutted path that disappeared into the woods. Pike had a hunch that if there was a still around here, supplying moonshine to the store, it would be located somewhere up that path and not too far off.

The store itself appeared to be deserted, but that proved not to be true. As Pike reached the river bank on that side, a man stepped out onto the building's porch, pointed a rifle at him, and said, "That's far enough, mister."

CHAPTER 15

Pike reined his horse to a stop with the water still flowing around the animal's hooves.

"Take it easy, friend," he said as he moved both hands a little to make sure they were in plain sight. He recognized the rifle the man held as a Sharps Big Fifty. A buffalo gun, the weapon that hunters used to lay waste to the vast herds that had spread over the Great Plains from the Texas Panhandle all the way up into Canada. A slug from a Sharps could do more than bring down a buffalo.

It could blow a hole the size of a fist clean through a man.

"I don't recollect us ever bein' introduced, so I don't hardly reckon you could call us friends," the man on the porch said. "Who be ye, and what's your business here?"

"If that's the way you greet all your customers, I don't imagine you do much trade here."

"You let me worry about how much trade I do. I'll ask you again, who be ye?"

The man was short and thickset, with curly gray

hair and a close-cropped beard of the same shade adorning his jaws. Bushy eyebrows lowered as he squinted over the rifle's barrel at Pike.

"Name's Smith," Pike drawled.

"Hah! Tell me another one."

Pike lifted his reins a little and said, "Listen, if you don't want my money, I'll just take it and go somewhere else to ease my thirst—"

"Hold on, hold on." The man lowered the rifle a little but kept it pointed in Pike's general direction. "I don't reckon it matters what your name is. Who told you that you could get a drink here?"

"Does *that* matter?" Pike asked. "I figured a man selling moonshine wouldn't be so inquisitive about his customers."

"I never said I sold moonshine," the man responded immediately. "You never heard me say that."

"Blast it, I'm not the law!" Pike burst out, starting to get a little impatient now. "As a matter of fact, I've cooked plenty of 'shine myself. I'll do it again if that's what it takes to get a decent drink in a county full of idiots who'd vote against it!"

The man frowned at him for a moment longer, then pointed the Sharps at the ground and said, "All right, come on in. You sound like you're tellin' the truth, and if you ain't, I'll just blow a hole in you. Deal?"

Pike chuckled.

"Deal."

He nudged his horse into motion again and rode up onto the bank in front of the store. There was no hitch rail, but the bearded man said, "You can tie your horse to the signpost."

Pike did so and stepped up onto the porch. He followed the man into the "stoar."

Inside were several sets of shelves with goods on them, as well as barrels full of beans, coffee, and flour. Shovels and axes and other tools hung on the walls. Pike was willing to bet that most of the business was transacted over the bar in the back of the room, though.

The man went behind the bar and set the Sharps on it, positioning the rifle so that he could still grab it and point it at Pike in a hurry if he needed to.

"Didn't mean no offense out yonder, ye understand, but a man's got to be careful. There's always some busybody wants to nose around in his business."

That made Pike think about the farmer he had talked to before riding on to Nelson's Ford. He nodded, put a silver dollar on the bar, and said, "I'm not looking for trouble, just something to drink."

"I got that." The man reached under the bar, brought out a jug and a tin cup. He pulled the cork on the jug, carefully poured clear liquid into the cup, and slid it across the bar to Pike. In the same motion, he made the dollar disappear. "That'll buy you four shots."

"Obliged," Pike said. He lifted the cup to his lips and drank down the moonshine in it.

It set fire to his gullet and burned all the way to his stomach. He had a strong constitution, so he managed not to show what he was feeling, but this was some of the rawest stuff he had ever sampled.

"What'd ye think?" the proprietor asked as Pike set the tin cup on the bar.

"Did you boil down a gator and add what was left to the mash?"

"Haw!" The man slapped a hand on the bar as he laughed. "It's got a kick, don't it?"

"That it does, amigo." Pike pushed the empty cup toward the man. "Since it hasn't burned a hole in my belly yet, I reckon I'll have another."

"Best be careful. It can sneak up on ye and lift your scalp just like an Injun."

Pike was sipping the second cup of 'shine when he heard hooves thudding on the ground outside, as well as the creak of wagon wheels. The sounds stopped, and a moment later a man stepped up onto the porch and came inside.

"Howdy, Josiah," he greeted the proprietor. "I got the stuff, and I'm ready to go get started on the next run."

The bearded man, Josiah, glared at the newcomer and said, "Blast it, Massey, are ye blind? I got a customer here."

"Yeah, but he's drinkin' 'shine, ain't he? So he must be all right."

Pike looked over his shoulder at the man, who turned out to be a tall hombre with his hat crammed down on a wild thatch of straw-colored hair. He had two old cap-and-ball pistols stuck behind his belt, positioned for cross-draws.

"Don't mind me," Pike said. Echoing what Josiah had said earlier, he added, "I keep my nose out of other folks' business."

"See?" Massey said. "Nothin' to worry about."

"Well, then, get on with ye and do what you're bein' paid for," Josiah snapped.

"I will, soon's I get some supplies. I'm gonna be out there in the woods a while, you know. I need some salt jowl and some coffee and—"

"All right, all right, I'll put together a bag of provisions for ye."

Josiah started doing that while Pike and Massey eyed each other. After a moment, Massey stuck out his hand.

"Tom Massey's my name," he said. "Glad to meet ya."

"Smith," Pike lied. "It really is my name."

"Oh, I don't doubt it. I've knowed lots and lots of Smiths."

"Headed out in the woods to cook some 'shine, are you?" Pike ventured.

"That's right. You know anything about it?"

Pike leaned his head toward Josiah and said, "Like I told your boss earlier, I've cooked plenty myself, back in the old days."

"Josiah ain't my boss," Massey declared, which prompted an irritated growl from the bearded man. "We both work for the same fella, name of—"

"Name of Shut Your Dadgum Mouth," Josiah said. "We've never seen this fella before, and you come in here flappin' your jaws like . . . like . . ."

Pike drained the last of the white lightning in the cup and set it on the bar again, then said, "Don't worry about me, boys. I'm harmless as a kitten, and I've got to be on my way."

"You got two more shots comin'," Josiah said.

"You fellas have one apiece on me," Pike told him. "I'll stop in again, next time I'm in these parts."

Josiah just grunted. Massey said, "So long, Smith."

As Pike was headed out the door, he heard Josiah

say quietly to Massey, "You watch him and make sure he's gone. I don't want him followin' you."

"Don't worry, Josiah. He'd never find the place."

A smile tugged at Pike's mouth. Finding the still was exactly what he intended to do.

First, though, he was going to make the moon-shiners believe that he had left. He untied his horse's reins, mounted up, and crossed the river to pick up the narrow trail again. He continued following it to the southeast until he was well out of sight of the store and tavern in the clearing.

Just to make sure, he pushed on even farther, going around numerous bends in the river before he started looking for a place to ford it again. He wouldn't find anywhere as good as the crossing up-stream, but he was confident that his horse could swim the Brazos if it had to.

After a while, Pike found a spot where he could tell that the river was shallow enough. He could see the rocky bed about a foot under the water. The Brazos could be treacherous; stretches of quicksand lurked here and there. So he crossed carefully, let-ting the horse be sure of its footing every time it put a hoof down before proceeding.

There was a deeper channel in the center of the stream where the horse had to swim for about twenty feet. Pike took off his gunbelt and held it over his head to keep the revolver out of the water. When they reached the far bank, he dismounted, took off his clothes, and wrung them out as much as he could before putting them back on and turning upstream toward Nelson's Ford.

The damp clothes were annoying, and he knew they wouldn't dry very fast in the thick shadows under the trees. That wasn't going to stop him from getting on with what he had set out to do.

With no trail through these woods, he had to move slower and backtrack from time to time when gullies or fallen trees blocked his way. It took him almost an hour to work his way to the vicinity of Nelson's Ford.

He came across the wagon track through the woods. Even though Tom Massey should have traveled along it well before now and Pike thought it was unlikely he would encounter anyone, instead of following the rutted trail he continued his laborious journey through the woods, paralleling the track.

After a while he smelled woodsmoke. It gave Pike something else to follow besides just his instinct and sense of direction—both of which had seldom let him down.

After a while he came to a steep bluff, an unusual formation in this mostly flat part of Warbonnet County. It was too steep for a horse, although he figured he could climb it on foot, Pike thought as he frowned at the slope.

The smoke seemed to be coming from beyond the bluff, which didn't make any sense. If it originated at the still, Massey had to have been able to reach the spot with the wagon.

Pike dismounted, tied his horse to a tree, and patted the animal on the shoulder.

"I'll be back in a spell," he told the horse, then turned to the bluff and started to climb, finding footholds and handholds where the sandstone jutted out.

The bluff was about twenty feet high, so it didn't take Pike long to scale it. When he reached the top, he catfooted through the trees and brush, still following his nose toward the source of the smoke.

After a few more minutes, he heard someone humming and knew he had to be almost on top of the still. Kneeling, he parted the brush and peered through the gap he'd created.

The still was sitting about twenty yards away in a clearing. The fire he'd smelled wasn't burning underneath the copper boiler connected to a couple of barrels. The mash in the boiler would have to sit for a while before it was ready.

Instead the flames crackled merrily inside a ring of rocks in front of a shed-like shelter made of branches. Tom Massey hunkered beside the fire, spooning coffee into a pot and getting ready to put it on to boil.

The wagon sat a few yards from Massey, at the edge of the camp. It was proof there was a hidden trail up here. Massey had commented to Josiah that the place was hard to find, so Pike wondered if they had concealed the trail with brush that could be moved aside. He had seen such hide-outs before.

As Pike knelt there, he pondered his next move. He could gun down Massey from here without any trouble, but he'd never been a bushwhacker and would never stoop that low. Maybe he could decoy Massey away from the still somehow, long enough for him to slip into the camp and bust it up . . .

The decision was taken out of Pike's hands by the

crack of a branch behind him. He pivoted swiftly and saw that a man had just stepped out of the trees. The way he was pulling up the straps of his overalls indicated that he had been answering one of nature's calls in the brush. He stopped short, his eyes bugging out as he saw Pike kneeling there.

From Pike's vantage point, the burly moonshiner looked as big as a bear. And like a bear, he suddenly roared an angry challenge and charged.

CHAPTER 16

Since Pike was already low to the ground and the man was rushing blindly ahead, Pike threw himself at his attacker, turning so that he hit the man's legs with his left shoulder and swept them out from under him.

The man's angry bellow turned to an alarmed shout as he pitched forward, out of control. He crashed headlong into the brush, and from the pained note his yelling took on, there must have been quite a few briars woven among the branches.

Pike rolled and came up on his feet. The big man was still yelling as he thrashed around and tried to free himself from the stickery vines.

Over by the fire, Massey jumped up and shouted, "Otis! Otis, what's wrong?"

Otis finally got loose from the briars and surged upright. Blood streaked his hands and face where the thorns had scratched him. He shook his shaggy head, looking more like a bull buffalo now than a bear. He stumbled toward Pike, who stepped back and drew his gun.

"Hold on there, mister," Pike warned. "I don't want to shoot you."

Otis didn't stop. He growled like an animal and picked up speed and momentum as he came at Pike. As big as Pike was, he still didn't want Otis getting his hands on him. He fired while Otis was still a few yards away.

The bullet drilled cleanly through Otis's left thigh, about halfway between knee and hip. He screamed as the leg folded up under him and dumped him on his left side.

Massey crashed through the brush with a shotgun in his hands. Pike dived to his left as Massey fired one of the Greener's barrels. The second barrel thundered as Pike rolled desperately. The buckshot tore up the ground where he had been a heartbeat earlier.

He came up on a knee and leveled the Colt at Massey as the moonshiner fumbled to reload the scattergun. Massey had a couple of shells in his hand and had broken open the weapon.

"Don't do it," Pike warned. "Just drop it, Massey, and I won't have to kill you."

"Dadgum it, Smith, I trusted you," Massey said. "I can't let you steal the boss's moonshine or do anything to his still. It'd be worth my life if I did."

"It's liable to be worth your life if you don't drop that shotgun."

Massey smiled sadly and shook his head. Then, as fast as he could, he shoved the shells into the barrels and snapped them shut as he raised the scattergun.

Pike could have shot him two or three times in

the seconds that it took Massey to do that. He held off, hoping the man would see reason, but as the twin barrels lifted toward him, he squeezed the trigger.

The Colt boomed before Massey could fire. The bullet struck him in the right shoulder, shattering it. He fell back a step, crying out in pain as he dropped the shotgun.

A rustling sound made Pike spin around. Despite the injury to his leg, Otis had managed to crawl closer and now lunged at Pike, reaching out to grab his ankle. The big man heaved and Pike went over backward, landing hard enough that it knocked the breath out of him and left him stunned for a few seconds.

Grunting with the effort, Otis scrambled after him. He had to drag the bleeding, useless leg behind him, but that didn't seem to slow him down much. He grabbed the wrist of Pike's gun hand and slammed it against the ground. The Colt flew out of Pike's grasp and landed several feet away.

Otis tried to get his hands around Pike's throat. Pike recovered just in time to raise his arms and fend off the attempt. He shot a short, sharp punch into Otis's face, causing blood to spurt from the moonshiner's nose as the blow landed. Otis's head rocked back as he yelled in a mixture of pain and anger.

He levered himself up with his arms and his good leg and flopped forward like a fish to land across Pike, pinning him to the ground with greater weight. This time he managed to close his left hand around

Pike's throat. Pike hammered a fist to the side of Otis's head without much visible effect. The man was as strong and durable as an ox.

Pike was pretty strong himself and had plenty of experience in bare-knuckles, no-holds-barred brawls. He splayed his right hand across Otis's blood-smeared face and dug fingers for his eyes. Otis jerked his head back to avoid them, and that loosened his grip enough for Pike to writhe free. He rammed his shoulder against Otis's chest and pushed himself off the ground with enough strength to roll the larger man onto his back.

Planting a knee in Otis's belly, Pike heaved himself up, clubbed both hands together, and swung them in a tremendous blow that caught Otis on the jaw and twisted his head far to the side. Pike lifted his arms again and brought his fists down in the middle of Otis's face in a piledriver of a punch that cracked bones and knocked Otis out cold.

Hearing heavy breathing, Pike jerked his head around and saw Massey struggling to lift the shotgun with his left hand. Massey's right arm hung bloody and limp from his wounded shoulder. Pike spotted his gun lying on the ground and dived for it.

He scooped the Colt from the dirt, tilted it up, and triggered, hoping the barrel hadn't gotten clogged when Otis knocked the weapon out of his hand. The gun roared a fraction of a second before Massey jerked both triggers on the shotgun. The twin barrels went off with a thunderous explosion and flame spouting from both muzzles.

Massey dropped the shotgun and fell back, pawing

with his left hand at his throat where Pike's bullet had ripped through it. Crimson flooded between and over his fingers as blood pumped from the severed veins and arteries. Massey spasmed a couple of times, arching up off the ground as he did so, and then with a last grotesque gurgle, he slumped down and didn't move again.

Pike put his free hand on the ground and pushed himself to his knees. He looked over at Otis and grimaced. In Massey's pain- and anger-wracked state, he hadn't paid enough attention to where he was aiming the Greener. The double load of buckshot had shredded Otis's face, turning his already bloody and broken features into something that didn't even look human. Pike looked away.

He had seen plenty of death in his time. This was an ugly one.

Pike got to his feet and reloaded the Colt. All of his senses were still on alert. He figured Massey and Otis must have been alone here at this moonshining camp. If anyone else had been around, the shooting would have drawn their attention. But he didn't want to get taken by surprise again, so he would continue to be cautious.

He pouched the iron, found his hat and put it back on, and started to look around the camp. Finding an ax that Massey and Otis probably had used to construct their flimsy shelter, he took it over to the still and began chopping holes in the barrels so they couldn't be used again. He used the ax on the copper boiler and battered it to pieces. He hacked the shelter apart as well.

The men had rigged a rope pen for the mules that had pulled the wagon up here. Pike let them loose. More than likely they would wander off and some farmer would find them and give them a home.

That left the wagon to deal with. He followed the ruts back to the edge of the bluff, where from this angle he was able to see the trail he had known had to be there. It ran up the face of the slope at an angle. Trees that grew along the outer edge would make it difficult to see from below.

He went back to the wagon, took the brake off, and got in front of it. Bracing his shoulder against it, Pike began to shove. The wagon resisted for a moment, but then the wheels started to turn as it rolled backward. Pike kept pushing.

He didn't stop until the back wheels went over the edge of the bluff and the wagon tipped up to follow them. The wagon turned over, and the racket of its crashing descent down the steep slope filled the air. Pike went to the edge and looked over to see that the heavily damaged wagon had come to a stop resting against some trees.

Destroying the wagon was a mite on the petty side, he knew, but he wanted to inflict as much damage as he could on Solomon Henshaw's operation. He would have spared the lives of the two moonshiners if he could, but Massey hadn't left him any choice except to defend himself, and Otis had just plumb run out of luck.

Pike walked down the trail to the bottom and found a crude gate formed out of sections of brush lashed together, the sort of thing he'd suspected they might use to conceal the way up the bluff. He pushed it aside and headed back to the place where he had left his horse.

He was reaching for his mount's reins when the skin on the back of his neck prickled. He didn't know if his ears had heard something that hadn't registered on his consciousness, but he obeyed the sudden impulse to throw himself to the side.

At that same instant, the ear-pounding boom of a heavy caliber weapon rolled through the woods. Pike saw a sapling the size of a man's wrist sawed in two by the slug ripping through it.

He dropped to a knee and palmed out his Colt as he spotted a small cloud of white smoke drifting from some brush. He squeezed off a couple of swift shots in that direction and heard a man yell in pain. Pike kept his gun leveled as the gray-bearded man called Josiah reeled out of the thicket.

Pike wasn't surprised. From the sound of the rifle, he had figured it was Josiah's Sharps. The storekeeper and moonshiner still had hold of it, but as he stumbled forward, he dropped the Sharps to press both hands to his belly, where at least one of Pike's bullets had driven deep.

Josiah crumpled and rolled onto his back. Pike approached carefully, keeping his gun trained on the man. Josiah stared up at him with pain-widened eyes and gasped, "Y-You! I heard the shots . . . and knew it had to be . . . you!" He moaned. "That idiot . . . Massey . . ."

"Solomon Henshaw won't be getting any more white lightning out of that still," Pike said, and from the surprise he saw in Josiah's eyes, even as the man was dying, he knew that his thrust had found its target.

"He'll . . . kill you . . . you son of a—"

"You ask him how much luck he had doing that," Pike said, "when you run into him in hell."

CHAPTER 17

Josiah lapsed into unconsciousness right after that but took quite a while to die. Pike stayed with him until he was gone, partly because it seemed like the decent thing to do, partly because he had a habit of not leaving wounded enemies behind him, even badly injured ones like this.

You never knew when a man might recover *just* enough to pose a threat again.

But once Josiah was dead, Pike mounted up and rode off, heading northwest toward Warbonnet. Three of Solomon Henshaw's men were dead, and the still was destroyed. That was a good enough day's work.

Some tender-hearted souls might say he should have loaded Josiah on a horse and tried to get medical attention for him, but Pike knew that wouldn't have done any good. A man with two slugs in his belly wasn't going to survive.

Besides, the bullet from that Big Fifty would have blown his head clean off if it had hit him, so he wasn't inclined to feel much sympathy for the man who'd done his best to kill him. That was the reason he hadn't buried Massey or Otis, and he didn't put Josiah in the ground, either.

Pike stopped in Warbonnet and found Andy Burnett in the sheriff's office. After exchanging greetings, Pike said, "Remember what you told me about there being a still somewhere down around Nelson's Ford?"

"Yeah," Andy said, suddenly wary. "What about it?"

"You don't have to worry about it anymore."

Andy's eyes narrowed.

"Pike, what have you done?"

"What I said I'd do. I'm trying to run Solomon Henshaw's moonshining ring out of Warbonnet County."

Andy sighed and said, "I'm gonna need to fetch Cyrus Malone and tell him to take his wagon out there, aren't I?"

"It wouldn't hurt," Pike said with a shrug. "From what I saw, there'd been some trouble."

"But you're not admitting to causing that trouble, are you?"

"I'm just a citizen making a report of something suspicious," Pike said as he turned to leave the sheriff's office.

He thought he heard Andy start to say something behind him, but then his friend just sighed.

Right about now, Andy might be starting to regret unleashing Pike on the forces of lawlessness in the county. He might even be thinking the cure could turn out to be worse than the illness . . .

Pike wouldn't know about that. As always, he

just figured he had a job to do—and he intended
to do it.

Not many things scared Carl McConnell, and he
wouldn't have admitted it now, but his nerves were
stretched pretty tight as he dismounted in front of
the palatial mansion on a hilltop just north of Clarkston, the county seat of Chaparral County.

The house behind the wrought-iron fence and
neat lawn rose three stories, and that upper story
was capped with cupolas and even a widow's walk.

At least, that was what McConnell thought they
called those things. Being a Texan, he wasn't that
familiar with the architecture of the northeastern
seacoasts.

Solomon Henshaw's family had made their fortune in whaling, fishing, and shipping. A decade
and a half earlier, he had come to Texas as one of
the thousands of carpetbaggers who had flooded
into the former Confederacy following the end of
the War of Northern Aggression.

Most of those carpetbaggers were only interested
in money and power. Henshaw wanted those things,
too, of course, but he had also left Massachusetts
and come down here because certain unsavory pro-
clivities of his made the rest of his family want him
as far away from them as possible, so the stain of his
activities wouldn't rub off on them.

In the years since, Henshaw had built an empire
of sorts in Chaparral County. In addition to buying
up notes, then repossessing and selling property—

the most common business practice among Yankee carpetbaggers—he dealt in stolen goods, brought in opium from China, owned two houses of ill repute in Clarkston and another in Bolivar, and before the local option election that had turned the county dry, he had operated half a dozen saloons and road-houses. It galled him that he'd had to shut down those lucrative establishments, so right away he had gone whole hog into moonshining.

McConnell had worked for Henshaw most of that time, starting out as a gun for hire whenever Henshaw needed to intimidate someone—or dispose of them entirely. Taking orders from a Yankee rubbed McConnell the wrong way a lot of the time, but he had lost his farm over in East Texas to another carpetbagger, and his wife had left him, taking their young'uns with her, so he'd been at loose ends and looking for a chance to let out some of the rage he felt.

Time spent as a Confederate cavalryman had taught McConnell how to ride and shoot and fight, so he put those talents to use doing whatever he could, and that had led him to Solomon Henshaw. His skills and ruthlessness allowed him to rise until he was Henshaw's right-hand man.

He tied his horse's reins to a ring on an iron post that matched the fence, then opened the gate and went up the walk to the front porch. A tasseled cord hung by the heavy, ornately carved door. It rang a bell somewhere inside when McConnell tugged on it.

A middle-aged black man in a dark suit opened the door and ushered McConnell in. McConnell took off his hat as he stepped inside, but when the man reached for it, he said, "No, I'll hang on to it." A grim smile touched McConnell's lips. "I may be leaving in a hurry."

"I understand, sir," the man said as he gestured for McConnell to follow him out of the foyer and into a hallway. "You're the bearer of bad tidings today?"

"They ain't good," McConnell said.

The servant led McConnell to the double doors that opened into Henshaw's opulently furnished library and study. McConnell had been there plenty of times before. The servant knocked, and when a grunted query came from inside, he opened one of the doors and said, "Mr. McConnell is here to see you, sir."

"Send him in," Henshaw rumbled.

Still holding his hat, McConnell stepped into the library. The door closed behind him.

Solomon Henshaw sat behind a large desk, a fat black cigar smoldering between the first two fingers of his right hand. A tendril of smoke curled up in front of his florid face, which was dominated by a rock-like shelf of jaw. His dark hair was graying, except over his ears where it had already turned white.

To McConnell's right, set against the wall, was a small bar where a lovely young woman in a low-cut gown was pouring amber liquid from a crystal carafe into a thin-stemmed snifter. Solomon Henshaw wasn't just about to drink the same moonshine his men cooked and now sold in two counties. He had fine brandy brought in specially from New Orleans.

The woman came out from behind the bar and carried the snifter over to the desk. It would have been more accurate to call her a girl, since she still had a few years to go before she would be out of her teens. She had long, raven-black hair that contrasted sharply with her pale skin. Henshaw had had *her* brought in specially from New Orleans, too.

"Thank you, Lucille," he said in his gravelly voice as she placed the brandy in front of him. "You can go now. I'll see you later for supper."

"Of course, *M'sieu* Henshaw," she murmured. She went out past McConnell, favoring him with a slight smile as she passed by, as well as the scent of her perfume. He looked straight ahead stolidly, knowing that it was unwise to pay too much attention to Henshaw's young ladies.

Henshaw picked up the snifter in his left hand and drank down the brandy. Sometimes he liked to smell the liquor and savor it and talk about how fine and expensive it was. Today, clearly, he just wanted it warming his belly.

He put the cigar in his mouth, clenched his teeth on it, and said around the cylinder of expensive tobacco, "All right, what's the bad news today, Carl?"

"Josiah Wilson, Tom Massey, and Otis Nunley are all dead," McConnell said. "The still that Massey and Nunley have been operating was busted all to pieces, and whoever did that ran their wagon over the edge of the bluff and wrecked it, too. I just happened to be riding down to check on them today, else we might not have known about it for a while."

"The same man who stole that strongbox from

Grant and Blake was responsible for this outrage, too?"

McConnell shook his head and replied, "Could be, but I don't have any way of knowing that, boss."

Henshaw took the cigar out of his mouth and leaned forward with a scowl on his face.

"I do," he said. "My gut tells me it was the same man. There can't be two men in Warbonnet County brave enough—or stupid enough—to defy me like that."

"You're still convinced whoever stole the strong-box came from Warbonnet County?"

A bark of scornful laughter from Henshaw.

"No one in Chaparral County would dare cross me like that."

McConnell hoped his boss was right about that, but he didn't see how they could know for sure.

However, he'd had another thought while riding out here, so he supposed he might as well go ahead and get Henshaw's opinion.

"I can think of somebody we know in Warbonnet County who might do something like ride right into Bolivar and steal that money. He's gun-handy enough to have killed Wilson, Massey, and Nunley, too. I'm talking about Pike Shannon."

Henshaw leaned back in his chair again and chewed the cigar for a moment before saying, "Shannon has a reputation as a daring, dangerous man. He proved that by the way he played Doak Ramsey and I against each other."

"And it's well deserved, from what I know of him," McConnell replied. "He's hired out his gun in scrapes all over the West. From what we were able to find out, he and his family didn't start cooking 'shine after they got rid of Ramsey, but our information could've been wrong. They might not want you moving in and competing with them."

"Find out what Shannon's been up to," Henshaw snapped. "If he's behind these new troubles that have been plaguing us, we may have to take special steps. Perhaps even call in some additional help."

"I can handle Shannon," McConnell said, irritated now that it seemed like his boss was doubting his abilities.

"Just look into it. If he's the one doing this, I'm not going to allow him to get away with it. We'll stop him—whatever it takes."

McConnell nodded. It wouldn't do any good to argue with Henshaw. The man had money and power and was used to getting his own way. He demonstrated that by waving McConnell out of the room without any parting words.

The black servant was waiting in the corridor. He said, "You're not running, so I assume your meeting with our mutual employer went well."

"I wouldn't say that," McConnell responded. "But he made it pretty clear what I need to do."

Maybe the best way to do it would be to just go ahead and kill Pike Shannon. If they did that and the trouble stopped, then they would know Shannon had been to blame for it, wouldn't they?

And whether Shannon was responsible for what had happened already or not, his mere presence in

Warbonnet County was a threat because they never knew when he might move against them.

Yeah, McConnell mused as he mounted up and rode back down the hill toward town, killing Pike Shannon was the way to go.

CHAPTER 18

Pike didn't know how long it would take for Solomon Henshaw to find out about what had happened down at Nelson's Ford, but he didn't want to ease the pressure he was putting on Henshaw's operation. Andy had told him about reports of possible moonshining activity around the community of Galena, in the southwestern part of the county, so Pike figured he would take a ride down there and see what he could turn up.

He was saddling his horse when Torrance came into the barn, made a disgusted sound in his throat, and said, "I see you're riding out again today."

"And what business is that of yours?" Pike replied coolly.

"Oh, none, I suppose," Torrance said with a dismissive wave of his hand. "We've had this conversation before, haven't we? Dougal and I keep the ranch running, and you go off and do . . . whatever it is you do."

Pike's jaw tightened. He knew that, despite Torrance's words, his brother was trying to bait him into an argument. He wasn't having any of it. Torrance would understand later, when this was all over, that Pike was just trying to help Andy Burnett. Until then, Pike didn't really care what Torrance might think.

"I'll be back when I'm back," he said as he mounted up. He turned his horse and rode out of the barn.

He almost ran right into Belle Ramsey.

They reined in at the same time, so their mounts didn't collide. Belle, wearing jeans and a man's flannel shirt with the sleeves rolled up on her tanned forearms, was riding astride. The stock of a Winchester saddle carbine stuck up from its scabbard beside her right knee.

Her auburn hair was pulled back and tied behind her head. The chin strap of the flat-crowned brown hat she wore was taut. The scar on her face didn't keep her from being attractive enough to take a man's breath away, Pike thought. She could almost distract him from the mission he was setting out on today.

Almost.

As it was, she delayed his departure from the ranch, because he stopped and said, "Morning, Belle. What brings you out here?"

"I was invited to come and visit, remember?"

"Well, sure, you're always welcome here." Pike became aware that his brother had come out of the barn. "Isn't that right, Torrance?"

"Of course," Torrance said. "I'll take your horse if you'd like, Belle, and you can go on over to the house. I know there's coffee left from breakfast. I'm sure Ma and Nessa will be happy to see you."

"Thank you, Torrance." Belle smiled at him for a second, then looked at Pike. "Where are you going?"

"Have to take care of some business," he replied, deliberately adopting a gruff tone.

Her chin lifted. She said, "I'll come with you."

"I don't reckon that's a good idea," Pike said with a frown. "You came to visit my mother and sister, didn't you?"

"I came because I'm tired of sitting around War-bonnet. But if you don't enjoy my company . . ."

"Now, hold on, hold on. I didn't say that. It's just that I'm going to be pretty busy today and might have to do some hard riding—"

"That's right," Torrance broke in. "Pike's off on another of those mysterious errands that are keeping him so busy these days."

"Mysterious errands?" Belle repeated with a finely arched eyebrow. "I hadn't heard anything about that."

Pike cast an irritated glance toward Torrance then said, "That's because I keep my business to myself, unlike *some* people"—he looked at Torrance again—"who like to stick their nose in where it's not needed. Or wanted."

"Well, I still think I'd like to ride along with you, at least for a while."

Pike didn't want to sit there arguing with her. He thought it was a little rude of her to just invite her-self along like that, but he couldn't see any way to refuse without insulting her.

And for some reason, he didn't want to do that.

He supposed he didn't have to take action today against any moonshiners he found operating around

Galena. He could consider this just a scouting trip. That way, he could keep Belle safe.

And to be honest, after the past few days, spending some time with Belle Ramsey would be a welcome respite from trouble.

"All right, but no complaining," he told her. "Like I said, there may be some hard riding."

"Honestly, Pike Shannon," she said, "have you ever known me to complain about hard riding?"

He opened his mouth to respond to that, then closed it, frowned, and glanced at Torrance, who was smirking to beat the band and obviously struggling not to laugh.

Pike lifted his reins and pulled his horse around a little harder than he'd intended to.

"Come on," he growled.

He rode out, not looking back to see if Belle was following him. He heard her horse's hoofbeats and knew that she was.

He didn't want to be a jackass to Belle just because Torrance got under his skin, so after a minute he slowed his mount and let her pull up alongside him.

"Where are we headed today?" she asked brightly.

"Ever heard of a place called Galena?"

"That's a little town southwest of here, isn't it?"

"Calling it a town is being generous, from what I remember of the place. More like a wide spot in the trail."

"Why are you going down there?"

"Just taking a look around," Pike said. "Might be some business opportunities in those parts."

She looked sideways at him and asked, "What

sort of business? Pike, do you plan to get back into moonshining?"

"I didn't say that." Something about her tone intrigued him. "Why? What would you think about it if I did?"

"I don't know. I mean . . . it's sort of a tradition in your family, isn't it? And mine as well? And you didn't exactly promise that Texas Ranger you wouldn't. You said you'd have to wait and see. That doesn't sound to me like you've closed any doors."

It didn't, did it? He hadn't given any serious thought to taking up moonshining again after the war with the Ramseys because he'd been ready for some peace and quiet by then, and after Andy Burnett had been elected sheriff, he'd resolved to steer clear of lawbreaking, out of respect for his friend.

But maybe there was some way the family could get their hands back in the game without causing any complications for Andy . . .

He was going to have to think about that, Pike decided.

For now, he said, "I don't plan to do any moonshining around Galena. From what I hear, somebody else may already be doing that, though."

"That could be a problem for the sheriff."

"Yeah." Pike figured he could risk telling her part of the truth. "That's why I'm going down there. I thought I could scout around a little, maybe find out something for him."

Belle's eyebrows rose.

"You're working for the sheriff? That would make you—"

"No," Pike said sharply. "No, it doesn't. Not hardly.

I'm no deputy. I'm just an hombre doing a favor for a friend. Andy doesn't even know about it."

"Oh. Well, I'm glad you trusted me enough to tell me what *we're* doing."

He started to tell her that she was just riding along for the company, that she didn't have any part of the job he had taken on. But she'd probably been trying to bait him into a response like that, so she could argue with him and wind up getting her way. Better just to ignore that little comment, he told himself.

So he changed the subject and started telling her about some of the horses he and Torrance and Dougal had been working with on the ranch. To be honest, his brother and grandfather actually *had* been doing most of the work lately, but Pike still considered himself a horse rancher, too.

The miles and the hours passed pleasantly as they talked not only about horses but about Pike's family. Belle dropped hints that she wanted to hear about some of the adventures he had had while he was gone from Warbonnet County, but he didn't take the bait. He'd done some things he wasn't that proud of, and for some reason he didn't want to admit that to Belle. At its best, his life while he was away had been a mite sordid.

They reached Galena around midday. It was a little more than the wide spot in the trail Pike had called it. It was a wide spot in *two* trails that intersected here. A business stood on each of the four corners. According to the signs on the buildings, they were Merle's Grocery, Willett's Blacksmith Shop, Tip-Top Mercantile, and Hebden's Café. In addition, a dozen houses were scattered around the tiny settlement.

Pike nodded toward the café and said, "How about we get something to eat?"

"Sounds good to me," Belle replied, then asked quietly "You think somebody at one of these businesses is selling moonshine?"

"That's what I intend to find out."

A couple of horses and a wagon team were tied up in front of the café. Pike and Belle tied their mounts with the others and went inside the frame building.

There was nothing fancy about the café. Instead of individual tables, it had two long, rectangular tables with benches beside them and no counter, just a door into the kitchen.

A heavyset man with a red face and fair hair waved them toward the tables and invited, "Have a seat anywhere, folks. Got beef stew, collard greens, and cornbread today. I'll fill up some plates and bowls for you."

"Seems like we don't have any choice in what we eat," Pike said with a smile as he and Belle sat down. They took off their hats and placed them on the bench.

"That's fine as long as the food's good," Belle said.

The burly proprietor, who introduced himself as Matthew Hebden when he came back, set the full plates and bowls in front of them, then fetched cups of coffee to go with the meal. Pike and Belle dug in. The food was good, and so was the coffee.

Pike looked around at the other three customers.

The lone man at their table was obviously a farmer and no doubt went with the wagon outside. The other two, who sat at the far end of the other table, looked like cowboys.

Belle was the only woman in the place. Pike saw the young punchers sneaking admiring glances at her and frowned at them to let them know it would be best for them not to get too bold. They seemed to get the message, because they looked back down at their plates.

Hebden came over as they were finishing their meals and asked, "How was everything, folks?"

"Really good," Pike told him. "I was wondering about something, though. You wouldn't happen to have anything a mite stronger to wash it down with, would you?"

Hebden laughed and said, "I already brew my coffee strong enough to get up and walk around on its hind legs."

"Well, that's not *exactly* what I meant," Pike said with a smile.

"Oh." Hebden frowned. "Oh!" He shook his head emphatically. "No, sir, not here. That's against the law. If that's what you want, you're gonna have to look for it elsewhere."

"I understand, I promise you. No offense meant."

"Galena's a law-abiding community. Except for—"

He stopped short and cast what appeared to be an involuntary glance through the front window at the business on the opposite corner, which was Merle's Grocery.

"That's fine," Pike said in a conciliatory manner. "It's always best to be law-abiding."

He felt a little like a hypocrite as those words came out of his mouth, and judging by the way the corners of Belle's mouth twitched slightly, she was trying not to laugh at hearing him say such a thing. He took out a silver dollar and handed it to the proprietor.

"We're much obliged to you, Mr. Hebden."

"I'll get your change—"

"No, you keep it. Food that good's worth it."

Hebden shrugged. Pike and Belle picked up their hats and left the café, pausing outside to put their headgear back on.

"You're going over to that grocery store and see if you can buy some moonshine, aren't you?" Belle asked as she tightened her hat's chin strap.

"Reckon I am," Pike said.

The store wasn't any busier than the café had been. From the looks of things, Galena was a pretty sleepy place most of the time. Pike and Belle went inside and waited until the owner finished bagging up some beans for a woman. When she left, they were the only ones in the place other than the proprietor.

He turned to them and asked, "Something I can do for you folks?"

He was a tall, thin man with a shock of graying hair, spectacles, and a nervous habit of rubbing his hands together. Pike smiled and said, "I was told you were the man to talk to about getting something to drink around here."

"Sure, we've got bottled sarsaparilla and other phosphates—"

"Now, you know that's not what I meant, friend."

The man rubbed his hands together harder.

"Look, I don't want any trouble," he said. "But some stranger comes into my place of business and starts making insinuations—"

Pike was weary of this already. He took a five-dollar gold piece out of his pocket and said, "Look, will this cover the cost of a jug or not?"

The man licked his lips. He started to reach for the coin, stopped, then took it. He gestured with his head toward the counter at the back of the store, then led Pike in that direction while Belle waited near the front.

"I'll bet it was Hebden over at the café who sent you here, wasn't it?" Merle said over his shoulder. "He thinks he's better than everybody else." He went behind the counter. "Wait here. I'll be back in a minute."

He went through a door into another room. When he returned, he didn't have a jug, but he carried a couple of bottles with clear liquid in them.

"I'll wrap these up in some burlap for you—"

"Hold on," Pike said. "For all I know, that could be water in those bottles."

Merle shrugged and pushed one of them across the counter.

"Try it for yourself."

Pike pulled the cork and tilted the bottle to his mouth. The liquid was moonshine, all right, smoother than what he'd had at Nelson's Ford but not up to the quality of the 'shine the Shannons had always produced.

He nodded and replaced the cork. Merle wrapped the bottles in burlap and tied twine around the bundle. He was about to hand them over but hesitated.

"You're not a lawman, are you?"

"A little late to be asking that, don't you think?" Pike said. He laughed and shook his head. "I give you my word, friend, I'm not a star packer, just a fella who has a thirst now and then."

"All right, I—Oh, shoot, here comes Mrs. Simpkins. If, uh, you wouldn't mind taking that and going on . . ."

Pike said, "Sure. Much obliged to you." He turned and walked back to Belle, and as they left the store they passed a sour-faced, elderly lady in a sunbonnet who was coming in. Pike pinched his hat brim and nodded to her as they went by, saying, "It's a mighty fine day, isn't it, ma'am?"

Belle was laughing as they went outside and walked toward the café where their horses were still tied.

"You're terrible, you know that," she said quietly. "That old woman looked like she'd been sucking lemons all day."

Pike patted the burlap bundle he had tucked under his other arm and said, "Maybe I should have offered her some of this. Might have gotten that puckered-up expression off her face."

Belle grew more serious.

"Are you going to tell Andy about this? That man's breaking the law by selling moonshine."

"I'm breaking the law by having it in my possession."

"That's different. By the way, what are you going to do with that?"

"Figured we'd pour it out on our way back to Warbonnet."

"Not without letting me sample it!" Belle objected.

"Really?"

"I'm a Ramsey, aren't I? I know good 'shine when I taste it."

"Well . . . I suppose we could have a drink or two before we pour it out."

"You'd never get Sophie Truesdale to do that!"

"I haven't tried to get Sophie to do anything, as I recall," Pike said.

"You'd be wasting your time, more than likely, with a thin-blooded girl like her."

Pike didn't figure it was a good idea to pursue that subject, so he didn't. Instead he stowed the burlap-wrapped bottles in his saddlebags, and they mounted up to ride back toward Warbonnet.

"To answer the question you asked earlier," he said as they ambled along the trail, "I know who's selling the stuff in Galena, but I don't know who's supplying old Merle back there. I might wait and see if I can find out about that before I talk to Andy."

"How? By keeping an eye on the place?"

"That's what I was thinking," Pike said. "And before you can ask, no, I don't need any help."

"It might be interesting to work on the side of law and order for a change," Belle said.

Pike might have argued with her, but he looked back and saw that they were well out of sight of the settlement by now. He reined in and reached into his saddlebags to take out the bundle.

"You can have a taste of this," he said as he pulled one of the bottles loose and held it up, "but then we really ought to—"

The bottle seemed to explode in his hand, showering him with glass and white lightning, at the same time as the crack of a rifle shot filled the air.

CHAPTER 19

Pike didn't know if he was hit, but he was more worried about Belle. He dropped the jagged neck of the bottle he was still holding and jerked around to see her trying to get her suddenly skittish mount under control. As far as he could tell, there wasn't any blood on her clothes.

A second shot blasted just as he lunged to grab her horse's reins and help her. The bullet whined past his head. This time he could tell the shot came from a clump of post oaks fifty yards farther along the trail.

Pike didn't waste any time. He caught hold of the reins and hauled Belle's horse around.

"Go!" he shouted at her when the animal was pointed in the right direction. "Get back to Galena!"

To make sure of that, he yanked his hat off and slapped it against the horse's rump. The horse leaped ahead in a gallop, forcing her to grab the horn to stay in the saddle.

Pike whirled his own mount and charged toward the trees where the bushwhacker lurked. He was between Belle and the rifleman and intended to stay in that position, shielding her with his own body and that of his horse.

He pulled his Colt and fired over the head of the running horse, not expecting to hit the rifleman at this range with a handgun, but he hoped he could distract the sorry bushwhacker, anyway.

Pike was about halfway to the trees when the rifle cracked again and he heard the horrible sound of a bullet striking flesh. His horse's front legs folded up instantly, dropping the animal in a grotesque, rolling sprawl.

Pike barely had time to kick his feet free of the stirrups before he found himself sailing forward through the air. He landed hard enough on the hard-packed trail to knock the wind out of him and rattle his teeth, but that was better than being pinned under the horse.

His momentum rolled him over a couple of times, and as it did, a bullet plowed into the ground where he'd been a split second earlier and kicked up dust and dirt.

Pike had held on to the Colt. He came up on both knees and his left hand and triggered another shot at the trees, then surged onto his feet and dashed toward the nearest cover. It wasn't much, just a grassy little hummock, but it was better than nothing. He dived behind it and stretched out full-length on his belly.

The rifle cracked again. Dirt showered on him as the bullet struck the hummock. Pike grimaced. Being careful not to raise up too high, he plucked some cartridges from the loops on his shell belt, opened the Colt's cylinder, and replaced the rounds he had fired.

He was pinned down here, he thought bitterly. If the ambusher was smart and careful and patient, he could work his way around to a position where he had a clearer shot at his intended target, firing now and then to make sure Pike kept his head down and didn't try to move.

Twenty yards to his left was a fallen tree that would provide better cover. He could try to leap to his feet and make a run for it, but if the fella in the trees was any kind of a shot, Pike knew he would never make it . . .

More shots suddenly blasted through the air, these coming from behind him and to his left. He grated a curse, thinking there was a second ambusher and now they had him trapped in a crossfire.

No bullets landed near him, though. In fact, the shots stopped coming from the trees. He twisted his head around and saw that the second rifleman was atop a small hill and seemed to be firing toward the trees, not him.

That was a friend up there, Pike realized. But he wasn't in the clear yet, because if he stood up, the bushwhacker could still pick him off.

No shots had hit the hummock since the second rifleman began peppering the trees with lead. The shots from the hilltop continued. Pike risked a glance over the little mound of earth. He saw tree branches jump as bullets whipped through them. Some of the slugs sent bark flying from tree trunks.

The rifle on the hill fell silent. As the echoes rolled away, Pike heard rapid hoofbeats from the direction of the trees. Had the bushwhacker given up his ambush and decided to flee? Pike thought he saw a faint haze of dust in the air, as if kicked up by a horse's hooves as its rider lit a shuck out of there.

He wasn't sure enough of that to risk stepping out into the open just yet. Instead he waited.

The shots from the hilltop didn't resume. After a few minutes, he heard a horse approaching on the trail and turned his head to see Belle Ramsey riding toward him. Belle had the reins in her left hand and the short-barreled Winchester saddle gun clutched in her right.

"Pike!" she called. "Pike, are you all right?"

He cast a glance toward the trees, thinking that the bushwhacker might still be lurking there and would take a shot at her, but nothing of the sort happened. That was a pretty good indication that her bullets had chased the varmint away.

Colt in hand, he pushed himself to his feet and walked back along the trail to meet her.

"I thought I told you to head for Galena," he said.

"And if you believed I'd ride off and abandon you, just because somebody was shooting at us, you're a bigger fool than I thought you were, Pike Shannon."

The defiant words, accompanied by a toss of her head, didn't surprise him a bit. In fact, as soon as the shooting had started from the hilltop, his first thought had been that Belle had doubled back and was getting in on the fight. That was exactly the sort of thing she would do. The fact that he'd been right didn't give him any particular sense of satisfaction, though.

She looked along the trail and exclaimed, "Oh, your poor horse!"

"I know. The son of a gun shot him right out from under me." Pike's voice took on a grim note as he added, "That's another mark against whoever was in those trees. I've already got a score to settle with him for trying to kill me, and putting you in danger, too."

"You're sure he was shooting at you?"

"You're not likely to have anybody gunning for you, are you?"

"I can't think of anybody," Belle admitted. "But why would someone be trying to kill you? I mean, I'm sure you have a lot of old enemies . . ."

More than enough, Pike thought, but he didn't believe an old grudge was what had prompted this bushwhack attempt. He thought it was more likely that Solomon Henshaw suspected he was responsible for what had happened at Bolivar and Nelson's Ford and had sent someone to kill him or at least keep an eye on him.

If he was being trailed by one of Henshaw's men when he'd gone to Galena and started poking around, it would be obvious that he intended to disrupt the moonshining operation in this area, too. That would have been enough to paint a big fat target on him.

The theory made sense, but Pike had no proof of it—yet. He wasn't going to stop his efforts. The fight at Nelson's Ford had been enough to make this personal, not just a favor for a friend. Having his horse shot out from under him, along with bullets whipping around Belle, just made it worse.

He was going to make Solomon Henshaw pay for this.

Those thoughts flashed through Pike's mind. He didn't feel like going into all those details with Belle, so to answer her question he just said, "I've been shot at enough that I know when a bullet's aimed at me. Which means you won't be taking any more of these rides with me for a while. Keeping company with me is just too blasted dangerous."

"Don't you think that's up to me?" she said. "Anyway, it looked to me like I was the one who pulled *your* fat out of the fire just now."

Pike couldn't argue with that. If not for Belle taking a hand, he'd still be pinned down behind that mound of dirt. She wasn't through lending him a hand, either.

"I hate to ask it of you, but your horse is going to have to carry double back to Warbonnet. I didn't see anyplace back in Galena where I could rent or buy another mount."

"Neither did I," she said. "You need some help getting your gear?"

Pike shook his head and said, "No, I can manage. It's my responsibility."

He was sweating hard by the time he got the saddle off his fallen horse. He had to carry it as he climbed up behind Belle on her mount. Balancing the saddle against his leg with one hand, he slipped the other arm around her waist.

He was uncomfortably aware of how close they were, and Belle probably was, too. It was going to be a strained ride back to the Shannon ranch.

Pike just hoped that the bushwhacker was long gone by now.

The black servant tapped deferentially on the library door and, at Solomon Henshaw's response, opened it and said, "Mr. McConnell is here, sir."

"Fine," Henshaw said. He sat back in his chair and raised his eyebrows in surprise at the sling Mc-Connell wore and the bandage wrapped around the man's left arm. "What happened to you?"

"Pike Shannon happened to me," McConnell snapped. "Or rather, Shannon and that redheaded witch Belle Ramsey."

McConnell wasn't expressing himself with the proper amount of respect and humility, but Henshaw was curious enough to let that pass for now. He had ordered McConnell to keep an eye on Pike Shannon and make certain he was the one sticking his nose into the moonshining operation down in Warbonnet County. Henshaw wanted to know how that had led to McConnell being injured.

"Sit down and tell me about it," Henshaw said as he nodded toward the comfortable red leather chair in front of the desk. "Would you like a drink?"

"I could use one," McConnell said. He settled himself in the chair.

Henshaw looked over at a divan near the bar where Lucille was lounging. He nodded to her, and she got up to pour a drink for McConnell. She raised her finely arched eyebrows questioningly as she touched the carafe of brandy. Henshaw nodded.

Lucille poured the drink, brought it to McConnell, and bent low enough as she handed it to him that he had a good view of a considerable amount of creamy flesh. He saw it—a man would have had to be blind not to—and appreciated it, Henshaw noted.

Henshaw took no offense at that. He enjoyed it when other men looked at his women, because he knew they were *his*. It was the same as if a visitor admired a fine piece of horseflesh or a valuable painting on the wall.

McConnell swallowed some of the brandy. Color came back into his face, which had been rather washed out when he entered the library. He said, "I followed Pike Shannon down to Galena, in the southwestern part of Warbonnet County. A fella name of Merle has been selling 'shine for us out of his store there."

Henshaw nodded and said, "I know that. Go on."

"I figured Shannon wouldn't have done that unless he's the one behind all the trouble, so I decided to put an end to it right then and there. I waited for him on the trail back to Warbonnet."

Henshaw sat forward and said, "You ambushed him?"

"That's right. Shannon's too dangerous to let him keep roaming around meddling in our business."

Henshaw frowned. He wasn't too happy about McConnell taking it on himself to kill Shannon without being ordered to . . . but on the other hand, that showed initiative, and it was true that Shannon was dangerous.

"Where does Belle Ramsey come into this?"

"She was with him."

"Were you going to kill her, too?"

"Didn't see any need to do that," McConnell said. "If I'd plugged Shannon, I would have let it go at that. Killing a woman would've stirred up the county more than I figured you'd want."

Henshaw nodded slowly and said, "You were right about that. But I assume you *didn't* kill Shannon?"

"I had a bead drawn on him," McConnell said with a bitter edge in his voice, "but he had a bottle of that 'shine he bought in Galena in his hand and he moved it so that the sun reflected off it right into my eyes, just as I pulled the trigger. That threw my aim off just enough."

"Bad luck," Henshaw said.

McConnell downed more of the brandy and said, "Yeah. But I kept trying. I killed his horse, and I had him pinned down when somebody else opened fire on me. Had to be the Ramsey girl. He'd sent her galloping back toward Galena, but she must have circled around."

He nodded toward his injured arm.

"She got lucky and drilled me. I was bleeding like a stuck pig and knew I had to get out of there and get some help before I bled to death. I found a farm, told them some story about accidentally shooting myself, and the woman bandaged it up good enough for me to get back here to Clarkston and have the doc tend to it."

The story had come spilling out of McConnell. Now he sighed, lifted the snifter, and drained the rest of the brandy.

"Shannon's got to die," he said heavily. "That's all there is to it."

"It certainly appears that he's the cause of our troubles," Henshaw agreed, "and I don't have any objection to him dying. However, that seems like a pretty big job, considering that you're injured."

"I can handle Shannon," McConnell flared defensively.

"There's no shame in getting a little extra help. Have you ever heard of a man named Ben Grayle?"

"Sounds familiar," McConnell responded curtly. "Hired gun, isn't he?"

"That's right. Once I knew we might have to deal with Pike Shannon, I did some looking into his background these past years while he was away from Warbonnet County. He and Grayle were on different sides in several conflicts."

"Range wars, you mean."

"Precisely."

"You figure he hates Shannon? Seems to me that gun-wolves like that don't take it personally who they go up against."

"Perhaps not most of the time, but Shannon seriously wounded Grayle in a shoot-out in Montana several years ago. Grayle was flat on his back for six months before he recovered. He hates Shannon, all right."

"So you're going to send for him." McConnell sounded resigned to that now.

"That's right. And in the meantime, I have some other ideas about how we can make life more difficult for Pike Shannon and his family." Henshaw smiled. "He's going to be sorry that he ever decided to involve himself in my affairs. Very sorry indeed."

CHAPTER 20

Pike's family wanted to know why anybody would have shot his horse out from under him like that.

"I don't know," he told them. "Maybe whoever it was figured on robbing Belle and me."

"The shots just came out of nowhere," Belle said, backing up Pike's story. He was grateful to her for that. "We're lucky we made it back alive."

Fiddler said, "For goodness' sake! Is this country ever going to get civilized, so that people can go out for a ride without having to worry about somebody ambushing them?"

"Life is always going to be dangerous," Torrance said, "as long as greed and anger are part of human nature."

For once, Pike couldn't argue with his brother. He had seen enough during his time as a hired gun to know that the balance between good and evil was a precarious one in this world—and the scale was liable to tip to the bad side at any time, with little or no warning.

Since it was late in the afternoon by the time they got back to the ranch, Mary insisted that Belle stay for supper, and then it just made sense for her to spend the night. There was an extra bedroom that once had belonged to the oldest Shannon son, Tyree, so having enough room wasn't a problem. Belle agreed.

If anybody found the idea of a Ramsey spending the night under the Shannons' roof a little odd, nobody brought it up.

It was nice seeing Belle at breakfast the next morning, Pike thought. He realized he could get used to that.

After breakfast, he saddled her horse for her. As she was about to mount up, he said, "I appreciate everything you did yesterday, Belle. I reckon you saved my life. I owe you."

"You don't owe me anything, Pike," she told him. "I'm just glad I was there to help." A smile curved her lips. "You may not have noticed, but I'm handy to have around."

"Yeah, I'm starting to get that idea—"

Pike wasn't sure what else he would have said—or done—next, because at that moment, Torrance came into the barn, whistling a tuneless melody.

"Do you plan on staying around here and getting a little work done today, Pike, or are you going off gallivanting around the countryside again, getting shot at?"

The warm, if confusing, feelings Pike had been experiencing evaporated instantly, replaced by annoyance at his brother.

"I didn't plan on getting shot at yesterday," he snapped.

"We lost a good horse, not to mention Miss

Ramsey being in danger. Whatever it is you're up to, Pike, maybe you ought to consider putting a stop to it before somebody really gets hurt."

"And maybe you ought to consider minding your own business." Pike's jaw jutted out defiantly as he said it.

Torrance took a step closer, his chest swelling as he took a deep breath and glared. Pike moved away from Belle's horse and clenched his fists.

Belle said, "If you two are going to strut around clucking at each other like a couple of banty roosters, I'd just as soon not be here to see it." She put her foot in the stirrup and swung up. Pike would have helped her, but she was mounted before he could do so. "I'll see you in town sometime, Pike. Torrance, my thanks to you and your family for your hospitality."

He nodded and said, "You're welcome anytime, Miss Ramsey."

Pike said, "Belle, wait a minute—"

"So long," she interrupted. She reined her horse around and heeled it into a lope that carried them out of the barn and into the morning sunlight. Her hat hung behind her head by its chin strap, and the golden rays made her auburn hair flash like fire.

Pike watched her go. Behind him, Torrance muttered, "You're a blasted fool."

Pike couldn't argue with that, either.

Pike didn't ride to Warbonnet that day or for a couple of days afterward. He didn't have anything definite to tell Andy Burnett, other than where moonshine was being sold in Galena.

If Andy went out there and arrested Merle, Solomon Henshaw would just find somebody else in that part of the county to sell his white lightning. It was more important to find out who was cooking and distributing the stuff.

And although he hated to agree with Torrance about anything, he *had* been neglecting his share of the work around here. If he was going to be part of the family again—and he wanted to be—he needed to pitch in more.

After working with his brother and grandfather for a couple of days, though, Pike's restlessness grew to the point where he knew he was going to have to ride out and take up his campaign against Solomon Henshaw again. Maybe by now, Henshaw wouldn't have men trailing him.

Or maybe he would. Pike would just have to take that chance.

Before he could saddle up and leave the ranch, though, Fiddler came into the house and said worriedly, "Pike, there's a fellow out there talking to Dougal, and he seems to be very upset about something. I think you should step outside before there's trouble."

Pike was standing beside the kitchen table, drinking the last of the coffee in his cup. His mother was over by the stove.

Mary turned around and said, "Oh, my heavens. What now?"

"I don't know, Ma, but I'll find out," Pike said as he set his empty cup on the table.

As he followed Fiddler out through the living room, he snagged his gunbelt from the peg where it hung near the door and buckled it on as he stepped out onto the porch.

A rawboned man in a high-crowned black hat stood in front of Dougal, poking a finger against the older man's chest. That was a bad idea, because Pike could tell from the blood turning his grandpappy's face a bright red that Dougal was about to explode.

"—could've killed us all," the visitor was saying in obvious anger. "What in blazes were you thinkin', tryin' to pass that poison off as moonshine?"

"If you'd let me get a blasted word in edgewise—" Dougal began.

"There ain't no excuse," the man interrupted. "No excuse at all! You could've killed us all—"

"You said that already," Pike broke in as he went down the steps. His thumbs were hooked in his gunbelt, with the right hand near the Colt's walnut grips.

The visitor glanced at him, clearly annoyed at the interruption, then looked again and frowned.

"You're that gunslinger," he snapped. "You just hold your horses there, mister. I ain't armed."

He lifted his empty hands out to his sides to demonstrate that.

"Maybe you shouldn't come around pestering your elders and throwing your weight around if you're not going to pack iron," Pike said. The man looked vaguely familiar to him, as if he might have seen him in Warbonnet sometime, but other than that, the visitor was a stranger. "We don't know each other, do we?"

"No, but I know who you are." The man waved, the gesture taking in his surroundings. "I know who all you Shannons are."

Dougal said, "Then you ought to know we aren't gonna stand for anybody comin' on our place and causin' trouble."

"I ain't the one peddlin' poison and callin' it white lightnin'," the man replied with a sneer.

Torrance had already ridden out to check on some of the horses, or else he would have been right up in the man's face by now, Pike was sure. Dougal was about to be.

Pike kept a tight rein on his own temper as he came closer and asked, "Mister, what in blazes are you talking about? None of us sold you any white lightning."

"Not you directly, but you cooked it and got fellas to drive around sellin' it."

"You're loco," Dougal said. "We ain't cooked any 'shine in months."

"Then why did the hombre say that it came straight from a Shannon still?"

"How in tarnation should I know?" Dougal yelled as he crowded forward. "Idiots can say anything!"

Pike got between him and the stranger. Dougal was liable to start throwing punches, as worked up as he was, and they didn't need that.

Pike glanced over at the house and saw that Mary, Fiddler, and Nessa were standing on the porch, looking worried. Trying to sound reasonable, he said, "Look, friend, I want to get to the bottom of this as much as you do. Why don't you come over to the house and have a cup of coffee? Then you can tell us all about whatever happened to get you worked up like this."

"What happened was that your family tried to poison me—"

Pike held up a hand to stop him.

"Let's sit and drink some coffee first," he suggested again. "If we all lose our tempers . . . it's not going to go well."

There was just enough menace in his voice to get through to the upset visitor. The man glared at him for a long moment, then nodded and said, "I reckon that'll be all right. I could use some coffee."

"You're lucky my grandson's feelin' hospitable," Dougal snapped. "I sure ain't."

Pike motioned unobtrusively for Dougal to be quiet and led the stranger over to the house.

"Have a seat there on the porch," Pike told him. "Ma, can we get some coffee?"

"I'll bring it right out," Mary said. She ushered Nessa back into the house. Fiddler remained on the porch. Dougal stomped off to the barn, snorting like an old bull as he went.

The stranger lowered himself gingerly into one of the rocking chairs. He looked stiff and uncomfortable at first but gradually relaxed a little. Pike propped a hip against the railing along the front of the porch.

Mary brought out cups of coffee for each of them. As the visitor took his, he said gruffly, "Thank you, ma'am."

"You're very welcome," Mary told him. "We're always glad to have company here on the ranch."

She went back into the house. Pike sipped his

coffee and said, "Why don't you start by telling me your name? Your face looks a mite familiar, but I don't reckon we've ever been introduced."

"I'm Royce Gallagher," the man said. "Got a spread north of town."

"The Box G," Pike said. "I've heard of it. Probably ridden across your range before, to be honest."

Gallagher waved a hand and said, "That's fine. I don't mind anybody cutting across as long as they're respectful and don't hurt anything."

"Well, I wish we were meeting under better circumstances, Mr. Gallagher, but why don't you tell me what's got you so riled up this morning?"

"It was what got me so sick yesterday," Gallagher said. "And not just me. Three of my hands were sick, too, just as bad as I was. I thought we were all gonna die."

"After drinking moonshine you believe *we* made?"

"That's right. Fella came around on a wagon, you know, a peddler—"

"A whiskey peddler?"

"Well, he didn't have that written on the wagon," Gallagher said acerbically. "Liquor's against the law in this county, you know that. He had all sorts of other things, pots and pans and horse liniment and knives and gadgets and what not, and when I went to run him off, he dropped a hint about havin' something mighty good to drink, too. That's when he said he got it from you folks and that he was sellin' it for you all over the county." Gallagher shrugged. "I used to hear how good Shannon moonshine was, but I never had any. So I took a chance and bought a couple bottles off him. I sure wished I hadn't."

"Clearly, though, you didn't die," Pike said. "I'm guessing none of your ranch hands did, either."

"No, we all got over it," Gallagher admitted grudgingly. "Still feel like we've been stomped on by a mule team this morning. I decided I'd ride over here and tell you you ought to be ashamed of yourselves for cookin' up something that makes folks so sick."

Pike took a drink of his coffee and then said, "You can believe this or not, Mr. Gallagher, but that 'shine didn't come from here. We don't have any stills. We're out of the moonshine business."

He didn't add "for good." He wasn't prepared to go that far.

Gallagher frowned up at him and asked, "Then why did the fella claim he was sellin' your 'shine?"

"I don't know," Pike said, although to tell the truth he had an inkling of the reason behind the deception.

During the war with Doak Ramsey and his family, Pike had pulled a similar trick, dosing moonshine so that it would make folks sick and then passing it off to Solomon Henshaw's representatives as Ramsey product. His goal had been to create a rift between Henshaw and Ramsey, and he had succeeded in that.

He'd made sure that the doctored 'shine wasn't bad enough to kill anybody, though. If what Gallagher was telling him was true—and Pike had no reason to doubt the man—it seemed likely that Henshaw was playing turnabout.

Pike wasn't convinced that Henshaw would be as

careful. Henshaw wouldn't care if some Warbonnet County folks got sick or even died, as long as he could strike at the Shannons that way.

Pike went on, "This peddler told you he was selling the stuff all over the county?"

"Well . . . he indicated as much. I don't remember his exact words. To tell you the truth, Shannon, I was so sick that a lot of yesterday is just a blur."

"I'm sorry about that, Mr. Gallagher, I really am. I give you my word, that 'shine didn't come from us, and I'm going to try to get to the bottom of who's really cooking it."

Gallagher thought about that for a moment and then slowly nodded.

"I reckon I believe you," he said. "When you find out, what are you gonna do about it?"

"I'm not sure yet," Pike said. "But I can tell you this. Whoever's behind this isn't going to like it when I catch up to him."

CHAPTER 21

Andy Burnett looked up from the desk in his office and said grimly, "I was just fixin' to ride out to the ranch and have a talk with you, Pike."

"Let me guess. You've been getting reports about somebody selling moonshine that makes people so sick they feel like they're going to die."

"Worse than that. There are a couple of people over at the doc's office who are so bad off with the blind staggers, he says they may not make it, and the relatives who brought them in say they got that way after drinking what was supposed to be Shannon moonshine."

Pike's jaw tightened as he stood there in front of the sheriff's desk. He felt like he'd just been slapped across the face.

"You don't believe that, do you, Andy?"

With a frown, Andy leaned back and said, "What I believe is that Dougal's been cookin' 'shine long enough that he'd never make the mistake of lettin' a run get tainted like that. That's true of Torrance, too. I figure even you know better, and you weren't around the family business as long as those two."

Indeed, Pike knew good and well that the first part of a run could be poisonous and was always discarded. That precaution would be second nature to his brother and grandpappy.

But it was moot, because, as he said to the sheriff, "I swear up one way and down the other, Andy, that none of us are cooking 'shine these days. We haven't since that trouble with Doak Ramsey. The Shannons are honest horse ranchers now."

Andy nodded and said, "I'm glad to hear it."

"Yeah, but do you believe it?"

Andy looked a little offended at that question. He said, "If I swore something to you, Pike, wouldn't you take me at my word?"

"Yeah, sure," Pike admitted.

"Well, then, give me as much credit. If your family's not the source of this bad liquor, then where's it coming from?"

Pike turned a chair around, straddled it, thumbed his hat back, and said, "I reckon you know the answer to that as well as I do."

"Henshaw," Andy said heavily.

"Yeah. He's figured out that I'm the one who's causing trouble for him down here in Warbonnet County, and he wants to get back at me and my family."

Even though Pike had told Belle he wasn't going to fill Andy in on what had happened at Galena until he found out more information, this new development changed things. He spent the next few minutes telling the sheriff about the ride he and Belle had taken to that small settlement and the ambush that had been waiting for them when they left.

"You can see why I already had a mighty big grudge against Henshaw," Pike concluded. "Now it's not just the fact that Belle was in danger and I lost a good horse. He's smearing mud on my family's good name. I'm not going to stand for that, Andy."

"I don't blame you. But what are you going to do?"

"I want to find that peddler and put a stop to what he's doing. In the meantime, when anybody reports that Shannon moonshine is being sold again, I'd appreciate it if you'd set 'em straight. Tell them you've checked it out, and it's not true."

"I can do that," Andy said, "but I can't guarantee that folks will believe me. Like it or not, Pike, your family *does* have a reputation, and it's hard to live that down." His voice took on a rueful tone as he added, "I saw that for myself, with my own reputation, when I was running for sheriff. Once folks tar you with something, it doesn't wash off easy."

Pike knew his old friend was right about that. To be honest, the idea that people would believe the Shannons were back in the moonshining business didn't bother him as much as the fact that they were willing to believe his family was incompetent or uncaring enough to produce bad liquor. It was an insult to their pride.

Solomon Henshaw would have known that. It was why he had hatched the scheme.

Pike suddenly wondered if Henshaw was trying to goad him into doing something foolish. Pike had used that tactic on his own enemies in the past, so he wouldn't put it past Henshaw.

But even if he *was* playing into the hands of the man from Chaparral County, he couldn't let this stand.

"Warbonnet County's a big place," Andy went on. "I'm not sure how you're gonna find that peddler. But if I hear anything about him, I'll let you know. I'll try to tamp down the sentiment that's rising against your family, too."

"I'm obliged to you for that," Pike told him. "I don't know how I'm going to find him, either, but I've got to try."

"What about finding out who's selling the stuff over around Galena?"

Pike rubbed his chin and said, "Maybe one will give me a lead to the other."

Pike brought his horse to a stop in front of Merle's Grocery in Galena and dismounted. He had been at peak alertness during the ride down here, but he hadn't seen any signs of an ambush, and his instincts told him he wasn't being followed. After so many years of living on the knife edge of danger, he trusted his gut more than just about anything.

He went inside and found Merle waiting on a middle-aged woman accompanied by two teenage girls. The girls eyed Pike with frank admiration, but he tugged down the brim of his hat and ignored their boldness.

When the three of them were gone, Pike stepped up to the counter.

"What can I do you for?" Merle asked automatically, then looked closer at Pike and went on, "Say, I remember you." He got a sly look on his face. "You want a couple more of those special bottles?"

"Not exactly. I want to know who you're getting them from."

Merle got a dubious look on his face and said, "Oh, now, I don't know if it would be a good idea to say—"

Pike reached across the counter, grabbed Merle by the shirtfront, and jerked the man toward him.

"I think it would be a very good idea," Pike said, "and I'm not in any mood to argue about it."

Merle was scared, and that fright showed in his wide eyes. But he was stubborn, too, and said, "Hey, you can't . . . you can't come in here and push me around in my own place!"

"Tell me what I want to know, and I'll leave you alone."

Merle shook his head.

"I don't dare—"

"Then ask yourself who you're more afraid of right now: the man who's selling you that white lightning . . . or me?"

Pike kept his grip on Merle's shirtfront with his left hand and dropped his right to the butt of the Colt.

Merle grimaced, swallowed hard, and said, "He . . . he's a big fella, got a mustache and a craggy face, calls himself—"

"Grant," Pike interrupted again, expressing in his voice the disgust he felt. "Norvell Grant."

"You . . . you know him?"

Pike let go of Merle's shirt, gave him a little shove back from the counter.

"Yeah, I know him." Norvell Grant wasn't the new lead he'd been hoping for.

"I guess you figure on buying directly from him now, don't you? It's getting so a businessman like me can't even make an honest living."

Merle sounded petty and aggrieved now, which made Pike feel a little less guilty about handling him roughly. Not to mention him referring to selling moonshine as making an honest living.

Pike started to turn away, but he paused and took a longshot.

"Did you ever see anybody else with Grant?"

Merle sniffed and said, "There's usually another fella with him. Mostly a skinny, redheaded hombre, but it's not always the same one."

That would be Ruel Blake. Again, not a bit of help to Pike.

But then Merle offered, "The last time he came by, he had Doc Fergus with him."

"Who's Doc Fergus?"

"You know, the fella who used to have the medicine wagon that came through these parts once or twice a year. Put on a show, sold bottles of medicinal tonic." Merle's voice dropped to a conspiratorial level. "If you asked me, that so-called tonic that was supposed to cure all sorts of ailments had more of a kick to it than the stuff I buy from Norvell Grant these days!"

"Yeah, a lot of that snake oil was mostly alcohol," Pike agreed.

"So I guess it makes sense Doc's helping sell moonshine now, when he's not out on his wagon peddling pots and pans."

That perked up Pike's interest right away. He said, "So Doc Fergus sells pots and pans? He's just a regular peddler now instead of a medicine show man?"

"Yeah, he had to give up selling the tonic when he got in trouble up around the Red River someplace. Some folks got sick on it, I heard. So now he sells a little bit of everything instead and, I guess, helps out Grant now and then."

And peddles tainted moonshine out of his wagon while claiming it came from a Shannon still, Pike thought. Doc Fergus had to be the man he was looking for.

"Where can I find him?"

"The doc?" Merle frowned and looked confused. "Shoot, I don't know. I haven't seen him in a while. I don't know if he's even in this part of the country anymore."

Pike was willing to bet that he was. But as Andy Burnett had said, Warbonnet County was a big place.

"Does Grant come by here on a regular schedule?" Pike asked. That was the case with Edgar Bennett's trading post, so it was likely Grant handled his deliveries in Galena in a similar manner.

"Every couple of weeks," Merle replied. "He was here yesterday."

Pike bit back an exasperated curse. He didn't want to wait two weeks just on the off chance that Doc Fergus might be with Grant the next time.

"You can't tell me anything about Fergus or where to find him?"

Merle shook his head and said, "Sorry. Now that I've spilled the beans about where the 'shine's coming from, there ain't no point in being coy about it, I reckon. So I'd tell you if I knew, mister." He glanced nervously at the gun on Pike's hip. "I swear I would."

"All right," Pike said. He was wasting his time here. He turned to leave.

"Hold on a minute," Merle said when Pike was halfway to the front door.

Pike stopped and turned.

"You happen to remember something?"

Merle still looked nervous. He said, "You've got to promise this won't come back to cause me trouble."

"As far as I'm concerned, I was never here today. That good enough for you?"

Merle sighed and said, "Reckon it'll have to be. I remember one time when Doc came by here, not with Grant, you understand, but in his peddler's wagon, and he said something about a place called the Blue Top. It took me a minute to come up with the name. I don't know where or what it is, but Doc made it sound like he went there pretty often, if that name means anything to you, mister."

It didn't, but it was still a thread that might lead Pike to Fergus, no matter how slender. He said, "I'm obliged to you."

"I hope you were telling the truth about keeping my name out of this, whatever it is. That Grant is a bad fella. He's got the meanness in his eyes. Doc's always grinning and friendly, but I don't think he'd like being crossed, either."

"I'll remember that," Pike said, but in reality, he didn't give a hang what Doc Fergus liked or didn't like.

As a matter of fact, when he caught up to Fergus, he intended to do some things that the fella was likely to downright hate . . .

CHAPTER 22

After supper that night, Pike caught Fiddler's eye and motioned with a lean of his head for the older man to follow him out onto the porch. Fiddler hesitated, because he usually helped Mary with the dishes after the evening meal, but then he stepped out onto the porch where Pike was leaning against the railing.

"Something wrong, Pike?"

"No, I just want to pick your brain for a minute."

"I'm not sure what sort of crop you'll get," Fiddler said with a chuckle. "After spending so many years soaked in booze, my brain isn't the most fertile field anymore."

"I think you underestimate yourself," Pike told him. "You seem sharp enough to me."

"Well, perhaps . . . but not what I once was."

Pike didn't want to dwell on the past, but the question he had for Fiddler centered around that part of the man's life, so there was no avoiding it.

"Back when you were drinking, you knew most of

the places in the county where you could get some moonshine, right?"

"Oh, yes, I got around," Fiddler replied. "Not just moonshine, either. Before the local option election, there were plenty of places that served liquor of all kinds. Scotch, bourbon, rye, brandy, vodka . . . I especially liked a jot of rum now and then . . ." Fiddler sighed nostalgically. "I wouldn't go back to those days, you understand, not after I've tried so hard to quit. And of course, having met your mother . . . but you don't want to hear about that, do you?"

"Just as soon not," Pike said.

"Certainly. But since we've established that I'm quite familiar with all the places in Warbonnet County where a man could partake, what is it you want to know?"

"Ever hear of one called the Blue Top?"

"Why, of course," Fiddler answered without hesitation. "It's a roadhouse . . . well, a café now, I suppose . . . down near Warbonnet Peak."

Pike shook his head and said, "I don't recall it."

"Well, it wasn't there when you lived in Warbonnet County before, and I don't imagine you've had a reason to go there since you've been back. It was a good place in its time. There's a large open area under the trees next to it, and the owner used to have dances there. I've played the fiddle on more than one such occasion, playing in return for, ah, appropriate compensation."

"A jug of who-hit-John?"

"The laborer is worthy of his hire," Fiddler replied solemnly. "It says so in the Good Book."

Pike laughed softly.

"You scrape a fiddle about as well as anybody I ever heard, so I suspect you earned every bit of it."

"Why are you asking about the Blue Top?" Fiddler wanted to know.

Pike wasn't sure how much detail he wanted to go into, so he said, "I heard that a fella I'm interested in used to spend time there."

"Who might that be?"

"A peddler called Doc Fergus."

"The good doctor!" Fiddler exclaimed. "Yes, I'm acquainted with him. And you're right, I've seen him on a number of occasions at the Blue Top. That was his headquarters, so to speak, when he would come through this area with his medicine wagon."

Out of curiosity, Pike asked, "Did you ever try any of his special tonic?"

Fiddler smiled and exaggeratedly licked his lips.

"Indeed, I did. And it was good for what ailed you."

"Did you know that he's still in these parts?"

"Not with the medicine wagon, surely," Fiddler said. "I heard that he got into some trouble because of it . . ."

Pike nodded and said, "I heard the same thing. He's got a peddler's wagon now and sells a lot of different things." He decided to go ahead and explain. "Including tainted moonshine he claims comes from one of our stills."

Fiddler's eyes widened in shock. He said, "That's terrible! The scoundrel! Why in the world would Doc do such a thing?"

"Because Solomon Henshaw is paying him to," Pike replied flatly.

Fiddler looked at him for a moment and then nodded slowly. He sighed and responded, "I hate to say it, but Doc always did have enough of a mercenary streak that he would do practically anything if the price was right. I don't want to believe that he would work for Henshaw and try to hurt your family . . ."

"But you don't really doubt it, do you?"

"No," Fiddler said. "Not really." He paused. "What are you going to do about this, Pike?"

"I want to find this Doc Fergus and put him out of business."

"You're not going to kill him, are you?"

"I'd just as soon not," Pike said again. "But whatever it takes, I'm not going to let him keep on throwing mud on the Shannon name."

"An admirable goal! I'll do whatever I can to help." A thoughtful look appeared on Fiddler's face. "Say, why don't I show you where the Blue Top is? If anyone there knows where we can find Doc, they won't be as suspicious if I'm doing the asking, since it's well-established that he and I are acquainted."

Even though Pike's first impulse was to tell Fiddler that he couldn't come along, the more he thought about it, the better the older man's idea sounded.

"How would you like to take a ride over there with me tomorrow?"

"Of course," Fiddler answered with his usual enthusiasm. "I'm happy to do anything I can to help the

Shannon family, Pike, you know that." He glanced toward the open front door and lowered his voice. "Should I . . . pack iron?"

Pike shook his head and said, "I don't reckon that'll be necessary. Any shooting needs to be done, I'll do it."

Mary wasn't too happy about Pike involving Fiddler in what she called "his crusade."

"If you get that poor man killed, I'll never forgive you," she told Pike the next morning when she cornered him in the kitchen after breakfast.

"I'm just trying to get a line on a fella," Pike said. "There shouldn't be any trouble."

"Trouble has a way of popping up around you like a thunderstorm in the spring, and you know it, Pike Shannon." She shook a finger at him. "You just remember what I said."

"Yes, ma'am, I will."

The two of them set out a short time later on horseback. Fiddler wore one of Dougal's broad-brimmed straw hats to keep the sun from blistering his mostly bald pate. The hat was slightly too big and sat down on top of his ears, but that was better than a sunburned noggin.

Fiddler shifted a little in the saddle and said, "My, I haven't ridden a horse in quite some time."

"We could've brought the wagon."

"No, no, that seems like too much trouble, not to mention it might slow us down. Don't worry about me, I'll be fine."

As the miles fell behind them, however, Pike could tell that Fiddler was getting more uncomfortable.

"Why don't we rest these horses for a spell?" he suggested.

"You think that would be a wise idea?"

"I do."

"Then I defer to your experience," Fiddler said as he pulled back on the reins.

They dismounted in the shade of some trees beside the road. Without being too obvious about it, Pike looked around for any signs that someone might be following them. He didn't see any, but that didn't mean their trail was clear of followers. Somebody might be hanging back and staying out of sight most of the time.

From where they were, they could see Warbonnet Peak, the big mesa that dominated the skyline in the southern half of the county. The town of Warbonnet lay between the Shannon ranch and the peak, but Pike was taking a different road today that skirted the town and would get them to their destination sooner.

After a few minutes, they mounted up and started riding again. Fiddler said, "I know what you were doing back there, Pike, and I appreciate it. I'll never be a hard-riding, hard-fighting hombre such as yourself."

"It takes all kinds in this world, though," Pike told him. "We need fellas who are good fiddle players, too, and smart to boot."

"Be that as it may, if we do happen to encounter any trouble, it's fully my intention to . . . how do you say it? Back your play?"

"I appreciate that. But the best way you can help

is to keep yourself safe. Ma would pure-dee kill me if I let anything happen to you."

"Then we'll endeavor to keep your dear mother happy."

"Sounds good to me," Pike agreed.

Warbonnet Peak, despite being level on top, had no buildings on it because the sides were too rugged for wagons to make it up there and no water was available. Even getting a horse to the top was difficult.

A man on foot could make it, though, and because of that, the Indians who had roamed this part of Texas in years past had used it as a favorite lookout spot. With the surrounding land being relatively flat, the peak was tall enough that a keen-eyed watcher could see for miles around from the top of it. Its popularity with war parties had given the peak its name, and from that had come the names of the town and the county.

At the western edge of the mesa's base sat a squat stone building with tiles of blue slate on the roof. A few other buildings were located in the shadow of the peak. One was a blacksmith shop, another was a church, and the rest were rough frame cabins where people lived.

"Does this little community have a name?" Pike asked Fiddler.

"Not really. Some people call it Ebenezer, because that's the Ebenezer Baptist Church over there."

"The Blue Top doesn't look very busy."

In fact, there were no saddle horses or wagon teams tied up at the hitch rack in front of the stone building. This tiny settlement was even sleepier than Galena.

Pike and Fiddler rode slowly up to the Blue Top and dismounted. Fiddler sighed in relief when his feet were on the ground again. They tied up and went in.

The thick stone walls and scarcity of windows gave the shadowy interior a welcoming coolness after the heat of the day. Candles mounted on a wagon wheel "chandelier" flickered and cast uncertain light over the room, which had a rough wooden floor. To the left was an L-shaped counter with a door to the kitchen behind it. To the right were tables. The place might be a café now, but to Pike's experienced eye, it was easy to see from the layout that the Blue Top had started its life as a saloon.

A heavyset man with dark hair, heavy beard stubble, and what seemed to be a permanent scowl on his face stood behind the counter, wearing a once-white apron over his work clothes. Fiddler greeted him by saying, "Luther, my friend! How are you?"

The man's scowl deepened as he said, "Fiddler? Is that you? Ain't seen you in a coon's age."

"Yes, I've been quite busy."

"If you're here lookin' for whiskey, we don't sell it anymore. It's against the law. I can cook you up a steak and some taters, if you want."

"I know about the law." Fiddler let out a solemn, mournful sigh, then his expression brightened as he went on, "But I've heard that there are certain places where, if a man is suitably discreet, he can still partake—"

Luther interrupted him with a shake of the head.

"Maybe, but not here," the man said. "Sorry, Fiddler. You were always a good sort, and when you resined up your bow, you could get some mighty fine tunes outta that fiddle of yours, but I ain't goin' to jail."

"Having spent more than my share of time incarcerated, I can certainly sympathize. My friend and I will take those steaks, though."

Fiddler cocked a quizzical eyebrow at Pike, who nodded. They were here for information, and they'd be more likely to get it if they didn't act like that was the reason for their presence.

Luther retreated to the kitchen and came back ten minutes later carrying a couple of plates. Each plate had a steak on it, charcoaled on the outside and bloody in the middle, as well as a pile of soggy potato chunks.

Pike looked at the unappetizing food and thought that a jug of moonshine certainly would help wash it down.

He and Fiddler both ate determinedly, however, as Fiddler reminisced with Luther. The man must have been bored before they got here, because he seemed to enjoy the conversation, although it would be difficult to tell that from his habitual glower.

"Remember Joe Foster?" Fiddler asked. "My, what a character he was! Whatever happened to him? Is he still around?"

Luther shook his head and said, "Naw, the consumption got him a while back. Just about wasted away to nothin' before he kicked the bucket, the poor devil."

"What about Jeb Blackstone?"

"Even worse! He married a hatchet-faced widow woman and moved to Dallas."

Fiddler shuddered and said, "What a terrible fate."

He asked about a few more old acquaintances from his drinking days before saying without a hint of anything different in his voice, "I haven't seen old Doc Fergus in a long time. Surely he's not still in these parts."

"Doc?" Luther repeated. "Sure he is. He comes by here now and then. More often, here lately, I'd say. Fact is, last time he was here he told me he'd probably be by today."

"Really?" Fiddler murmured. "Perhaps we'll wait for him. It would be nice to see Doc again. He's still peddling pots and pans and whatnot?"

"Yeah." Luther lowered his voice. "Actually, if you've got a thirst, Fiddler, I hear tell that Doc might have something on his wagon you'd like."

"Really?" Fiddler said again as his bushy eyebrows climbed up his forehead.

"That's right. You've got to keep it outta here, though. I meant it when I said I don't intend on breakin' the law and goin' to jail."

"Well, of course. If my friend and I conduct any such transactions with Doc, we'll make certain that they take place outside."

"Speakin' of your friend . . ." Luther gave Pike a meaningful look. "You ain't introduced us."

"This is Bill Smith," Fiddler said easily.

Luther nodded and said, "Pleased to meet you . . . Smith."

His voice made it clear he didn't believe for a

second that was really Pike's name, but it was equally
obvious that he didn't care.

"Same here," Pike said as he returned the nod.

"Appears that you won't have long to wait," Luther
went on. "I think I hear Doc's wagon coming now."

Pike turned his head toward the door, which was
still partially open from when he and Fiddler had
come in. He heard hooves clomping on the hard-
packed road, along with the rattle and squeal of a
wagon jolting along.

Some clanging noises accompanied the usual
sounds, and after a moment Pike realized they came
from pots and pans banging together as they swung
from hooks on the sides of the wagon bed. He had
encountered other peddlers and recognized the
racket.

Fiddler said, "Perhaps we should go out and
meet him."

"No, let's just wait here," Pike said. He wanted a
good look at Doc Fergus, and more than likely, the
man would pause to let his eyes adjust to the dimness as soon as he stepped into the Blue Top.

The hoofbeats and the other noises came to a
stop outside. Pike heard a man saying something in
a low voice and realized that Doc Fergus was talking
to his team of mules, as a man would do if he was by
himself a great deal of the time.

Heavy footsteps approached the entrance. The door
swung back farther, spilling more early-afternoon
sunlight into the café. A short, bulky figure stepped
inside. The newcomer was just a silhouette at first,
but that was enough to tell Pike that he wore a
long duster and a derby hat. He took the hat off

and smacked it against his clothes, revealing a bald head and tufts of white hair that stuck out like wings above each ear. Doc Fergus put the hat back on and stumped toward the counter with a grin on his round, beefy face.

"Howdy, Luther," he said. "How's about fryin' me up a chunk o' cow—"

He stopped short at the sight of Pike and Fiddler standing at the counter. Fiddler said, "Hello, Doc. It's your old friend—"

"I know who you are, Fiddler," Doc Fergus rasped. His beady eyes swung over quickly to Pike and widened in surprise. "And you, too, you son of a—"

He didn't finish the epithet because he was too busy clawing for a holstered gun under the long coat he wore.

Chapter 23

Pike could have outdrawn Doc Fergus and drilled him. The man wasn't fast on the draw at all.

But that wouldn't have served his purpose, so instead he acted swiftly but not lethally. He sprang forward, and as Fergus cleared leather, Pike chopped down with the side of his hand on the older man's wrist. Fergus yelped in pain as his fingers opened and the gun thudded to the floor.

A swipe of Pike's boot sent the gun spinning away. Fergus used his other arm to push his coat back and closed his fingers around the handle of a sheathed knife on his left hip. Before he could draw the blade, Pike hit him with a hard, straight right that sent Fergus staggering back through the open door. His feet got tangled up and he sat down hard.

"Pike, look out!" Fiddler cried.

Pike whirled and saw that Luther had come out from behind the counter. He held a mallet in his raised right hand as he rushed at Pike, obviously intent on bashing his brains out.

Pike bent low and went under the blow as it fell.

The mallet struck his left buttock. The impact stung but didn't do any real damage. Pike wrapped his arms around Luther's knees and heaved upward, grunting with the effort as he straightened. Luther yelled in alarm and went over Pike's back. Pike heard him crash to the floor.

Stepping back, Pike drew his gun and stood where he could cover both Luther and Doc Fergus, the latter through the doorway. He glanced over at Fiddler and said, "Thanks for the warning."

"I couldn't let him hurt you," Fiddler said. He shook his head. "I suppose Luther's going to hate me now. I sided with someone who's a stranger to him."

Even stunned as he was, Luther must have heard that. He rolled onto his side, groaned, and pushed himself up on an elbow. Propped there, he shook his head, groaned again, and said, "Blast it, Fiddler, that's no way to treat an old friend!"

"I know, and I'm sorry, Luther, but you gave me no choice."

Luther's glare was as dark as a spring thunderstorm as he looked at Pike.

"Bill Smith, my hind foot!" he said disgustedly. "Who are you really, mister?"

"Name's Pike Shannon," Pike drawled.

A look of surprise replaced the glare on Luther's face.

"One of the moonshinin' Shannons?" he asked.

"That's right. At least we used to be. We're out of that business now."

As usual when he said something like that, Pike felt a little pang inside. It still seemed wrong for his family not to be cooking 'shine, but he supposed nothing ever stayed the same in life.

Luther managed to make it to a sitting position and asked, "Why'd Doc try to gun you?"

Telling the truth might actually be the best course of action this time, Pike decided. He said, "Because he's been going around the county selling tainted moonshine and claiming it came from a Shannon still." Pike's voice hardened. "The Shannons never sold bad 'shine and anybody who claims we did is a blasted liar. Anybody asks, you tell 'em that, Luther."

"Leave me outta your feuds," Luther muttered. He pushed himself awkwardly to his feet. "Sorry I tried to stove your head in. I didn't know what was goin' on. I was just stickin' up for a customer."

"I understand that," Pike told him.

Fiddler added, "We're sorry to involve you, Luther. We didn't know we were going to find Doc here today. We were just looking for information about him. Running into him was a stroke of luck."

"Not for Doc," Luther said. He leaned his head toward Fiddler. "You're runnin' with the Shannons now?"

"The family has befriended me," Fiddler replied. "I owe them a great deal."

Luther frowned and said, "If I didn't know better, I'd say you was sober, Fiddler."

"Indeed I am. And I intend to stay that way."

Luther scratched his beard-stubbled jaw.

"Well, I'm happy for you about that, I reckon. Even though it's hard to think of you bein' sober."

Just outside the door, Doc Fergus was beginning to come around. Pike hadn't knocked him out cold,

but the punch had stunned him for several minutes.
Now he sat up as Pike stepped out of the Blue Top.
Fergus looked at the gun Pike pointed at him. The
peddler spewed curses.

Pike let it go on briefly, then said, "That'll be about
enough, mister. If anybody's got a right to do any
cussing, it's me, seeing as how you've been going
around trying to destroy my family's good name."

"I don't know what in blazes you're talkin' about,"
Fergus blustered.

"Then why'd you slap leather as soon as you laid
eyes on me?"

The peddler scowled but didn't say anything.
There wasn't a good answer to the question Pike had
just asked him.

Pike motioned with the Colt's barrel and said,
"Get up."

Fergus hesitated, then clumsily climbed to his feet.

"Go on over to your wagon."

Fiddler and Luther came out of the building as
Pike followed Doc Fergus to the wagon, which was
hung with pots and pans, kitchen utensils, and tools.
There were doors on the sides, and Pike knew that
if they were opened, he would see built-in shelves
stacked with other goods.

"What's he gonna do?" Luther asked quietly.

"I don't know," Fiddler replied. He sounded a
little worried.

When Pike and Fergus were standing beside the
wagon, Pike demanded, "Where's that tainted white
lightning?"

"I tell you, I dunno what—"

Fergus stopped short as Pike tilted the Colt's barrel toward his face.

"Here's your choice," Pike said in a tone of quiet menace. "You can get the stuff out here, or I'll just have Fiddler unhitch those mules, then I'll burn the whole wagon. That'll get rid of it for sure."

"You can't burn my wagon!" Fergus objected. "You're loco! That's my livelihood."

"Then you should have stuck with peddling instead of working for Solomon Henshaw." The sudden flicker of fear and recognition in Fergus's eyes told Pike that he was right. He went on, "It's up to you. Lose the moonshine or lose everything."

Faced with that choice, Doc Fergus did the only thing he could. He went to the back of the wagon, opened a door there, and reached in to take out a jug.

"You still claim you don't know what I'm talking about?" Pike asked.

Fergus stood there in surly silence.

"Drink it, then."

Fergus's eyes widened. He said, "What? You mean . . . this?" He hefted the jug.

"That's exactly what I mean. Pull that cork, tip it up, and take a nice long drink, Doc. Get a good healthy swallow of that white lightning."

"I . . . I don't reckon I want to—"

Pike squeezed the Colt's trigger. The gun boomed, and the jug flew apart in Fergus's hand, leaving him holding just the loop on the jug's neck. The contents splashed over his belly and legs. He let out a frightened yelp and jumped backward.

"Got any more jugs in that wagon?" Pike asked when the shot's echoes died away.

Fergus threw the broken piece of jug aside and practically dived into the back of the wagon. He brought out another jug.

"Pour it out on the ground," Pike ordered.

Fergus did as he was told. With Pike's gun pointed at him, he took four more jugs from the wagon, one by one, and emptied them all. The moonshine formed a glistening pool on the ground as it began to soak into the dirt.

Finally, Doc Fergus looked at Pike and said, "That's all, Shannon. I swear it."

"Step back," Pike told him. "Fiddler, take a look in there and see if there are any more jugs."

Fiddler peered inside the wagon. After a moment, he turned to Pike and shook his head.

"I don't see any," he reported.

"Good. You step back, too."

When Fiddler had done so, Pike fished a lucifer out of his pocket and snapped it to life on his thumbnail. He tossed the burning match into what remained of the pool of whiskey.

The stuff went up with a violent *whoosh!* It caused Fergus to leap back even more and cry out in alarm. He looked at Pike and said, "You could'a singed my dern eyebrows off!"

"You're lucky I don't make you dance on those flames as they burn out," Pike snapped, "after what you tried to do to my family. Now, you run on back to Henshaw and tell him his plan didn't work. Nobody's going to ruin the Shannons' reputation for cooking the best white lightning in Texas, even if we're not in that line of work anymore. You understand what I'm saying to you, Doc?"

"Yeah, yeah, I understand," Fergus muttered.

"All right. Get this wagon out of here and head back to Chaparral County."

"What about my gun?"

"I'll leave it with Luther," Pike said. "You can pick it up the next time you come through these parts peddling your wares." He paused. "And that had better not include any moonshine. Because if I hear even a whisper about you trying to pull that stunt again, I really will burn that wagon next time, Doc . . . with you in it."

Fergus climbed onto the wagon seat. Fiddler untied the mule team for him, and Fergus soon had the vehicle rolling away from the Blue Top. He sat hunched over on the seat, looking miserable.

Luther had already retrieved Fergus's gun. He frowned at Pike and said, "You took advantage of my good nature, mister. I don't appreciate it. And I don't want your business, neither."

"We still owe you for those steaks," Pike said.

"Forget it. I don't want your money." Luther looked at Fiddler. "And you sure have changed. I don't reckon the old Fiddler would've turned on his friends like that."

"You mean when I was a sodden drunk?" Fiddler asked with a hint of anger in his voice. "I'm sorry you feel that way, Luther, but Doc's been working for a bad man, trying to harm some good people. People who have been mighty kind to me. So I'm not going to apologize for trying to help them."

Luther still glared, but after a few seconds, he said grudgingly, "All right. I reckon I can see why you'd do that." He paused. "If you ever want to come down here and play that fiddle o' yours again, folks still have dances over yonder under the live oaks, a couple of times a month."

"I'd be welcome?"

"I expect so." Luther shrugged. "I don't plan on runnin' my mouth about what happened here today."

Pike said, "Except for the part about the Shannons not cooking any bad 'shine and not selling any, either. You can tell anybody about that, and I'd take it kindly."

Luther didn't respond to that, just went back into the building. Pike and Fiddler untied their horses and turned the animals to the northwest, back toward the Shannon ranch.

"We've put a stop to that little scheme of Henshaw's, at least for now," Fiddler commented as they rode. "I'd call that a good day's work."

"Maybe," Pike said. "I reckon it all depends on what Henshaw tries next."

CHAPTER 24

Carl McConnell had never liked the imperious way Solomon Henshaw summoned him to the big house on the hill just north of Clarkston, but he liked Henshaw's money just fine. So he put up with Henshaw's arrogant manner. Henshaw was the boss, after all. He called the shots.

This time, instead of the black butler, it was Lucille who opened the front door to McConnell's knock.

"Where's . . ." McConnell started to say, then his voice trailed off as he realized he didn't know the servant's name. All the time he'd been working for Henshaw, all the occasions on which he had visited the house and been greeted by that calm, middle-aged gent, and he'd never heard Henshaw call the man by name. And Henshaw certainly hadn't introduced the servant to McConnell. Such a thing would never even occur to a man like Henshaw, who saw people as tools to be used, more than anything else.

"Come in," Lucille said gravely, ignoring the question McConnell hadn't finished asking. The dress she wore today wasn't quite as fancy as her usual garb, but the neckline still dipped to reveal a considerable amount of cleavage, which was common. She lowered her voice to a half-whisper and added, "Solomon isn't in a good mood, exactly, but at least it's improved a little, thank heavens."

Henshaw had been furious a few days earlier when Doc Fergus showed up unexpectedly and reported what had happened with Pike Shannon at the Blue Top. McConnell happened to be there to hear Fergus's story, too.

Henshaw had ranted and raved and gotten so red in the face that McConnell had worried he'd have an attack of apoplexy right then and there. He had told Fergus to get out, and once the peddler was gone, Henshaw had sworn vengeance on Pike Shannon for thwarting his plans yet again.

"How the devil does he do it?" Henshaw demanded. "How is he always in the right place at the right time to ruin everything I try to do?"

McConnell didn't figure his boss really wanted an answer to that question, and anyway, he didn't have one to offer Henshaw. He didn't know how Shannon managed to be such a pain in the rear end, either.

Now, McConnell looked closer at Lucille, spotting the faint bruise on her cheek despite the powder covering it. That was a sure sign Henshaw was tiring of her. When he'd had a girl around for a while, he started getting more impatient with her and losing his temper.

All of them believed they would be the one who was different, McConnell thought. But it never played out that way. Sooner or later, McConnell was summoned to the mansion to take them to the railroad station, put them on the spur line to Fort Worth, and give them a little money.

That was the way it went with the lucky ones, the ones who didn't annoy Henshaw *too* much. The ones who were unfortunate enough to get on his bad side . . .

The less McConnell thought about that, the better.

McConnell hoped that Lucille would be one of the lucky ones, then shoved that out of his mind and asked, "What lifted the boss's spirits?"

"The man who arrived a little while ago."

"What man would that be?" McConnell asked, although he had a pretty good idea he already knew the answer.

"He said his name was Grayle."

Lucille shivered a little, as if she didn't like what she felt when she thought about Ben Grayle.

The hired gun had made good time. Grayle had been in Wichita when he wired back, the telegram McConnell had sent having caught up to him there. Of course, the way the railroads were spreading out all over the country these days, it didn't take nearly as long to get from one place to another as it had used to.

Lucille motioned for McConnell to go on down the hall to Henshaw's library, then closed the front door behind him.

"He's expecting you," she told him. "Just knock and go on in."

McConnell did so. As he walked into the library, he saw Henshaw behind the desk and another man sitting in the chair where McConnell usually sat. This hombre had his right ankle cocked on his left knee, drawing attention to the fancy, expensive black boots he wore.

His black trousers had a sharp crease in them. He sported a black leather vest over a white shirt, and a string tie with a turquoise clasp was fastened around his neck. His black gunbelt had two holsters attached to it, each occupied by an ivory-handled revolver.

A black frock coat and a flat-crowned black hat were hung on a hat tree just inside the library door, completing the man's outfit.

The stranger's strong white teeth were clamped firmly on a cigar that McConnell recognized as having come from the humidor on Henshaw's desk. That meant the cheroot was an expensive one, too.

A hawklike nose and piercing, deep-set eyes completed the man's features, along with the thin-lipped mouth. His dark hair was cropped close. He had the look of a predator about him.

McConnell hated him on sight. Dandies like that always rubbed him the wrong way. But he had to admit, Ben Grayle had quite a reputation as a ruthless gunman. He had hired on to fight the private wars of cattle barons, mining tycoons, and railroad magnates all over the West. The fact that he was still alive and approaching middle age in such a dangerous profession testified that he was one tough son of a buck.

But so was Carl McConnell, even if he didn't have Ben Grayle's notoriety. He hooked his thumbs in his gunbelt and stood there in hipshot arrogance as the two men in the library turned their heads to look at him.

"There you are, Carl," Henshaw said with a trace of impatience and annoyance in his voice.

"I headed right on out as soon as I got word you wanted to see me," McConnell replied. "Don't know how I can get here any faster than that."

Henshaw gestured impatiently and said, "Never mind." He nodded toward the man sitting in front of the desk. "This is Ben Grayle."

McConnell grunted and said, "Figured as much."

Grayle took the cigar out of his mouth and held it between the first two fingers of his left hand.

"It's good to meet you, too," he said dryly, with an infuriatingly confident smile. "You'd be Carl McConnell. I've heard of you."

That eased McConnell's irritation slightly, knowing that Grayle had heard of him. He had a reputation, too, and it would be a good idea for Grayle not to forget it.

McConnell nodded curtly, said, "Grayle."

Behind the desk, Henshaw said, "Don't arch your back and spit and hiss like an old tomcat, Carl. We're all on the same side here, you know."

"Sure, boss."

To show that he wasn't intimidated, McConnell turned and ambled over to the bar. Henshaw and Grayle both had glasses with a couple of inches of amber liquid in them sitting on the desk, so he figured he ought to have some brandy, too.

He picked up a glass, splashed liquor into it, and turned to see Henshaw glaring at him. Other than the baleful look, Henshaw ignored McConnell's defiance. He said, "Sit down, Carl. We have things to talk about."

McConnell took another chair from against the wall and placed it in front of the desk. He wasn't going to sit off to the side. He took a sip of the brandy and said, "I reckon you want to talk about what we're gonna have Grayle here doing."

"*You* won't have me doing anything," Grayle said. "I take orders from Mr. Henshaw."

"Both of you stop it," Henshaw snapped. "Carl, I didn't send for Ben to hurt your pride, no matter what you may believe. I just want to put a stop to Pike Shannon's interference in my affairs, whatever it takes."

"There's one sure way to do that," Grayle said.

"We've tried that," Henshaw said with a meaning-ful look at McConnell.

"With all due respect"—and Grayle's tone made it clear that he meant *no* respect whatsoever—"*I* haven't tried that. Not yet."

"Pike Shannon's a hard man to kill," McConnell rasped. "You ought to know that. From what I hear, the two of you have been on opposite sides several times in the past. If killin' him is so easy . . . why's he still drawing breath?"

"Just because we were on different sides doesn't mean I ever found him in my gunsights. We can't always pick and choose our targets, McConnell. You ought to know that."

Henshaw leaned back in his chair, puffed on the cigar for a few seconds, then said, "Killing Shannon isn't enough. He's defied me, and I want him punished for that. I want to make an example of him, and his friends and family, so that if anyone in Warbonnet County starts thinking about standing up to me, they'll decide against it because of what happened to the Shannons and their friends. Can you handle that, Ben?"

Grayle solemnly regarded the glowing coal on the end of his cheroot and nodded.

"I can. I brought ten men with me and have eight more coming who should be here within a few days. And these are good men. Top-notch fighters. I'd put them up against anybody short of a company of Texas Rangers." Grayle gave Henshaw an intent look. "There's not a company of Texas Rangers in Warbonnet County, is there?"

"There aren't *any* Texas Rangers," Henshaw replied. "I heard that one of them was poking around down there before Doak Ramsey was killed, but he never did anything, and once Ramsey was dead, there was no reason for him to stay around. I have contacts in the state government in Austin who will let me know if any Rangers are headed this way."

"Well, then, we don't have to worry about that. Give me a list of Shannon's relatives and friends, and we'll get started on making him wish he had never crossed you."

McConnell frowned and said, "You're just going to ride down there and start shooting people?"

Grayle clamped the cigar between his teeth again and asked around it, "You know a better way to get somebody's attention?"

CHAPTER 25

Sam Crow was a happy man, although you wouldn't know it to look at his solemn face. He just didn't believe in going around grinning all the time, although he could have. He had a good farm, a pretty wife, a teenage daughter who was beautiful, respectful, and well-behaved, and a pair of boys, eight and ten, who were full of piss and vinegar, as all little boys should be.

Sam's skin was just coppery enough that it, along with the name Crow, made people suspect he was a half-breed. Sam never mentioned the subject one way or the other because he just didn't believe it mattered. The important thing was that people didn't give him trouble because of it.

Leaning on the handles of his plow, he used the sleeve of his homespun shirt to wipe sweat off his face as he rested the mule Absalom for a minute. Rested himself, too, since it was a hot day here in north-central Texas. The sky was a pale blue where it showed through gaps in the thick white clouds. Sam wished he had a drink of cool water.

As if by magic, his daughter Lita appeared, emerging from the shadows underneath the trees at the edge of the field planted in sorghum. She had a glass jar in her left hand, and even though Sam couldn't make out the details at this distance, he knew the jar would have beads of sweat on its slick outer surface, formed by the cool water inside.

Lita's long black hair was parted in the middle and fell in waves around her face and then down her back. She wore a plain cotton dress that clung to her figure, already womanly despite the fact she was only in her mid-teens.

As she walked through the field toward Sam, she called, "Ma thought you'd be needing this about now, Pa."

"Your mother is right, as always," Sam responded. He smiled. His children had a way of making his usual dour nature disappear momentarily.

But it came crashing right back as he spotted movement behind Lita and saw several men on horseback ride out from under the trees.

He didn't recognize them at this distance, but alarm bells went off inside his head anyway. He waved to Lita and called, "Hurry up, honey."

She picked up her pace, and as she came up to him, she said, "You must be really thirsty."

He had forgotten all about that. What he wanted was to get himself between his daughter and those men on horseback.

"Go on over to the other side of the field," he told her as he took the jar from her. "My shotgun's leaning against a tree there."

"Your shotgun?" Lita said with a frown. "Why do you need your shotgun?"

"I don't. You get it and move on back in the trees. If there's trouble, you run, hear? Go to the Bear Cave and hide."

"Trouble? I don't—"

"Just go," Sam snapped.

She looked a little hurt for a second, but then she glanced over her shoulder and caught her breath as she saw the riders. They had started into the field, and they weren't being careful about where their horses stepped, cutting across the rows instead of following them.

"Go!" Sam said again, and this time Lita did what she was told. She started out walking, but after a few steps she broke into a run toward the trees.

Sam sipped water from the jar. It was cool and tasted good. He had a fine well. But he didn't really notice much about the water right now. It was just wet in his mouth as he watched the four men approach him.

He dropped his right hand to the knife sheathed at his waist. It was more of a tool than a weapon, but it was all he had. He hadn't expected trouble to find him in the middle of a sorghum field.

The man in the lead was tall and lean; that was evident even while he was in the saddle. He wore a black suit that had to be hot on a day like this, but Sam didn't see any sweat on the man's face under the flat-crowned black hat.

The other three wore typical range clothes, but

he could tell by looking at their hard-planed faces that they weren't cowboys.

Sam glanced over his shoulder and saw Lita disappearing into the shadows under the trees on that side. He hoped she had found the shotgun.

The four men reined to a stop with the black-suited man slightly ahead of the others. His face reminded Sam of an ax blade as he nodded and said, "Afternoon. Would you be Sam Crow?"

Sam tried to answer but found himself too choked to get any words out. He covered that by taking another drink from the jar. Then he was able to say, "That's right. And I'd be obliged to you if you're a little more careful when you ride out. You did some damage to my crop there."

"Did we?" The man looked back over his shoulder for a second, then gave Sam a cold smile. "I don't reckon it'll matter all that much."

His hand flickered toward the ivory-handled gun holstered on his right hip. He was fast, really fast, but Sam had been watching for a move like that and his reflexes were pretty quick, too. He flung the jar of water at the man's face and dived to the side.

The gun boomed, and blended with it was a curse that ripped from the hatchet-faced man's mouth. Sam didn't know where the bullet went, but he could tell he wasn't hit.

He rolled, pulling the knife as he came back up. He was to the horse's side now. He raked the blade across the animal's hip, cutting deeply enough to make the horse let out a shrill sound of pain and rear up as the gunman tried to swing the revolver toward Sam. The gun blasted again. The bullet whined past his head.

There was no cover out here in the middle of the field, but Sam darted to the side so that the spooked horse and its rider were between him and the other three men, so they couldn't open fire on him. He lunged at the black-suited man, reached up, and caught hold of his arm. Sam packed a lot of strength in his stocky figure. He hauled the man out of the saddle and sent him crashing to the ground.

The plowed earth cushioned the man's fall, but he was still stunned momentarily. Sam bent down and jerked the other gun from the left-hand holster. He was under no illusions that he could win a shoot-out with these men, who had the look of hardened killers about them, but if he could ventilate one or two of them and slow down the others, that would give Lita a better chance to get away.

He spun toward the men still on horseback and lifted the gun. He was out in the open enough now that they could risk shooting at him, but he was a moving target as he cut across the field. The gun roared and bucked in his hand as he triggered a pair of shots at the men who obviously had come here to kill him.

He didn't have time to see if he had hit any of them. Something struck him a hammerblow, high on the left side of his chest, and knocked him off his feet. He went down in a hard sprawl.

His left side and arm were numb, but he was able to make his right arm work enough to lift the gun again. Before he could pull the trigger, the black-suited man loomed over him and kicked his right wrist. Sam cried out as the gun flew from his grip.

Then the black-suited man, hatless now, brought his foot down on Sam's wounded shoulder and pinned him to the ground, causing agony to explode through him.

"Go get that girl!" the man ordered. "Bring her back here." He had retrieved his other gun, and he pointed it down into Sam's face as he went on, "You can have some fun with her, but her pa's going to watch . . . before I kill him!"

No bears roamed this part of Texas. Maybe they had once, but if so, that was long ago.

The Bear Cave was a small, hollowed-out spot in the side of a hill that Lita and her father had discovered while they were exploring the family's farm a decade earlier. The little girl had seen it first and had started to scamper inside, but Sam had called after her, "Better not. There might be a bear in there."

She'd looked back at him and asked skeptically, "Really?"

"I don't know," Sam had said, even more solemn than usual. "I wouldn't risk it, just on the off chance that there *is* a bear. It's best if you can manage it so all the surprises in your life are good ones."

"Instead of bears."

"Exactly."

So ever since, the place had been known to them as the Bear Cave, and it was a special spot that only the two of them knew about. Eventually, Sam had brought along a lantern on one of their little jaunts and they had explored the cave, which was barely big enough to deserve the name, a round space roughly four feet in diameter that went back into the hillside maybe a dozen feet. There was no sign that a bear or any other wild animal had ever made a home in it, although it was a good place to find worms.

Today, with her heart slugging crazily in her chest, Lita crawled backward into it until her feet hit the far end. Then she lay there with the shotgun in front of her, pointed toward the entrance. She curled her fingers around the stock but didn't touch the triggers, just as her father had taught her. You never put your finger on the trigger unless you were ready to shoot.

She had flinched as she ran through the woods at the sound of gunshots behind her. A time or two, she'd almost turned back, but the knowledge that her father wouldn't have wanted her to do that kept her moving forward.

So did the fear that roiled inside her, although she didn't want to admit that even to herself.

Now she lay there in the close confines of the Bear Cave and listened to her pulse hammering inside her head.

She hadn't gotten a very good look at the four men who had ridden into her pa's sorghum field, but she was confident she had never seen them before. The gunfire proved that they hadn't come there for any good purpose. Somehow, her father had realized their evil intentions right away; that was why he'd sent her running here to hide.

Tears ran down Lita's cheeks. She started to whimper but suppressed the urge and told herself she needed to be as quiet as she could. That might be important, if the bad men came to look for her.

Had they killed her father? Had they done anything to her mother and little brothers? Lita didn't know, but the possibility of all those things terrified her. What if she were the only one of her family left alive? Even if she survived today, how could she possibly go on by herself?

She had to bite her lower lip to keep from sobbing. She closed her eyes and rested her forehead against the cool dirt where she lay. The heat of the day hadn't penetrated the Bear Cave.

She didn't lift her head until she heard horses. The steady thudding of their hoofbeats slowly came closer.

A man called, "You see any sign of her?"

"No, not yet, but she's got to be around here somewhere."

"I don't know, kids can run pretty fast."

"From what I saw of her, she ain't no kid. Looked pert near like a grown woman to me."

Lita swallowed a terrified moan that tried to well up her throat. Silence was more important than ever with those searchers close by. Even the sound of her heart thumping in her chest seemed too loud to her. They were bound to hear it.

The horses kept moving, though, and after a minute or so Lita realized the hoofbeats were going away instead of coming closer. The men hadn't spotted the Bear Cave, and now they were riding off to search somewhere else. Lita was relieved by that realization, but the fear for her family still remained.

With a rattle that made her gasp and jump, rocks and dirt suddenly showered down over the cave's entrance. Somebody was sliding down the hill above her. A terrified grimace twisted Lita's face as a pair of booted feet and denim-clad legs suddenly appeared in front of her in the opening.

"Hey, fellas!" a man shouted. His voice sounded like he had his hands cupped around his mouth. "There's a little cave over here in this hill! I'm gonna have a look!"

The blood roared inside Lita's head, fueled by fear. She didn't wait. She didn't want to give the men on horseback time to turn around and ride back.

She just tightened her grip on the shotgun, shoved it toward the man's legs, and pulled the triggers.

CHAPTER 26

Andy Burnett was on his way to his friend Sam Crow's farm when he heard gunshots not too far away.

The sheriff reined his horse to a stop and frowned. It wasn't that unusual to hear a shot out here in the countryside, or even several shots. Folks hunted. They had to shoot rattlesnakes and copperheads.

The shots Andy heard didn't come from a squirrel rifle or a varmint gun, though. Those distinctive booms were handguns going off, and a flurry of such shots usually meant trouble.

The worst of it was that the ruckus sounded like it was on the Crow family's farm.

Andy put his horse into a run. He couldn't think of any reason why a gunfight should be going on at Sam's place. Sam had given up moonshining and was just a peaceful farmer with a nice family these days. When Andy had been elected sheriff, he had asked Sam to come to work for him as a deputy, and Sam had turned him down flat. He had seen enough trouble during the war with the Ramsey clan to last him the rest of his days, he said.

That didn't stop Andy from dropping by to see his old friend now and then, which was what he intended to do today. It wasn't strictly a social visit, though. Andy spent a lot of time just riding around the countryside, visiting with folks and making sure that trouble wasn't trying to sneak up on Warbonnet County.

The quickest way to Sam's farm was straight over a sparsely wooded hill directly in front of Andy. As he galloped up the slope, he spotted a saddled but riderless horse at the top. He wasn't sure, but he thought he heard, over the drumming of his horse's hooves, a man calling out to somebody.

Then there was a muffled roar somewhere close by. It sounded like a shotgun going off, but there was something odd about it, something hollow and echoing.

There was nothing muffled about the man's scream that came right on the heels of the blast. It ripped through the air and was full of shock and agony.

Andy charged over the hilltop and saw a man thrashing around on the ground and kicking legs with bloody, shredded calves. The white of bone showed through the gore.

A girl with long dark hair scrambled to her feet and ran along the slope on this side, never looking back as brown legs flashed under the dress she was holding up. Even though her back was turned toward Andy, he recognized her as Lita Crow, Sam's daughter.

About two hundred yards away, two men on horseback rode hard toward the hill, leaning forward in their saddles and slashing their reins against their horses.

Every instinct in Andy's body told him those men were more trouble galloping straight at him. He looked at the man still rolling around on the ground and yelling. The hard-featured, beard-stubbled face resembled every drifting hardcase Andy had ever seen. There were plenty of faces just like it on the stack of wanted dodgers in the desk drawer in his office.

The fact that Lita was running away like that told Andy how frightened she was. He urged his horse after her, cutting across the face of the hillside.

"Lita!" he called after her. "Lita, it's me, Andy Burnett!"

In her fright, maybe she didn't hear him, or she just didn't believe him. But within moments, he caught up to her, and as the horse drew closer to her, she jerked a wide-eyed glance over her shoulder.

She stumbled and slowed as she recognized him. Andy leaned down from the saddle to wrap his left arm around her and swing her up off the ground.

As he did, he felt the wind-rip of a bullet past his head and knew with a cold feeling in his belly that if he hadn't leaned down to pick her up when he did, he'd be dead right now.

He lifted her onto the horse's back in front of him. Her arms went around his neck and she clung to him as she pressed her face against his chest.

"Hang on!" he told her. "I'll get you out of here."

Her head jerked up.

"No!" she cried. "You've got to go back and help my pa!"

That made the cold ball inside Andy's stomach expand even more. He didn't know what sort of trouble Sam was in, but it had to be pretty bad.

"Where is he?"

"Back in the sorghum field! I'll show you!"

Actually, Andy knew from previous visits which field Sam had planted in sorghum, and he was familiar enough with the farm to know, as well, that two armed and angry men were between them and that field.

As if to emphasize that fact, when he threw a look over his shoulder he saw powder smoke spurting from gun barrels as the pair of men thundered after them.

Under different circumstances, he might have reined in and put up a fight. Running away from trouble stuck in his craw. But right now, Lita was his responsibility. He had to get her to safety.

Unfortunately, she realized what he was doing and started to squirm in his grip.

"Go back! Go back!"

Andy muttered a curse and tightened his arm around her. If she wasn't careful, she was going to slip off the horse's back and fall to the ground. If that happened while they were galloping along like this, she stood a good chance of breaking an arm or leg—or her neck.

"Stop that!" he said. "I'm just tryin' to save your life!"

"But if the rest of my family is dead," she sobbed, "I don't want to live!"

Andy had been too busy to think about Sam's wife and the two boys. Lita might have a point there. If those varmints were trying to kill her and Sam, they might have gone after the rest of the family, too.

He looked around to see where they were and then abruptly hauled his horse to the right, aiming for a saddle in the gently rolling hills. That route would take him back toward the cabin where the Crow family lived. He didn't have to go through the sorghum field to reach it.

That meant abandoning Sam to whatever fate had befallen him there, but Andy knew his friend would want the rest of his family to be safe, if at all possible.

"I'm takin' you home, girl," he told Lita. "Hang on!"

The gunman's loathsome words cut through the sea of pain that threatened to drag Sam Crow down into its depths. He looked up at the gun muzzle, which seemed as big around as a cannon from this angle, and the hateful face above it.

"You hear that, redskin?" the man went on. "My men are going to have some sport with your little girl, and then I'll blow your brains out. Who knows, maybe we'll take her with us. Or maybe I'll just cut her throat."

Sam raised his other hand, clutched his wounded shoulder, and whimpered as tears ran freely down his face. The gunman laughed. Sam turned his head to the side in apparent shame and rolled his body slightly in that direction, too.

"Don't . . . don't hurt me any more, mister," he

gasped. "You can have my daughter. Whatever you want, I'll do it. Just don't . . . kill me."

"Anything?" the man taunted.

"Anything!" Sam said.

The gunman seemed to be considering it for a second, but then he chuckled again and said, "Sorry, redskin. I can't make any deals with you, no matter how attractive a morsel that girl of yours is." His voice hardened. "You're Pike Shannon's friend, and you've got to die."

The mention of Pike surprised Sam enough it almost disrupted the submissive act he was putting on. While pretending to beg for his life, he had put himself in a better position to fight back, and that was what he intended to do, wounded shoulder and all.

He didn't have to wait long for his chance. He heard a distant boom that sounded like his old shotgun, followed by a flurry of gunshots. Those reports made terror explode inside him, because he figured Lita was fighting for her life against the men who had gone after her. They might be shooting her right now!

He lunged toward the gunman's legs. Wrapping his uninjured arm around the man's calves, he surged up. The gun roared. Sam felt the heat of the bullet as it ripped his shirt and burned along the skin of his back. Then the gunman was upended and went over backward into the sorghum.

In the heat of the moment, Sam didn't really feel the pain from his injury, but his left arm hung limp and useless and that threw him off balance as he tried to go after the gunman. He slipped and fell, struggled to get back to his feet.

While he was doing that, his hand fell on the empty glass jar in which Lita had brought the water to him a short time earlier. He scooped it from the ground and swung it in a looping blow at the gunman's head.

The jar landed with a crash and shattered. At the same instant, the man's gun blasted again, this time so close to Sam's ear that he was deafened, and the world seemed to spin crazily around him.

Instinctively, he rolled away and landed on his wounded arm, causing so much pain that he almost blacked out. His muscles refused to work. He expected to feel a bullet slam into him at any second, putting him out of his misery.

That didn't happen, though, and when he finally forced himself to raise his head and blink through pain-fogged eyes, he saw the gunman trying to grab the horse's reins. The man's hands were empty. He had dropped his gun and probably couldn't find it because a sheet of blood covered his face, including his eyes. The gore came from a gash that the breaking jar had opened in the man's forehead.

Sam spotted the ivory-handled gun lying on the ground and tried to crawl toward it. His skull still throbbed, and he could barely move.

Hoofbeats thudded close by. The gunman had managed to haul himself into the saddle. He rode toward Sam, clearly intending for the horse to trample him.

Desperation overcame pain and uncooperative muscles. Sam flipped to the side. The slashing hooves barely missed him. Sam thought the would-be killer would turn his mount and try again, but the man kept riding, hunched far forward in the saddle. Sam realized he must have done some significant damage when he hit the hombre in the head.

Just because the man was fleeing didn't mean that Sam was safe, though. He might still bleed to death or die just from the shock of being shot. He needed help.

But even more, he had to find out what had happened to his daughter. Lita might need him, and he wasn't there for her.

Slowly but surely—and painfully—he climbed to his feet. His hearing was starting to come back now. He still had a ringing in his ears, but he was able to make out the fading hoofbeats of the gunman's horse as the man rode away, heading north.

Sam turned to the west, the direction Lita had gone, and stumbled in that direction. He grimaced, lifted his right hand, and pressed it to the bloody wound in his left shoulder.

He had gone about twenty feet before his strength and his balance deserted him. He tried as hard as he could to hang on to consciousness, but it slipped away from him and he pitched forward on his face, out cold.

Andy looked back after realizing he hadn't heard any shots for several minutes and saw that the pursuers were no longer behind him and Lita. He didn't know how far back they had given up the chase—and he didn't relax because he wasn't sure but that this was a trick of some kind.

A few minutes later, the two of them came in sight of the farm. Lita twisted around so she could get a better view.

"Everything looks all right," she said.

Andy had been afraid maybe the marauders had set fire to the cabin, but that worry had lessened when he didn't see any smoke. As Lita said, everything appeared normal around the place.

"There's my ma!" the girl suddenly exclaimed. "Look! She's hanging up washing on the line in the back."

Hearing the horse approaching, Millie Crow turned away from her washing and shaded her eyes with her hand as she looked at the newcomers. She must have recognized her daughter perched on the horse in front of Andy, because she suddenly lowered her hand and hurried to meet them.

"Lita!" she called. "Lita, are you all right? Andy, what's going on here? What's Lita doing with you?"

"Oh, Ma!" Lita cried. "There were these awful men! I'm afraid they hurt Pa!"

Millie raised her arms to help Lita as Andy swung her down from the horse's back.

"Are your boys here, Millie?" he asked tightly.

"Yes, they're . . . they're in the barn. Andy, I thought I heard shots a little while ago. What—"

"I'm gonna find out," Andy told her. "Keep an eye on the kids. All of you get in the cabin. Is there a gun in there?"

"My pa's Henry rifle," Lita said. Now that she was home and had seen that the rest of her family was all right, anger was beginning to replace the fear. Andy could see that on her face and hear it in her voice. "It's loaded, and I know how to shoot it."

"Go fetch your brothers and get inside the house," her mother told her. "Andy, what can I do?"

"Just stay safe. I'll go see about Sam."

With that, he hauled his horse around and heeled it into motion again. He rode fast toward the sorghum field.

Along the way, he checked that his gun was still in its holster. The stock of a Winchester stuck up from a saddle sheath under his right leg. That was comforting, too.

He halfway expected to run into the other riders, but he hadn't seen any sign of them by the time he reached the field. Right away, though, he spotted a dark shape lying in the dirt near the edge of the field.

"Sam!" he exclaimed as he headed in that direction.

It was Sam Crow lying there, all right, no doubt about that, Andy saw as he dismounted while his horse was still moving. He stumbled slightly, recovered his balance, and ran through the soft dirt to Sam's side.

Sam was lying facedown. Andy took hold of his shoulders and carefully turned him onto his back. From Sam's shoulder almost down to his waist, the left side of his shirt was dark and wet with blood. He had lost plenty of the life-giving fluid.

But he was breathing, Andy saw to his great relief.

He could even hear the breath rasping in Sam's throat.

He needed to get his friend back to the cabin so Millie could get that shirt off him and see just how bad the wound was. Andy was trying to figure out the best way to lift Sam onto the horse when Sam's eyelids fluttered open. He looked up, seemingly unable to focus for a moment, but then his gaze locked on Andy's face.

"An . . . dy!" he gasped. He tried to reach up and grasp Andy's arm with his good hand, but he lacked the strength. His arm fell back to the ground.

"Take it easy, Sam," Andy told him. "I'll get you home and Millie can patch you up."

More than likely, Sam was going to require more medical attention than that, but getting him home was a place to start.

"L-Lita . . . ?"

Andy was expecting that. He said, "She's safe, and so are your wife and the boys. Those fellas who shot you are all gone."

He glanced around as he said that, hoping that he was right and none of the gunmen had doubled back.

"You have to . . . tell Pike."

That took Andy by surprise.

"You mean I should tell Pike you got shot?"

"N-no. Tell him . . . the varmint shot me . . . because I'm Pike's friend!"

CHAPTER 27

Pike, Torrance, and Dougal leaned on the corral fence and watched Nessa working with one of the half-broke colts. In the past, they had tried to persuade her that she shouldn't risk life and limb like that, but eventually they had realized they were wasting their time.

Besides, Nessa had a good touch with the horses, and she was a lot lighter than all of the male Shannons. She was sticking to the saddle like a burr as the horse capered around inside the corral.

The sound of approaching hoofbeats made Pike look around. He spotted a rider on the lane leading to the ranch headquarters and after a second recognized him as Lem Cranepool, one of Andy's deputies.

As Cranepool came closer, Pike was able to make out the grim expression on his face. The deputy looked like something was wrong, and Pike's first thought was that something had happened to Andy Burnett. Being sheriff was a dangerous job . . .

Pike stepped away from the corral, prompting Torrance to look around and say, "What . . . ?"

Pike met Cranepool and asked, "What brings you out here, Lem?"

"Sam Crow's been shot," the deputy replied bluntly as he reined his mount to a halt.

Pike caught his breath. He felt like he'd been punched in the face.

"How bad? Is he dead?"

Cranepool shook his head and said, "No, but he's in piss-poor shape. Doc Faulkner says Sam lost a heap of blood and the bullet tore up the muscles in his shoulder mighty bad. But there's at least a good chance that he'll pull through."

"Well, that's a relief, anyway. He's at the doctor's house?"

"Yeah."

"I'll have to ride in and see him," Pike said.

"You'll have to ride in and talk to the sheriff, that's what you'll have to do," Cranepool said. "That's why he sent me out here. He told me to fetch you."

Pike didn't care for the idea of being fetched, but at a time like this, he wasn't going to argue over words.

"I'll saddle a horse. Before I do, though . . . Who shot Sam?"

Cranepool shook his head and said, "I don't know the details. I just know that Andy wants to talk to you."

"Fair enough," Pike muttered as he turned away.

Torrance had followed him over to meet the deputy. As Pike headed for the barn, his brother said, "Did I hear right? Sam Crow was shot?"

"That's what Lem said."

"Who'd do a thing like that?"

"I intend to find out," Pike said, then added, "And when I do, they won't be happy about it."

"Maybe I should ride into town with you," Torrance suggested.

Pike shook his head. The first thing he had thought when Cranepool told him Sam had been shot was that this had something to do with his crusade against Solomon Henshaw. Maybe he was being too quick to think that the world revolved around him, Pike warned himself, but the idea made sense in a way. He and Sam were good friends. Sam had been Pike's ally in the battle against Doak Ramsey. If Henshaw wanted to hurt Pike by going after his friends, that could have put a target on Sam.

"I think it might be better if you stay here."

"Why? Because there's a chance somebody will come after us?"

Pike might not always get along with his brother, but he knew that Torrance was pretty sharp. He said, "There's always a chance trouble might crop up."

"Especially when your brother's a hired gun with a lot of enemies, who believes in solving problems with bullets," Torrance replied, nodding slowly.

That air of smug moral superiority rubbed Pike the wrong way, but again, this wasn't the time to worry about it. He went on into the barn and quickly got a saddle on a chestnut gelding, one of the horses he often used as a saddle mount.

When he rode out of the barn, Cranepool was over by the house, standing on the porch steps and drinking from a glass of water that Mary had given him. Fiddler was there on the porch, too, with a concerned expression on his face.

When Pike rode over, Mary said, "Deputy Cranepool says that Sam Crow has been hurt. Do you know if Mrs. Crow and their children are all right, Deputy?"

"They're in town, ma'am. They came in with the wagon that brought Sam to the doc's house. As far as I know, they're all right."

"You make sure of that, Pike," Mary said with a stern look.

"Yes, ma'am," he replied.

"Tell them that if they need a place to stay, they can come out here."

Cranepool said, "I don't reckon that'll be a problem, ma'am. Ol' Sam, he's well liked in Warbonnet. Folks'll be sure his family's taken care of."

"Well, just remember what I said," Mary told Pike, who nodded.

He and Cranepool started toward town. Pike tried to find out more from the deputy, but either Cranepool honestly didn't know anything else or had been instructed by the sheriff to keep his mouth shut. When they reached Warbonnet, Pike didn't know any more than he had when they started for town.

"Andy said for you to go on to Doc Faulkner's," Cranepool said as they neared the courthouse and the sheriff's office. "He was gonna wait there for you and keep an eye on Sam."

"Thanks, Lem."

"Just doin' my job." Cranepool paused. "Sam's a good fella. I hope he's gonna be all right."

So did Pike.

A few minutes later, he drew rein in front of the one-story, whitewashed frame house where Dr. Preston Faulkner's medical practice and living quarters were located. A number of obviously curious townspeople stood outside the picket fence that bordered the yard. Pike was sure word had gotten around that Sam Crow had been shot and brought here. Folks wanted to know how he was doing and find out the details of what had happened. News of any kind was always important in a frontier settlement.

The bystanders got out of Pike's way, though, when he tied up his horse and moved through the crowd. Pike wasn't disliked here in Warbonnet, exactly, but he did have a reputation as a man not to be interfered with.

One person who didn't step aside was Belle Ramsey. She stood beside the gate and said, "As soon as I heard that Sam had been shot, I figured you'd show up sooner or later."

"Sam's my friend. And Andy sent for me."

"I'm coming in with you."

Pike didn't see any point in arguing. Belle would just ignore him, anyway.

"I'll bet she doesn't tell *you* no," Belle said under her breath as they went up the walk.

Pike had no idea what she meant by that, but he figured it out quickly enough when the front door swung open in response to his knock and Sophie Truesdale stood there with a stern look on her face.

Pike wasn't all that surprised to see Sophie. He knew that she assisted the doctor from time to time.

She didn't have any formal training as a nurse, as far as he was aware, but evidently she was good at taking care of people.

Pike took off his hat and asked, "How's Sam?"

"He's sleeping right now."

"Sheriff Burnett wanted to see me."

"Yes, I know." Sophie looked at Belle. "But I don't believe he sent for you, too."

"I'm with Pike," Belle replied curtly.

Sophie looked at Pike and quirked an eyebrow, obviously waiting for him to pick a side in this disagreement.

Thankfully, he didn't have to, because at that moment, Andy Burnett said from inside the house, "Pike, is that you? Come on in."

Sophie stepped aside to let Pike pass, and as he did, Belle came with him. Sophie frowned but didn't try to stop her. Pike figured Belle had tried to get in earlier, and Sophie had refused entrance to her.

Andy was standing next to a door on the other side of the doctor's waiting room, hatless and wearing a weary look on his face. He nodded and said, "I'm glad you're here, Pike."

"What happened?" Pike asked tersely. "Did somebody raid Sam's farm?"

"That's exactly what happened. Four men showed up while Sam was plowing, getting ready to plant more sorghum. His girl Lita happened to be with him. Sam figured the fellas were up to no good and told her to run off. One of them shot Sam and the others chased after Lita. She had Sam's shotgun and was able to wound one of the varmints. Then I happened to show up and got her away from there. I took her home and then went to find Sam.

"All those gun-wolves were gone. Even though Sam was wounded, he fought back against the one who shot him and hurt the fella so much, he took off for the tall and uncut. I reckon the other three pulled out, too, because I didn't see hide nor hair of them. I carried Sam back to his place, and then we put him in the wagon and brought him here to the doc's as fast as we could."

As Andy wound up that recitation, Pike nodded and asked, "Do you have any idea who those fellas were?"

"That's what I'm hoping you can tell me."

"Me?" Pike said. His thoughts went back to the theory that had crossed his mind earlier, that the attack on Sam Crow had something to do with Solomon Henshaw.

"Sam was able to tell me a few things," Andy said. "According to him, the hombre who shot him came right out and told him it was because he was your friend."

Rage welled up inside Pike and threatened to boil over. What Andy had just said all but confirmed the idea Henshaw was behind this violence.

Belle put a hand on his arm. The touch calmed Pike enough he was able to get his anger under control and asked, "What else did Sam say?"

"He described the man who shot him. Said he wore a black suit and hat and a white shirt. Hawk-faced hombre who carried these."

Andy turned and gestured toward a small table behind him that Pike hadn't been able to see until now. Lying on that table were two revolvers, both of them sporting ivory grips.

"I found them out there at the field, where the fella dropped them," Andy went on. "You know anybody who looks like that and carries guns like these, Pike?"

With his pulse hammering in his head, Pike nodded and said, "Yeah, I do. His name is Ben Grayle. He's a gun for hire. Our trails have crossed a few times." Pike paused. "Always on opposite sides."

"Is there a reason for that?"

Pike shrugged and said, "Just the way things worked out, I guess. Grayle never cared who he worked for, as long as the price was right." He drew in a breath. "Sad to say, too many times I never did, either."

"Well, if I had to guess, I'd say that right now he's workin' for Solomon Henshaw. I don't know of anybody else who has a good reason to send hired killers after your friends."

"My friends," Pike repeated. "That would include you, too, Andy, as well as Will Fisher and the Dawson brothers. All of you helped me take on Doak Ramsey. Henshaw knows about you."

"I'll send deputies out to warn Will and Cloyd and Hebner to be careful for the time being," Andy said. "How many men do you reckon this fella Grayle might have with him? Just those other three?"

Pike shook his head.

"Ben Grayle always liked having the odds as much on his side as he could get them. And he has the same sort of contacts I do. He wouldn't have any trouble finding a dozen men, or more, who'd be willing to work for Henshaw."

"Sounds like we've got our work cut out for us, then." Andy sighed. "At least Sam said that he hurt Grayle before the varmint took off. Maybe he's in bad enough shape that he's out of the fight."

"We can hope so, but if he's not, things are liable to be even worse. I know Ben Grayle. Having somebody fight back against him . . . losing those fancy guns of his he values so highly . . ." Pike's voice was grim as he went on, "When he strikes again, he's really going to be out for blood."

"He was gonna kill Sam and probably wipe out his family, too," Andy pointed out. "I don't see how anybody could be more bloodthirsty than that."

"If there's a way," Pike said, "Ben Grayle will find it."

CHAPTER 28

It was a council of war in Solomon Henshaw's library.

Henshaw paced back and forth on the expensive rug, his head wreathed by coils of smoke from the cigar on which he puffed angrily.

Ben Grayle was in the leather chair in front of the desk. A bandage around his head covered the deep cut, which had required a number of stitches from the doctor in Clarkston when Grayle and his men got back there. Two plain revolvers with walnut grips rested in his holsters instead of the fancy ivory-handled guns.

Carl McConnell stood over by the bar, leaning one elbow on the hardwood as he sipped clear liquid from a glass. No brandy this time; the drink was from a particularly good run at one of Henshaw's stills.

When McConnell arrived at the Henshaw mansion a short time earlier, the black butler had opened the door to his knock and escorted him to the library. He'd seen no sign of Lucille. He wondered whether she was still here. He hadn't taken her to the train station—or had to deal with her in any other way.

For now he would hope that she wasn't around simply because of the seriousness of the situation.

Henshaw stopped his pacing, glared at Grayle, and said, "Four professionals, and all you have to do is kill one half-breed, his squaw, and their brats. Instead you come back with a man who's crippled, and you yourself look like you're on death's door!"

"Head wounds always bleed a lot," Grayle said tersely. "It looked worse than it really was."

"Evidently it was bad enough to keep you from doing the job you set out to do."

McConnell's eyes narrowed as he kept a close watch on Grayle. The gunman didn't cotton to being talked to like that. It hurt his pride. A gunman with hurt pride sometimes felt that the only way to address that problem was with hot lead.

McConnell was ready. If Grayle looked like he was even thinking about reaching for a gun, McConnell intended to draw first and kill him.

At the same time, McConnell thought that Henshaw ought to watch his mouth. Henshaw believed that his money insulated him from any consequences of the angry words he spoke. Most of the time that was going to be true, but a man couldn't count on it *all* the time. Especially when dealing with a gun-wolf like Ben Grayle.

Grayle had a glass of white lightning, too. He sipped from it and then said, "What's important now is what we're going to do next. I'm not going to let some bad luck make me run scared."

"Maybe you'd better take more men with you next time," Henshaw replied with a sneer.

McConnell didn't particularly want to defend Grayle, but he figured he'd better defuse this situation. Keeping his employer from getting ventilated by an angry gunslinger could be considered part of his job.

"Grayle's right, boss," he spoke up. "Crow ought to be dead, but he's not, and that's just bad luck. He'll be laid up for a while in town, where it wouldn't be easy to get at him. So . . . there are other targets we can go after."

Grayle glanced in his direction, gave him a clearly reluctant nod of thanks for stepping in.

Henshaw chewed his cigar some more, then said in a slightly mollified tone, "All right. What's your plan, Grayle?"

"First of all, I'm going to send for more men, as long as you're willing to pay for them. The time may come when we're going to need to make some bigger moves against Shannon."

Henshaw thought about it and nodded.

"There's plenty of money to be made in War-bonnet County, so it's worth some investment," he said. "More than that, it's a matter of making sure these blasted Texans are too scared to stand up to me in the future. They need to know who their betters are."

McConnell, who had been born and raised in

Texas, took a drink of moonshine to wash down the irritation he felt at Henshaw's arrogant statement.

"I'll pay, as long as it doesn't get out of hand," Henshaw went on to Grayle. "What else?"

"I'll go after some of the other names on the list you gave me." Grayle shrugged. "I'll take a few more men with me next time."

"To make sure you're not done in by . . . bad luck."

The white bandage on Grayle's head stood out more as his face flushed with anger. But with a visible effort, he kept a tight rein on his temper and nodded.

"That's right. We'll wait a couple of nights, then make a move."

"Why wait?" Henshaw wanted to know.

"It'll be a new moon," Grayle said. He smiled thinly. "They'll never see us coming."

Cloyd and Hebner Dawson were both tall, a little stoop-shouldered, and prematurely gray-haired. Cloyd was the older by a couple of years. The left side of Hebner's face was covered with puckered, pinkish scars, the ugly aftermath of burns he had suffered in a fire that resulted when Doak Ramsey's men blew up the brothers' still the previous year.

Since then they had given up moonshining and gone back to farming on land that had been in their family since the days when Texas was an independent republic. Cloyd and Hebner had been born on that land.

Now they were a couple of old bachelors, set in their ways, rather dour by nature but staunch allies whenever their friends needed help.

The whitewashed frame farmhouse had replaced the log cabin originally built by the Dawson brothers' father. It was surprisingly homey inside, considering that no female had set foot in it since the death of their mother. Yellow lamplight glowed in the windows.

Outside, the sun had been down for a while and the heat of the day was fading. A breeze drifted through the open windows, stirring the curtains and bringing with it the sudden baying of a hound.

The brothers sat in rocking chairs on opposite sides of a fireplace that was unused at this time of year. The lamp on the mantel cast its light on the books they were reading: Hebner, the Bible; Cloyd, a much thinner, yellow-backed dime novel. The hound's caterwauling made both men look up from the pages.

"Somethin's got ol' Brutus stirred up," Hebner said.

Cloyd set his book aside.

"I'll go see about it."

"I can go—"

"You just go on with readin' the Scriptures," Cloyd said. "That book o' mine's just a bunch of hoohah about some fella chasin' a bunch o' stagecoach bandits." He snorted. "Judgin' by how it's wrote, the hombre who come up with the words don't know one end of a horse from the other. Prob'ly doped up on that there opium whilst he was scribblin'."

While he was talking, Cloyd reached up over the

fireplace and took down one of the Winchesters that hung there on pegs driven into the wall. He worked the lever enough to make sure there was a round in the chamber, then snapped it closed and turned toward the door.

Andy Burnett had ridden by a couple of days earlier to warn them that somebody might be looking to cause trouble for Pike Shannon's friends and allies. Sam Crow had been attacked and wounded by gunmen who had also threatened his daughter.

That was shocking news to the Dawson brothers, but they were too stubborn to change their ways. They weren't the type to hunker down in fear.

"Be careful," Hebner said now. "Not much moon out there tonight. Nights like this was when the Comanches liked to come skulkin' around, back in the old days."

"The Comanch' ain't give any trouble for nigh on to a decade," Cloyd said.

"I didn't say there were any Comanch' out there, just that it's the kind of night they liked to raid. These days, there are other things out there just as dangerous."

Cloyd reached the door.

"More'n likely it's just a blamed skunk that's got that fool hound stirred up—"

He was swinging the door open and stepping out onto the porch as he spoke. The light was behind him, making him a perfect target.

He saw muzzle flashes, but they barely had time to register on his brain before bullets smashed into his chest and drove him backward off his feet.

"Cloyd!" Hebner yelled as he leaped out of his chair. The Bible fell to the floor at his feet. He started to take a step toward his brother as Cloyd lay there on his back, twitching and kicking. Red stains spread across the front of his faded work shirt.

A bullet whined past Hebner's ear, causing him to change course. He grabbed the other rifle off the pegs above the fireplace and flung himself to the floor. The barrage from outside continued, slugs filling the air like angry hornets as they shattered the windows, chewed pieces out of the walls, and set both chairs to rocking from their impacts. By sheer luck, they all missed the lamp on the mantel.

Staying as low as he could, Hebner crawled close enough to reach out and grab Cloyd's shirt collar. He tugged on it and tried to pull his brother out of the open doorway.

Cloyd had stopped moving, though, and was dead-weight now, literally. Hebner sobbed as he saw Cloyd's eyes staring lifelessly at the ceiling.

He gave up and let go. Cloyd was beyond help—but he was also beyond hurting. Hebner scooted backward and then rolled so that he was partially behind an old desk. It would give him a little cover, anyway.

Not enough, though. Clearly, the men outside intended to kill both of the Dawson brothers and would shoot the house to pieces if they had to, in order to accomplish that.

The whining of bullets ricocheting off the stones around the fireplace filled the room, along with the racket of gunshots. Instinctive terror forced Hebner to lie there as flat as possible with his head down.

As seconds that seemed like minutes dragged by, the fear he felt began to recede. He looked across the floor at his dead brother. As far back as he could remember, he and Cloyd had been together. They weren't twins, but the bond between them was very similar to that.

Now Cloyd was gone, not because of anything he or his brother had done to bring disaster down on their heads, but simply because a greedy, power-mad man like Solomon Henshaw had ordered it. Hebner had no doubt of that.

And while there was a small part of him that wanted to blame Pike Shannon for forcing the issue, he knew it wasn't really Pike's fault, either. Somebody had had to stand up to Henshaw. There was no telling the amount of misery a criminal like Henshaw would have brought to Warbonnet County in the long run, if his ambitions were allowed to run unchecked.

With all that fear, grief, and shock roiling around inside him, the anger that suddenly bubbled up was too much for Hebner to withstand. It combined with the other emotions and burst in a white-hot explosion that drove him to his feet without him fully comprehending what he was doing.

The men outside would shoot him so full of holes that he'd look like a sieve, but he would take some of them with him. With a furious roar on his lips, he leaped over his brother's body and charged out

the door, levering and firing the Winchester as fast
as he could.

Pike rode slowly through the night with Lem
Cranepool beside him. The two men had stopped
by Will Fisher's place earlier in the evening to make
sure Will and his family were all right, and now they
were headed for the Dawson brothers' farm to check
on Cloyd and Hebner.

These evening patrols had been going on for several days now, ever since the attack on Sam Crow, who
continued to mend under the care of Dr. Faulkner
and Sophie Truesdale. Sam had been gunned down
in broad daylight, but Pike had a hunch Ben Grayle
wouldn't do that again. After being stopped once and
injured when his intended victim fought back, Grayle
would be more stealthy next time.

That was Pike's thinking, anyway, and Andy Burnett agreed with him. Andy didn't have enough
deputies to blanket the entire county, but it seemed
prudent to keep an eye on the most likely targets for
Grayle and Henshaw's wrath.

Since Pike knew his own actions had played a part
in bringing on this trouble, he felt it was only right
that he pitch in and try to keep anyone else from
getting hurt. He still refused to allow Andy to deputize him, but he was willing to make the rounds with
Cranepool on an unofficial basis. Andy and some
of the other deputies were spread out in different
locations, checking on men who had sided with

Pike in the war against the Ramsey clan, since they were known to be Pike's friends.

So far there had been no more trouble in the county—but Pike knew better than to believe that would last.

The sudden blast of gunfire somewhere not too far away shattered the warm, peaceful evening and made Pike stiffen in the saddle. Shot after shot roared, all but confirming his worst expectations.

"Come on!" he called to Cranepool as he dug his boot heels into his horse's flanks. "That's coming from the Dawson brothers' farm!"

Leaning forward in their saddles, the two men charged along the hard-packed dirt road that ran between fields of corn, sorghum, beans, and cotton. They could still hear gunshots over the drumming of their horses' hooves.

After a few minutes they came in sight of the farmhouse, as well as the nearby barn, chicken coop, hog pen, and corrals. Orange flashes of muzzle flame were visible from various places of conceal-ment as half a dozen riflemen poured lead into the house.

The front door was open, allowing lamplight to spill out. Pike thought he spotted someone lying on the floor just inside the door. His jaw tightened with anger.

Both men reined in and pulled Winchesters from saddle sheaths. As Pike worked the lever of his re-peater, Lem Cranepool said, "As a lawman, I really ought to give those varmints a chance to surrender."

"I'm not toting a badge," Pike snapped. "And it

looks to me like one of the Dawson brothers is down, just inside the door. They must have killed him when he started to step out onto the porch."

"Yeah, I think you're right," Cranepool agreed with a grim note in his voice. "You're sayin' we don't owe those skunks any consideration?"

"We don't owe them anything except a chunk of hot lead."

With that, Pike brought the Winchester to his shoulder. Only a thin sliver of moon hung in the sky, so it didn't cast much light, but the tongues of flame from the attackers' weapons were enough to pinpoint them.

Pike drew a bead on a man who crouched behind a parked wagon as he shot at the house. He squeezed the trigger.

The man arched his back as Pike's slug smashed into him between the shoulder blades. The bullet drove him forward against the wagon's sideboards. He bounced off the vehicle and toppled backward.

Pike was already swinging his rifle to the left, searching for another target, before the man he had just shot even hit the ground.

To his right, Cranepool opened fire as well, his rifle cracking swiftly and steadily. Pike downed another of the attackers, who, judging by their lack of reaction, hadn't yet realized that they were under assault from behind.

Then a tall figure appeared in the doorway, fire spitting from the rifle in his hands as he charged out of the house. That was the other Dawson brother, Pike thought, taking the fight to the attackers because he was convinced he was going to die but wanting to take some of the varmints with him.

Cloyd or Hebner, whichever one it was, had taken only a couple of steps before he stumbled, pitched forward, and tumbled down the porch steps to the ground. Pike didn't know how badly the man was hit, but he knew the remaining attackers would shoot him to doll rags while he lay there unless they were distracted.

Pike kneed his horse forward and whooped loudly as he continued shooting. The saddle of a running horse was no place for accuracy, but Pike managed to drill another of the ambushers as the man stepped around a corner of the chicken coop to see what was going on.

Cranepool sprayed lead around the farmyard, too. Pike saw another attacker go down.

In the chaos of battle, on such a dark night ripped apart by muzzle flashes, with the stink of burned powder filling the air, it was almost impossible to know for sure what was going on. The raiders wouldn't be able to tell how many men were counterattacking them. But they were bound to realize by now that some of them were down and likely would never get up again.

That was enough to make them cut their losses and run. Between gun blasts, Pike heard a man shout, "Let's get outta here!" Figures darted through the shadows. Seconds later, Pike heard the swift rat-aplan of hoofbeats as the killers threw themselves into saddles and lit a shuck.

He threw a few more shots in their direction as he was torn between chasing after them and checking on the Dawson brothers. His worry about Cloyd and Hebner won out. With Cranepool beside him, he rode quickly to the house and swung down from the saddle.

"Keep an eye out, Lem," he said. "Some of those buzzards might double back."

"I'll be ready for 'em if they do," Cranepool promised grimly.

Pike ran to the man who had fallen at the foot of the porch steps. In the light that came through the open door, he saw that the man was moving around, evidently trying to struggle to his feet, but he wasn't having much luck.

Pike dropped to a knee beside him and put a hand on his shoulder.

"Take it easy, Hebner," he said. The scars on the older man's face made it easy to tell which brother he was. "From the looks of the blood on your overalls, it looks like you've been shot in the leg."

In general, the Dawson brothers were quiet-spoken men, not given to ranting and raving. But a blue streak of profanity poured out of Hebner's mouth now. Pike couldn't blame him for that.

When Hebner paused to take a breath, Pike asked, "Do you know how bad Cloyd's hit?"

"He's dead," Hebner said in a hollow voice. "Dead as he can be."

Pike took a sharply indrawn breath, then said, "Are you sure?"

"Plumb certain. The lowdown skunks shot him at least three times in the chest. I got a good look at his eyes. He's gone, Pike. Gone."

Pike's hand tightened on Hebner's shoulder.

"I'm sorry," he said. "But we need to get you in the house and have a look at those wounds of yours."

"Who's with you?"

"Lem Cranepool, one of Andy's deputies."

"I know Lem. Good man." Hebner paused. "Did you do for any of the scum?"

"We sent two or three of them straight to hell, at least."

Hebner sighed, closed his eyes, and said, "Good."

CHAPTER 29

It was easy enough to see what had happened. Even though he'd been shot, luck had been with Hebner. He'd been hit low by a bullet that passed cleanly through his right thigh and another that grazed the outside of the same leg. That had been enough to knock him off his feet and send him tumbling down the porch steps—and that fall meant the rest of the lead scything through the air had gone over him and hit the house instead.

It was hard to call anything that had happened good fortune, though, when Cloyd Dawson was dead. As Hebner had said, he'd been shot numerous times in the chest and must have died within seconds of being hit, if not instantly.

While Pike was roughly bandaging Hebner's wounds after carrying him inside and placing him on the bed in one of the other rooms, Lem Cranepool took a lantern and checked on the men they had shot. He came back to report, "They're all done for, Pike. Three bodies." A note of disgust came into his voice. "Their pards just rode off and left 'em. Never looked back."

"Gun-wolves like that don't have pards," Pike said. "Just fellas fighting temporarily on the same side."

He didn't mention that, for all too long, he had fit that description himself.

"How's Hebner?"

"He'll be all right, I think. We'll need to load him in the wagon and take him into town so the doctor can do a better job of patching him up." Pike glanced at Cloyd's body, which they had moved away from the door and covered with a blanket. "We'll send Cyrus Malone out here to take care of Cloyd." He paused, then asked, "Those dead men outside, one of them didn't happen to be a hawk-faced fella dressed in a black suit and hat, did he?"

"Nope. Is that Ben Grayle you just described?"

"Yeah. I figured he got away, if he was actually here. Grayle's got a habit of doing that. He always slithers away, like a snake in a pile of rocks."

"One of these times, you'll come up against him head-on, and that'll be the end o' Mr. Ben Grayle."

Pike didn't say anything. He honestly believed he was faster on the draw than Grayle, but with something like that, you could never be sure until the time came . . .

Andy Burnett sighed and said, "This thing is getting too big for us, Pike. I think I'm gonna have to ask for help from the Texas Rangers."

"You think the governor will send in a company of Rangers?"

"He might. We've had unprovoked attacks on two families in our county. Two men are wounded, and one's dead. I'm not trying to shirk my responsibility as sheriff, but this is starting to sound like a job for the Rangers, all right."

They were in Andy's office in the courthouse, the morning after the attack on the Dawson brothers' farm that left Cloyd dead. The body was down at Cyrus Malone's undertaking parlor now, and the funeral would be that afternoon.

The three gun-wolves who had been killed in the fighting were laid out at Malone's place, too. Earlier that morning, Pike and Andy had gone down there to study their faces, then returned to the sheriff's office to go through the stacks of wanted posters in Andy's desk.

Pike had thought he might recognize them from past acquaintance, since they'd been in the same line of work as him, but he didn't know any of them. That wasn't a real surprise. Neither was the fact that they didn't find any wanted posters matching the dead men.

"All that means is that they've never been charged with anything serious enough to get their faces on reward dodgers," Pike had commented.

Now he told Andy, "You do whatever you think is best, but after everything that's happened, I'm not waiting for somebody else to get around to cleaning this up. It's time to take the fight to Henshaw."

"I thought that's what you'd been doing by inter-fering with him making and selling moonshine down here. Seems like that's already pushed him pretty far. Far enough to bring in a killer like Ben Grayle."

Pike shook his head and said, "We've been fighting him in Warbonnet County. It's time to take the battle to his home ground."

"You're going to attack him in Chaparral County?" Andy asked in surprise.

Dryly, Pike responded, "It might be better not to tell you exactly what I plan to do, Andy. After all, that's still a sheriff's badge pinned to your shirt. You're sworn to uphold the law."

"Are you saying you intend to break it?" Andy asked with a frown.

"I'm saying Solomon Henshaw's going to be sorry he hurt my friends."

Like Warbonnet County to the south, Chaparral County was dry because of a local option election. Pike knew that Henshaw operated pretty openly all over the county, though. Most, if not all, of the local authorities were probably on his payroll.

Despite that, no businesses sported signs announcing that liquor was available there. There were no saloons or taverns, as such. But if folks wanted to know where they could get a drink, it probably wasn't hard to find out.

One such place, Pike suspected, was the café in Bolivar where Norvell Grant and Ruel Blake had delivered the money they'd collected to Carl McConnell, Henshaw's chief lieutenant. Pike tied his horse to a hitch rail in front of the building next door to the eatery that night.

MUNSEY'S CAFÉ read the sign on the building. Pike stepped up onto the boardwalk and glanced through the front window. The café had a dozen tables and men sat at all of them. Some were eating, but others were playing cards and drinking from cups that Pike suspected didn't have coffee in them.

Others sat on stools at a counter on the right of the room. A door at the far end of that counter undoubtedly led into the room where McConnell had met with the two henchmen.

Pike studied the men inside the café but didn't recognize any of them. Maybe they wouldn't recognize him, either. He tugged his hat brim down and went in.

The aproned man behind the counter was tall, skinny, and bald as an egg except for a sweeping longhorn mustache. He nodded as Pike took a seat on one of the stools.

"What'll it be, friend? Got a pot of son-of-a-gun stew in the kitchen."

"That'll do fine," Pike said. "Especially if you've got something good to wash it down with."

"Arbuckle's?"

"I was thinking of something a mite stronger."

The man got a canny look on his face and said, "That'll run you a little more."

"Fine by me, as long as it's not too unreasonable."

"Oh, we always try to be reasonable here in Bolivar. You just sit there and I'll be right back."

The man went through a swinging door into the kitchen. Appetizing aromas drifted out while the door was open. Pike looked through the momentary gap and saw not only a stove but a stack of crates in a far corner, as well as a rear door.

He'd be willing to bet those crates contained jugs of white lightning from Solomon Henshaw's stills.

A man stood up from one of the stools farther along the counter and drifted over to where Pike sat. He brought his "coffee" cup with him, carrying it in his left hand.

Without taking a seat on the empty stool next to him, the man set the cup on the counter, leaned an elbow beside it, and drawled, "I don't recollect seein' you in here before, mister."

"Reckon that's because I never set foot in this place until tonight."

"New to Bolivar, are you?"

"That's right."

The man was stocky, with curly brown hair peeking out from under his pushed-back hat. The holstered Colt on his right hip was set at an angle so the butt leaned forward. A man who packed his iron like that was putting on a show. He wanted folks to think he was a bad hombre.

But that didn't mean he wasn't actually fast on the draw.

"Name's Ned Stockdale," the man went on.

Pike nodded and said, "Pleased to meet you," but didn't offer his own name.

Stockdale noticed that. His eyes narrowed a little, but before he could say anything, the counterman came back from the kitchen and set a bowl of stew in front of Pike, along with a cup. Pike could smell the moonshine in it.

Stockdale picked up his own cup and swirled the

contents a little before drinking from it. That cup didn't have coffee in it, either.

Pike nodded to the counterman and said, "Obliged. How much do I owe you?"

"Two dollars."

Pike cocked an eyebrow and said, "Must be mighty good stew."

"The best you'll find in Chaparral County."

Pike slid a couple of silver dollars across the counter. The man made them disappear.

"What brings you to these parts?" Stockdale asked.

"Just passing through," Pike said.

"Is that so? You look like the sort of fella who might be in the market for a job."

Pike took his time about answering. He ate a couple of bites of the stew—which actually was very good, as well as quite hot—and then sipped from the cup. The 'shine was smooth and potent. Henshaw's stills produced a decent run of white lightning.

"I said—"

"I heard what you said. I'm not some cowpuncher riding the grub line."

Stockdale grunted and said, "That's not the sort of job I was talking about."

Pike had been looking around the room as unobtrusively as he could ever since he'd come in here. Of the eighteen men in here, only Stockdale and three others struck him as possible members of Ben Grayle's gun crew. Most of the others looked tough enough, but they were Chaparral County tough, not the sort who had sold their guns in dozens of bloody wars from one end of the frontier to the other and managed to live through those clashes.

"Who's hiring?" Pike asked, still sounding casual about it.

"You know Ben Grayle?"

"Know of him."

"Well, he's looking for good men to help teach some hillbillies down in the next county to respect their betters. He's up against a troublemaker called Pike Shannon."

"Is that so?"

"You want to know how much the job pays?" Stockdale asked.

Slowly, Pike shook his head. He said, "No, that's not necessary."

"Why not?"

Pike said, "Because I wouldn't work for a lowdown skunk like Ben Grayle no matter how much money he offered me."

Stockdale's already beefy face flushed even darker. He said, "Who in blazes do you think you are?"

"My name's Pike Shannon," Pike said, and although he hated to waste good stew, he scooped up the bowl from the counter and rammed it into Stockdale's face as hard as he could.

CHAPTER 30

The stew was still pretty hot. Stockdale bellowed in pain, surprise, and anger as he staggered back a step and clawed at the gun on his hip while he pawed at his face with his other hand.

Pike came up off the stool and used the momentum of that movement to put plenty of power behind the punch he threw. His fist crashed into Stockdale's beard-stubbled jaw. The impact drove the gunman backward off his feet.

The three men Pike had pegged as being likely members of Grayle's bunch leaped to their feet and grabbed for their guns. As he pivoted away from the fallen Stockdale, his Colt seemed to appear in his hand almost as if by magic.

Flame spouted from its muzzle. One of the gunwolves doubled over as the slug struck him in the belly and drove deep into his guts. He had just cleared leather. The gun fell unfired from nerveless fingers.

Pike's gun roared again. A second man spun off his feet, hit in the chest.

The third man actually got a shot off. The bullet sizzled past Pike's ear. He triggered again and the third man's head jerked back as the slug left a red-rimmed hole in his forehead and bored into his brain.

Stockdale had recovered enough to try to get to his feet, although he was still sputtering from the stew that had gone up his nose and down his throat and choked him.

Pike lashed out with his right leg. The heel of his boot caught Stockdale on the jaw and drove his head back so far that a sharp crack sounded. The kick had broken his neck. He fell back to the floor, limp as a dishrag.

All that had happened so quickly, in just a handful of heartbeats, that the other men in the room hadn't been able to react until now. But some of them no doubt worked for Solomon Henshaw and weren't going to let some stranger just waltz in here and kill four of the gunmen also on Henshaw's payroll. Shouting angry curses, they lurched up from their chairs and started their draws.

Pike probably could have killed another one or two of them without much trouble before they brought him down. Instead he leaped onto the counter and rolled over it. The counterman had already dived to the floor back there to get out of the line of fire. Pike almost stepped on him.

He shouldered through the door into the kitchen and let it swing closed behind him. As it did, shots blasted and bullets smacked into the swinging panel.

Pike darted to the corner where the crates were

stacked up and shoved hard against them, toppling three onto the floor. They fell with a splintering crash, and he heard glass shatter inside them. Liquid began to seep out from the wreckage. The sharp tang of moonshine filled the air.

The men in the café's main room continued shooting. They could have rushed the door into the kitchen, but they were probably worried that Pike would be waiting on the other side to shoot them in the face. Some of the bullets punched through the door, but none of them came too close to Pike as he went to the back door and used his left hand to fish a lucifer out of his shirt pocket. He snapped the match into life with his thumbnail and tossed it onto the spreading pool around the broken crates.

The white lightning caught fire and flared up with a loud *whoosh!*

A key was in the lock of the back door. Pike twisted it and turned the knob. With the Colt still in his right hand, he slammed two shots through the swinging door, then bolted out the back. He heard men yelling in alarm in the café's main room and knew they must have smelled smoke, maybe even heard the crackling flames as they started to spread.

Pike darted through the shadowy alleyway, then ran along the narrow passage between the café and the building next door. He figured the gunmen would be too busy trying to put out the fire to pursue him.

However, a couple of them had been smart enough to anticipate his actions. As he reached the street, the pair burst out through the café's front door. One of them shouted, "There he is!" Shots hammered from their guns, accompanied by jets of orange flame.

Pike whirled and crouched. He had only one round left in his gun, and he didn't figure those two hombres would stop and give him time to reload. He aimed at the one who was slightly in front and pulled the trigger.

That man grunted, stumbled, and fell, sprawling in the boardwalk so that his companion almost stumbled over him. That was enough to throw off the second man's aim. His next shot whined high over Pike's head.

Before the man could pull his gun back down level, Pike had charged him and closed the gap between them. The barrel of Pike's empty gun cracked down on the man's wrist and caused him to cry out in pain as he dropped his weapon. Pike swung his gun in a backhanded blow that landed with stunning force on the man's jaw.

Then Pike lowered his shoulder and bulled into the man, forcing him back through the café's front window. The glass shattered and sprayed inward as the man fell through it.

Smoke was billowing out of the kitchen now from the fire Pike had started. He saw a number of men standing around looking upset and perplexed. The rest had to be in there trying to put out the flames.

The ones in the main room swung around in surprise at the sound of the breaking window. A man spotted Pike on the boardwalk and yelled, "It's him! It's Shannon!"

A second later, a thunderous volley of gunshots

rolled out from their guns, aimed through the broken window at the spot where Pike had been a split second earlier.

He was already springing toward his horse, though, and he yanked the reins loose and leaped into the saddle while the men inside the café were still shooting madly through the window. He turned the horse away from the hitch rail and kicked it into a run.

Men began to boil out of the café as Pike galloped along the street. They fired after him, sending round after round into the night. None of the bullets found Pike or his mount. The horse continued running with a strong, steady stride.

The shooting died away. Pike looked back and saw faintly in the light from inside the café that several men were mounting up to come after them. He wasn't worried about them catching him. He had picked the horse underneath him for its speed and stamina.

Within minutes, he had left Bolivar behind and was riding steadily southward toward Warbonnet County. He looked back over his shoulder from time to time and was glad that he didn't see an orange glow in the sky.

He felt a little bad about starting a fire to cover his getaway. Fire was the most dreaded disaster in every frontier settlement. The wind was still tonight, however, and there was an open lot on one side of the café, the alley on the other. With no other buildings attached to it, and with that many men in the place to fight the flames, Pike had been confident they could keep the blaze from spreading.

That load of moonshine was destroyed, though, and since it was likely that Solomon Henshaw actually owned the café, Pike wasn't going to feel too bad about however much damage was done to the place.

This was just one more thrust in the ongoing war, though, and Pike knew it. Henshaw would be furious when he found out. It would make him more determined than ever to hurt Pike, to destroy him if possible.

He rode on through the night, figuring his next move—and he had a hunch that Solomon Henshaw was probably doing the same thing already.

Ben Grayle wasn't around when Carl McConnell reported the latest news to Henshaw.

Lucille was, and in fact, she was the one who answered his knock and let him into the house. Even though it was none of his business, McConnell was glad to see her since she hadn't been there during his past few visits. He knew better than to get attached to any of Henshaw's girls, but her absence had puzzled him.

Her face was a little drawn and her eyes seemed sunken deeper than usual. He wondered fleetingly if she'd been sick. Then he dismissed her from his thoughts because Henshaw's reaction to Pike Shannon's latest escapade occupied his attention instead.

Henshaw wore a silk dressing gown and his normally sleek hair was mussed from sleep. Clearly he and Lucille had turned in early. She had on a filmy gown that hinted at the curves underneath it. McConnell had to work not to make too close a study of her shapely form.

"This in intolerable," Henshaw declared as he paced back and forth in front of his desk. He didn't have a drink or a cigar this time. He was too upset for either. "We can't just keep going back and forth with Shannon, upping the stakes each time."

"I agree with that," McConnell said. "Seems to me like the best way to stop things in their tracks is to just go ahead and kill him." He raised a hand to forestall a protest as Henshaw stopped pacing and turned to glare at him. "I know, boss. We've tried that. *I* tried that. I admit that I failed. But we've got more men at our disposal now. If we send enough guns after Shannon, he can't stop them all."

"You're talking about Grayle and his men."

"I don't like the man, even if he did manage to kill one of Shannon's friends last night," McConnell said bluntly. "He also managed to get three of his own men killed, and four more went down tonight. But they're here and you're paying them, so you might as well get some use out of them."

Henshaw rubbed his jaw as he frowned in thought. After a moment he said, "You're right, Carl. It's time we stopped pulling our punches."

McConnell wouldn't have called wounding Sam Crow and killing one of the Dawson brothers pulling their punches, but he knew what Henshaw meant.

"Get Grayle out here to the house," Henshaw went on. "I want him to send for more men. When we make our next move, it's going to be with an army. I'm talking about forty or fifty guns, at least."

McConnell frowned and said, "That's a lot of firepower, boss. What do you plan on doing, attacking the whole town?"

McConnell wasn't completely serious in asking the question, but Henshaw looked straight at him and said, "That's exactly what I'm going to do."

CHAPTER 31

Pike wasn't sure how Henshaw would react to his foray into Bolivar, but he wasn't expecting what happened during the next week.

Nothing.

He and Lem Cranepool, along with some of Andy's other deputies, continued their nightly patrols, but as early summer settled over Warbonnet County, peace reigned. Sam Crow was up and around, getting better by the day. Cloyd Dawson had been laid to rest in the cemetery behind the First Baptist Church. His brother Hebner was still recuperating at Dr. Faulkner's home. None of Pike's other friends had been attacked.

"Do you think Henshaw's given up?" Andy Burnett asked late one afternoon when Pike dropped by the sheriff's office while he was in town with Mary, Nessa, and Fiddler, picking up supplies. Pike had left his mother and sister and the little man down at the general store while the things they bought were loaded in the wagon.

They were planning to stay and eat supper in the

hotel dining room before heading back to the ranch. They wouldn't get home until well after dark. Pike hadn't been sure that was a very good idea, but since it had been a while since Mary and Nessa had been to town, he hadn't had the heart to say no when Mary suggested the trip.

Pike responded to Andy Burnett's question by shaking his head and saying, "I'll believe that when I see it."

"Yeah, but we're *not* seeing anything," Andy said. "That's kinda the point. It's been more than a week since Cloyd was killed, and I heard rumors about some sort of ruckus up in Bolivar the night after that. No trouble since then. If Henshaw hasn't called it quits on this war . . . then what's he up to?"

"I wish I could answer that," Pike said. "When he does make his next move, it'll be bad."

He left the courthouse and went along to the café to say hello to Sophie. The place was busy with the beginning of the evening rush, but she greeted him with a smile. She also looked a little wary.

"Are you bringing trouble with you this evening, Pike?"

"Not a bit of it!" he replied. "Ma and Nessa just came into town to pick up a few supplies, and Fiddler and I came along with them. It looks like things have settled down again, and that's just fine with me."

That was stretching the truth, of course. He had been blunt with Andy about the continuing danger from Ben Grayle and the rest of Henshaw's hired killers, but he didn't see any reason to worry Sophie.

"I hope so," she said as she poured him a cup of coffee without asking. "I have some pie for you, too."

He grinned and said, "It's like you read my mind."

She laughed softly and told him, "It's not as if you're all that mysterious, Pike Shannon. You never come in here without wanting coffee and pie."

"My ma's liable to fuss at me for ruining my supper, you know."

"Well, I won't mention it to her if you don't."

"We've got a deal," Pike said.

When Pike left the café a few minutes later, after enjoying a slice of apple pie and a cup of excellent coffee, he saw a man he didn't recognize loitering on the boardwalk in front of the saddle shop a few doors away.

That didn't mean anything, of course. Warbonnet was a big enough town that folks Pike didn't know passed through here all the time. And there was nothing special about this hombre. He was probably just a cowboy looking for a job.

Pike forgot all about the fella when he ran into Belle Ramsey less than a block away. The sight of her in a dark green dress with her auburn hair loose around her shoulders was enough to keep him from thinking about anything else.

"Been paying a visit to Miss Truesdale?" Belle asked.

"How'd you know?"

"That pleased-with-yourself look on your face is kind of a dead giveaway."

"I just stopped by to say hello," he admitted.

"And get some pie and coffee, I expect."

Pike shrugged. He wasn't going to apologize to Belle for enjoying Sophie's food—or her company.

A rider went by in the street. Pike glanced at him, recognized him as the man he'd seen loitering on the boardwalk a few minutes earlier. There was still nothing unusual about the nondescript hombre, no reason for Pike to notice him at all . . .

But despite that, the skin on the back of Pike's neck prickled faintly, as if some instinct was trying to warn him of some danger. He couldn't have said what prompted that reaction, but he was too experienced to ignore it.

He looked back at the café for a second, then took Belle's arm.

"Why don't you walk down to the store with me?" he suggested. It was crazy to think that something might happen in the middle of town like this, even with night coming on, but Pike trusted his gut. He wanted to get Belle off the street. Once she was at the store, Fiddler could look after her while he went to check on Sophie. He knew he had just left her, but he wanted to be sure she was all right.

"A walk to the store doesn't sound very exciting," Belle said. Despite that, she fell in step beside him. "I was thinking maybe the two of us could rent a buckboard sometime and drive out into the country for a picnic. I know some places along the river that would be good for that."

"So do I," Pike agreed. The thought of sitting on a blanket with Belle, on a nice grassy riverbank, was mighty appealing to him. "That sounds mighty nice, Belle. As soon as we're sure that things have settled down—"

"When you and Solomon Henshaw have settled your differences, you mean?" Belle's voice took on an edge. "I don't figure that will happen until one of you is dead."

"Let's don't talk about that this evening."

Belle looked like she wanted to argue, but then she nodded and said, "All right. We'll just look forward to better days."

"Sure."

When they reached the store, Fiddler was his usual charming self as he greeted Belle by saying, "Why, hello, Miss Ramsey! You look beautiful, as always."

"Thank you, Fiddler."

Mary and Nessa hugged Belle, and Mary said, "Fiddler's right. Land's sake, you get prettier every time I see you, Belle."

"I agree," Nessa said. She smiled mischievously at her brother. "Don't you think that's true, Pike? Doesn't Belle get prettier all the time?"

"I've always thought Belle looked just fine," Pike said, not letting his sister's teasing put a burr under his saddle. "At least, ever since she grew out of being a freckle-faced, spindle-legged colt."

"Freckle-faced?" Belle repeated. "Why, Pike Shannon, I'll have you know—"

Pike was enjoying this banter, but he couldn't shake the uneasy feeling he'd had earlier. He interrupted and said to Belle, "Why don't you stay here and visit with Ma and Nessa and Fiddler for a few minutes? I'll be right back."

Belle looked at him with narrowed eyes.

"Where are you running off to, Pike?" she asked. "You forget something at the café, maybe?"

Pike didn't answer that question directly. He just said again, "I'll be back," and left the store.

As he walked down the street, he wondered what

exactly he was going to say to Sophie. What he wanted was for her to close up the café and come back with him to the general store, so he could have both her and Belle in one place where he could look out for them.

At this time of day, though, Sophie would have to chase out customers and lose business if she closed. She was liable to argue about that, and he couldn't blame her for doing so.

But if he told her he just had a hunch that something bad might happen, she'd probably scoff at him. Sophie was too practical and hardheaded to believe in hunches.

Pike still felt that cold prickle on the back of his neck, though. Without him even thinking about what he was doing, his right hand strayed to the gun on his hip, and his fingertips brushed the Colt's walnut grips.

Carl McConnell leaned forward in his saddle in anticipation as he heard the horse approaching.

Beside him in the gathering darkness under the trees, Ben Grayle said, "That'll be Seeger."

"Might not be," McConnell cautioned.

Grayle's snort was an eloquent expression of the contempt he felt.

"I don't know who else it'd be out here, at this time of the evening," Grayle said.

The two men sat just inside the shadows of a line of post oaks growing at the base of a flat-topped hill a couple of miles north of Warbonnet. Farther west, a hill like this would be called a mesa, but here it was just a hill, the same sort of geological feature as Warbonnet Peak, only on a much smaller scale.

What was important was that with the trees and the hill to protect them from view, nobody was likely to notice the forty-four mounted men who waited there, out of sight of the road that ran between War-bonnet and Bolivar. The most recent arrivals among them had drifted into Clarkston over the past couple of days, in answer to telegrams Grayle had sent summoning more men willing to sell their gun skills.

Grayle went on, "It'll be good and dark in another half-hour. Most folks are home by now, eating supper or at least getting ready to."

"Maybe," McConnell grunted.

He still wasn't sure this planned attack on War-bonnet was a good move on Henshaw's part. He understood his boss's frustration, and when you came right down to it, Henshaw *was* the boss, so McConnell would follow his orders. When he took a man's money, he rode for the brand.

But raiding the town, killing a bunch of innocent folks, burning down some of the buildings . . . that was going to attract a lot of attention across the state. Sure, Henshaw wanted to terrorize the inhabitants of Warbonnet County so they'd never dare stand up to him again, but such an atrocity was liable to bring in more lawdogs than anybody could deal with, even Ben Grayle and the large pack of gun-wolves he had assembled.

McConnell had tried to hint around about his concerns, but Henshaw was too angry to listen. He just wanted his revenge on the county to the south and all its inhabitants—especially Pike Shannon.

And not only was Shannon in Warbonnet this evening, so were his mother and sister and his friend Fiddler. Orrie Seeger, Grayle's scout, had been keeping an eye on Shannon and had followed the group from the ranch to the settlement, then reported back to Grayle. Then Grayle had sent Seeger, who had the sort of face you forgot five seconds after looking at him, into Warbonnet to take a look around.

Grayle probably was right about the approaching horseman being Seeger. A moment later the rider drew rein on the trail and whistled like a bobwhite. That was the agreed-upon signal to announce his identity.

Grayle edged his horse out from the shadows. McConnell was only slightly behind him. Seeger rode over to join them.

"Nobody in town acts like they're expectin' a thing, Ben," Seeger reported. "Folks are just goin' about their business and settlin' down for the evening."

"Shannon's still there?" Grayle asked sharply. His hatred for Pike Shannon was plain to hear in his voice. He had recovered from the clout on the head Sam Crow had given him, but his pride was still wounded, and he blamed Shannon for that, as well as the men he'd lost in the raid on the Dawson brothers' farm and the shoot-out at Munsey's eatery and 'shine joint in Bolivar.

"Sure. He went to the café and flirted with the blond gal who runs it, then met up with some red-headed girl who was just as pretty except for a scar on her face."

McConnell said, "The girl with the scar is Belle Ramsey. It was her family that Shannon fought a war with a while back, but he gets along just fine with Belle. Better than fine, from what I hear."

Grayle smiled thinly in the fading light and said, "Is that so? Well, if we get a chance, we'll teach Miss Ramsey that it's not a good idea to get friendly with Pike Shannon." To Seeger, he went on, "Where's the rest of his bunch?"

"The ones he came in with are at the general store. From what I saw, Shannon and the redheaded girl were headed in that direction when I rode out."

Grayle nodded curtly and said, "We can't afford to waste any time, then. We don't want Shannon and his family leaving town before we strike."

"You mean to attack now?" McConnell asked.

"That's right."

"It'll be good and dark in another half-hour—"

"We don't have a half-hour," Grayle broke in. "I'm not going to take a chance on Shannon getting away from me again. He dies tonight." He turned his head to look at McConnell. "Go tell the men we're ready to move."

McConnell had to tighten his jaw and force himself not to tell Grayle to give them the order himself. He was no man's lackey, and certainly not Ben Grayle's.

But in the interest of keeping the peace—for now—McConnell nodded and turned his horse. He called softly to the shadowy mounted figures, "All right, fellas, it's time. Follow me."

The line of gunmen surged forward, riding through the gaps between the post oaks and emerging into the last vestiges of dusk like gray phantoms. Grayle and McConnell took the lead as they turned toward Warbonnet. Orrie Steeger dropped back to join the others. The nondescript little man might not look like much, but according to Grayle, he was an efficient, ruthless killer.

They all were, McConnell thought. The citizens of Warbonnet were going about their business peacefully this evening . . .

With no idea that hell was riding toward them.

Chapter 32

"Back already?" Sophie asked with a slight frown as Pike came into the café.

He looked around. She had eight customers at the moment, and none of them looked like they were almost finished with their meals. If he asked her to tell them all to leave, she would call him loco.

Maybe he could approach it from another angle. He said, "My ma and Nessa would like to see you. They haven't gotten to say hello and visit with you for quite a while."

"Well, tell them to come on down here, then. I'd like to see them, too." Sophie paused. "Although to tell you the truth, Pike, I never have been that close to the rest of your family."

"Maybe it's time we remedy that. They're still at Strickland's store. You could step down there for a minute—"

"Have you not noticed?" Sophie asked with a crisp note of annoyance in her voice now. "I have customers."

"I know, I just thought—"

"Ask them to come down here," Sophie interrupted him. With a smile, she added, "In fact, why don't all of you have supper here? It'll be on the house."

That would be a way to get all of them in the same place so he could keep an eye on them, Pike decided. They didn't have to eat dinner at the hotel, after all. Fetching Mary, Nessa, Fiddler, and Belle would take more time, but it might be the best solution.

"All right," he said, nodding. "I reckon we can—"

He didn't get to finish, because at that moment gunshots blasted somewhere in Warbonnet.

Silverware rang against plates as several of the diners dropped knives and forks in surprise. Sophie gasped. Pike swung toward the door and barked, "Everybody hunt cover and stay there!"

Sophie called, "Pike, wait!" but he didn't slow down. He pulled his gun as he shouldered through the door. Down the street, men on horseback thundered toward him, firing at the buildings on both sides as their mounts surged forward underneath them.

Pike dived behind a nearby water trough as the bullet wave washed toward him. Several slugs thudded into the sturdy trough, and more lead whined through the air just above it. Hoofbeats pounded past. The raiders never slowed down.

Pike pushed himself up far enough to look over the top of the water trough. A stray slug plunked into the water, splashing him. He snapped a shot back at the straggler who had just fired at him and saw the man sway in the saddle. Pike couldn't be sure he'd hit the raider, but he thought he probably had. The man didn't fall but galloped on after the others.

They rode all the way to the end of the street, shouting and shooting as they charged through Warbonnet. The hail of bullets shattered dozens of windows. The riders slowed as they came to the outskirts of town. Pike saw that and knew they were about to regroup, turn around, and roar back through Warbonnet.

It would take them a moment to start that second assault, though, and Pike intended to put that time to good use. He was closer to the café than the general store, so he leaped to his feet and ran back there.

Sophie was peeking anxiously over the counter when he came in. She said, "Pike! Are you all right?"

"Fine," he said. "Anybody hurt in here?"

He looked around the room. The people who had been peacefully eating their supper earlier were now sprawled on the floor, some of them with shards of glass scattered around them from the bullet-busted windows. A couple of men had turned one of the tables on its side and were hunkered behind it.

"They're shooting up the buildings along the street," Pike said. "Go out the back door and stick to the alleys, and you might be all right. Head back to your homes."

One of the men behind the table lifted his head and asked, "Don't we need to fight back?"

"If you have guns and you want to, nobody's going to stop you," Pike told him. "But those are professional killers out there."

He had no doubt in his mind that the raiders

were led by Ben Grayle, and Solomon Henshaw had sent them to wreak havoc in Warbonnet.

This was the next step in the series of hostilities *he* had initiated, Pike thought.

He indulged in that pang of guilt for about half a second before he thrust it away. It was Henshaw, McConnell, Grayle, and the rest of their bunch that had targeted innocent folks. Pike had confined his opponents to men who were paid to fight, men who had chosen to take up the gun and risk their lives. The wanton destruction going on in Warbonnet this evening was *not* his fault, in any way, shape, or form.

Hoofbeats welled up again outside. Pike yelled, "Keep your heads down!" and vaulted over the counter. He grabbed Sophie and pulled her to the floor with him as another barrage of gunfire slammed into the front of the café.

The gun-thunder seemed to go on forever. Sophie huddled against him. He tightened his arm around her as shudders ran through her. She pressed one ear against his chest and covered her other ear with a hand, clearly trying to shut out the terrifying sounds.

In reality, those endless moments passed in a matter of only seconds. Then the gunfire receded as the attack progressed on down the street. The echoes began to fade away.

As they did, Pike heard another sound that made alarm bells go off in his brain.

Hoofbeats thudded on the boardwalk just outside the café. One of the marauders was about to ride his horse right into the place. Pike was certain that if he did, he would murder some of the frightened customers.

"Stay down," he told Sophie. She clung to his arm for a second as he pushed himself up, then her hands slipped off his sleeve.

As his head rose above the level of the counter, he saw a man bending low in the saddle as he forced his horse through the door. The fit was a tight one, and the horse didn't want to come in the building, but the raider cursed and raked the animal's flanks with his spurs. As he cleared the doorway, he straightened and started to swing the gun in his hand toward the townspeople lying on the floor.

That was when he spotted Pike rising from behind the counter.

The man tried to jerk his gun back in that direction but had no chance to do so before Pike triggered twice. The pair of bullets drilled into his chest and drove him backward out of the saddle. The horse reared up in alarm, completing the job of dumping the man on the floor just inside the entrance. He lay there in a tangled heap.

Panic-stricken from the shooting and the mingled smell of blood and powder smoke, the horse began to jump around, overturning tables and wrecking chairs. The café's customers had to scramble wildly to avoid being stepped on by the iron-shod hooves. The horse was bound to hurt itself or some of the people if this continued for very long.

Pike put a hand on the counter and vaulted over again. He rammed his Colt back in its holster and lunged to grab the horse's trailing reins. As he hauled the animal's head down, Pike spoke in calm, steady tones. The human voice and the strong, steady touch on the reins brought the horse back under control again.

"Everybody get out the back while you can," he told the townspeople.

They hustled to do so, all except Sophie, who stood up behind the counter and said, "I'm staying with you, Pike."

That was all right with him. Keeping her with him was what he had intended all along. He led the horse toward the door and managed with some effort to get the animal to step over the body of its former owner and then go on outside, onto the boardwalk again.

The shooting hadn't stopped, and as the horse bolted away, Pike looked up the street and saw the gang of gunmen regrouping again at the far end of town, getting ready for another charge. He turned and hurried back to Sophie, who had come out from behind the counter.

Taking her right hand in his left, he said, "Come on."

"Where are we going?"

"I have to find out if my ma and Nessa and Fiddler are all right. We'll see if we can make it to the store."

He was concerned about Belle, too, but he didn't mention that.

They went out the back door and ran through the shadows of the alley behind the buildings. Once Sophie tripped on something, cried out, and would have fallen if not for Pike's strong hand grasping hers. He put his other hand on her arm to steady her and asked, "Are you all right?"

"Y-yes." Gunfire flared up again, out on the main street. "Pike, they're going to kill everybody in town!"

"No, they're not," he declared grimly. "They're not going to kill us."

He wished he knew if the same was true for his mother, sister, and friends. They would find out soon enough, he told himself.

Other people were scurrying for safety behind the buildings. As gunshots continued to slam, a stray bullet came through one of the gaps and struck a man running for his life ahead of Pike and Sophie. He cried out, stumbled, and pitched forward. Sophie exclaimed, "Pike, we have to help him."

"Press yourself against the back wall of that building," he said. "You ought to be safe there."

Sophie started to argue but then did as he said. Pike hurried forward, ignoring the danger of another bullet coming through the gap, and dropped to a knee beside the fallen man. Even in the bad light back here, he saw the dark, spreading pool around the man's head and knew he was wasting his time. He felt for a pulse in the man's neck anyway.

"He's gone," he called softly to Sophie a moment later. "There's nothing we can do for him. Come on."

The attackers had moved on down the street again, so he thought it would be safe for her to cross the open space between buildings, but he held his breath anyway until she was beside him again and he grasped her hand.

Several nerve-wracking minutes later, they stood in the mouth of an alley across the street from their destination. Pike could tell that all the windows in the front of the store had been shot out, leaving just jagged edges of glass, but he had no idea how much damage was done inside—or who had been hit by all that flying lead.

He motioned for Sophie to stay back, then eased out far enough so he could look along the street. The guns were silent now. Had the raiders left, satisfied with the havoc they had wreaked on Warbonnet?

Then he spotted them down at the far end of the street, a dark mass of men milling around on horseback. More than likely, they were just reloading. But that would give him and Sophie a chance to make it to the store. He grasped her hand again and said, "Let's go."

They took off running across the street, Pike holding back a little so Sophie could keep up with his long-legged strides.

Somebody in the gang spotted them and yelled, and guns began to roar again as the marauders charged them. Bullets kicked up dust from the street, several of them coming perilously close to Pike and Sophie. Pike considered sweeping her up in his arms and carrying her, thinking that he might be able to move faster that way.

Before he could do that, a man stepped out onto the store's front porch with a rifle in his hands.

Chapter 33

Pike's first impulse was to whip out his Colt and fire at the man. His hand even started in the direction of the gun butt.

But he stopped as he recognized the man on the porch as Andy Burnett. The sheriff brought the rifle smoothly to his shoulder and started cranking off shots as fast as he could work the repeater's lever.

He was aiming down the street at the charging marauders. Pike glanced in that direction and saw several of the men topple out of their saddles as Andy's deadly fire raked the front ranks. That onslaught of lead slowed the charge and gave Pike and Sophie time to reach the porch. Pike bounded up the steps, practically carrying Sophie now.

Andy lowered his Winchester enough to yell, "Get inside!" then triggered three more swift shots. With his arm around Sophie, Pike reached the open double doors and plunged inside. Andy was right behind them. He kicked one door shut, grabbed the other and slammed it. Pike heard bullets thud against the panels.

"Pike!"

That was his sister Nessa's voice. He looked around and saw her running up one of the aisles toward him. She appeared to be unharmed, but he waved for her to stop and said, "Get back! Stay at the back of the store! It's safer there."

Nessa hesitated, then retreated. Pike pushed Sophie after her.

"Get behind the counter," he told her, "and keep your head down."

He turned to Andy Burnett. Both men crouched behind shelves full of merchandise that provided some cover from the bullets that still zinged through the broken windows.

"What are you doing in here?" Pike asked.

"Happened to be in the street making my rounds when all Hades busted loose," Andy replied, "and this was the closest place to duck into." His voice grew even more grim as he went on, "This is more of Henshaw's work, isn't it?"

"I'd bet a hat that it is," Pike replied. "That's got to be Ben Grayle's bunch out there shooting up the town. Looks like he's recruited even more gun-wolves to back him up." He glanced toward the rear of the store and added, "You don't happen to know if Belle and my ma and Fiddler are all right, do you?"

Andy nodded.

"I laid eyes on all them, along with Nessa, after I ran in here," he said. "They looked to be fine, just scared, and I can't blame 'em for that."

Both of them ducked instinctively as a slug whined particularly close, then Andy went on, "How many of them do you reckon are out there?"

"From what I saw, thirty or forty. But I wasn't taking any time to count."

"Yeah, I was thinking the same thing," Andy said, his tone glum now. "Those are pretty high odds for two men to be taking on."

"But you're thinking about going out there and doing it, aren't you?"

Andy glanced down at the badge pinned to his shirt.

"This star says it's my duty to do that."

"It's not your duty to get killed, badge or no badge," Pike said. "And that's what'll happen if you go out there and take them on face-to-face. We can do more damage if we hit them from the shadows."

Andy considered that for a second and then nodded.

"All right. Out the back?"

"Yeah," Pike said.

They straightened and ran to the back of the store. Half a dozen heads popped up from behind the counter. Pike was relieved to see his mother and Fiddler. Nessa was beside Mary, and Sophie was beside her. Belle was next to Fiddler, and at the end of the line was burly John Strickland, the store's proprietor. Evidently Mary, Nessa, Fiddler, and Belle had been the only ones in the store besides Strickland when the attack started.

"Pike!" Mary exclaimed. "Are you all right, son?"

"I'm fine," he assured her. "Anybody hurt back there?"

"No one was hit," Belle said, "but not from lack of those varmints trying."

Pike grabbed a couple of Winchesters from a display rack on the wall and put them on the counter.

"Nessa, Belle, I know the two of you can shoot. Mr. Strickland, do you have ammunition back there?"

"You dang well know I do!" the storekeeper replied. He lifted the double-barreled Greener he'd been holding below the level of the counter. "Got old Matilda here, too, and I don't mind usin' her!"

Pike jerked his head in a nod and said, "Good. You two girls load those rifles and keep them ready. If anybody you don't know starts in the front door, shoot them."

Grimly, Nessa and Belle returned his nod.

"Andy and I are gonna go see if we can whittle down the odds some," Pike went on.

Mary stood up and leaned over the counter to grasp his arm.

"Pike, stay in here where it's safer," she urged. "Those men are bound to get tired of shooting up the town pretty soon, and then they'll leave—"

"After killing some more innocent people," Pike broke in. "I don't reckon we can stand by and let that happen without trying to stop it."

She looked intently at him and then said, "No, I reckon you can't. You wouldn't be your father's son if you could. But you can be careful, can't you?"

"That's a quality Shannons aren't exactly known for," Pike said with a grin, "but I'll try."

"You, too, Andy," Mary called after them as they went to a door at the end of the counter that opened into a back room. "Try not to get your head shot off."

"Sure will, ma'am," Andy said, politely pinching

the brim of his hat as he followed Pike out of the store's main room.

Enough light came through the open door to allow Pike and Andy to make their way through the stack of crates, bags, and boxes of supplies stored back here. Pike heard a fresh burst of gunfire from the street and hoped that the others were keeping their heads down.

He found the rear door, opened it, and with Andy following closely behind him stepped out into the dark alley behind the store.

They moved around the building's rear corner into the pitch-dark passage beside it, then cat-footed to the front. The street was empty, and from where they were, they couldn't see the raiders, but sporadic shots still sounded down at the far end of town.

"How many times do you reckon they're gonna ride back and forth shooting like that?" Andy asked quietly.

"I've seen Grayle lead attacks like this before," Pike replied. "He probably won't be satisfied to shoot up the town and leave it at that."

"What do you mean? You don't think he'd . . . burn it, do you?"

"It's happened before," Pike said grimly. "I've ridden up to more than one settlement that was just ashes after Ben Grayle got through with it."

Uncharacteristically, Andy cursed in a low, bitter voice. On the frontier, anybody who would use fire as a weapon was considered the lowest of the low.

"We've got to stop 'em, but blast it, I don't see how just the two of us can do it!"

"We can make a start on it now," Pike said. "Here they come again!"

They pressed themselves against opposite corners of the opening between buildings and leveled their guns, Pike with his Colt and Andy holding the Winchester he'd used earlier. As the rumble of hoofbeats welled up in the street, a rolling tide of gun-thunder mixed with it to create a symphony of chaos and destruction.

In the midst of that terrible racket, the crack of Andy's rifle and the boom of Pike's revolver went unnoticed at first. They weren't the only people in Warbonnet fighting back, either. Pike saw muzzle flashes from the windows of several other buildings. The defiant citizens had to duck for cover, though, as a terrific onslaught of lead hammered the storefronts.

Several of the gunmen either swayed in their saddles as they were hit or toppled completely off their charging horses. That drew some attention from the killers. A concentrated barrage of bullets forced Pike and Andy to leap back farther into the shadows and throw themselves to the ground. For a few seconds, it was a hornet's nest inside the dark passage as dozens of slugs ripped through the air.

Then the gang was past again. Pike and Andy scrambled to their feet, stepped out into the open, and sent a few more shots after the gun-wolves.

"Andy!"

The shout made them turn around quickly and level their weapons. They lowered the guns, though, as they recognized Lem Cranepool hurrying toward them. The middle-aged deputy was limping pretty heavily but moving fast anyway. The left leg of his trousers was dark with blood where a slug appeared to have creased him.

Two men followed closely behind Cranepool. Pike was a little surprised to recognize Lester Scroggins, Andy's opponent in the election several months back, and Fritz Durham, the troublemaker who hadn't wanted Andy running for sheriff in the first place.

All three men carried rifles. As they came up to Pike and Andy, Cranepool asked, "Are you boys ventilated?"

"No, but they came too close for comfort plenty of times," Andy replied.

Cranepool jerked his head toward his companions and said, "I ran into Lester and Fritz, and we been tryin' to mount a defense against those varmints. Seen the two of you blazin' away at 'em and figured we ought to join forces."

"That's right," Scroggins said. "No hard feelings about anything that happened back in the campaign, Andy. With the town in trouble, we've all got to pull together."

Andy looked at Durham and said, "You feel the same way, Fritz?"

"Yeah, sure," Durham responded with only a trace of reluctance. "No hard feelings. Things just get heated up during an election campaign."

"Or a horse trade, eh?"

"We can worry about that another time," Durham said. "Right now, we need to stop those men from hurting anybody else."

Pike looked along the street. The guns were silent at the moment, but he knew they wouldn't stay that way long. He and Andy and their new allies were still outnumbered. It was only a matter of time until Grayle's crew renewed the attack.

Cranepool said, "While I was hunkered behind a rain barrel, I overheard the fella who seems to be the boss yellin' at some of the others. They're fixin' to start workin' their way through town, goin' from business to business and house to house, cleanin' 'em out along the way."

"That's nothing but wholesale murder," Andy exclaimed.

"And I wouldn't put it past Ben Grayle for a second," Pike said. He thought fast, and as he glanced along the street to where the Warbonnet County courthouse stood, an idea came to him. The courthouse, with its thick stone walls, was probably the safest place in town, as well as the easiest to defend.

"Lester, Fritz," he snapped, "spread out. Get some other men to help you, and go through town as much as you can. Tell everybody, men, women, and children, to gather inside the courthouse."

"That's good thinking," Andy agreed. "We'll make our stand there. We need to keep those hombres occupied, though, so they won't start their sweep too soon."

Pike nodded and said, "That's what you and Lem and I will be doing."

"You sure about this, Andy?" Scroggins asked.

"It gives us the best chance to save the most people," Andy said.

"Then that's what we'll do. Come on, Fritz."

The two men hurried away on their desperate

errand. Pike, Andy, and Cranepool turned toward the gang of killers.

"We'll need to take the fight to them in order to keep them busy," Pike said.

"Lem and I will do that," Andy said. "You get inside the store and start your folks toward the court-house, Pike."

Pike glanced at the nearby storefront. He hadn't forgotten about the people in there, but he felt like he ought to be siding Andy and Cranepool.

The deputy said, "Andy's right. Tend to that, and then you can join us. I guarantee, there'll still be plenty of varmints to kill when you do!"

CHAPTER 34

Just as Pike was about to go through the general store's front door, he recalled the instructions he had given to Belle and Nessa and called out, "Don't shoot! It's me, Pike."

He went in to find his sister and Belle Ramsey standing behind the counter at the back of the store with Winchesters trained on the door. Strickland was there, too, holding the scattergun he called Matilda. All three lowered the weapons as they recognized Pike. Mary, Fiddler, and Sophie peered over the counter.

"Pike, you're all right," Mary said, sounding as if she found that a little hard to believe.

"What about Andy?" Belle asked.

Pike nodded and said, "He's not hurt, either, or at least he wasn't when we split up." A burst of gunfire came from up the street. "I can't guarantee what's going on now, though."

"Why did you come back here?" Fiddler asked. "I thought you were going to fight those outlaws."

Pike didn't answer the question directly. Instead he said, "Grayle's going to sweep the town building by building. We're trying to get as many people as we can to fort up inside the courthouse."

"That's a mighty fine idea," Strickland said. "It was built in the days when folks still had to worry about fighting off the Comanches, so it's strong."

"I want all six of you to head down there right now," Pike went on. "Go out the back. Nessa, you and Belle lead the way. Mr. Strickland, I'd be obliged if you and Matilda would bring up the rear."

Strickland brandished the Greener and nodded.

"We sure will," he declared.

Pike added, "Lester Scroggins and Fritz Durham are rounding up folks and telling them to get to safety, and they've probably recruited some help since I saw them. Be careful not to shoot any of them. All those gun-wolves are strangers to these parts, though, so if you see anybody you don't recognize who looks threatening, don't hesitate to open fire."

Belle and Nessa nodded in understanding. As they ushered the others out from behind the counter and toward the door to the back room, Nessa asked, "What are you going to do, Pike?"

"Andy and Lem Cranepool are trying to keep Grayle's bunch occupied, and from the sound of it, they're doing a good job. I'm going to go help them."

He waited until everyone had gone out through the back, then stepped through the front door and, in a crouching run, started toward the sounds of battle.

Carl McConnell stood in an alcove where the entrance to a saddle shop was set back a few feet from the boardwalk. Ben Grayle was with him. The gunman had a thin black cigar clenched between his teeth. The orange glow from the coal at the end of the smoke faintly illuminated his hawkish visage.

"I didn't expect these sheep to put up quite as much of a fight," Grayle rasped. "I've lost half a dozen men."

"Did you figure folks would just roll over and let you kill them?" McConnell asked harshly.

"This isn't the old days. People have gone soft."

"It's been less than ten years since the army beat the Comanches up at Palo Duro Canyon and ended that threat," McConnell pointed out. "Most of the folks in Warbonnet *remember* those old days you're talking about. And if they're not pioneer stock themselves, they come from it."

Grayle puffed angrily on the cigar and made it glow brighter.

"This is Shannon's doing," he said. "He's the one who rallied them. I'd bet anything on that."

"Probably," McConnell agreed. "But I don't see that it matters who's responsible for them putting up a fight. We've already done a heap of damage, and unless we want to lose more men, we ought to call it off and head back to Clarkston now."

Slowly, Grayle shook his head.

"We're not going anywhere," he said. "Not until we've taught this town a lesson it'll never forget. That's what Henshaw's paying me for . . . and I always deliver value for payment received."

McConnell thought Grayle sounded a little loco.

He said, "What are you gonna do? Kill everybody and burn Warbonnet to the ground?"

Grayle didn't say anything. After a few seconds, McConnell looked at him and realized that was exactly what the hired killer intended to do.

The two of them had retreated when fierce fire from the defenders of Warbonnet had sent bullets whistling too close to their heads. Since then the shooting had become sporadic. Grayle's men were waiting for the order to resume charging up and down the street, shooting wildly.

It was McConnell's belief that that tactic had run its course. Evidently, Grayle agreed with him, because he'd had his men hold off momentarily and just fight back against the citizens who were trying to stand up to them.

One of the gun-wolves ran up to the alcove and said to Grayle, "Boss, it looks like folks are retreating to the courthouse. A few men are trying to keep us busy while others round up the townies."

Smoke from the cheroot wreathed Grayle's head as he nodded.

"Good, good," he said in obvious satisfaction. "I had a hunch that idea would occur to them sooner or later."

"Why is that good?" McConnell demanded. "I've been in the Warbonnet County courthouse. The walls are solid rock and a foot thick! You'd need a cannon to shoot through them." He paused. "You don't have a cannon in your back pocket, do you, Grayle?"

"I don't need a cannon." To the subordinate who

had reported the news, he said, "Tell the boys not to put up too much of a fight. Let those people fort up in the courthouse, just like Shannon wants. That little trick is going to backfire on him."

McConnell frowned and said, "Just what is it you're planning to do, Grayle?"

Around the cigar clenched between his teeth, Ben Grayle said, "Those stone walls may not burn . . . but everything inside them will."

Pike ran along the boardwalk, then dropped to one knee behind a water barrel. A few feet away, Lem Cranepool stood in an alcove with his rifle at his shoulder, firing around the edge of the wall beside him.

"Where's Andy?" Pike called to Cranepool.

"Across the street," the deputy replied. "He's got Harvey Billings from the blacksmith shop with him. Harv's got that old Sharps of his."

A resounding boom from the other side of the street told Pike that Billings was bringing his old buffalo rifle into play.

"We ran into Harv on the way up here, and he wanted in on the action," Cranepool continued as he thumbed fresh cartridges through his repeater's loading gate. "We got those varmints bottled up around the saddle shop and Tompkins' Apothecary. I figured they'd have tried another charge by now, but they've just been tradin' shots with us. Maybe they're tired or runnin' low on ammunition."

Pike doubted if either of those things was true.

Grayle would have something else up his sleeve. It was just a matter of time until he tried some fresh atrocity.

Every moment of delay was a chance for more people to reach the safety of the courthouse, though, so Pike wasn't going to complain.

He saw a muzzle flash and ducked as the bullet slammed into the water barrel. He snapped a shot back at the gunman but had no way of knowing if he hit the varmint.

"Cover me," he called to Cranepool. "I'm going to talk to Andy."

"Sure thing," the deputy replied. He opened up on the hired killers at the end of the street, spraying lead in their direction as he worked the Winchester's lever.

Pike burst out from behind the barrel and sprinted toward the opposite boardwalk, zigzagging as he did so in order to make himself a more difficult target. Even so, and even with Lem Cranepool keeping up a steady covering fire, several bullets from Grayle's bunch kicked up dirt near Pike's feet as he ran.

Luck was with him and he made it without being hit, though. He bounded into an alley mouth. The corner of the building next to him shielded him from the gun-wolves' fire.

Andy crouched behind a nearby parked wagon. Harvey Billings was using a water trough for cover. Andy called, "You hit, Pike?"

"Nope," Pike replied. "You?"

"Not so far." Andy chuckled. "I've given up counting how many times they've come close, though."

"Looks like we've got people making it into the courthouse all right. We can't help anybody who's caught beyond this point, but it appears most of the town will be able to fort up there."

"How long do you reckon we'll need to keep that bunch of killers bottled up?"

"Another ten or fifteen minutes ought to do it. The word to gather at the courthouse probably spread pretty fast. Most folks ought to be headed that way, if they're not there already."

Even as Pike spoke, a sense of unease stirred inside him. Andy had referred to keeping Grayle's crew of gun-wolves bottled up. As many of them as there were, that would have been impossible if they really wanted to break out of this end of town. As Pike considered that, his worry deepened.

Grayle was up to something. Pike didn't know what it was, but he suddenly had a hunch they were doing exactly what Grayle wanted them to do.

However, at this point there were no other good options. And every hired gunman they drilled was another who wouldn't kill any more innocent folks.

For the next quarter of an hour, the back-and-forth shooting continued. Fritz Durham showed up to join Pike and Andy in peppering the gunmen with bullets, then Lester Scroggins came to the mouth of a nearby alley and called, "Time to pull back, boys! Everybody we could find is in the court-house, except for a few stubborn holdouts who wouldn't leave their homes."

Pike understood that feeling. Those folks were afraid that the gang might try to loot the town or even burn it, and they wanted to protect what was theirs.

But possessions, even homes, didn't do anybody any good if they were dead.

From behind the wagon, Andy said, "The rest of you head on out. I'll stay here and keep the varmints busy for a little while longer."

He punctuated that order with another shot, but the rest of the men didn't budge from the spots where they had taken cover.

"I reckon we all go or nobody goes," Pike said.

"That's right," Scroggins said. "I want to keep you alive, Andy, so I can run against you again when your term is up . . . and beat you next time!"

Andy lowered his rifle and laughed.

"You fellas are stubborn as all get-out," he said. "All right. Let's all light a shuck for the courthouse."

He waved to get Lem Cranepool's attention across the street and conveyed the order through gestures. Cranepool waved back to show that he understood. The defenders began an orderly retreat, dashing from cover to cover, then stopping to fire back at the gang of killers while the next man made his move.

When they reached alleys that would lead them away from the main street, they hurried along those narrow passages and then raced for the courthouse.

Riflemen were posted in the windows of the three-story stone building. They were ready to cover the withdrawal of Pike and the others, but that wasn't necessary. The gun-wolves had stopped shooting. An eerie quiet fell over Warbonnet.

Pike didn't expect *that* to last long.

Men inside swung the courthouse doors open as Pike approached. He led the group of defenders inside. The men who were already there slammed the doors behind them.

Mary, Nessa, Belle, and Sophie were waiting for Pike. Mary put her arms around him and asked, "Are you hurt?"

"Not a bit," Pike assured her.

"How in the world did you manage that?" Fiddler said. "It sounded like the Battle of Chickamauga out there!"

"Luck's been with us." Pike nodded toward Andy, Cranepool, and the rest of the men who had been with him. "Nobody was hit except Lem, and he's just got a bullet graze on his leg. He'll be all right." He looked around the courthouse lobby, which was packed with people. "How many folks are here?"

"A couple of hundred, I'd say," Nessa replied. "I was going to try to keep count, so we'd know how many *didn't* make it, but I had to give up after a while."

"I'm glad my wife and kids are out at my farm," Andy said. "That's safer than being in town tonight." He frowned. "Isn't it? That's all of Henshaw's bunch out there, right?"

Pike said, "We don't have any way of knowing that for sure, but it's bound to be most of them, anyway. My hunch is that's all. This attack on the town is like a knockout punch in a bare-knuckles brawl. Henshaw wants to end the fight tonight, even if it means wiping out Warbonnet."

"But that's insane!" Fiddler said. "This whole thing started because Henshaw wants to sell moonshine down here in this county. If he wipes out the county seat, it's going to hurt his business!"

"You're asking for common sense from a Yankee who thinks he's above the law and better than all us white-trash Texans," Pike said. "Henshaw can't abide the fact that somebody is standing up to him. He's got to win. That's the most important thing to him."

Once again, Pike felt a pang of unease at the knowledge that his harassment of Henshaw's moonshine operation was what had started this. Henshaw and his minions were the ones who had escalated it into murder and open warfare, though, he reminded himself. It was up to him and his allies here in Warbonnet to bring that war to an end by defeating Ben Grayle and the rest of Solomon Henshaw's hired killers.

He turned to John Strickland and said, "Who's taken charge of the defense here in the courthouse?"

"Reckon I have," the burly storekeeper replied. "I told Abe Millworth he ought to, since he's the mayor, but he said it'd be better if I did, since I was a colonel back during the war and commanded troops in battle."

Pike hadn't known that about Strickland, but he wasn't really surprised. A lot of men who had been in the war never talked about it much.

Strickland went on, "I had the fellas who brought guns with 'em spread out and cover the windows. I figure that bunch will be attackin' sooner or later, but I believe we can hold 'em off in here."

"That's the plan," Pike said.

Mary said, "I seem to recall that there's a kitchen down in the basement."

"There is," Andy said. "It's next to the cell block.

There's not much to it, but the jailer brews up coffee there."

"That's just what I was thinking," Mary told him. "I ought to go down there and get a pot on to boil right now."

"That's a good idea," Pike said. "From the looks of things, this is going to be a long night . . ."

CHAPTER 35

The next half-hour was surprising for what *didn't* happen. No attack on the courthouse was forthcoming.

However, from the third-floor window where Pike ascended to take a look at the town, he spotted furtive movement in several places. He walked across a hallway to a room on the other side of the courthouse and studied the streets of Warbonnet from that vantage point.

Before long, he discerned more of those stealthy maneuvers. Even though full night had fallen and he couldn't make out any details, he had a pretty good idea what was going on.

The gang of killers led by Ben Grayle was surrounding the courthouse.

Obviously they had something in mind for the people who had sought sanctuary here, and it wasn't going to be anything good. Pike didn't doubt that for a second.

He went back downstairs to get a cup of that coffee his mother had been preparing. Belle met him at the foot of the main staircase with a steaming cup in her hand.

"I reckon you must've read my mind," Pike said with a smile as he took it from her. He sipped the coffee and immediately felt the bracing effects of the hot, strong liquid.

"I believe there's an old saying, or a quote, about great minds thinking alike," Belle replied with a smile of her own.

"If there is, Fiddler could tell us about it, but I think that'll wait until another time."

Belle sat down and patted the marble step beside her.

"Sit with me for a minute, Pike. I've been thinking about something."

He sat down, grateful for the chance to take it easy for a few moments in good company.

Belle tempered that gratitude by saying, "This isn't going to work."

"What isn't?"

"Forting up like this. Don't get me wrong, heading for the courthouse was the best thing we could do at the time. Otherwise, that bunch out there might have slaughtered half the town. But now they have all of us trapped here."

"That occurred to me," Pike admitted. "And from what I've seen, they've surrounded the place. I figure they intend to lay siege to it."

"What we need," Belle said, "is some help."

"Yeah, but where will we get it?"

"I intend to go fetch it," she declared.

Pike stared at her for a couple of seconds before he said, "You can't mean that."

"Sure I do. I know this town. I can slip out of here, get hold of a horse, and ride to your ranch. Torrance and Dougal are there, aren't they?"

"They are," Pike said, "but the two of them wouldn't be enough help to make a difference."

"But there are other people out there in the county. Friends of yours like Will Fisher and Sam Crow. Plenty who'd be willing to come and fight." Belle laughed, but the sound had a grim note to it. "You know how contentious folks are in Texas. Counties have gone to war before over less than this. All I need to do is spread the word that a bunch of gunmen from Chaparral County have attacked Warbonnet, and people will be coming out of the weeds for a chance to whip them."

"That could be," Pike allowed. "But the important thing is, you're not going to do it. Trying to sneak out of here like that is just too dangerous."

She sat up straighter and frowned at him.

"That's not really your decision to make—"

"Then we'll find Andy, and he can order you to forget about it. He's still the sheriff, after all."

"So what do we do?" Belle wanted to know. "Sit here and let them starve us out?"

"It won't come to that. Somebody who's still out there is bound to go for help."

But would they, Pike asked himself. Those citizens who hadn't taken refuge in the courthouse probably were hunkered down in their homes, praying that they and their families would survive the night.

Come morning, folks might risk trying to find some help—but would Ben Grayle hold off for that long before attempting whatever it was he had in mind?

Pike doubted that, and he knew that whatever Grayle was planning would be bad. But even so, he wasn't going to allow Belle to risk her life like that.

"One of the men can go," he said. "Let me think on it."

Belle stood up and said, "You're a stubborn man, Pike Shannon. You always have been, as long as I've known you."

She walked off with her back stiff.

Pike sighed and took another drink of the coffee, which was starting to cool off now.

Someone sat down on the step beside him. He looked over and saw Sophie Truesdale smoothing her skirt around her legs as she drew her knees up slightly.

"Belle looked upset," Sophie commented. "Of course, I don't blame her. It's terrible what's happening out there tonight." A shudder went through her. "I hate to think about how many people have already been hurt or . . . or killed."

"Too many," Pike said. "And we'll be mighty lucky if we make it through the night without there being more."

The two of them sat there in silence for a moment before Sophie said, "Belle looked like something more than that was bothering her, though."

Sophie was being nosy, Pike realized. He didn't know if she was jealous of Belle, and at a time like this, it seemed pretty ridiculous to worry about such a thing. Human beings didn't get to pick and choose which emotions popped up when, though.

"She had an idea, and I told her it wasn't a good one."

"What did she want?"

"She thought she could sneak out of the courthouse, slip through the ring of gunmen Grayle's thrown around us, grab a horse, and ride to fetch help. I told her that one of the men might try that, but she wasn't going to."

Sophie smiled and said, "Now I understand why she looked like she did. She didn't care for being told what she could and couldn't do."

"Maybe not, but I'm not just about to let her go off and try something loco that might get her killed."

Sophie looked away and asked, "How much longer is this standoff going to last?"

"Hard to say," Pike replied. "But I have a hunch that whatever Grayle tries next will come before morning. He'll know that he can't keep us penned up in here forever."

"I'm scared, Pike."

He drained the last of the coffee from the cup, set it aside, and put his arm around Sophie's shoulders.

"It's going to be all right," he told her.

He wished he could be sure he'd be able to keep that promise.

Belle Ramsey knew the courthouse fairly well. She had been in it several times when her cousin Doak was the sheriff and was aware that at the back of the basement cell block was a narrow flight of stairs leading up to a barred door opening into a partially sunken alcove on the building's rear side.

That exit was used for taking out the bodies of prisoners who had died while in custody—which had happened more frequently than usual while Doak Ramsey was in office. Several of his deputies had been little better than brutal animals.

Even before Doak had been elected, though, prisoners sometimes hanged themselves or died of natural causes. Cyrus Malone was able to pull his undertaker's wagon right up to the building and fetch them out that way.

When she thought no one was looking, Belle went down the stairs to the basement, past the little kitchen, through the cell block, and up those narrow steps, hoping that Andy Burnett hadn't changed anything since taking over—such as padlocking that exit door.

She had to work by feel since it was dark back here. There was a lamp burning in the jail kitchen, but the glow from it didn't reach this far.

She needed only a moment to discover that the heavy bar holding the door closed was still in its brackets. No lock had been added. Belle grasped the bar and, grunting with the effort, lifted first one end of it and then the other. She lowered it carefully to the steps so it wouldn't make a racket and draw attention, not that she believed anyone had noticed her coming down here.

This would teach Pike Shannon to believe he could just blithely give her orders and have her follow them. More important, if she succeeded in what she planned to do, she would be helping to save scores of innocent people.

The door was made of thick wood banded with iron strips. She turned the latch and pulled it toward her. That was a bit of a struggle, too, since the door was pretty heavy. But after a moment, it swung back onto the landing at the top of the steps. Belle opened it just wide enough for her to slip out into the warm night air.

Three broad stone steps led up to ground level from the sunken entrance. The shadows were thick here, so Belle froze for a long moment as she peered into the darkness and listened intently.

She didn't see or hear any sign of the hired killers, although she knew that some of them had to be lurking out there not far away. But the post oaks and live oaks grew up fairly close to the courthouse and cast shadows of their own. Belle took a deep breath and slipped through that murky gloom like a phantom.

She had covered about fifty yards across the courthouse lawn, darting from tree to tree, and had almost reached the nearest side street, thinking that in another few moments she would have reached safety . . .

When a hand came out of the darkness, clamped painfully around her upper right arm, and a harsh voice said, "Hold on there, missy. Where in blazes do you think *you're* goin'?"

CHAPTER 36

"What do you think you're doing?" Carl McConnell asked Ben Grayle as they stood at the counter in the now abandoned general mercantile store a couple of blocks from the Warbonnet County courthouse.

"Putting together some little presents for Shannon and his friends," Grayle replied as he set a can of coal oil on the counter. He had been pouring the black, greasy stuff into glass bottles he had scavenged and emptied off the store's shelves. "Stuff some cloth wicks in these, light them, throw them through the windows, and before you know it, the inside of that courthouse will be a big old bonfire."

"That's a mighty harsh thing to do."

"We're in a mighty harsh business," Grayle said. "These things work really well. I got the idea from the Pinkertons."

McConnell frowned and said, "The detectives?"

"They're the ones who tossed a bomb into Jesse James's house in Missouri and blew up his kid brother and his ma. It was a different type of explosive, but the principle's the same. If you want somebody to come out, blow up the place he's hiding or set it on fire."

"You're gonna chase everybody out of the courthouse and gun them down while they're trying to escape that fire."

Grayle shrugged.

"They can stay inside and burn up if they want to. Doesn't matter to me. All I know is that by the time I'm finished with Warbonnet, anybody who's left alive will never dare cross Solomon Henshaw again."

McConnell couldn't contain the anger he felt at Grayle's casual tone. He burst out, "By grab, you're taking this too far. I've killed men who had it coming, and I've killed some who maybe didn't have it coming, but that's what the boss wanted anyway. But this is too much. You're talking about killing women and kids, maybe hundreds of them."

"As much lead as we've thrown around this town tonight, you think none of it found any women or kids?"

Wearily, McConnell scrubbed a hand over his face.

"I didn't care for that, either, but at least it wasn't a massacre like what you're talking about! I'm not going to stand for—"

With a whisper of steel against leather, one of Grayle's guns came out of the holster faster than McConnell's eyes could follow it. McConnell found himself looking down the weapon's barrel.

"You'd better be mighty careful what you say next, McConnell," Grayle told him in a silky, vicious tone. "If I think you're turning on your partners . . .

disobeying our employer's orders . . . why, I'll just kill you myself, right here and now."

For a few long, tense seconds, McConnell didn't say anything. Then he growled, "Put that iron up, Grayle. I'm not double-crossing you or the boss. I don't play the game that way. But that doesn't mean I have to like every hand you deal, either."

Grayle grunted, did a show-off twirl of the gun, and slid it back into leather.

"You don't have to like it, but you'll play it out to the end, and you'll watch your mouth, too."

"Fine."

McConnell managed to get the word out, but even as he spoke, he was thinking that the next time Ben Grayle tried to pull a gun on him, one of them was going to die.

Nodding toward the bottles full of coal oil, McConnell went on, "When do you intend to make that move?"

"Not for a while yet. In fact, I figure it would be a good idea to wait until closer to sunup. Let them stew and fret the rest of the night. By that time of the morning, they'll all be tired and their guard will be down. They won't be able to put up as much of a fight when we move in."

McConnell actually agreed with that strategy. If they were going to follow Grayle's vicious plan, they might as well give it the best chance to succeed.

"There's only one thing that bothers me," Grayle mused.

"What's that?"

"I always believed that someday, Pike Shannon and I would have a chance to settle the question of which one of us is faster." Grayle shook his head. "Now it's more likely that somebody else will shoot him down like a dog, or else he'll burn up in that courthouse." The gunman laughed. "But either way, he'll soon be dead, and I'll settle for that."

Belle gasped and tried to pull her arm free from the gunman's grip. He was too strong, though. She couldn't get loose.

"Please," she said. "I . . . I just want to get out of here."

She made her voice sound pathetically frightened instead of letting it reveal the anger she actually felt. She wanted her captor to believe that she wasn't really a threat. If he underestimated her, she'd have a better chance of turning the tables on him and getting away.

And if she could hurt or even kill this gun-wolf in the process, then so much the better.

It didn't seem to be working, though. The man's grip didn't loosen. He jerked Belle roughly along with him and called in a quiet voice, "Hey, Denbow, look what I got."

The man dragged Belle behind a couple of post oaks growing close together. The trees screened them from the view of anyone in the courthouse. Another man waited there. He said, "Who's that, Stevens?"

"Don't know, but I'm gonna take a look."

Belle flinched as the man used his other hand to snap a match to life and held the flame up close to her face to reveal her features and thick auburn hair.

"Dang, she's a pretty one, whoever she is," the gunman called Stevens said. "Claims she wants to get away. What do you reckon she'd be willing to do for us if we was to let her go?"

"Forget about that," Denbow snapped. "Grayle said no deals . . . and no prisoners, remember?"

That made a cold ball of fear congeal in Belle's stomach. Men such as these wouldn't hesitate to kill her.

A new voice said sharply, "Let her go!"

The surprise accomplished what Belle's strength hadn't been able to do. The gunman's grip loosened on her arm as he turned quickly and drew his revolver with his other hand. She jerked free from him, clubbed her hands together, and swung them against the side of his head with all the strength in her lithe young body.

The hammering blow knocked the man to the side. Belle brought her hands down on his wrist and jolted the gun out of his grasp. As it thudded to the ground, she lowered her left shoulder and bulled into him.

The man was already off balance and wasn't able to brace himself for the impact. Belle's charge drove him back into the other gunman, who cursed as he tried to shove Stevens aside and draw his own gun.

Belle whirled away from them and bent to scoop up the gun Stevens had dropped. It wasn't lying there on the ground anymore, though. The shadowy figure who had spoken in a familiar voice had picked it up already.

Belle's eyes had adjusted enough to the dimness that she was able to make out Sophie Truesdale's long, fair hair. The gun barrel waved wildly as Sophie thrust the weapon at the two men.

Since Belle was already bent over, some instinct warned her to dive to the ground. Sophie pulled the trigger. Flame spurted from the gun's muzzle as it roared. One of the men grunted and reeled back.

Sophie stood there futilely pulling the trigger, but the gun didn't do anything else. It was a single action, Belle realized. Stevens had cocked it as he drew, as an experienced gunman would, and it hadn't gone off when it hit the ground. But it wasn't going to fire again until the hammer was drawn back, and Sophie wouldn't know to do that.

Belle did, though. She surged up, plucked the gun from Sophie's hands, and cocked and fired two-handed. Even in this bad light, the range was so close that she couldn't miss. She slammed three swift shots into the gun-wolves, knocking them back against the trees. They hung there like that for a second, then pitched forward limply.

As Belle stood there with the gun still held in front of her, Sophie clutched at her frantically, hysterically.

"You shot them!" she said. "You shot them!"

"They would have shot us," Belle said. "And you opened the ball." She lowered the gun and used her left hand to take hold of Sophie's arm. "Settle down!"

Belle knew that Sophie must have followed her out of the courthouse, although she wasn't sure why, and sending her back into the building wasn't an option. Those shots were going to draw a lot of attention in a hurry. She tugged at Sophie and went on, "Come on. We have to get out of here!"

Sophie hesitated.

"I'm scared!"

"You'll be a lot worse than scared if you don't come on," Belle said.

Already, she heard men shouting and footsteps pounding toward them. She thought about leaving Sophie here, but she couldn't do that. For a split second, she considered walloping the other girl with the gun and carrying her away from the courthouse, but that wasn't feasible, either. All she could do was pull on Sophie's arm.

Suddenly, Sophie lurched into motion. Belle let go of her, and they rushed side by side through the shadows. Belle hoped they wouldn't run right into one of the trees and bash their brains out.

She also hoped it wouldn't take them long to find some horses, because she knew they had only minutes to get away from here. Maybe less . . .

McConnell and Grayle were still in the general store when one of Grayle's men came in to report on the shots they had heard a few minutes earlier.

"Stevens and Denbow are dead," the man reported grimly. "We found their bodies out back of the court-house, drilled twice each."

"Then somebody must've gotten out of there," McConnell said. "Likely they'll try to fetch help." He turned to Grayle. "That means we need to go ahead and launch that attack you've got planned now, instead of waiting until later."

Grayle shook his head.

"Nobody's going to be able to round up enough help in this county to make any difference. We'll wait and strike when I said."

A frown creased McConnell's forehead. He said, "You're taking a mighty big chance, aren't you? I still don't like what you've got in mind, but it's time to finish this blasted thing."

"Henshaw put me in charge," Grayle snapped. "We'll do things the way I say. That means we attack when I give the order, not before."

McConnell could tell that if he pushed Grayle any further, he would be forcing a showdown, and he wasn't ready for that. Not while the menace of Pike Shannon and his friends remained. That had to be taken care of first.

"You're the boss," he said.

"That's right," Grayle replied with a self-satisfied smirk. "I am."

For now, McConnell thought. For now . . .

CHAPTER 37

"What in blazes is that?" Andy Burnett asked as he and Pike heard the sudden flurry of gunshots from somewhere outside the courthouse. The shots sounded to Pike as if they came from behind the building.

"Could be they're getting ready to rush us. Come on."

They hurried to a window in a darkened rear office where one of the townsmen was posted with a Spencer carbine. Andy asked him, "What's going on out there, Phil?"

"I don't know," the man replied, sounding puzzled. "There were just four shots, first one and then three more in a hurry, and after that, nothing. I saw some muzzle flashes behind the trees over yonder, but honestly, whoever it was didn't seem to be shooting at us."

Pike said, "Maybe one of the citizens who didn't take shelter here in the courthouse was trying to fight back against Grayle's bunch."

"If he did," Andy said, "more than likely he got himself killed."

"More than likely," Pike said, but at the same time, an idea stirred in the back of his head. As it formed more fully, he hoped that he was wrong.

There was one way to find out. He left Andy watching out the window and went in search of Belle Ramsey.

He started by checking with his mother and sister, but Mary and Nessa hadn't seen Belle recently. As it turned out over the next fifteen minutes of questioning the citizens, neither had anyone else in the courthouse.

Even more alarmingly, Sophie Truesdale appeared to be gone, too. Pike wasn't too surprised that Belle was no longer in the courthouse. He could easily imagine her being stubborn enough to try to sneak out and go for help, as she had suggested, even though he had told her not to. But she wouldn't have taken Sophie with her.

Sophie *might* have seen what Belle was doing and followed her, he realized. The friction between the two young women could have caused Sophie to be suspicious enough of Belle to do that.

As those thoughts went through Pike's mind, the shots out back of the courthouse took on a more worrisome significance. If Belle and Sophie were together, they might have encountered some of Grayle's men and been captured.

Or they might be lying out there dead.

When he had first returned to Warbonnet County months earlier, Pike had been locked up in the jail. He cast his mind back to that time, trying to remember the details of the cell block. He found Andy again and asked, "There's a door out the back from the cell block downstairs, isn't there?"

"Yeah, but it's got a mighty sturdy bar on it," the sheriff replied. "Nobody's gonna get in that way."

"I'm not worried about somebody getting in. I think somebody went *out.* "

Andy stared at him, clearly not understanding.

Pike said, "I'm going to go have a look," and turned toward the stairs.

"I'll come with you," Andy said as he hurried to catch up.

Moments later, they found the half-sunken exit door unbarred. It was pulled up tight, so that no one outside could tell by looking at it that the bar was off on the inside, but clearly someone had left the courthouse this way and pulled the heavy door shut behind them.

"Who in the world . . .?" Andy muttered. "Somebody double-crossing us, working with Grayle?"

Pike shook his head.

"If that was the case, they'd already be in here wiping us out. No, Belle and Sophie did this."

"Belle and—" Andy stared even harder at him. "But *why?*"

"Belle got it in her head that she could ride to the ranch and get help from Torrance and Dougal," Pike explained. "And from Will and Sam and others in the county, too."

"Well, somebody who knew what they were doing could round up a pretty good bunch of reinforcements, that's true."

"Yeah, but you heard those shots earlier," Pike

said bleakly. "Those girls could have run into trouble right away, too. That's a lot more likely."

"But that means they might be . . ."

Andy's voice trailed off as he looked horror-stricken.

"Yeah, they might," Pike said. He heaved a sigh. "And I don't see any way of finding out, short of going out there and maybe getting killed ourselves. No, Andy, the thing that makes the most sense is putting this bar back on the door so nobody can sneak in that way. Give me a hand with it."

The two big men handled the heavy bar easily, lifting it and settling it into its brackets.

"Better not say anything about this to Ma or Nessa," Pike warned. "That would just upset them, and we don't *know* anything happened to those girls."

"I understand," Andy nodded. "When it gets to be morning, maybe we can find out more."

"Maybe," Pike said.

Then they went back upstairs to wait and see what Ben Grayle was going to do next.

Time dragged by in the courthouse. All the lamps had been turned low. Exhausted people stretched out wherever they could and went to sleep. Children cried and fretted but gradually settled down. As happened in any crisis when there wasn't an immediate physical threat to deal with, a certain numbness set in. Most people could maintain a high level of tension for only so long.

Pike had the sort of experience that the citizens of Warbonnet could thank their lucky stars they had been spared. He knew what it was like to have his life depend on staying alert, and although he was undeniably weary, he had no real trouble staying awake.

He sat next to one of the front windows on the ground floor with a rifle. After a while, he took out his pocket watch and opened it. Almost four o'clock. In less than an hour, it would start getting light. He wouldn't have thought that Grayle would hold off on attacking for this long . . .

Pike stiffened with alarm. Like all good Texans, he had been brought up on stories of the Alamo and how the valiant defenders had held out for thirteen days, until early in the morning of March 6, 1836, they had been overrun by the Mexican army under the command of the dictator Santa Anna. That attack had come right around four o'clock, when folks' readiness to fight ebbed at its lowest.

He leaped to his feet. Warning bells went off in his mind. He called to the other men dozing around the windows, "Wake up! Open your eyes, blast it! They'll be coming any minute now!"

He would have felt foolish if nothing had happened. But he didn't have to worry about that, because at that moment, thunder crashed outside. Gun-thunder, as dozens of rifles and revolvers opened fire at the same time.

Pike leaped to the window and brought up his Winchester, but he had to duck back as a storm of lead ripped through the opening. Everywhere else in this part of the courthouse, he saw people hitting the floor. Bullets sizzled through the air, ricocheted and whined, chewed chunks out of the walls. It was a concentrated effort, and Pike knew Grayle's men couldn't keep it up for very long without having to reload.

He edged closer to the window and risked a glance out. A man on horseback galloped across the lawn toward the courthouse. He held something in his hand that was burning. Pike knew instantly what was going on.

Grayle was going to try to set fire to the courthouse.

Pike thrust the rifle out the window and tried to draw a bead on the rider, but before he could squeeze off a shot, a slug whipped past his ear, no more than an inch away. Another hit the side of the window and sprayed splinters into his cheek. Some of them almost went into his eye. He had to draw back.

As he did, he caught a glimpse of the man in the saddle throwing the flaming object as he wheeled his horse around to flee. Pike didn't know where the thing went, but he had a hunch Grayle's man had aimed it at one of the shot-out windows on the second floor.

A moment later, shouts of "Fire! Fire!" confirmed that guess. Similar yells came from elsewhere in the courthouse. That wasn't surprising. Grayle wouldn't have trusted the task to just one man. He wanted to make sure the Warbonnet County courthouse burned.

Pike's jaw was a tight, grim line. He should have seen this coming. Ben Grayle was utterly ruthless, and he didn't care how many people he killed in order to accomplish what he set out to do. Pike knew that Grayle's men were just waiting out there for those inside the courthouse to flee from the flames—then they would shoot them down as they ran outside.

The only chance anyone had to escape was if Pike and some of the other men could keep Grayle's gun-wolves busy enough they wouldn't have time to commit mass murder. That meant a head-on assault, a suicidal charge that might break the circle of killers and open a route for at least some of the citizens to escape.

"Andy!" he called to the sheriff. "We have to go out there!"

"I know!" Andy replied. "Lem, Fritz, Lester! Come on!"

"Fiddler!" Pike said. "Grab a gun and come with us!"

The little man nodded, but paused long enough to take hold of Mary's arms and plant a kiss on her lips. Then he picked up a revolver and joined Pike and the others at the front doors.

"Ready?" Pike asked. The other men nodded grimly.

Pike lifted his right foot and kicked the doors open. With him in the lead, firing as rapidly as he could work the Winchester's lever, they rushed out. The roar of guns was deafening. Pike emptied the rifle, cast it aside, and knelt momentarily behind a barrel to fire his Colt at the ring of killers before running forward again.

It was a mad, glorious charge. Pike fully expected not to survive it. But as the chaotic seconds ticked past, he realized that the return fire from Grayle's men wasn't as intense as he expected. In fact, although there was still a lot of shooting going on, not much of it seemed to be directed at Pike and the men with him.

"What's going on?" Andy yelled. "How come they're not filling us full of lead?"

"Because they're fighting somebody else!" Pike exclaimed as he realized that was true. Gray, predawn light had started to filter into the sky, and it was enough for him to see men on horseback charging around the courthouse square, the guns in their hands blazing as they riddled the hired killers with bullets. Pike caught a glimpse of one barrel-chested rider he recognized instantly.

Torrance!

The arrival of his brother on the scene could mean only one thing: someone had summoned help.

Belle and Sophie. Had to be.

Pike let out a triumphant whoop.

"The guns of Warbonnet County!" he shouted to Andy, who let out a Rebel yell in response.

"We'd better see to getting everybody out of the courthouse!" Andy said.

"You and the others do that," Pike told him. "I'm going after Grayle."

"Pike—" Andy began, but whatever word of warning he might have voiced next went unsaid, because Pike was already gone, heading toward the area where the battle had shifted.

CHAPTER 38

As he ran toward the street, Pike thumbed fresh rounds into his Colt. He saw his grandfather Dougal charge past on horseback, firing a rifle as he did so. Pike spotted Sam Crow and Will Fisher among the reinforcements, too, along with several other men he recognized.

Grayle's men had gone from having the upper hand to being caught in a crossfire in the blink of an eye. But they were professional gunmen, hardened fighting men who weren't going to give up just because circumstances swung against them. Luck could always change again.

Pike wanted to make sure that it didn't in this case. He snapped the Colt's loading gate closed and drew a bead on a bearded gun-wolf who suddenly reared up and pointed a rifle at him.

Pike and the gunman fired at the same time. Pike felt the wind-rip of a slug past his ear. Close, but not close enough. At the same time, the gunman rocked back, dropped his rifle, and pawed at his chest where

Pike's bullet had driven deeply. He toppled to the side like a tree falling over.

Pike swung to find another target and drilled a hardcase who was about to shoot one of the mounted reinforcements in the back. That man jerked around in the saddle, saw the hired killer pitching forward with Pike's bullet between his shoulder blades, and spotted Pike standing not far away with smoke still curling from the muzzle of his gun.

The shock of recognition made Pike catch his breath. He knew that stern visage dominated by a strong beak of a nose. The man's broad-brimmed hat rested on crisp dark hair. Pinned to the breast of his shirt was an equally familiar badge, a silver star set inside a silver circle.

That was the emblem of the Texas Rangers, and the man wearing it was Walt Scott. *El Aguila*, some called him down along the border. The Eagle.

And he was a friend, of sorts, to the Shannon family, having met them in the aftermath of the war against the Ramsey clan. Now he was back in War-bonnet, and judging by the Ranger badges that Pike spotted on several of the other men who had come galloping in to turn the tide, he had brought some comrades with him.

Scott ticked a finger against the brim of his hat in acknowledgment of what Pike had done, then turned his horse and plunged back into the battle. The black-butted gun in the Ranger's fist spouted flame as his lead raked the hired killers and drove a couple of them off their feet.

Pike was looking for Ben Grayle himself, but he didn't find the man. He traded shots with another of the gunmen. As that hombre doubled over and collapsed from Pike's bullet in his belly, the gunfire died away all around the courthouse square. Pike saw a number of Grayle's men throwing their rifles and pistols down and sticking their hands in the air in surrender. They'd had enough.

The Rangers and the rest of the reinforcements swarmed around the prisoners. Pike reloaded his gun, his fingers moving instinctively and automatically, as he watched Walt Scott dismount and stride toward him, followed by Torrance and Dougal. Relief welled up inside Pike as he saw that his brother and grandfather appeared to be unharmed.

Pike pouched his iron, threw his arms around Torrance, and pounded him on the back.

"I don't reckon I was ever as glad to see you as I am now, big brother," he said.

"I'm happy that you made it through all right, too," Torrance said.

"Where are Belle and Sophie? They're the ones who brought you here, right?"

Torrance nodded and said, "We left them outside of town. Belle wanted to come in and fight alongside us, of course, but Ranger Scott assigned a couple of men to stay with them and hog-tie them if they gave too much trouble."

Pike grinned at Scott and said, "I'll bet they weren't happy about that."

"No, but I don't care too much," the Ranger replied. "Those young ladies had already done enough, escaping from the courthouse the way they did and riding hell-for-leather out to your ranch to bring help. It was a stroke of mighty good luck that I was there, along with the patrol I brought up here from Austin to settle things down."

"You heard about all the trouble that's been going on in these parts, eh?"

Scott cocked an eyebrow and said wryly, "Trouble that you seem to be smack-dab in the middle of, as usual, Pike. That's why we traveled first to your ranch and camped there last night. Yes, the Rangers keep a closer eye on things than you might think. You'd probably be wise to remember that."

Dougal asked, "Where are Mary and Nessa and Fiddler? None of them are hurt, are they?"

"They weren't the last time I saw them," Pike said.

The three Shannons went in search of their family members while Scott returned to the task of helping the other Rangers round up the gunmen who had surrendered. Normally, those men would have been locked up in the jail, but when Pike glanced at the courthouse, he saw smoke still rolling out through the broken windows, and flames still leaped and danced inside.

The Warbonnet County courthouse was going to need extensive repairs. It might even have to be completely rebuilt inside.

That was one more mark against Solomon Henshaw's name. One more score to settle . . .

"Fiddler!" Dougal exclaimed as they caught sight of the little man in the crowd. Fiddler had his right hand clamped to his upper left arm, and blood showed through his spread fingers. "Dang it, you're hurt!"

"Not too badly, I believe," Fiddler replied. "Although I will admit that it's quite painful. Hurts like blazes, in fact."

"Let me take a look," Torrance said.

A quick examination revealed that the wound was a deep bullet crease, messy but not life-threatening. While Torrance was doing that, Mary and Nessa pushed through the crowd.

"Thank heavens you're tall enough that you're easy to spot, Pike," Mary said. "Where's—Oh, my Lord! *Fiddler!*"

She grabbed his shoulders and stared in horror at his bloody arm.

"I'm all right, my dear," he assured her. "The wound is a minor one, or so Torrance tells me, and I believe him."

Mary looked at her older son and said, "You patch him up good, you hear me?"

"Of course, and we'll have the doctor take care of it properly as soon as we can," Torrance said.

With a worried look on her face, Nessa said to Pike, "What happened to Belle and Sophie? I haven't seen them in a long time."

"They're all right," Pike told her. "They're the ones who got away and rode to the ranch to fetch help. They weren't expecting the Rangers to be there, but it was sure lucky they were."

The presence of the Ranger troop had swung the tide of battle quickly. Without them, defeating Grayle and his men would have been a much more difficult—and bloodier—proposition.

Pike left his family fussing over Fiddler and

walked across the lawn to the area where Walt Scott and the other Rangers had herded together all the prisoners. The light was better now; the sun wasn't up yet, but the eastern sky was orange and gold. Pike scanned the faces of the two dozen prisoners, looking for two in particular—Ben Grayle and Carl McConnell.

He didn't see either of them.

Scott noticed what he was doing and joined him, saying, "You look a mite disappointed about something, Shannon."

"I was looking for Ben Grayle, who headed up this crew of killers, and Carl McConnell, who's Solomon Henshaw's right-hand man."

"Henshaw being the hombre who's responsible for all this hell-raising?"

"Yeah. I don't know how much you've been told, but he runs all the moonshining up in Chaparral County and wanted to move in down here, too. Andy Burnett and I tried to stop him, and that led to what's happened here."

Pike nodded grimly toward the courthouse, where the fire inside the thick stone walls finally appeared to be dying out. The roof hadn't collapsed, which was something of a surprise.

"There are fifteen or twenty dead men scattered around," Scott said. "Could be the two you're searching for are among them. Let's have a look."

The sun was peeking over the horizon by the time Pike and Scott finished checking the bodies. They hadn't found Grayle or McConnell. Although Pike hadn't seen either man during the fighting, he felt confident they would have been on hand for the battle. Their absence could mean only one thing.

"They got away," he said bitterly. "Maybe just the two of them, maybe they took some of the others with them, but when they realized the odds had turned against them, they abandoned the others and lit a shuck."

"You reckon they headed back up to Chaparral County?" Scott asked.

Pike nodded and said, "They would ride to Clarkston—that's where Henshaw's mansion is—and report to him."

Scott hooked his thumbs in his gunbelt and said, "Then I'll be heading for Clarkston, too, along with some of my men. Henshaw's going to answer to the State of Texas for what he's done."

"I'll be coming with you."

"You're not a Ranger, Shannon, or any other kind of lawman, are you? This is our business now, not yours."

Pike looked squarely at the older man and said, "Then you'll have to arrest me to keep me from coming along."

"Or maybe . . . deputize you?"

Pike drew in a deep breath. The thought of wearing a lawman's badge still went against the grain for him, but he wasn't going to let anything keep him from going after Henshaw, McConnell, and Grayle.

"Call it whatever you want," he said, "as long as we get on the trail of those varmints and give them what's coming to them."

CHAPTER 39

The sun was up, a brassy orange ball hanging low in the eastern sky, when Carl McConnell and Ben Grayle dismounted in front of the mansion atop the hill just north of Clarkston. Four of Grayle's men were with them, having also fled from the debacle in Warbonnet.

"Stay out here," Grayle snapped at them. "We'll be leaving soon."

"Running like rats out of a burning building, eh?" McConnell said. "Appropriate, considering what you did down there."

The atmosphere between the two men had been tense but mostly silent during the ride up here. Now Grayle turned sharply toward McConnell, and his hand hovered above his gun butt. McConnell was ready to slap leather, too.

With a visible effort, Grayle relaxed.

"Go to hell," he said. "How was I supposed to know the Rangers would show up like that with no warning?"

"If you'd made your move earlier instead of

waiting, like I suggested, it wouldn't have mattered. We'd have been done and gone before the blasted Rangers ever got there, and some good men would still be alive. That's what I intend to tell the boss, too. If you think he's going to pay you the rest of what he promised and just let you ride away—"

"Forget it," Grayle snapped. "I don't take money I didn't earn. I'm just going to tell Henshaw what happened, and then he can find somebody else to deal with Pike Shannon." A bitter curse came out of the gunman's mouth. "I've never seen anybody as lucky as Shannon!"

"Or maybe he's just that good," McConnell muttered contemptuously as he started up the walk toward the house. "Better than you, obviously."

He had taken only a couple of steps when some instinct warned him. He stiffened and tried to turn as he clawed at the gun on his hip, but he was too late. As angry and worked up as he was, he had made a stupid mistake, and now he was going to pay for it.

He heard the crash of the shot, felt the smashing blow of the bullet in his back, and then he was falling forward, toward the flagstone walk.

He never felt the impact as his face struck one of the stones. His bullet-drilled heart had already stopped, and blackness without end swallowed him whole.

Solomon Henshaw and Lucille were still in their dressing gowns, about to eat breakfast in the sumptuous dining room, when the shot rang out. Henshaw frowned and snapped at the black butler, "See what that's about."

The servant nodded and slipped out of the room. He was back less than a minute later, looking frightened as he said, "Mister, uh . . . Mr. Grayle is—"

"I'm right here, Henshaw," Grayle said as he pushed the butler aside. "I've come to let you know that I'm not working for you anymore and neither is McConnell."

Anger brought Henshaw to his feet. He demanded, "What the devil are you talking about?"

"Everything went wrong down in Warbonnet," Grayle replied with a shrug. "We managed to set fire to their courthouse and kill some of them, but most of my men are dead, too, and those who aren't have been arrested by the Texas Rangers."

"The Rangers!" Henshaw repeated in a roar. "You've brought the Rangers down on me?"

"Not yet. A few of us got out while we could and headed back up here. The Rangers may be coming this way pretty soon, though."

"Damn you!" Henshaw raged. "All you had to do was teach those people a lesson—"

"They didn't want to be taught," Grayle said.

"Where's Carl?"

The servant spoke up, saying, "Mr. McConnell, he . . . he's lying out there on the walk—"

Savagely, Grayle backhanded him and knocked him against a sideboard. He drew his gun as he turned toward Henshaw again. Lucille gasped in alarm at the sudden violence and the threat of more.

"McConnell had a big mouth, and he was a fool,

to boot," Grayle said. "You don't want to be foolish, too, Henshaw. Just give me all the money you have here in the house, and I'll be on my way."

Henshaw stared at the gunman for a few seconds, then said, "You're robbing me like a common thief?"

"I'm a hired killer," Grayle said with a thin smile. "You didn't expect a paragon of virtue, did you?"

"You won't get another penny from me," Henshaw said coldly as his lips curled in a sneer.

"Well . . . maybe I'll take the girl with me, instead."

Henshaw let out a derisive snort.

"Take her!" he said. "I'm tired of her, anyway."

Lucille stared at him in horror.

For a moment, Grayle appeared to be considering it, but then he said, "No, I believe I want the money. I'm sure if I kill you, this servant of yours will be too scared not to show me where it is." Grayle lifted his gun. "So, tell me, Henshaw . . . What's it going to be?"

Before Henshaw could answer, one of the other gun-wolves rushed into the room and said, "Riders coming, Ben. They look like the Texas Rangers!"

Walt Scott brought four of his fellow Rangers with him, leaving the rest of the patrol in Warbonnet to deal with the prisoners and make sure order remained restored. Andy Burnett put John Strickland, Lester Scroggins, and Mayor Millworth in charge of getting all the injured citizens to Dr. Faulkner's office so the doctor could start giving them medical attention. Fritz Durham formed a bucket brigade to throw water through the courthouse windows and make sure all the flames were extinguished inside the gutted building. No fires had been started elsewhere in town, but repairing the courthouse was going to be a mighty big job by itself.

Dougal and Torrance had wanted to come with Pike, but he'd told them to stay there and help out in Warbonnet. The town looked like a war zone this morning, and some of the people were wandering around like they were shell-shocked. It was going to take a while for everybody to get over this attack, too.

Pike was confident that he was leaving everything in good hands, though, as he rode north with Walt Scott and the other Rangers.

They had gotten fresh horses in Warbonnet, so they were able to push north at a brisk, steady pace. When they crossed the county line and rode through Bolivar, the settlement wasn't stirring much this early in the morning. People who were on the street, though, stared at the group of grim-faced lawmen as they rode past.

Not surprisingly, no one tried to stop them.

The sun came up while they were between Bolivar and Clarkston, so when they reached the county seat, the place was coming alive for the day. People were out and about on the street, and the Rangers got the same startled, slightly nervous reaction from them that they had gotten from the citizens of Bolivar.

Pike didn't know if the folks who lived here were aware of just how crooked the county's richest, most powerful inhabitant was, but from the faintly guilty glances some of them cast toward the Rangers, he had a hunch they were. The state lawmen showing up like this didn't bode well.

A man with a big gut and a balding head under his pushed-back hat stepped out into the street and held up a hand for Pike and his companions to stop. He had a star pinned to his vest.

"Hold on there, boys," he called. "I'm Jim Kessler, the sheriff of Chaparral County. Mind tellin' me what the Rangers are doin' here in my bailiwick?"

Walt Scott gave him a curt nod and said, "I'll give you a straight, honest answer, Sheriff. We've come to arrest Solomon Henshaw, Carl McConnell, Ben Grayle, and any more of that bunch we find."

Kessler's round face paled. He swallowed hard and said, "Arrest Mr. Henshaw? I . . . I'm not sure if you can do that—"

"Reckon this badge says I can," Scott drawled. "I understand you may feel like you owe some allegiance to Henshaw, Sheriff. He probably helped you get elected." His voice was quiet as he went on, "Do you intend on trying to stop us?"

"N-no. No, sir, I don't. You're . . . uh . . . you're the Rangers. I reckon you've got . . . more authority than I do."

"I'm glad you can see your way clear to cooperate with us." Scott nodded again. "We'll be moving on. And I'd appreciate it if you didn't try to send word to Henshaw and warn him that we're coming."

"He'll know," Pike said. "As soon as McConnell and Grayle talk to him, he'll know."

They heeled their horses into motion again, leaving the hapless local lawman standing there staring glumly after them. He had been elected by the voters, at least with a pretense of legality, so he ought to still have a job when this was over, but he would have lost the true power behind him. He might try to stay on as sheriff, or he might just slip away and put Chaparral County behind him.

Pike didn't care either way, as long as the man didn't interfere with them.

As they approached the hill where Henshaw's mansion was located, Pike lifted a hand and motioned for Scott to rein in. The Rangers came to a stop. Pike said, "Henshaw may have guards out, and even if he doesn't, Grayle and McConnell will be with him, along with we don't know how many of those hired killers. So I'm going to circle around and come in the back, see if I can take them by surprise."

"And maybe end this without a lot more killing?" Scott said.

Pike thought about everything that had happened and said, "I can't make any promises about that."

"There's such a thing as justice," Scott snapped. "It usually involves a trial with a judge and jury."

"Usually," Pike said, "but not always."

Scott studied him intently for a moment, then said, "Comes down to it, you're still a civilian. I'm not going to give you any orders, Shannon. But don't push me. You don't want to wind up on the wrong side of the law from me."

"Fair enough," Pike said. He turned his horse away from the road and headed off at an angle that would take him around the hill. He stayed in the trees and brush as much as possible so that if anyone was watching from up there, they would be less likely to see him skirting around this way.

He had never been here before; Solomon Henshaw had moved in and had the mansion built while Pike was away from Texas. But his instincts allowed him to find his way around the hill, climb a steep, wooded ridge, and approach the imposing dwelling from behind.

He didn't see any guards on this side of the house. Leaving the horse tied to a gazebo—a *gazebo*, of all things!—he moved quietly to a rear door and tried the knob. It turned under his hand, and he eased inside.

He found himself in a room used for storage that was attached to the kitchen. As he cat-footed toward the front of the house, he heard voices somewhere not too far away. They sounded angry. He wondered if there was trouble between Henshaw and his subordinates. Ben Grayle always looked out for himself above all others, so it wouldn't surprise Pike if Grayle and Henshaw had had a falling-out.

He came to a swinging door and paused to listen. The voices were in the room on the other side of it. He heard harsh tones that must belong to Solomon Henshaw. For all the enmity Pike felt for the man, he had never laid eyes on him or heard his voice.

He knew Grayle's smooth, menacing tone, though, and as he eased the swinging door open a crack, the gunman demanded of Henshaw, "What's it going to be?"

Before Henshaw could answer, a door opened and

a man's alarmed voice announced, "Riders coming, Ben. They look like the Texas Rangers!"

Pike took that as his cue. Gun in hand, he kicked the swinging door open, stepped into a sumptuously furnished dining room, and called, "Hands up, all of you!"

CHAPTER 40

Pike's keen eyes took in the scene instantly. Five people were in the room: Ben Grayle, one of his hardcases, a middle-aged black man in servant's livery, an attractive, dark-haired young woman in a dressing gown, and a tall, imperious-looking hombre, also in nightclothes, who had to be Solomon Henshaw.

Pike had never expected Grayle to surrender. Walt Scott might not like it, but Pike had circled around and entered the mansion alone because he knew the time had come for him and Grayle to settle things.

Grayle already had his gun in his hand. There would be no tense showdown, no fast draw with life and death riding on a man's nerves and muscles. Grayle whirled, and the gun he held geysered smoke and fire and racket. Pike crouched slightly and squeezed the trigger of his own Colt. The gun bucked against his palm as it roared.

All in the same shaved fraction of time, less than a heartbeat, Pike felt the heat of Grayle's bullet against his cheek as it narrowly missed. His own slug smashed into Grayle's chest and jolted the gunman back a step. Grayle didn't fall or drop his weapon, though. Iron will kept him on his feet as he fought with the rapidly spreading weakness in his body to get off another shot.

Even as Grayle took that backward step, Pike was swinging his gun toward the other man, who had clawed his iron out of leather. He was fast enough to get a shot off but hurried it just enough that the bullet missed Pike and thudded into the swinging door behind him. Pike fired.

The man grunted and rocked back. He caught himself, but his knees buckled. His gun clattered on the polished hardwood floor as he dropped it, and he followed it a second later, falling forward on his face.

Even seriously wounded, Ben Grayle was a bigger threat than Henshaw, Pike decided, so he pivoted again as Grayle rasped, "Damn you! I'm . . . faster . . ."

Grayle's finger started to whiten on the trigger. Pike shot him between the eyes. Grayle crashed to the floor without firing another shot.

"You're deader, anyway, that's for sure," Pike told him.

The sound of a gun being cocked made him turn swiftly toward Henshaw. The man had a pocket pistol in his hand. It was aimed at Pike's head, and at this range, the gun was accurate enough to be deadly.

Henshaw didn't pull the trigger, though. Before he could, there was a flicker of movement behind him and a high-pitched cry of pure rage. Henshaw's eyes widened as he took half a step forward and his gun hand drooped. He tried to turn around as he gasped, "Lu . . . Lucille!"

Pike saw the knife buried in Henshaw's back. The girl had scooped it up from the table and driven it into Henshaw's body with all her strength.

"Wh . . . why?" Henshaw managed to say.

The girl stared at him, fury in her eyes.

"You can ask that?" she demanded. "After the things you did to me? The way you treated me? The way you were ready to throw me away to save yourself and your precious money?"

Henshaw dropped the pistol. He swayed as he stared at her in shock.

"Don't look so surprised," Lucille said. "You had it coming."

Solomon Henshaw folded up in a heap and didn't move again.

Even with all that going on, a part of Pike's brain had been aware of guns going off outside. Now he heard boot heels clomping on the floor and spurs jingling as someone approached the dining room. Gun in hand, Ranger Walt Scott stepped into the room and looked around quickly.

Pike slid his Colt back into its holster and asked, "Everything all right outside, Scott?"

"Yes, we've got two dead gun-wolves and another prisoner," Scott said.

"Is the prisoner Carl McConnell?"

"Don't know the man. What's he look like?"

"Middle-aged, craggy face, white hair."

Scott shook his head and said, "That hombre

was dead when we got here. He'd been shot in the back."

"Probably by Grayle," Pike muttered as he looked down at the dead gunman. "That's the sort of thing he'd do."

"That's Grayle, I take it?"

"Yeah."

"And this other fella?"

"One of the men who worked for him," Pike said. "I don't know his name."

Scott nodded toward the crumpled figure in the dressing gown, with the knife in his back, and said, "That would make this gentleman Solomon Henshaw."

"I suppose so," Pike said. "We were never actually introduced."

Scott cocked his head quizzically and said to the girl, "Did you put that knife in his back, miss?"

The black servant had been brushing and straightening his suit. Before the girl could respond to Scott's question, he stepped forward and said, "Miss Fletcher struck the fatal blow in defense of this gentleman's life, sir. Just as the gentleman shot those other two to save himself as they were trying to murder him."

"You'd testify to that in a court of law?"

"Absolutely," the butler replied. "Neither Miss Fletcher nor this other gentleman had any other choice but to do what they did."

Scott grunted and then nodded. He said to Pike, "I reckon that means you're in the clear." He looked at the young woman. "Both of you."

She sighed and sank into one of the chairs beside

the table as if all her strength had suddenly deserted her. Her head slumped onto her arms and she began to cry.

Pike didn't know what Solomon Henshaw had done to make the girl hate him that much. He figured he didn't want to know.

All he really wanted right now was to go home and be with his family and friends.

That evening, Belle Ramsey joined the Shannons for supper at their ranch. After returning to Warbonnet with Walt Scott and the other Rangers, Pike had spent the day helping restore things in town to normal as much as possible, working alongside his mother, Nessa, Torrance, Dougal, Belle, Sophie Truesdale, Sheriff Andy Burnett, Sam Crow, and his other friends. Even Fiddler, his arm bandaged and resting in a black silk sling, pitched in, helping deliver food that Sophie prepared in her café for volunteers.

Men who had been in the war talked about how this was like what had happened when the ravaging Yankee army swept through southern towns. The destruction was not nearly as bad or widespread, of course, but the citizens of Warbonnet were shaken to their core by the losses they had suffered.

It would take a while, Pike knew, but Texans were strong and resilient. Other than the repairs to the courthouse, which probably would be going on for a long time, the town and the people who lived there would be going about their business again very quickly. He was confident of that.

After supper, Pike was sitting on the front porch with Dougal, Torrance, and Fiddler when Belle came out of the house. She had been helping Mary and Nessa clean up after the meal. Pike noticed how quickly the other three men came up with excuses to go back inside after Belle joined them and sat down next to Pike on the swing that hung from the porch roof.

"If I didn't know better," he said, "I'd think those three hombres are trying to play Cupid."

"You think so?" Belle asked.

"I said, if I didn't know better."

"Oh. Well, it's good to know such a thing never entered their mind . . . or yours."

They sat there quietly for a moment. Pike was considering putting his arm around her shoulders when he sat up straighter, instead. He had heard a horse coming along the lane toward the house.

So had Belle. She stiffened beside him and asked, "Who could that be?"

"Don't know," Pike murmured, "but maybe you should go back inside."

"I'm not going to run and hide just because someone is riding up. That's not the kind of person I am, Pike Shannon."

"Reckon I know by now what kind of person you are, Belle."

"What kind is that?"

He was saved from having to answer by a familiar voice that called, "Hello, the house!"

Pike stood up and said, "Come on in, Ranger."

Walt Scott rode up to the porch, and in the light that spilled through the open doorway, he reined in, nodded to Pike, and pinched his hat brim to Belle.

"Miss Ramsey," he greeted her politely.

"Hello, Ranger Scott," she said.

Pike asked, "What brings you out here?"

"I just wanted to tell you that I'll be headed back to Austin with some of my men, first thing in the morning. I'm going to leave a few of them in War-bonnet for a while to give Sheriff Burnett a hand. We found enough records in Solomon Henshaw's office to know pretty much everybody in Warbonnet County who was involved in trying to bring his moonshining operation down here, and the sheriff intends on putting them out of business."

"I don't think Andy will have too hard a time doing that," Pike said. "Especially with some Rangers backing him up." He paused, then added, "Before you know it, Warbonnet County will be a plumb law-abiding place again."

"You sound like you're a little disappointed by that."

Pike shrugged and said, "A man gets in the habit of something, and it's hard to set aside."

"Like breaking the law?"

"You said that, Ranger, not me."

"Speaking of the Rangers . . ." Scott reached up to the pocket of his bib-front shirt and took some-thing out. "That's another thing I wanted to ask you about." He held out his hand. The light from the house glinted on the star-in-a-circle that lay on his palm. "I haven't offered this to you officially . . . until now."

"And I haven't turned you down officially until now," Pike responded without hesitation.

Scott laughed and tucked the badge away in his pocket again.

"I was almost a hundred percent sure that's what you'd say, but I wanted to ask anyway."

"You've got your answer." Pike leaned his head toward the door. "Why don't you go on in and say hello to the folks? There should still be some coffee in the pot, and I'll bet my ma could rustle up a piece of pie."

Scott swung down from the saddle, looped his reins around the hitch rail in front of the porch, and came up the steps.

"Unlike some people, I know when to accept a good offer," he said with a grin. He went on into the house, taking off his hat as he did so.

"Pike Shannon, Texas Ranger," Belle mused. "You don't like the sound of that?"

"It gives me the fantods," Pike said.

She looked at him and said, "If somebody else was to make you a good offer, would you accept it?"

"I reckon that would depend on what it was . . . and who was offering."

She patted the seat of the swing beside her and said, "Why don't you sit down here, and we'll talk about it."

*Keep reading for a special preview
of the next Johnstone epic!*

A KNIFE IN THE HEART
A HANK FALLON WESTERN

As both a prisoner and an undercover operative, U.S. Marshal Hank Fallon has faced down some of the most vicious, terrifying, cold-blooded thieves and murderers in the West. Now Hank is finally free and he's got no intention of setting foot inside a jail ever again.

But the new federal prison being constructed in Leavenworth, Kansas, needs a warden and Hank is the right man for the job. He's got the scars to prove it—and to keep the peace. But keeping these lawless hornets in their nest is no easy feat. And when several escape before Leavenworth is at maximum security, they take Hank's family hostage.

To save his wife and baby daughter, Hank will have to get as down and dirty as the devils he's pursuing—and they won't be taken alive.

Look for **A KNIFE IN THE HEART** *on sale now!*

CHAPTER 1

They come at him, just as they always do—at least six men, wearing the striped uniform of inmates. Harry Fallon can't see their faces, and even if he could, it's not like he knows these hardened lifers. He doesn't even remember the name of the prison where he has been sentenced. Joliet? Yuma? Jefferson City? Huntsville? Detroit? Alcatraz? Cañon City? Laramie? Deer Lodge? But a bad memory is the least of his problems right now.

He stands with his back against the door of six-inch cold iron, no bars, just a slit for a peek hole so the guards can check in every now and then. Ahead of him, to his left, are the cells on the fifth floor. Hands extend between the bars and rattle tin cups against the iron. The doors remain shut. Inside, prisoners chant some dirge or hum, mixed with curses and laughter, but all that proves hard to understand with the racket the cups make against the rough iron. To his right, there's a metal rail about waist-high, and beyond that, the emptiness for thirty yards to the other row of cell blocks. Five stories below, the stone floor of this hellhole called a prison. And just in front of him, the six men, faces masked, but intentions clear. The knives they have—fashioned from the metal shop, or the broom factory, or the farms where they work—wave in hands roughened by a life of crime, followed by life sentences.

"Hey!" Fallon shouts through the slit in the iron, but dares not look through the opening. He can't take his eyes off the six killers. By now, they are less than ten feet from him.

"Hey!"

Nothing.

The big brute in the center of the gang laughs.

Of course, there's no guard here. Not now. Fallon has been behind the iron long enough to know that guards and prisoners have the ability to make a few deals when it comes to taking care of prisoners neither guards nor convicts like. A guard decides to head to the privy at a predetermined time, a trip that'll take a good long while, and it just happens to coincide with other guards needing to find a cigarette, or a toilet, or happening to be escorting another inmate to see the warden.

Handy.

Right now, there's probably not a guard anywhere in this particular house.

So six cons, armed with shivs, start to smile.

If only Fallon could recall where he is, what he's in for, why these men want to kill him. If only Fallon could remember *anything*.

My God, he thinks, has he been sent to prisons so many times his brain has become addled? Has he been hit on the head, suffered . . . what is it they call that . . . amnesia? Yeah. Amnesia. All right, at least he can remember some things.

He remembers something else, too.

Because one of the faceless men before him whispers a growling, "Take him," and the thug on Fallon's right charges, laughing, slashing with the blade, and Fallon leaps back, against the cold stone of the wall, feeling and hearing the tearing of cloth but not of flesh. His intestines aren't spilling out of his belly—yet.

The remaining five killers merely laugh.

The big fellow, eyes black, face pale, almost not even a face at all, pivots, cuts up with the blade, but Fallon uses his left forearm, to knock hand and knife away. The man's face, or what passes for a face, seems surprised. A moment later, Fallon is driving his right hand, flattened, hard against the killer's throat. The crack is almost deafening. The man's eyes bulge in shock, and the blow drives him back, back, back, till he slams against the iron railing at the corner, the end of the passageway. Fallon tries to grab the knife, but both of the men's arms start waving as he tries to regain his balance, as he tries to remember how to breathe.

But he can't. Spittle comes between his lips. He's like a whirlwind now, and the other five men, outside of the cells, watch in fascination and amusement. Even those still inside their cells are transfixed. All they do is hold their tin cups outside the bars. Fingers grip other bars as they watch, laugh, hiss, joke, and pray.

The man moves farther over the rails. He opens

his mouth as if to scream, but he can't scream. He can't breathe. He can't do anything but die. Fallon has learned several things in prison, including how to crush an attacker's larynx.

The shiv drops over the side. Damn. Fallon could have used that to defend himself against the other five killers.

The arms stop waving, and then the faceless man starts to slip over. His mouth opens as though to scream, but he cannot scream, either. A second later, and he's suspended in the air, prison brogans pointing toward the hard ceiling, and then there is nothing.

A long silence follows, stretching toward infinity, before the sickening crunch of a body seems to shake the prison house to its very foundation.

Fallon's heart races. He wets his lips, turns back toward the five other men. The shuddering of the passageway ends, and the man in the center, who might have a mustache and beard, although that appears to be against the prison policy—whatever house of corrections Fallon is in—walks to the edge, puts his hand on the rail, peers over. He spits saliva, which drops toward the corpse, broken and bloody, and stares sightlessly toward the impenetrable ceiling.

Fallon knows because somehow he, too, has moved to the railing, to see the man he has just killed, another kill for a onetime lawman turned killer. The man's dead eyes seem to follow Fallon as he turns back to the five men. The leader spits again, wipes his mouth, and slowly turns to stare at Fallon.

As though on cue, the tin cups resume their metallic serenade. The grinding has now been picked up across the chasm. Prisoners there have likewise resumed raking cups against the bars. And so have the prisoners on the floors below. The noise intensifies. Surely the warden can hear this from wherever his office or house is. Fallon can hear nothing else but the grinding, pounding, insane bedlam of hell.

The noise becomes deafening. Fallon breathes in deeply, watches the five men now back to staring at him. They could rush him, should rush him, for there's no room for Fallon to move, and he can't take down five men when they have knives and he has nothing but . . .

He takes a chance, steps forward quickly and as a tin cup rattles from one bar to another, Fallon strikes hard with his left hand against the wrist. The damned fool should have kept his hand and cup inside his cell. He thinks he hears a scream, but the fingers release the handle, and somehow Fallon has the cup in his own hand.

That prompts a laugh from the leader.

"You think a cup is a match for a blade?" the big faceless man asks.

The killer closest to the cell laughs. But that stops when Fallon steps forward and smashes the man in the face with the hard, cold tin cup.

Fallon quickly steps back, taking it all in, seeing the man, his nose gushing crimson, his lips flattened and bloody, spitting out teeth and saliva, and stumbling in a wild spin. An arm hits the man nearest, him, and pushes him against the leader, who steps back against the fourth man, who jolts the fifth killer to the railing. And now that man is screaming, screaming out for mercy from God, but God cannot hear any prayer in a prison, especially with cups grinding cell doors after cell doors, and just like that, the fifth killer has gone over the edge, plummeting like a rocket, but he can scream, and his cries overcome the drone of metal on iron, until a sickening crunch below silences him.

But not the sound of cups.

The fourth man catches the railing, looks over, and mouths, "Oh, my, God," before turning to Fallon and charging.

Fallon feels the blade as it cuts into his side, but his right hand rams the cup into the man's temple, and the man falls to his knees. The knife comes up, just as Fallon jabs his kneecap into the man's jaw. The blade sticks in up to its makeshift handle of hardened lye soap, deep in Fallon's thigh, and then the man goes down, tries to come up, and Fallon kicks him over the railing.

"Get him!" one of the men calls.

Fallon turns, blinks, confused and angry. Three men have been hurtled to the floor five stories below. There should be only three more inmates outside of their cells, but somehow the doors must have opened, and there are dozens, maybe hundreds. It's as though every prisoner in this whole cell block has been turned loose on the alley. Fallon rips the knife out of his leg with his left hand. Blood sprays the striped trousers of the men as they cover the few feet separating him. He has a short blade and a tin cup. They have knives and clubs and rocks.

He has no chance, and soon they have him, his cup and knife thrown to the floor. He smells their sweat, feeling blows against his arms, back, head, neck. Cursing them as they curse him, he tries to free his arms, his hands, his legs, but there is nothing for him to do.

A moment later, he is at the iron railing. Now he glances through the opening in the slit of the door, and he sees the faces of the guards, and the guards are laughing, too, shouting.

"Toss him overboard, boys!"

Which they do.

Fallon looks below as the stone floor rushes up to greet him. He sees the bloody, crushed, lifeless bodies of the three men he has killed on this day. Their eyes remain open, as well as their mouths, and he can hear these dead men laughing at him. One says, "Join us Fallon . . . in Hell."

And the stones are there to greet him, and send him to the fiery pit.

Where Harry Fallon knows he belongs.

He screams.

CHAPTER 2

His own scream woke him up.

Fallon tried to catch his breath, feeling suddenly freezing, and realized sweat drenched his night robe. While trying desperately to catch his breath, he noticed his right arm was up, crooked, and his clenched fist trembled. He held a pair of scissors. Fallon stared as early morning light seeped through the curtains of the parlor of his home. He waited until he stopped shaking, could breathe normally, and stared at the scissors.

Sobs came somewhere down the foyer beyond the formal parlor.

A woman's voice soon whispered, "It's all right, baby. It's all right. Papa just had another bad dream."

He lowered his hand, swung his bare feet over the chaise. Feet on the rug, he managed to swallow, and gently laid the scissors down on the side table. How he had managed to find them was beyond him, but thank God, he prayed, he was sleeping in the parlor.

Sleeping in the parlor. One more time. Instead of in the bedroom with his wife.

Fallon planted his elbows on his thighs, buried his face in his hands, and waited until he stopped shaking, bits and pieces of the nightmare returning to him, but only in fragments. He didn't need to remember every single detail. It was the same damned nightmare he always had. A few things might change: the location, the number of inmates, how men were trying to kill him, or execute him. Sometimes he knew the men, the crazed killer named Monk from Yuma; the leader of the riot from Joliet; The Mole from Jefferson City; even John Wesley Hardin from Huntsville. Mostly though, they were cretins and monsters and blurs of men, often without faces, but always trying to kill him. In the worst of the dreams, they were about to succeed before he woke up. On the good nights, he woke up quickly before his own shouts awakened his family . . . one more time.

This, he knew, was no way to live. Not so much for his sake, but for Christina and the five-year-old girl, Rachel Renee.

He managed to stand, ran his fingers through his soaking hair, looked at the chaise and tossed a blanket on it, hoping the wool would soak up the sweat. The chaise had belonged to Christina's grandmother. He would hate to ruin it, like the leather-covered sofa he had slept in one night that he had ripped apart with a paper opener he happened to find in his sleep.

As long as he didn't start sleepwalking. God, wouldn't that be awful?

He moved out of the parlor and into the hallway, stopped in the indoor bathroom to dry his face, comb his hair, drink a cup of water, and maybe make himself look halfway presentable, with luck mostly human, and then to the girl's bedroom. It was empty, her covers thrown off the little bed. Which is what usually happened.

Fallon took a few more steps, before pushing open the door at the end of the hallway.

Christina Whitney Fallon sat in the four-poster bed, hugging Rachel Renee tightly, kissing the top of her dark hair. Dark hair like Fallon's, not the soft blond of his wife's.

Both stared at him in silence.

"Good morning," Fallon said, realized the absurdity of such a greeting, and sighed. "Sorry."

"It's all right, Papa." Rachel Renee's voice trembled.

"Are you all right?" Christina asked. Her voice was noncommittal, professional, like she was interviewing a witness or a suspect from her days just a few years back as an operative for the American Detective Agency in Chicago.

"Bad dream." He shrugged. "The usual."

"Were there monsters?" Rachel Renee asked.

By then, he had managed to cross the room and sat at the end of the bed. "Yeah," he said. "Daisies and licorice."

Rachel Renee laughed, and that made Fallon breathe a little easier, if not quite relax. He even thought he saw a twinkle in Christina's eyes.

"Daisies and licorice aren't monsters, Papa," the girl said with bemusement. "Those are nice things. My favorite flower. And my favorite breakfast."

"Breakfast?" Christina now laughed.

The day might be all right, Fallon thought.

The precious little girl, one of the two loves of

Fallon's life these past few years, crawled from her mother and leaned against Fallon, still in the robe.

She quickly pulled away. "Oh, Papa, you stink."

Fallon tried to laugh.

"And you stink."

"That's what boys and men do, baby," Christina said.

"They're gross."

"Yes," her mother agreed. "Very much so."

"But I love you anyway, Papa." She came back, and tried to hug him. Fallon put his arm around her.

"What was the nightmare really about?" Rachel Renee asked.

Fallon looked across the room. It was a nice room, extravagant by Fallon's standards, a rented home—what Fallon would have considered a mansion back when he was a kid in Gad's Hill, Missouri—in the upscale section of Cheyenne, Wyoming. Fallon would have opted for something a little less presumptuous, but the governor insisted, as did the state senators—Fallon could remember when Wyoming was just a U.S. territory. Everyone argued that the United States marshal for Wyoming needed to live in a fine house. Especially since he had a beautiful wife, and, for the past four-plus years, a lovely little daughter.

Politics.

All politics.

That's what Fallon's life had become. Politics during the day. Nightmares for the night.

A hell of a life.

"Papa?" Rachel Renee pleaded.

Fallon hugged her tightly. "Oh, I'm not too sure. Dragons, I think. Maybe a unicorn."

"Are unicorns mean?"

"This one was."

"I know dragons are evil. They spit fire."

"Yeah, the two in my bad dream spit out a lot of fire."

"Where there any Indians?"

Fallon looked down at her. "Indians aren't mean like dragons and bad unicorns, or smelly boys and sweating old men."

"Janie Ferguson says Indians are real bad."

"Janie Ferguson is wrong." He tousled her hair. "You know, back when I was just a regular old deputy marshal, back in Fort Smith, Arkansas, I worked with a lot of Indians. Lawmen. Peace officers like me. Scouts. They were always good folk. Really good folk. So I don't think I met any real bad Indians."

"Honest?"

Not really. Fallon had arrested Indians, too, but not as many as the white men who tormented the Indian Nations across the western district of Arkansas. But those times had changed, and after what happened at Wounded Knee so many years ago, Fallon had decided that he'd bring up his daughter to understand that you could find good and bad in all kinds of people, no matter their skin, no matter their beliefs.

Although Fallon had a hard time thinking that for himself. Most of the men he had dealt with were rotten to the core.

As a deputy marshal, and then as an operative for the American Detective Agency—the latter a job he had been forced into—Fallon had worked with dregs. And some of the worst of the lot were men who supposedly represented law and order, like the president of the American Detective Agency, a soulless pitiful man named Sean MacGregor.

Often Fallon blamed MacGregor for these nightmares, for keeping Harry Fallon from being able to spend a night sleeping next to his wife—without having this fear that a nightmare would seize him and he'd wake up and realize that he had killed her by accident.

No way for a man to live. No way for a daughter to grow up.

On the other hand, Fallon might be having these dreams anyway, even if Sean MacGregor had not forced Fallon to go undercover into three of the worst prisons in America: Yuma in Arizona Territory, Jefferson City in Missouri, Huntsville and its prison farms in Texas.

Because long before that, Harry Fallon had spent ten years in Joliet, Illinois—for a crime he had not committed.

"You hungry?" Fallon asked his daughter.

"I'm always hungry," Rachel Renee said.

"What time is it?"

"Five-thirty," Christina answered. She started to rise. "I'll get some . . ."

"No." Fallon pushed himself up. "You two snuggle or at least get a few minutes more of sleep. I'm wide awake. Let me make some breakfast."

Christina smiled, and the baby girl crawled back to her mother, hugged her, and Fallon pulled up the sheets and blankets over them. He kissed Rachel

Renee's forehead, and looked into the hard eyes of his wife.

He kissed her forehead, too, pulled back, and mouthed, "I'm sorry."

Christina just nodded.

And Fallon walked out of the bedroom and closed the door.

One more time.

If this kept up, he realized, he wouldn't have a wife or a child with him.

He could blame that on the American Detective Agency, the prison system in the United States, and the men who had framed him and tried to ruin his life.

Tried? Hell, his life was still ruined, even five years after being pardoned. After being told he was free, with an appointment as U.S. marshal for the district of Wyoming.

Fallon knew what most prisoners knew. Once you had spent time behind the iron, you never could be completely free again.